April and May

By the same author

The Wild Card
In All Honour

April and May

Beth Elliott

ROBERT HALE · LONDON

ISBN 978-0-7090-9042-7

Robert Hale Limited
Clerkenwell House
Clerkenwell Green
London EC1R 0HT

www.halebooks.com

2 4 6 8 10 9 7 5 3 1

Typeset in 10¾/14½pt Palatino
by Derek Doyle & Associates, Shaw Heath
Printed in Great Britain by the MPG Books Group,
Bodmin and King's Lynn

In memory of dearest Atilay

PROLOGUE

London, November 1799

Rose smoothed down the skirts of her blue silk evening gown and studied the toe of her embroidered dance slipper, peeping out from under the elegantly pintucked hem. Too excited to stand still, she turned this way and that, admiring the floral arrangements and the sparkling chandeliers in the ballroom. She turned impulsively to her friend Jane and Jane's mother, Lady Carlyle.

'This is so wonderful,' she exclaimed. 'My first ball and in such a splendid setting. I know I shall enjoy every moment.' She paused to watch another group of young ladies arriving before turning back to Jane. 'When will they make the announcement about your engagement?'

'It will be after supper. Freddy will get the orchestra to play a few bars to call everyone's attention. And then. . . .' Jane clasped her hands and twirled round in excitement, causing her mother to glance at her in reproof.

'I do love him so,' Jane whispered to Rose behind her fan, 'and I think *you* are in a fair way to loving his younger brother.'

Rose gave a gasp. 'But I have only known him for a month. I-I like him very much, of course, but you know my family wants me to marry Hugh. My father's godson,' she added, when Jane raised her brows.

Jane said nothing, merely making her mouth prim. Rose fidgeted with her fan, put up a hand to pat her shining golden hair and grew hotter and pinker. Eventually she darted a glance at her friend to see Jane smiling at her broadly.

'I am so happy myself tonight,' said Jane, 'that I want you, my dearest friend, to be happy as well. And if you think it has escaped my attention that every time Tom visits us, he always looks around the room to see if you are there I assure you that you would be wrong. Moreover,' she went on ruthlessly, watching the blush deepen on Rose's cheeks, 'you always look up eagerly whenever the door opens, until Tom arrives. And then you both talk to each other endlessly.'

'We find we share so many ideas,' stuttered Rose.

'Well, now you can enjoy the opportunity to share a few more. Here come Freddy and Tom now. How fine they look.'

Rose turned her head eagerly. The two young men were advancing through the crowd. They were both tall and athletic looking with the same dark eyes and thick curly brown hair. Rose tried to remain demure and cool but her friend was right. She had only to see Tom for her heart to beat faster. A wave of pleasure swept over her at the knowledge that they could be together once more.

When Jane had written the news of her forthcoming betrothal and begged her old schoolfriend to pay her a long visit in Town, Mr Graham had been reluctant to give permission. He did not want his daughter to be influenced by what he called the empty-headed pleasure-seekers of London society. Rose, however, longed for some variety in her life. At last she had been allowed to make the journey under the care of her older and very sober brother, George and his new wife, Augusta, when they went to London on a visit to Augusta's parents.

Rose was determined to make the most of every precious minute of her stay. Jane's circle of friends was lively, pleasant and welcoming. Her future fiancé, the dashing Freddy Hawkesleigh, was handsome enough to make Rose feel slightly envious until the day when he brought his younger brother to call. Tom Hawkesleigh was even taller than Freddy. He had the same dark eyes and good looks, with an engaging grin and a warmth of character that instantly appealed to Rose.

No sooner had she and Tom been introduced than they became inseparable. It seemed as if they had always known each other. They discovered that they held similar opinions on everything, from painting to literature, from sport to music and on ideas for improving society, especially the lot of the lower classes.

Jane's words were still ringing in her ears as Rose watched Tom approaching. Even as he exchanged a word here and there while he worked his way through the groups of people, his eyes were on her and she could see the glow in them. She felt the response come from her very core and smiled happily at him.

'You see,' murmured Jane, 'you are opening like a flower in the sunshine.'

Rose pressed her hand to her lips as the truth shot through her. This warmth that overwhelmed her each time she saw him was love, just as Jane had said. It was not because he was so tall and so good-looking. The bond they shared had more to do with a sense of them being like two halves of one whole. It felt as if they had always understood each other's thoughts.

He reached her at last and raised his eyebrows with a comical expression of relief. A bow and a word to Lady Carlyle and Tom was holding out his hand to lead Rose into the set to dance and be happy.

'Charming dress,' he said in his deep voice that sent a thrill down her spine as usual. 'Makes you look like a nymph from one of those old paintings over there.' He nodded towards the wall. 'This pale blue is most becoming.'

Rose smiled back at him. He was so smart in his claret-coloured jacket and dazzlingly white linen. It was obvious he had taken extreme care over tying his cravat. His ivory-coloured breeches seemed moulded to his well muscled thighs. That thick brown hair with its sunbleached strands was much neater than usual.

9

She thought he looked very distinguished. She could smell the spicy cologne he used, mingled with the scent she had quickly come to recognize as his own and the fresh smell of clean linen.

The dance was lively and they did not speak, merely exchanging a look or a smile from time to time. When the final chord sounded, Rose was hot and breathless.

'Drink?' asked Tom. She nodded eagerly. He seized two glasses from a nearby waiter and they sipped.

Rose frowned at the glass in her hand. 'Tom, this is champagne. I am a debutante and this is my first ball. Lady Carlyle said I must drink nothing stronger than lemonade.'

He laughed. 'One glass will not hurt you. My brother is getting engaged tonight. You can ignore the rules on this occasion. Drink up!' He raised his glass to her then drained it in two gulps.

She sipped thirstily. It was not a very large glass after all. They danced again and at the end of it they drank more champagne. Rose began to find the room too crowded. The combination of the wine, the press of people and the heat from so many hundreds of candles in the chandeliers was overpowering.

'Why can they not open a few windows?' she murmured to Tom. 'There is no air in here at all.'

He was also looking rather hot. He nodded. 'I am sure my shirt points are wilting. It seems as if the whole of the *ton* has come to Freddy and Jane's ball. I say, Rose,' he added in concern, 'you have gone white. Come on, let us find a quieter spot for you.'

He grasped her firmly under the elbow and steered her towards the doorway. She was indeed feeling quite light-headed and let him lead her, leaning gratefully on his strength. He took her into a small side room and flung up the sash. Rose leaned out of the window and took in deep breaths of the cool night air.

'Better?' He turned his head towards her and his deep voice feathered across her bare shoulders. He was standing so close that her skirts were touching his trouser leg. He also breathed in the cool air gratefully. 'Phew! We needed that.'

She nodded, her eyes closed. The fresh air felt wonderful after the noise and crush of the ballroom. But Tom's large body so close beside her was making her feel giddy again. Then she felt his breath on her neck as he sighed. He grasped her arm.

'Rose. . . .' His voice was almost a groan.

She opened her eyes in alarm. 'What is it?' Without realizing, she placed a hand on his chest, moving even closer at the sight of the trouble in his face.

Tom did not answer at once. He gazed at her as if trying to imprint her features on his mind, from her blue eyes and straight little nose to the enchanting arch of her brows; from her sweet smile to her thick, golden hair, swept up in an elaborate style this evening and set off with a sky-blue ribbon to match her gown. She waited in growing anxiety.

'Tom, what is wrong? Why are you so distressed?'

His chiselled features looked tight, there were lines beside his mouth, which was set in a grim line. His eyes were narrowed. Even so, he was still devastatingly handsome and she felt the usual thrill of pleasure as she gazed at him. But now there was a chill in her heart. At last he heaved a sigh and turned away. He gripped the window sill with both hands. 'You know I am a soldier.'

She nodded, rigid with anxiety.

'I have received a message from my colonel,' he said in a low voice. 'In another week I must rejoin my regiment. We are ordered overseas again.'

Rose's deep-blue eyes widened in horror. Her throat closed up so that she could not speak. Life without Tom seemed impossible. She put up a hand to touch his cheek. She gave a shuddering sigh and the next instant Tom's arms were around her.

'Don't cry,' he whispered in her ear. 'I can manage if you stay calm.' He rubbed his cheek against her hair, then she felt his lips pressing a kiss on her cheekbone. Rose lifted her face and offered her lips mutely. He needed no further invitation. His mouth covered hers and she yielded to the sensation of delight, swept away in a drugging pleasure. Tom slid an arm round her shoulders, pulling her against him. Her soft curves moulded against his muscled form. The familiar smell and shape of him felt so right, Rose knew she had come home.

She was past thinking now, had forgotten why she was here; she only knew that she wanted this kiss to go on forever. She put her arms round his neck, pulling his head closer still. At once the pressure of his lips grew deeper, more fierce, calling for her to respond in kind. Rose felt an answering flame and kissed him back urgently, moaning with pleasure as his arms tightened around her. Her body came alive with a host of new sensations.

In some corner of her mind, however, she knew she should not be doing this. It took an enormous effort of will but she pulled back slightly. At once he relaxed his hold. They stared wildly at each other, panting hard. Rose swallowed convulsively. Wrong or not, she wanted Tom to kiss her again.

Both moved forward at the same instant and this time their kiss was more savage, more needy. It seemed to both of them that it was their last chance to bind themselves indelibly to each other. Rose slid her hands up from Tom's broad chest, up over his jaw and hard cheekbones into his thick hair. He gave a growl and pulled her even closer, one hand at the back of her neck.

The world had shrunk to the space within Tom's arms. Rose never wanted to leave this safe haven. Her legs were shaking and she clung helplessly against him. His breathing had become hoarse, slow with a beat of passion. He was brushing little kisses across her cheekbones, against her eyelids, then beneath her ear. A delicious pang shot down her whole body to her toes as he kissed the tender flesh in the hollow of her neck.

She trembled as his large hands slid down her back and clutched her against him. Then came the slide of her sleeve being pushed down. She gave a sigh of pure pleasure when he pressed his mouth to the delicate skin of her shoulder. Her head fell back as a sharp thrill pulsed through her. She felt his warm breath against her breast and heard him growl again.

Then, like cold water, came a sharp voice.

'How *dare* you conduct yourselves in such a disgusting manner?'

Tom lifted his head. His chest was heaving. Rose struggled to open her eyes. Her body was still shaken by waves of sensation. She could not stand alone and clung to Tom. He kept one arm round her waist and tried to pull her sleeve back up her shoulder with his other hand.

'Stand away!' the cold voice said again. 'Rose, you will come with me. You, sir, will remain here.'

By now, Rose had managed to take a shaky step back from Tom. She tugged at her dress with hands that trembled. Augusta, her sister-in-law, was glaring at her in outrage.

'I am sorry, Augusta, we did not mean—'

'Sorry! You behave like a trollop and you think *sorry* will excuse you? Adjust your dress properly. George and I will escort you home at once.'

'But I am staying with Jane. It will look very odd if I leave her home in the middle of a ball.'

'You will do as I say,' Augusta's thin bosom had swelled in indignation and her pale face was mottled with disapproval. 'You have brought disgrace upon the family—'

'That is too strong,' interrupted Tom, who was trying in vain to smooth his unruly hair. 'Perhaps you could give us a minute to explain—'

'There is nothing that can excuse your shameful conduct, sir! Be so good as to wait here. I shall inform your father.'

Tom shot her a glance of dislike. He turned to Rose. 'I am so sorry to have brought this upon you. I will call on you in the morning.'

Rose nodded dumbly. She wanted to put her arms round him again. She tried to convey her feelings by her look but Augusta grabbed her arm and pulled her out of the room.

'And do not think you will ever see him again, miss,' she hissed.

'Of course I will,' protested Rose, 'Did you not hear him say he will call—?'

'After such a disgrace, that is impossible. *You* cannot be trusted, and *he* is only a younger son!'

CHAPTER ONE

Constantinople, May 1804

The tall man in the silken robes and turban put the papers down on the table and placed a strong brown hand lightly on them.

'For these, I thank you,' he said, inclining his head to the two men seated opposite him. His keen eyes went from the ambassador, fidgeting with his snuffbox, to Tom Hawkesleigh. Tom sat very upright and kept his face impassive but his gaze was intent. Kerim Pasha permitted himself a slight smile. 'You have been very prompt and the plan you outline is extremely clear and detailed. His Majesty, Sultan Selim, will certainly be pleased to consider it.'

Tom quelled his sigh of relief. He maintained a politely interested expression while inside, his heart swelled with a fierce joy. He had worked non-stop to produce this plan in the two weeks since his first meeting with this powerful minister. The ambassador was desperate to beat the French bid for this task of modernizting the Turkish Army. It would never do to allow Napoleon's envoy such a glittering triumph.

'There is just one thing,' continued Kerim Pasha, causing Tom to crash back to earth, 'His Majesty would appreciate sketches – the more modern uniforms are such an important part of the scheme.'

'I felt it would be presumptuous of me to decide on that aspect of the matter,' said Tom, his deep voice rumbling even more than usual. 'Moreover, sir, I have to say that I am no artist.' He looked very directly at Kerim Pasha. The Turk's eyes narrowed in amusement, but his hawklike face remained impassive.

The ambassador cleared his throat. 'If you wish for some sketches, Your Excellency, Mr Hawkesleigh will supply them very shortly. They would just be suggestions, of course.'

'Of course.' Kerim Pasha nodded. 'But it is an integral part of the whole scheme. If we modernize our weapons and our tactics, we must have modern uniforms that are appropriate for using them.'

There was a moment's pause. Then, 'Right away, Hawkesleigh,' urged the ambassador. 'His Excellency and I can discuss further details while you come up with a few sketches.'

Tom checked the protest that rose to his lips. For God's sake, had the man not heard him say he could not draw? His nostrils flared with a burst of rage, but he bent his head to conceal it, stood, bowed to their guest and left the room.

He closed the door carefully, then a thunderous frown descended on his handsome face. Swearing bitterly under his breath he strode along the wide passageway. He glared around as he went, looking for some way to vent his anger. Tom paused on the threshold of his own office. His assistant was sitting at the desk, copying notes into a ledger. A gleam of hope came into Tom's eyes as he considered the blond head bent over the books.

'Can you draw, Seb?'

The young man looked up, his blue eyes wide open in astonishment. 'Draw? No,' he said baldly, 'not at all.'

'Get out then,' snarled Tom. He dropped into the chair hastily vacated by a bewildered and alarmed Sebastian Welland. Still scowling, he added, 'And just see that I am not disturbed.'

Half an hour later another balled-up sheet of paper hit the wall. Tom pushed back his chair with a frustrated sigh. He strode over to the window and frowned out at the embassy garden with its trees and flowering shrubs, but he found no inspiration there. He raked his fingers through his hair, banged his fist against the wall, muttered a few choice oaths and wheeled round, back to his desk.

'Oh Lord!' he exclaimed ruefully, looking at the number of balls of paper scattered around the room. Nothing he could draw would impress the Sultan. Tom's eyes narrowed as he thought of Kerim Pasha. He was one of the most powerful men at the court. Why could he not find a Turkish artist and instruct the man as to what was wanted? Tom made a wry grimace. Because he was just too intelligent. Everything had to come from the foreign advisers, so that if the Sultan and his chief officers did not like it, no blame would attach to Kerim Pasha.

From the tales Tom had heard, life at the Ottoman court was a perilous affair. Exile or even execution were not infrequent for ministers whose policies did not find favour with the more powerful viziers. And even he could be at risk if his plan for modernization became known to the more conservative generals. Those pashas had their own interests to protect, which was why all this was top secret . . . and at the same time the British were in competition with the French. There was so much prestige and money involved.

For Tom, it was the danger that added spice to his job. He much preferred these secret missions to life as an officer in the British Army. After the Egyptian Campaign, Tom had resigned his commission to fight for a while alongside the soldiers of the Ottoman Empire, or to travel in the Levant. To all appearances, he was just another young gentleman fascinated by an exotic way of life. But in reality his journeys were dictated by the Foreign Office, depending on where secret diplomatic missions were needed. They were mostly schemes to thwart Napoleon's attempts to extend French influence around the eastern Mediterranean.

In this current assignment, Tom felt privileged to work with Kerim Pasha. Although he had a ruthless streak, the man was truly devoted to serving his country. He had admitted in their discussions that the Ottoman Empire was crumbling due to the outdated military methods and weapons they were using. And this brought Tom back to his present predicament. His 'soldiers' drawn as a combination of circles and cylinders just did not look like inspiring new soldiers in new uniforms. The Sultan would laugh himself silly at these drawings. He leaned his forehead on his hand as he considered.

Suddenly he was aware that the door had opened. Looking up with a frown he saw that it was only Mehmet, bringing him a glass of *hoshaf*, the sharp tasting fruit juice so popular in Constantinople in the growing warmth of early summer.

'Can *you* draw?' Tom asked, holding out his glass for a refill.

Mehmet raised his chin to signal no.

Tom set his glass down with a snap. 'Well then, do not disturb me,' he growled, setting to work on another attempt. He frowned in concentration as he scratched out his little shapes on the page. From time to time he dashed a hand through his thick hair with its sunbleached golden streaks. Soon he looked as if he had been out in a high wind but he was not aware of the havoc he had wrought and in his current state of frustration, would not have cared anyway.

He became conscious that the door was open. 'Mehmet!' he thundered without looking up, 'pray close that door.'

There was the sound of someone clearing their throat. A soft, feminine sound. Tom jerked up his head and his dark eyes opened wide. Before him stood three shrouded figures.

CHAPTER TWO

Tom gulped and frowned at the empty glass. Just what had Mehmet put in the *hoshaf*? To his annoyance, a large blot was spreading over his sketch. With a sigh he set down his pen and looked up again reluctantly. Apparently it was not an illusion. The three dark shapes were still there.

Not for the first time he found himself wishing that he knew just what he was looking at. Some ladies wore only the lightest of silken veils and you could more or less look them in the eye. These three were completely hidden. He scowled. How dare they invade his office at such a time?

Behind them he spotted Sebastian Welland, making frantic gestures to him to stand. With a sigh, Tom rose to his full six foot three. There was a rustle as three heads shifted upwards beneath their wraps. From behind one of the veils came a sudden sharp intake of breath. Then silence. Tom's thick brows drew down as he glared from one to the other, waiting. Normally women did not appear in public offices, especially Turkish women. Was it some kind of plot to disrupt these delicate negotiations?

Sebastian now reappeared, together with Mehmet, carrying chairs. As he placed the seats for the visitors the young man stammered, 'Ladies, this is our special envoy, Mr Hawkesleigh.' Turning to Tom he quailed at the glare he received but persevered in his explanation. 'I know you said you were not to be disturbed . . . but . . . but the ambassador's guest is still here. . . .'

Tom glared again at his unwelcome visitors. 'I regret I cannot spare any time at present—'

At this, the smallest one put back her veil with an impatient gesture. Tom saw that she was fair-skinned and haired. She looked to be in her late forties and had a keen, scholarly air.

'Lady Emily Westacote,' she said briskly, 'and these are my two nieces.'

'Westacote?' echoed Tom. 'Sir Philip Westacote, the antiquarian. . . ?'

Lady Westacote nodded. 'Just so. I am his wife. And we are in need of help.'

'In what way, ma'am?' Tom knew his tone was less than cordial. She probably wanted permits to excavate some godforsaken ruin in a remote and bandit-infested area of the Levant. Surely it could wait half an hour. His frustrated gaze turned to the other two females. They had not removed their veils.

Lady Westacote followed his gaze. 'Girls!' she said reprovingly. At this the figure on her left raised her arms and put back the heavy veil to reveal a lovely face with huge pansy-brown eyes and shining dark hair. Tom's eyebrows lifted a little and Sebastian gaped in frank admiration. Then their heads all turned expectantly towards the last veiled figure. There was a pause,then very slowly she raised her arms. Tom could sense the reluctance with which she folded back her veil. Then he drew in his breath sharply. His brows met across his formidable nose in a deep frown.

The young lady met Tom's eyes. Her oval face was pale and mask-like. Her hair was the colour of ripe wheat, just as he remembered. Tom felt a kind of pressure on his heart. Of all the impossible coincidences. What could bring Rose Graham here?

'Allow me to present Mrs Rosalind Charteris,' Lady Westacote indicated the fair-haired girl, 'and her sister, Miss Helena Graham.'

Charteris! So she was married now. Tom could feel the blood draining from his cheeks. He kept his face impassive as he sketched a bow in the general direction of the young ladies. The surge of emotion and anger swamped him. For a moment he could not speak. Then he recovered enough to snap his fingers at Sebastian, who was still gazing from one beauty to the other. The young man gulped, nodded and disappeared, to return a few minutes later with Mehmet and the tray of glasses and fruit juice.

While Mehmet poured drinks for the ladies, Tom stole a look at Rose Charteris. She was every bit as lovely as his memory of her. That glorious hair, so silky and thick, her creamy skin and that provocative pink mouth. He clenched his jaw against the memory of their last meeting. In spite of the years abroad, he had not forgotten the feel of her in his arms. He instinctively knew how ill-at-ease she was. She had not expected to find him here. She was gazing around the room, not looking in his direction. His mouth twisted. So what! She had married another man. And why was he surprised at that? She had never answered a single one of the many letters he had sent her. His bitter thoughts were interrupted by Lady Westacote's voice.

'That was most welcome,' she was telling Mehmet, 'yes, indeed I will have another glassful. I have such a raging thirst.'

Tom's eyes narrowed as he watched her hand tremble when she took the glass and drank again. She dabbed at her forehead with a damp-looking handkerchief, but she was still in a fighting mood. She gave him a stern glare.

'Now, Mr Hawkesleigh, we are sorry to interrupt your important work' – Tom noted the emphasis she put on the word – 'but we are in a most uncomfortable situation and must needs throw ourselves on your mercy.'

Trouble! thought Tom with a sinking heart. He merely nodded, however, and Lady Westacote, needing no further invitation, hurried on. 'We have been in Egypt for some months as part of the latest antiquarian expedition. While the gentlemen went on an exploratory trip up the Nile, my nieces and I were working on hieroglyphs in Cairo. But once the men had left, we were harassed and intimidated until we were forced to leave.' She pressed the handkerchief to her lips and tried twice to speak, but ended up shaking her head and covering her eyes.

Mrs Charteris squeezed her aunt's hand. 'Do not distress yourself, Aunt,' she said in the soft, melodious voice he remembered so well. 'I will explain.' She glanced up at Tom from very blue eyes and then looked away again. 'We had to leave our home in Cairo very suddenly. We managed to embark on a British frigate that was coming here. But the captain cannot take us any further. And we do not know what has happened to the rest of our party. My uncle and . . . and all our companions. . . .' She faltered to a stop and caught her bottom lip in her teeth. Her face was even paler than before. Her hands twisted in her lap.

Tom had sunk back into his chair, but at this, he leaned forward, fists clenched. He stared at Mrs Charteris, his dark eyes burning. 'Are you saying that you have suffered violence at the hands of these scoundrels in Cairo?'

This time she met his gaze squarely. 'Oh, no, not physical violence, not us. Our servants did get beaten until most of them ran away. We knew then that we dared not stay any longer.'

'By heaven, ma'am,' rumbled Tom, thumping his big fist on the table, 'surely your menfolk knew better than to leave you with only a few local servants to care for you.'

Again she turned her blue gaze on him. 'The British Consul was supposed to oversee our safety, but he was called away urgently to Alexandria, so that left us without any protection. And the French are very much opposed to our work. We had collected a large number of artefacts and they were no doubt angry about that.'

Lady Westacote raised a shaking hand to her forehead and closed her eyes.

'My aunt has a fever,' added Mrs Charteris.

Her sister put an arm around her aunt and looked at Tom with those huge brown eyes. 'Please . . . we need to find a lodging at once.'

Tom clutched at his hair as he grasped the extent of their

problems. He looked at the three of them, huddled together for comfort and regretted his surliness when they first arrived.

'Lady Westacote appears to have Nile Fever. From what I saw of that when I was in Egypt, the best treatment is rest. But I will find a physician; there are medicines that help.' He stood up, his drawings forgotten. 'Where is your luggage? Have you come straight from the ship?'

The two girls looked up at him hopefully, but before either of them could answer there was a tap at the door and Kerim Pasha advanced into the room. All heads turned towards this magnificent figure, exuding power and authority.

Kerim Pasha reached Tom's desk and he stopped there. 'Pray pardon this intrusion, Mr Hawkesleigh,' he said in his cultured English accent, his voice as deep as Tom's but with a more velvety tone. 'I am aware that there is an emergency and I wished to assure you that my business can wait a few days longer.' He touched the sheet of paper with Tom's sketch on it and raised an eyebrow. There was an infinitesimal pause before he turned towards the newcomers, placed a hand on his heart and bowed courteously. 'I could not leave, however, until I discovered whether or not I could be of help.'

His hawklike face with its neatly trimmed beard betrayed nothing but polite interest. He turned an expectant gaze on Tom, who felt a rush of hostility. He did not like this man seeing the ladies when they were so vulnerable. He clenched his fists behind his back. 'Your Excellency, may I make known to you Lady Westacote and her nieces, Mrs Charteris and Miss Graham. They have just arrived from Cairo.'

Kerim Pasha inclined his head. Tom noticed the slight flare of his nostrils. 'Ladies. You were part of the British expedition.'

It was a statement, not a question. Tom's jaw clenched. *The cunning devil, he knew everything.* How had he discovered these ladies were here in his office? Of course, Mehmet must have told him. And what did he want from them? Tom's lips compressed as he studied the man's face for a clue. It had to be information. It

23

had better be for information, he told himself grimly, darting a look at those two lovely faces.

All three ladies were dumbstruck at this vision of oriental magnificence. Kerim Pasha was tall and broad-shouldered, his splendid physique revealed by the blue tunic with the sash emphasizing his trim waist. His long legs were encased in loose-fitting pantaloons tucked into well polished knee-high boots.

Typical! thought Tom sourly. They had forgotten all their woes, sensing the power of this newcomer. And how long would it take Kerim Pasha to find out what he wanted to know from them? Tom groaned inside. If he was to find them a home for that night, he needed to set to work quickly. Such things had to be negotiated and Turkish homeowners liked to spend hours bargaining.

These ladies were weary and travel-stained and one at least was seriously ill. Tom knew from his own time in Cairo that this fever could be deadly if neglected. But for the moment Lady Emily had recovered her composure. The two girls were looking at her anxiously as she explained to Kerim Pasha how they had been chased out of their home.

'I am horrified at such events as well as by the distress this has caused you, madam,' that gentleman was saying. 'I fear we have endless trouble with that part of our empire. But I will see what I can do to help the other members of your expedition.'

Helena drew a deep breath and clasped her hands at her bosom. 'Oh, sir, is it possible – from this distance.'

Kerim Pasha gave a dismissive wave of his hand. 'There are ways.' He turned to Tom. 'I am deeply concerned by the plight of these unfortunate ladies. For the honour of my people I must make amends.'

Tom's hopes rose. Would the Pasha send his own men to find a lodging? But the Turk's next words took everyone by surprise.

'It would greatly honour myself and my family if you would agree to stay in my humble home while you are in Constantinople.' He looked from Tom to Lady Westacote. Rose darted a quick look at Tom but saw Kerim Pasha's eyes on him, daring him to object.

'Then that is settled.' The Turk smiled. 'My servants will convey your luggage. I will arrange for a carriage and my sister, Latife, will come to escort you. It is not very far.'

Rose again looked at Tom with a question in her eyes, but then her aunt slipped sideways onto the floor in a faint.

CHAPTER THREE

The day was going to be warm. Rose stirred from her chair to check on her aunt once again. Lady Westacote was sleeping quietly at last. She had been very restless and feverish but the bitter drink that their hostess, Latife Hatun, had prepared, now seemed to be having an effect. Rose tiptoed over to glance at Helena. Her sister was sunk in the sleep of exhaustion. She had insisted on sharing the job of nursing the invalid, but, as their aunt gradually quietened, Rose, quite unable to sleep herself, persuaded her sister to get some rest.

Now that her aunt no longer needed all her attention, Rose kept returning to that moment in the embassy office when she saw the man who had once meant all the world to her. She had seen the same shock and anger she felt mirrored in his eyes. What cause had *he* to be angry? Had he not walked away and disappeared without trace? He had never even sent a single letter to explain his absence.

At first she had been certain he would appear or at least write to her. But as the weeks lengthened into months, Rose sank into despair. It was made harder by her father's constant laments over the bad influence of London society. He forbade her to communicate with Jane any more. Isolated at home, watched over by her narrow-minded sister-in-law, Rose had been lonely and heart-sore.

Eventually the black misery had dulled into a deep ache that she learned to live with. Pride meant that during all that miserable time she had shown a calm face to the world. Had she been nothing but an agreeable way of passing the time for a young soldier on leave? The idea still hurt. Rose wiped her eyes angrily. Finally she had consented to the marriage her father had planned for her, with his godson.

Hugh Charteris had gained the rank of naval captain early in 1800 and the wedding followed before the end of the year. He was a quiet, correct man, more at ease on his man o' war than in society drawing-rooms. Rose had barely endured three months of married life when Captain Charteris was recalled to duty. Six months later came the news that he had died in action. His parents had shown no interest in offering Rose a home on their estate, which was encumbered with debt, due to their older son's reckless gambling.

Thankfully, by this time, Sir Philip and Lady Westacote and Helena had returned from a lengthy expedition to India. Aunt Emily insisted that Rose must stay with her in their lovely Tudor mansion by the banks of the river Thames near the market town of Reading. During their schooldays in Reading, the girls had sometimes stayed at Rivercourt with their kindly, if eccentric aunt.

That was where Helena had first become fascinated by the ancient languages her aunt studied. Rose, meanwhile, was happy in the peaceful atmosphere of the quaint old house and especially in the gardens that swept down to the wide river. Here she could sit and paint to her heart's content. It was exactly the kind of ancient building to appeal to romantically inclined schoolgirls. The dark corners, the inner courtyard, the gallery, all encouraged Rose to imagine touching scenes in times gone by.

When Rose joined them on their return from India, they were all very glad of her artistic skills. She sketched many of the items they had brought back with them. Her drawings were used to illustrate the papers they wrote for learned journals and for the lectures they frequently gave.

It was no surprise when Aunt Emily and Helena became

fascinated by the Rosetta Stone that had recently been placed on display in the British Museum. And when Sir Philip announced that he and his friend, the explorer Max Kendal, were setting up an expedition to travel to Cairo, Rose knew she would rather endure the heat and dust than return to the bleak life of her father's home. Indeed, the whole journey until recently had been an amazing adventure for them all. Cairo was a fascinating city and in spite of the heat and discomfort, even Rose had been awed by her visit to the pyramids at Giza. And it was a matter of pride that all the sketches she made for her uncle and aunt really were invaluable to them.

But the ladies had been forced out of Egypt and now here they were, completely out of their way in Constantinople, with Aunt Emily so ill. It seemed quite likely that Uncle Philip, Max Kendal and the other members of their group were in danger also. To crown it all, she thought bitterly, by some malign fate, the English official they met at the embassy in Constantinople was the one man above all others that she did not want to see. Rose gritted her teeth and rubbed her tired eyes.

A shadow moved behind her and she swung round. It was Latife Hatun, the younger sister of Kerim Pasha. This beautiful and elegant lady had welcomed them graciously and installed them on the top floor of the enormous mansion on the hilltop overlooking the sea. It was Latife Hatun herself who had prepared a medicine for Aunt Emily.

'How is she?' she whispered, nodding towards the bed.

'Sleeping at last,' whispered Rose in reply. 'Your bitter drink has brought her fever down.'

Latife nodded. 'Of course.' Her almond eyes considered Rose's weary face. 'But you have not slept. And now you have a visitor from your embassy.'

Rose jerked her head up. 'Surely it is too early in the day. . . .'

Her hostess lifted her chin in that negative gesture. 'Our day begins before the dawn. Come, my dear, he is impatient to speak to you.'

'Can I not send a message?'

'It is best if he sees you, I think. It will reassure him.' Her eyes crinkled in a smile. 'Although maybe not when he sees that you are dressed in harem clothes.'

Rose cast a glance at the yellow tunic and loose trousers she was wearing. She gave an answering smile.

'Take a shawl and go down to the *selamlik*. Fatma will show you the way. I will take good care of your aunt, have no fear.'

Rose draped the white silk shawl over her shoulders to cover the low neckline of her flimsy tunic. She grimaced as she ran a hand over her hair, pulled back in a long, thick plait. But no, she was not going to cover her head. That *would* give the messenger the wrong impression and cause alarm at the embassy. Feeling weary and cross, she followed Fatma down two floors to the reception room. She padded silently over the soft rugs that were spread everywhere. The elderly maidservant led her across a wide central hallway and pushed open the double doors at the far side.

'Salon,' she said, giving Rose's bare head a disapproving look as she stood aside for her to go in first.

A tall figure Rose recognized at once was pacing back and forth in the opulent room. His hands were clasped behind his back. His face seen in profile was rigid. Sudden alarm made Rose forget all the awkwardness of confronting Tom again.

'H-have you had bad news from Cairo?'

At the sound of her voice he whirled round and stood as if turned to stone. For a long moment he simply stared. At least it gave her time to find her composure. Her unruly heart was beating at a terrible rate. It must be due to her bitter anger at having to see *him* yet again. Rose kept her head high and stood straight and still. She forced herself to inspect him in the same way he was examining her.

There were subtle changes in him from the eager young man he had been. This was a man who had faced danger many times and triumphed, a man who carved his own path through life's hazards. And the years had made him even more handsome, his face so chiselled, his hair bleached blonder by the hot Mediterranean sun. His dark eyes, always expressive, were scorching her as he looked her up and down and down and up. His face darkened.

'So they have put you in the harem!' he growled at last.

She raised her brows. 'If you are referring to my garments, our kind hostess has given us fresh clothes while our own are laundered.'

'Yes but. . . .' He opened his hands in an impatient gesture. He glanced around and seemed to listen. His gaze came back to her. Rose understood. Of course, someone was listening to their conversation. She did not think that Fatma understood a single word of English, she was simply here for propriety.

'We have two rooms at the top of the house for ourselves. Remember that my aunt is ill.'

'How is Lady Westacote?'

Rose's lips twisted. 'Still very unwell. She passed a restless night but is sleeping now. Latife Hatun has made her a medicine which seems to be helping a great deal. *Have* you any news from Cairo?' Her voice trembled slightly.

'There has been no time yet.'

She dipped her head, thinking what would happen if the news was bad when it came. At last she looked up. He was watching her from under those thick brows.

'I thought that maybe a Turkish ship had arrived and someone had heard something. . . .' Her hands fluttered.

Tom shook his head firmly. 'The only ship to come in from Egypt was the one you arrived on. You can be certain that Kerim Pasha has already sent word that the members of your expedition must be protected.'

She nodded. 'I see.'

There was a long pause. She stared at a cypress tree through the window opposite. At length, Tom seemed to recall why he was here.

'I have come to convey to you the ambassador's concern. He

regrets he only learnt of your arrival after you had already gone to a Turkish home. Not,' said Tom honestly, 'that we could offer you anything to compare with this.' He glanced at the rich furnishings and costly ornaments. 'But he asked me to discover if you have any requests that we can fulfil.'

Mindful of the hidden listener, Rose spoke clearly. 'Pray thank the ambassador. We have been most warmly received here. Thanks to our kind hostess, my aunt is already much better. But if you will excuse me, I must return to her.'

She inclined her head briefly and turned away. She had not gone two steps when his voice checked her.

'No, wait . . . the ambassador has instructed me to call each morning to discover how you all go on.'

She half turned her head, just getting a glimpse of him as she nodded again. She slipped out of the room. On the other side of the door, she had to stand still briefly until her knees stopped trembling so violently. She made herself draw a deep breath and move forward again. Her back was ramrod straight. She had *done* it. She had looked him in the eye and not shown any emotion.

But he had been discomposed. Not that it was any pleasure to discover that she could still read Tom's thoughts as clearly now as when they had been such good friends in that other life long ago. Now she was so utterly weary that it was an ordeal to climb two flights of stairs. But she knew that Latife Hatun was waiting to be sure that the English embassy staff did not think the ladies had been kidnapped. Rose set a smile on her face as she began to follow Fatma one slow step at a time.

CHAPTER FOUR

Left alone in the salon, Tom unclenched his fists and shrugged his tense shoulders. He dashed a hand through the hair that was tumbling over his forehead. God, she was so lovely. He rubbed his aching head. Last night he had not slept. He had thought his busy life of intrigue and adventure had stifled the memories of the girl he loved. But one glimpse of her had let those memories flood out. And she was married!

Fool, he told himself, *of course she was married*. What other outcome could there be, especially for a beautiful girl? He gave an impatient gesture, as if shutting out the past. Drawing in a painful breath, he made for the door, flung it open and, squaring his shoulders, crossed the hall to the entrance door. It was open and two menservants were bowing low. A tall figure strode in. Tom halted, face to face with Kerim Pasha.

'My young friend!' Kerim Pasha's eyes were keen but he spoke smoothly. 'I can guess your errand,' he went on, a note of amusement in his voice. 'I trust all is well.'

Tom bowed. 'Thank you, Your Excellency, I am able to take a promising report to the ambassador.'

'Splendid! But please, before you do so, be so kind as to spare me a moment.' The Turk indicated that Tom should go with him back into the salon. 'You have not been offered refreshment? That must be remedied.' He snapped his fingers and one of the servants scurried away. He then spoke to another, who bowed and disappeared in another direction.

Now what was happening? The last thing Tom wanted at this moment was refreshment. It would choke him. He needed to vent his frustration in movement. But there was no escape. Gritting his teeth, he followed his host. Kerim Pasha led the way out onto the terrace and then to a white-painted wooden kiosk in the centre of the garden. They climbed the two steps and sat down facing each other on the low padded benches.

Flowering shrubs made a fragrant dapple of shade but there was nowhere for anyone to hide within earshot. Almost as soon as they were seated a man came hurrying up with a book. Kerim Pasha placed it on the bench beside him.

'First, the coffee,' he said. 'I find it stimulates the mind when important matters are to be discussed.'

'A wonderful beverage, sir,' replied Tom, wondering what was in that book and what matter needed such earnest discussion. Surely he was not going to offer to buy the girls. Tom gave his host a quick glance. He had seen the man's eyes light up when he saw the two beauties the previous day. And how smoothly he had spirited them away into his home. The ambassador had been incandescent when he found out. And here was Tom, caught in the middle of awkward negotiations as usual.

The coffee arrived. The aroma was mouth-watering and a couple of sips helped to clear Tom's throbbing head. He admired the kiosk and the garden. Kerim Pasha was graciously pleased. There was a gleam in his almond eyes. At last he set his cup down and his manner changed.

'Business,' he said. 'I regret the need for it on such a pleasant morning, but you and I are busy people, Mr Hawkesleigh. First let me assure you that I have sent word to Cairo. Whatever the situation at present – and let us hope this brave band of scholars and enthusiasts is large enough to deter possible thugs and evildoers – they will be under the protection of our officials and escorted by our soldiers so long as they remain in Egypt.'

Tom nodded. 'Thank you, sir. That will reassure the ladies.' He frowned. 'Provided, of course, that nothing has happened so far.'

Kerim Pasha made a dismissive gesture. 'No Egyptians will hinder them from digging in the sand.' His shoulders shook slightly. 'It is more likely to be the French who object to English antiquaries making important discoveries or acquiring treasures. And there, Mr Hawkesleigh, I hope they understand each other's tactics.'

There was a short pause, then he resumed. 'Speaking of tactics, I have informed His Majesty, Sultan Selim that the plan he is impatient to see will soon be ready. However. . . .' He stopped and picked up the book, opening it at a certain page. He leaned over and held it out to Tom. Tom saw a gilded and painted picture of an Ottoman army marching to war. It was very detailed and bright with colour. Men, horses, weapons, even the plants by the side of the road, everything was delicately observed and quite clear.

Tom stared at the picture. He felt his face going red. At last he looked up. 'I cannot draw like that, sir,' he added.

'Yes,' murmured Kerim Pasha with a wry smile, 'I did see your er . . . sketch yesterday.'

Tom sighed. 'I cannot find anyone able to do the drawings, sir. As you said, nobody must know what is being planned.'

Kerim Pasha leaned forward. 'No indeed. We must plan in secret. It will be a bloody business when the time comes. The old guard will never accept these changes and they will strike in anger and revenge. This is something that could put the lives of all foreigners in the city in danger.' His eyes were keen as lances. In that moment Tom saw just how vital the matter was.

Here was a proud general who could see how desperately his country's army needed reform if they were to hold on to their empire. And at the same time he was a diplomat and a man of vision with a wide culture.

Tom looked at him with renewed respect. He sincerely wanted to help. 'I have been most careful, sir. You now have the only copy of my report. I destroyed all my notes.' He hesitated. 'I – er – even destroyed all those sketches I made yesterday.' He heaved a sigh. 'I shall try again.'

Kerim Pasha gave a chuckle and gripped Tom's shoulder. 'Aha, *Ingiliz*! You are a man after my own heart. Such a pity that you are not a Turk.' He indicated the book of paintings. 'But I fear we must have more detail in the drawings. His Majesty will expect it.'

Tom nodded glumly. It was hopeless. Then a memory struck him and he raised his forefinger, his eyes brightening. 'Perhaps one of the young ladies could draw them. They are often skilled in painting. And they are well protected from curious eyes while they are here in your home.' *With so many guards round the place, all bristling with weapons.*

'Hmm. I wonder. . . .' Kerim Pasha mused while he delicately sipped his coffee. 'I will ask my sister to enquire if they draw.'

Tom only hesitated for a moment. 'Actually, sir, I know that one of them draws very well. I – knew her – slightly in London some years ago.' He was talking too fast. Why could he not be cool about her, dammit? And why should he care? She was a stranger now. Anyway, he was not revealing very much.

'I see.' Kerim Pasha stroked his chin. Just how much could he see, the cunning devil? Tom tried not to squirm as the grey eyes dwelt on him.

Kerim Pasha put down his coffee cup at last. 'And which one is it that you knew and who draws well? Such beautiful young ladies, but I only saw them so briefly.'

'The blonde one, sir. Mrs Charteris.'

'Very good. Perhaps when you make your duty call tomorrow morning, the ladies will be rested and the aunt in better health. Then you can discuss the drawings with Mrs Charteris. I regret to press the matter so much but time is short.' Kerim Pasha rose as he spoke. The interview was over.

Tom was glad to escape from the well-guarded *yali*. He strode out with his head high and marched off up the road with his usual long stride. But he was distinctly uneasy. True, Kerim Pasha had seen that he could not draw and he had admitted it. But he should not have involved Rose in this army business. Even if she had spurned him and married another man, he did not want to bring danger upon her.

How would she react to the request about drawing uniforms? He gritted his teeth. She was going to be furious that he had discussed her with the pasha. But if she agreed to do the drawings, they would enhance the report marvellously. Tom remembered – too well – how delightfully she had sketched the various members of their group of friends, that autumn in London.

Had he done wrong in drawing Rose and her drawing skills to Kerim Pasha's attention? If he had, the next few days were going to be difficult. Rose had a temper and he expected to be on the receiving end of her fury. He had nearly reached the embassy, but then he changed his mind and turned aside into the street that followed the downward curve of the hill, towards his own lodgings. Why he felt a sudden need to make sure that all was well he could not say. Instinct, born of many adventures, told him something was wrong.

He entered his rooms very quietly, on the alert for an intruder. There was nothing obviously wrong, nothing missing. But a careful examination of his table showed him that someone had been through his papers. Tom was meticulous about keeping everything in a certain order and he could tell that the papers and books had been moved.

The old man who owned the house had seen nothing. No visitors had called, he said. Why would anyone come looking for him here when it was known that the English *effendi* spent his days at the new palace in the main avenue?

CHAPTER FIVE

Rose awoke from a troubled dream in which she was fleeing armed men in the darkness. Since the terrifying time they had lived through in Cairo, this dream often troubled her sleep. She sat up with a jerk, heart thumping. She was bathed in sweat and her throat was dry. The room was unfamiliar. Had they kidnapped her? Then she remembered. They were in a safe haven in a mansion in Constantinople. She leaned her head on her knees while her heartbeat slowed. Then memory came back. Her aunt. . . ?

She leapt off the divan and at once saw Aunt Emily, lying on a bed close by the window. She was propped up against a mass of cushions. Rose took a step closer. Lady Westacote opened her eyes and smiled at her.

'Rose, dear,' she said in a feeble tone, 'at last you have woken up. Poor Helena has been looking after us both all day.'

'I was too tired to sleep,' said Rose, rubbing her face. 'It took ages for me to settle down. And now I need to wash.' She took her aunt's hand. 'But first, I am so glad to see you looking better – even if only a little. That drink has certainly reduced your fever.' She looked at the empty jug. 'Our hosts seem to know a lot about such illnesses.'

'We are in their debt.' Lady Westacote blinked away a tear. 'Helena has told me that the gentleman—'

'Kerim Pasha,' nodded Rose, 'has sent orders to Cairo to help

Philip and Max and all the team. You can imagine how that has relieved her mind. She was in such despair. . . .'

'It is a huge relief to all of us, dear ma'am. But I am not surprised that he should do so. He seems powerful enough to command anything he wishes.' She felt her aunt's forehead. 'Do not talk any more now, Aunt Emily, you are tired. I will come back and sit with you when I have washed.' She pulled at her sweat-dampened shirt and grimaced.

In the adjoining-room, as large and airy as the bedchamber, there were low, padded benches around three walls. The fourth, inside wall, had a fireplace in the middle, with wooden panelling each side. In the panelling were set rows of niches, all decorated with ornate carved woodwork.

Rose saw that Fatma was already waiting. The maid pulled open the concealed door by the fireplace. It led to a tiny room in which was a low marble basin and copper pots of steaming water.

'Oh, *yes!*' Rose gave a sigh of pleasure, Fatma laughed and handed her towels. The warm water did a lot to banish the lingering dream. Feeling fresh and clean again, Rose went to sit on a divan by the window. Fatma bore down on her waving a hairbrush. She was fascinated by the thick golden hair and brushed it carefully, smoothing away all the tangles and replaiting it.

Rose nodded her thanks. Fatma beckoned her over to the heap of garments in decidedly exotic styles and colours. Today Rose was more relaxed about wearing these harem clothes. The first time she had wondered just what dressing in such an oriental style was meant to signify. Now she felt that the clothes were suitable for the climate and for life in rooms furnished with divans rather than chairs.

Fatma was holding up a soft turquoise silk robe and looking a question. Rose smiled and took it, choosing a pair of loose trousers in a darker shade and a gauzy undershirt of white. Fatma gave a grunt of approval and added a fringed pink sash, winding it round and round her waist.

'Everything is so exquisite,' remarked Helena, who had just appeared. She yawned and stretched. 'I fell asleep on the balcony of all places.' She picked up a sleeveless jacket and showed it to her sister. 'Have you looked at the embroidery on these garments? Such delicate work. I mean to try and copy some of the motifs.' She put her head on one side and grinned at Rose's appearance. 'Very fine,' she said, her voice bubbling with laughter. 'You are ready to be introduced to a prince at the least.'

Rose made a face at her. 'Oh, and I think you will require a sultan, my dear. That almond-green robe sets off your hair and eyes to perfection. As if you did not know.'

Helena glanced in the little mirror on the wall. 'Well, I know how to make the most of any luxuries that come my way. And after being crowded in that tiny cabin on the ship, this is wonderful.' She waved her arm to indicate their living area. Leaving Fatma to tidy up, they went back to their aunt. She looked thin and tired but her eyes were clear and when she saw them she gave her old smile.

There was a stir at the doorway. In came their hostess, Latife Hatun, followed by several girls, carrying laden trays.

'We have brought chicken broth for the invalid,' smiled Latife Hatun. She cast a critical glance at Lady Westacote. 'Yes, the fever has gone for now. You must drink this,' she urged as the invalid shook her head. 'We need to strengthen you. Your nieces are anxious – and my brother has strictly charged me to restore you to good health. And to see that the young ladies are rested and well cared for. We must make you forget the nightmare you suffered in Cairo.'

At the word *nightmare*, Rose repressed a shudder. Her dream was still fresh in her mind. But she merely smiled at Latife. This lady was such a mixture of charm and imperious authority that it was impossible to resist her. She was of medium height and graceful, elegant in her dress and in all her movements. Like her brother, she spoke English with hardly a trace of accent. Rose wondered how they had learnt the language so fluently.

'Come, let us sit outside while your aunt drinks her soup. She does not need all of us watching her.'

They followed her onto the balcony. Rose noticed for the first time the pleasant green garden below. A long way below, thought Rose. They were on the third floor of this enormous mansion. If Kerim Pasha called this his humble abode, what must his country estate be like?

With a graceful movement, Latife swung her legs up on the long, high bench so she was sitting crosslegged. She settled her back against the cushion, then with an elegant gesture, invited the girls to join her. Arranging herself in a similar style, Rose decided that the loose trousers were exactly right for sitting cross-legged on a divan. She had to stifle a smile at the thought of how her old governess would have been scandalized. But she could not quite hide the smile.

'Something amuses you?'

Rose nodded and let the smile grow. 'I am smiling with pleasure. Now we are able to relax, thanks to your kindness.' She gestured towards the garden. 'The view is delightful, particularly the way the water sparkles through the cypress trees. Is that the boundary to your garden?'

A girl had arrived with tiny cups of fragrant coffee. Latife sipped delicately. 'It is,' she said at last, 'but I do not see why that makes you smile.'

'My sister is an artist,' put in Helena. 'When she smiles like that, it is because she has found a view she wants to paint.'

'Now I understand, Rose,' said her hostess. 'I may call you just Rose?' As Rose nodded, she continued, 'And Helena.' She leaned forward to smile at Helena who was seated next to Rose. 'We need not be formal amongst ourselves. Please, you must both call me Latife.'

They murmured polite thanks.

'So, please do paint this scene and I will watch you if I may? Such an agreeable change from our usual routine.'

'I fear our presence makes a great deal of work for you, Latife,'

Rose said, a little shyly. 'We must thank you for rescuing us at such short notice.'

Latife beckoned the girl forward to collect the empty cups. 'It is always a pleasure to have guests from abroad.' She smiled warmly at them. 'And you are very welcome here. It is not often that I can practise my English.'

Another servant appeared and whispered something to her mistress. Latife's eyes turned to Rose as she listened. Her face was smiling, but her brows rose in surprise. At last she nodded, said something and the little messenger departed. Latife stood up.

'Now I must explain. Rose, my brother is asking if you would be good enough to go down to that kiosk you can see there in the garden. He cannot come up here, of course.' Seeing the alarm in both girls' faces, she quickly added, 'No, no, do not worry. It is nothing to do with your menfolk.'

For the second time that day Rose followed Fatma down to the salon and this time out into the garden with its flowering shrubs. As she approached the kiosk, she saw a tall form rise to his feet. He was a fine figure of a man, lean and compact, yet his strength was obvious. Now she could see a similarity to his sister in the almond eyes and high cheekbones. His grey eyes sparkled as he watched her approach.

He bowed courteously, a hand against his heart in the Turkish fashion.

'So good of you to answer my plea, Mrs Charteris. I will not take up too much of your time.' He indicated that she should sit.

Rose looked about the little wooden structure with interest. The painted slats were arranged in a criss-cross pattern, light and pleasing. The roof was held up by four carved posts and all rails and bars had a scalloped edge. It was a very different type of summerhouse from an English one. She sat on the low cushioned bench. He sat opposite her. Fatma stood at a respectful distance, hands clasped in front of her.

Seated face to face, Rose felt the magnetism of this powerful man even more. He had such a controlled strength and was so good-looking that it would be hard not to enjoy studying his features. Wide forehead, aquiline nose, full but firm lips, a long face with a clearcut jawline. As an artist, she longed to draw him. She blinked as she realized that he was studying her just as keenly, a broad smile on his face now.

'It is as well I already know you are an artist and that artists study faces intently.'

Embarrassment brought the colour to her cheeks. Then she frowned. 'But I only just told your sister. . . .'

There was a flash of white teeth as he grinned. 'What is it that you say – ah yes! "A little bird told me".' His smile made an attractive crease down each cheek, she noted. He was bare-headed this evening, his hair shining blue-black in a gleam of sunshine. His blue robe showed off the powerful muscles of his chest and arms and emphasized his waist where the sash bound it tightly. She noted that he had shed his boots for soft leather slippers.

All in all, his presence was very masculine and very disturbing. After the emotional upset of meeting Tom again, with all the bitterness that had reawakened in her mind, Rose felt drained. This second encounter with a large and dominant male was very hard to endure.

'What I have to say now is very secret, Mrs Charteris' – she noticed that he did not seem to like giving her that title – 'and whether you agree or not to help me, I must trust you to keep the matter to yourself. In fact, I am putting you in danger just by telling you about it.' He raised an eyebrow and looked a question.

Rose frowned at him. 'Pray do go on, sir. I cannot judge until I know the whole.'

Kerim Pasha gave an approving nod. 'Thank you. You are courageous. But first I will say that it is your countryman, Tom Hawkesleigh, who told me you are an artist.' He raised his brows at the flash of anger in her blue eyes.

'H-has he been discussing m-me?' She half rose from her seat but Kerim Pasha's face told her she was giving too much away. His eyes had narrowed and his face was more hawklike than ever.

Rose forced herself to sink back on the cushioned bench. How silly she was to show her feelings now, when she had kept up a calm façade for so many years! Meeting Tom again had shaken her more than she realized. She uncurled her fingers and took a deep breath. 'It is a long time since I was acquainted with Mr Hawkesleigh.' Her voice sounded rather more high-pitched than usual. She cleared her throat. 'Perhaps he has exaggerated my talents.'

'I doubt that,' murmured Kerim Pasha. 'He was full of praise for your ability.' He leaned forward slightly, a twinkle in his eyes, 'But how angry this has made you. . . .' He waited and watched but she did not reply. He could see altogether too much, this clever man.

Eventually he resumed, 'Nevertheless, I would be deeply grateful if you could help us in this way. Mr Hawkesleigh would explain what is required.' He sighed. 'Sadly, he cannot draw very well at all' – he shook his head – 'and the pictures are vital to the huge plan we are undertaking.'

While he talked, Rose sat there, a tight little figure. She fumed, staring sightlessly out at the trees as the daylight faded. *Mr Hawkesleigh would explain.* . . . Surely he could tell she did not want to undertake anything that involved Tom. This work would mean several meetings with him and she could not bear that. She decided to refuse. She blinked and turned her head to look at Kerim Pasha, whose keen gaze had not wavered from her face.

At once she felt his power, his strong will and authority. And she knew that there was no choice. He had asked her, but that was simply a courtesy. This man was dealing with state policy at the highest level. That meant that Tom's work, whatever it was, was a vital piece of diplomacy between Britain and the Ottoman Empire. So, if she refused, she would be doing her country a very bad turn.

'Very well,' she said hoarsely, 'I have my painting materials. I will do this job for you.'

He did not move a muscle. She sat and waited. Tears threatened but she swallowed them down. Eventually he put a hand to his heart and inclined his head. 'You are very good. I would not ask it of you if I could not protect you. So long as you remain here you will be safe. The house is well guarded.'

She gave a little shiver, remembering again the nights in Cairo when unknown people had prowled around their house, banging on doors and shutters, sometimes snatching one of the servants and beating them cruelly. Then the screams would make the darkness even more threatening.

Kerim Pasha's deep, velvety voice recalled her to the present. 'When we deal in important policies, there is bound to be spying and opposition. Your countryman knows that someone is following him. But in this house there is no danger for you.' He rose smoothly to his feet.

Rose followed suit and looked up to his lean face, her eyes still wide with the fear she had endured in Cairo.

Kerim Pasha dwelt on her blue, blue eyes. His face softened. 'I assure you, my honoured guest, that nothing will be allowed to harm you or your companions while you are under my protection.' He bowed and indicated that she was to go first. Rose moved mechanically towards the step. Her heart was fluttering. She had had to rely on her own strength for so long. And now a man was actually offering to carry some of her burdens. It felt strange . . . and delightful.

CHAPTER SIX

The following morning Rose set off for her meeting with Tom, feeling heavy headed and desperately miserable. It would be best to act as strangers, she decided. After this meeting she would only need to see him once or at most twice, when the pictures were finished.

Fatma led her through the salon and out into the garden. A tall figure stood with his back to them, fidgeting by the entrance to the kiosk. He turned at the sound of approaching steps. The sun shone full on him. Rose glanced at his unruly hair, already rioting around his bare head. It seemed blonder than she remembered. Perhaps that was because he was very tanned.

His face was stern and cold as he subjected her to a careful examination, starting at her hair, which was mostly hidden under a fine gauze scarf with a beaded border, down the turquoise tunic and the thin cotton trousers to the soft kid slippers on her feet. Rose felt his gaze as if it touched her skin. He should not stare at her garments like that! She stiffened with indignation, her hands clasped tightly. Beside her, Fatma muttered something under her breath.

Tom himself was dressed impeccably. His clothes fitted his tall frame like a second skin and, apart from his hair, which was falling over his face as usual, everything about him was impressively smart. He made a small bow.

'The ambassador sends his compliments. He sincerely trusts

that your aunt's health is improving,' he said formally, moving aside and indicating that Rose should enter the kiosk.

'How kind of him to enquire,' she snapped, thinking that the ambassador could have taken the time to call on them himself. 'My aunt does indeed seem much improved. But this fever comes and goes, so we do not know what will happen next.'

'Yes,' said Tom, folding his long legs carefully so that he did not put his feet too close to hers. 'It can be very nasty. But with the help you are getting here, she should soon be back to full health.'

'I think she would need to know that Sir Philip and . . . and all our menfolk are safe before that will happen.' Rose's voice quavered. All three of them were frightened on that score, but trying to encourage each other to hope for the best. She felt Tom's eyes on her. There was still a chill in his gaze.

Rose lifted her chin. She reminded herself that coldness and distance were needed here. 'What are these pictures you wish me to draw, sir?' she asked frigidly.

Tom sighed. 'I am sorry to involve you. Believe me, if I could do otherwise, I would not ask you to do this. It is very likely to be a dangerous job.' He cast a glance around, staring at Fatma, who had perched on the entrance step.

'She does not appear to have the least grasp of English.' Rose assured him.

He shrugged. 'If Kerim Pasha says all is secure here, it must be so. He is one of the most powerful men in the Ottoman Empire. And he is in a hurry for a certain document. The one thing lacking is the illustrations. They are needed to give the Sultan a clear—' He stopped as Rose gasped and opened her eyes very wide. He nodded grimly. 'You heard me correctly. This is for His Majesty. He wants clear pictures of possible new uniforms for the troops. Horse and foot.'

Rose shook her head in disbelief. 'I arrived in this country three days ago. I know nothing of their uniforms. And you are asking me to provide expert sketches for the Sultan himself?' her voice rose on the word.

Tom glanced around uneasily. He grimaced. 'We have no one else we can ask. All hell could break loose if news leaks out to the wrong people.' He nodded at her, his dark eyes solemn. 'I do not want to frighten you, but there may well be counter plots – even riots, when these new ideas are made public. Now do you see why it has to be absolutely secret?'

What kind of business was she getting drawn into? For a moment she felt fear twist in her stomach. She pushed it aside. It was almost unheard of for such a task to be offered to a woman. And her artistic skills were considered to be superior. This was a challenge she would enjoy. But before she said yes she wanted Tom to beg a bit harder.

'Did you not see any Turkish soldiers in Egypt?' he was asking.

'No! I do not think so. . . . Well, how could I tell which were Turks and which Egyptians?'

'But the differences are quite clear,' he began, then, seeing her frown, he stopped. He eyed her uneasily. 'You know, this is a tremendously important piece of diplomacy for Britain. We *cannot* lose out to the French. The ambassador is so relieved that you will do the sketches.'

Silence.

The silence lasted so long that Fatma got up and looked to see if Rose was still there. Rose was sitting with her fists clenched, her mouth set in a straight line and her gaze, as on the previous evening, fixed on the cypress tree that swayed gently in the breeze off the sea.

Tom cleared his throat and scraped his booted feet across the floor into a more comfortable position. There was a wary expression on his face. This time he was not sure of her decision.

At last Rose turned her head towards him. 'I suppose,' she snapped, 'that this means I have no choice. It seems everyone is expecting me to do these sketches. Even the Sultan is waiting. And, of course, all the spies and felons who always get to know every secret.'

Tom chuckled. 'That's the spirit, Rose.' Seeing her face he

coughed and said, 'Apologies, I mean – *ma'am.*' His eyes narrowed.

Rose became even more frigidly formal. 'Please arrange for me to see what I am to describe. Type of jacket and trousers, colours, hats or helmets. I need some models to adapt from.' She stood up. 'Now, if you will excuse me, I am anxious to be with my aunt.'

Tom jumped up. 'Thank you,' he said, his voice warm with appreciation. 'You are doing your country a great service. And if you still feel reluctant, perhaps you could consider it also as a thank you to Kerim Pasha who is moving heaven and earth to get help to the members of your party in Egypt.'

He leaned back for her to leave the kiosk. Rose gave him a slight inclination of the head. As she stalked back towards the house, she looked up to the third floor balcony. Helena waved at her.

She had not refused although it had been a close-run thing! Tom stood by the kiosk and mopped his brow. Stuffing his handkerchief back into his pocket, he watched her walk gracefully away and disappear into the house. He let out his breath slowly. By her manner, she made it plain she wanted nothing to do with him. And yet he sensed that she still understood his thoughts and feelings as well as ever.

Perhaps she did not want her husband to suspect that she had ever entertained deep feelings for another man. Yes, he decided, that this must be the reason for her embarrassment. What a fool her husband was to leave such a beautiful woman without adequate protection. Tom walked slowly through the house and out of the front door into the road without noticing anybody as he went. He sighed. If only his situation had been more secure when he first met Rose in London.

But that chance had gone forever. He had stored his feelings for her away in a dark corner of his mind. The years of soldiering and spying had kept him busy, always on the move, outwitting villains and snatching success, often by a whisker, out of seemingly huge odds. He had scarcely spent four months in

England over the last four years.

It was a malign fate that had made their paths cross, especially when she was married. Tom kicked at a stone on the rough path. Was her husband happily digging up chunks of rock at some pyramid, more interested in antiquities than in his lovely wife? Now that he had seen her again, his feelings were alarming him. She was out of his reach, even more now than when she had been a young girl. He must control this stupid leap of the heart each time he saw her. Any pretty woman had that effect on him, he told himself. But he knew that was self deception. No other woman had ever stirred his feelings in the way Rose did. Tom wished the Turks had prize fights. He wanted to knock someone down.

CHAPTER SEVEN

She hated him! Oh, how she hated him. Revealing details about her to Kerim Pasha without a by your leave! He had made it impossible for her to refuse to do the sketches. It was obvious that Tom had not suffered in the years since they had met. He had lived a life of adventure and he looked well on it! He was so full of energy and confidence. And now he was an adviser to kings! No wonder he was dragging her into his schemes, so that his ambitious plans could succeed.

Rose fumed all the way back up to her room. How she wished she could put Tom in a similar situation. Before going into her apartments, she stood on the wide landing and dragged in a couple of calming breaths. She had to mask her anger from her sister and aunt. They knew nothing of this matter.

Helena had still been away at school in Reading when Rose had been bundled home from London in such disgrace, with endless reproaches from Augusta and lamentations from George. Augusta had talked of nothing else for months. Mr Graham, totally convinced that Rose had ruined herself, forbade her to leave the grounds of the manor or to contact any of her old schoolfriends.

'The best that we can hope for is that you will be forgotten,' he would repeat endlessly. 'And when the matter does die down, if it ever does, then perhaps we can do something with you.'

That something was marriage to his godson. Hugh Charteris was well enough in his way, a good naval officer if rather colourless in character. But he was not Tom. Rose still shuddered at the memory of that time. For months she had been certain that Tom would contact her but hope gave way to despair when there was no news from him. Eventually she had given in to the combined arguments of all her family and consented to the match with Hugh. It had seemed like an escape.

At this point, she resolutely shut the memories off. She shook her head, pasted a smile on her lips and opened the door. The living-room was empty so she went silently towards the inner room. The sight that met her eyes made her put her hands on her hips and shake her head in resignation. Her aunt was sitting up in bed against the pile of cushions. She had her hair brushed back under a lace cap and her spectacles were on her nose. Spread across the silk sheet was a row of books and pieces of paper.

'Whatever are you doing?' exclaimed Rose. 'I thought you were going to sleep for hours yet.'

'As you see,' said Lady Westacote, looking at her over her spectacles, 'I woke up feeling so much refreshed that I just had to get on with a bit of work. Do not shake your head at me, Rose dear. If I get tired I can always stop. But we must make haste to decipher these hieroglyphs before the French can do so.'

Helena appeared from the balcony, a pencil in one hand and a dictionary in the other. 'I wonder if this will help. . . .' she was saying, then she noticed Rose. 'Oh, are you back already?' She moved towards her aunt to show her the passage in the book.

Back already! It seemed to Rose as if she had been away for hours. But she knew that when the two of them started to work on any language question, they were lost to the world. And she felt so drained emotionally that she was glad they were wrapped up in their own work and did not look at her closely.

Silently thanking Latife's medicine for improving her aunt's health so quickly, she went out onto the balcony. She gazed down at the little kiosk. Such an innocent-looking structure, meant for the family to enjoy the sweet scents of the flowers while sitting in the shade. But in fact it was the meeting place to plan schemes that would shake the empire – if they ever came to pass.

Looking carefully towards the end of the garden, Rose could see a number of men in blue robes, walking slowly up and down outside the wall. The house was indeed well guarded. Kerim Pasha was beyond question a man of the highest rank and he was trusting *her* to work on a matter of such vital importance! Rose felt a thrill at the idea of her task. She would do her very best. But she would keep the work a complete secret. So she must start by establishing her reputation as an artist.

She deliberated, gazing absently at the blue water beyond the cypress trees. Of course! She blinked, her gaze sharpening. Since Helena had already put the idea in Latife's head, Rose would paint the view of the Golden Horn. In a very short time, she was at work. Her brushes and colours all set out, she was sitting at her easel with her sketchbook on it. And as she painted, her mind kept returning to Tom.

He had caused her so much grief, she would prefer not to have to see him ever again. Her first taste of love had been an awakening that thrilled her body and her soul. The many ideas they shared, their enthusiasm for all the challenges of life, had seemed to open a future of adventure and possibilities far beyond the usual restricted routine permitted to young ladies – especially by her father, grown much stricter since the death of their mother when she and Helena were barely ten and thirteen.

Well, she had come close to despair but she had fought and survived. She was determined that she was not going to fall in love ever again. That chapter in her life was closed by her own choice now! Rose's chest swelled in a deep sigh as she wondered why she seemed to pick the wrong man to be her partner each time.

Now she just wanted to be independent. Thanks to dear Aunt Emily, that was becoming a reality. With the money she earned for her drawings of ancient artefacts and sketches of archeological sites, Rose had enough to live on. It was a relief not to be dependent on anyone. Since her marriage, her father had never offered her any financial support. And Augusta, with her own growing family, never stopped hinting at the expenses of running the estate.

If only ... Rose delicately outlined the cypress trees in her picture. The sight of Tom that morning had upset her deeply. His thick, unruly hair, his strongly built frame, moulded into his blue jacket, all reminded her of the time she had been in his arms and thought she had reached paradise. She gave an exasperated sigh as she looked more closely at the branch she was painting. She hastily dipped her brush in the water pot and lifted off the too deep slash of green. She must stay calm and think only of her picture.

Rose was aware of the waft of jasmine perfume before she heard any sound. Turning her head, she saw Latife, smiling delightedly at the nearly completed painting.

'How quickly you are turning a blank sheet of paper into something beautiful.' Latife slid onto the divan, by Rose's side. 'Please, go on,' she urged. 'I shall enjoy watching.'

After a short silence, Rose remarked, 'We are profoundly grateful to you for your care of our aunt. She is so much better today.'

Latife gave a husky laugh. 'Do you call it better? She is working intently on her papers. She scarcely noticed me.'

Rose looked at her swiftly, but Latife was obviously amused.

'You are very understanding. My aunt – and my sister – get so wrapped up in their study of ancient languages that they would even forget meals if I did not remind them.'

'So you are the practical one in your family. And yet you,too,are an artist. Tell me, Rose, can you draw portraits as well?'

'Of course. Shall I draw you? A quick sketch so you can judge?'

Latife raised her chin in that 'no' gesture. 'Not like this. I would need to dress in better clothes.'

Rose opened her eyes wide. Latife's garments were all exquisite, made of sheer silk and stitched with fine embroidery. Her lustrous black hair was plaited and twisted into a complicated knot on top of her head. A little pink veil was pinned to it with a jewelled comb. The veil was long enough for her to pull over her hair and face if needed.

Rose smiled slowly. 'I cannot imagine that you could improve on your appearance.'

Latife waved a hand dismissively. 'You will see.'

The next morning, as agreed, Latife came to be painted. Aunt Emily was strong enough to get up and walk about the room. But already, she and Helena were discussing the probable meaning of two signs and Latife quickly made her way through to the more congenial company of Rose.

'Where is your picture of the sea?' was her first question.

For answer, Rose picked up the board against which her picture was pinned. It was finished. Latife studied it for a long while, occasionally glancing up at the real view then looking down at the drawing again with interest.

'Amazing.' she murmured. 'What skill you have.' She turned the picture so that Fatma, lingering in the doorway, could see it.

Rose smiled her thanks. 'I would be honoured if you would accept it.'

'Oh, I will gladly do that. Now, how must I sit?'

Rose put her head on one side. 'You are so beautifully dressed that we must display your clothes to best effect.' She considered the rich pink silk trousers and the little sleeveless jacket of wine-coloured velvet over a tunic of palest yellow muslin. Latife's hair was pulled up high to the crown of her head then allowed to fall in a braid over her shoulder. Plaited into the braid was a string of pearls, milky against the gleaming blue-black.

Rose went inside and came back with an armful of cushions and a copper bowl.

'Could you ask Fatma to find us a small table for the bowl?'

Fatma beamed and scurried away. She returned with another girl, carrying a carved wooden and mother-of pearl table between them. The other girl peeped at the picture and then at the view.

Finally she stared at Rose in admiration. Meanwhile, Rose had arranged the setting for her model.

'Please, could you sit here?' She showed Latife the place and position she wanted.

'Why must I lean against all these cushions?' Latife asked, in her husky voice. There was an extra gleam in her eyes. Rose could see she was excited by the prospect of having her likeness taken.

'It is for more colour and texture.' Rose settled behind her easel and began her sketch.

'You are a good model,' she remarked, 'you can hold the pose and not ask to move all the time.'

'I have had plenty of practice in sitting still,' said Latife. 'We spend much of our time attending on our older relatives, often just waiting to help when they call on us. And my mother was very strict. She still is!'

'Is your mother here?' Rose hesitated, her brush poised over the darkest browns on her palette, as she tried to decide on the shade for her subject's hair.

'Oh, no, she is away managing our country estate near Bursa. The children are there with her. Kerim's son and my own little son.'

'You must miss them.' Rose observed, hoping she was not prying, but keen to know more. So Latife had a husband and Kerim Pasha had a son!

'It is our custom. The boys must learn their duties as landowners.'

There was a short silence. Rose looked up and frowned. Latife had turned away. As Rose watched, her shoulders heaved. Then she turned back and Rose hastily bent her head over the palette and dabbed her brush into the dark blue, mixing and testing the resulting colour. She kept her head down, apparently absorbed in the task.

'Yes,' came Latife's voice, 'I wish my son could stay with me. He is only five years old. My brother's son is seven and he has no mother.'

Rose looked up at that.

'She died in childbirth – the second child,' explained Latife. 'So our mother is in charge of both boys.' She stood up. 'The day is growing hot. We should not stay out in the sun, we must protect our complexions.'

'I suppose it has got very strong,' said Rose, looking round in surprise.

Latife raised both hands. 'You said your aunt and sister get absorbed in their work. Now I know that you do as well.' She bent over the sketch. 'Do I really look so young? You flatter me. But that is enough for today.'

It was certainly cooler inside. Rose put her picture and materials on a table in the corner. When she had finished, she found their hostess talking to Lady Westacote.

'It is amazing,' her aunt was saying. 'I do feel so much more like myself already. You are all goodness to us. It would be a splendid opportunity for the girls.'

'I will leave you to tell them about it, then,' smiled Latife and she drifted gracefully out of the room.

'What did she say?' wondered Helena, who had been in the other room.

'Why, my dear girls, our kind hostess plans to take you out for a visit tomorrow.' She held up her hand as they both opened their mouths to protest. 'I am quite well enough now to stay here with Fatma. I shall start to write a paper on the papyri and other artefacts we have brought with us. When we are all back in London we shall be expected to give any number of talks on our expedition.' She said that without any tremor in her voice; a sure sign, thought Rose, that she was indeed stronger both in body and spirit.

Accordingly, the next day both girls came downstairs to meet their hostess in the salon. Latife surveyed them approvingly. 'How gracious of you,' she said. 'You have dressed with such taste. My friends will consider you to be most polite – as well as extremely pretty.'

She looked at Helena, who had chosen a robe of her favourite almond green and trousers and little kid slippers of straw colour. Her shining dark hair was piled into a knot on the crown of her head and set off by a bright red scarf twisted into it. The red was echoed in the wide muslin sash she had bound round her waist.

Latife's smile grew as she considered Rose, whose slender figure looked almost ethereal in a sky-blue robe over palest pink trousers. She had added a mid-blue velvet bolero, richly embroidered with silks and gold thread. A pretty little pink cap was perched on her fair hair, which she had allowed Fatma to arrange in a thick plait, decorated with blue ribbons.

'We so much enjoy dressing in these beautiful clothes,' said Helena, 'everything is both comfortable to wear and feels delightful.'

'You certainly make them look delightful, both of you.' Latife was already wrapped in a shimmering silk cape with very long, wide sleeves. She pulled the hood up over her hair and arranged a gauzy veil over her face. When the girls had done the same, they all went out of the salon and crossed to the large front door.

A carriage was pulled up right outside the door. At once, a strapping guard stepped forward to pull open the coach door. Once the ladies were settled inside he closed it, nodding at Latife's instructions. They set off with a jolt as the carriage wheels rumbled over cobblestones. The horses began to trot and the vehicle swayed alarmingly. Rose could see high walls hemming them in on either side. She peeped out through the latticed window and saw blue-clad men trotting along beside the coach. There had been a similar escort when Latife had come to the embassy to fetch them, she remembered. No doubt Kerim Pasha protected all his family with the utmost care.

They felt the coach turn a sharp corner and the horses strained as they pulled up a steep slope. Then there was another turn and the squeal of wood against wood as the coachman applied the brake. Now the slope was sharply downhill.

'Not much further,' said Latife. 'It is a roundabout way but the hills are so steep we have to use a longer route in the coach, for the sake of our horses. The next part of our journey is much smoother – at least, it should be, unless the sea is rough.'

Before Rose could ask which part of the shore they had reached, the coach stopped and the gigantic guard was swinging the door open. Latife descended, looking out at the expanse of water. She glanced back at the sisters. 'Ah, we are in luck, it is quite calm today.'

They were on a landing stage backed by a busy little square. It seemed like market day from the large numbers of people and goods. There was a mosque along one side and near it a large fountain with a shady roof jutting out over the structure. All around the square and behind it were houses similar to the *yali* in which they were staying, but not so grand. Larger houses were dotted up the hillside among trees and stretches of open grassland. In front of them lay the sea.

Rose had the impression that it was like a floating market. It was covered in boats, all full of moving figures. They were loading and unloading goods, or even selling things to people on the shore. Still more boats of all sizes bobbed along further out. She could see the men and oars moving in a steady rhythm, driving the boats along at a good speed. They were ferrying passengers across the channel. The air was full of noise, the flapping of sails, the shouts of the men, the cries of the market vendors and the squawking of seagulls. A youth carrying a huge case strapped over his shoulder came up to them, holding out a beaker. The huge guard waved him away, none too gently.

'Calm!' whispered Helena with a giggle.

Now their giant guard was pointing to a large, sleek vessel with gilded decorations along the prow. They stepped on board and followed Latife to a covered galley at the stern. Inside it was a large bench spread with mats and cushions.

'This is such a graceful boat. It makes me think of the Venetian gondola,' said Rose, a little breathlessly, grasping at the frame of the cabin to keep upright.

'So you have visited Venice,' exclaimed Latife, giving the sign to their guards that they were ready to set off.

'Oh.' Rose wobbled and toppled onto the cushions as the boat surged forward. 'That *was* sudden,' she said, adjusting her veils and wraps as best she could. 'No, I have only seen Venice in paintings. My uncle travelled there when he was young.'

Helena was still standing, clinging onto the frame of the cabin. She watched the rhythmic movement of the men and the oars. 'Oh, how terrible!' Her voice was shrill and horrified, causing Latife to break off what she was saying about the problems of visiting friends when they lived across the water.

'Is something wrong?' Latife asked.

' Tha— that boat.' Helena pointed a shaking finger. 'We nearly smashed into him. And here comes another . . . I am sure our oarsmen will hit it. See, it has disappeared under the bow. . . .' She pressed a hand to her mouth.

'Do not worry,' Latife said, amused. 'Look, there it is; he was not so close as it seems. This is a busy waterway. We are all used to dodging each other. Come, sit down. There will be no accidents.'

Rose shaded her eyes and gazed keenly ahead. 'Every day I have been looking at these huge buildings from afar. At last I am seeing them in more detail.'

Latife pointed out the various palaces and mosques, as well as the turreted walls of the Sultan's palace at the very end of the Golden Horn. Both Rose and Helena were thrilled. The scale of the buildings and the superb setting became almost overwhelming as they drew closer. Then their oarsmen swept into a little bay, quiet and green with tall trees that hid all the minarets and towers. It seemed as if they had reached open country. There was just one enormous red painted mansion with balconies that overhung the water.

'My cousin's home,' said Latife. 'This side is quite private but it is close to the heart of the city. The road is up there.' She indicated the slope at the back of the mansion. She led the way ashore and patted at her veils. 'Come and meet Princess Hulya. She is the wife of the Grand Vizier – the chief minister to the Sultan.'

CHAPTER EIGHT

The group of ladies was sitting on the divans drinking coffee when Latife brought her guests into the room. The delicious aroma hung in the air. The younger ladies rose with much fluttering of gauzy wraps and many exclamations of pleasure. There were a number of small children running around, but at the new arrivals, they all stopped what they were doing and went to cling onto their mothers' robes.

Rose and Helena saw all faces turn to examine them. They received smiles and gracious nods of approval. They curtsied in the English style to Princess Hulya, which caused even broader smiles. The princess indicated a divan close to her own and they sat down, doing their best to sit like the other ladies, cross-legged. The conversation started up again. Latife was answering endless questions and everyone was inspecting the sisters quite openly.

Before they could feel too embarrassed by such avid curiosity, a smiling girl offered them coffee. It was a welcome distraction. Rose was also curious. This was the first time she had been in a harem. She tried to take in all the details of the furnishings and decoration. She wondered how many of these ladies belonged to the family and how many were visitors.

There were a number of younger girls standing at the back of the room, watching eagerly and whispering to each other. She could see that her fair hair was the subject of many comments. Whenever a lady finished her drink, one of these girls would hurry to pick up the empty cup. Each time, the girl would glance timidly at Rose and Helena.

After the coffee cups had all been taken away, the girls returned to set plates of dried fruits and nuts by each guest. One or two of the ladies had hubble-bubble pipes, which were now lit. The scent of tobacco smoke mingled with the varied fragrances of the fruits and the lemon cologne that was offered to the ladies when their fingers became sticky after eating the figs and mulberries.

Their hostess was seated alone on a red-velvet-covered divan under the latticed window facing the garden. She was about the same age as Latife but considerably plumper, which made her appear older. Rose noticed that her clothes were extremely ornate and she was adorned with many strings of pearls and gold chains and bracelets.

All heads kept turning to the two English girls and everyone seemed to be asking Latife questions. At length, the princess declared, 'Mrs Rose, we say your yellow hair pretty – very much.' She smiled and inclined her head.

'Oh,' Rose was embarrassed, 'why, thank you, Your Highness.'

The princess gestured towards Helena but her voice was drowned by a sudden boom-boom, boom-boom and a prolonged blast of trumpets. Some of the small children started to wail and ran for their mothers again. Rose gave a start of alarm. It sounded ferocious. But Latife rose, curtsied to the princess and laid a hand on Rose's arm.

'How interesting for you,' she said, with a meaningful squeeze of her fingers, 'there is a military procession about to go past. Do come and see.'

Rose and Helena followed her across the wide room to an alcove and out onto a balcony, which was shaded from prying eyes by an intricate lattice in slats of varnished wood. The balcony overlooked the road and they could see out clearly.

'One of our most important officials is on his way to visit a special shrine,' explained Latife loudly and clearly, glancing round at the group of other ladies who had also come to see the spectacle. 'The escort will be most colourful with foot soldiers and cavalry And of course the military band is splendid, is it not?' Her face showed real pride.

'Yes,' said Helena, trying not to wince as the trumpets blared even more loudly. As the procession marched into view she put her hands over her ears. The huge drums were booming so loudly that the echoes bounced off the walls. The trumpets played a strange, eastern rhythm. It was wild, evoking a fierce, warlike people. None of the ladies so much as blinked although Rose felt the floor vibrating under her feet at the volume of noise from the instruments.

Then the marching soldiers turned their heads towards the mansion and roared out a song.

'They are saluting the Vizier.' Latife was forced to shout in Rose's ear to be heard.

The men swung along in a swirl of bright colours. Rose stared, fascinated at this unbelievably exotic sight. She took in all the details; the long skirts of the soldiers' robes, tucked back into their belts to make marching easier, the wide blue trousers, the white turbans wound over red caps, the enormous sashes stuffed full of knives and finally the red leather boots. It all made her feel she had slipped back in time.

She could not imagine these men fighting in the same battle as English soldiers in their trim modern uniforms. At last she understood why Kerim Pasha was so desperate for change. Indeed, why the Sultan wanted change and also how radical it would have to be. For the rest of the visit, Rose was absorbed by her thoughts. She thought it should be possible to keep the colours of the uniforms she had seen, while making them into modern jackets and trousers. But before she started, she needed to consult with Tom.

The rest of their visit dragged a little. The ladies ate pastries and sipped *hoshaf*. They chatted, some of them produced exquisite needlework and discussed it with each other as they sewed. Rose and her sister did their best to communicate and show an interest in everything. After a while the effort became tiring. The constant chatter of the ladies, the endless coming and going of the slave girls as they carried out their errands, began to irritate Rose. She found the smell of the scented tobacco in the water pipes sickly.

In spite of her best efforts, her mind wandered and her eyes began to glaze over. How long would this meeting last? Of course, for these ladies, it was an event simply to leave their own homes, so they were very happy to stay all day. If only she spoke their language, it would be so much more interesting.

At last, to her relief, she realized that Latife was on her feet and appeared to be taking leave of the princess. She nodded to Rose and Helena to rise also. They made their farewells, thanking the princess in English, which seemed to please her. She said something in her throaty voice, watching them closely.

'Princess Hulya says you are welcome to stay here with her as her guests,' translated Latife.

Beside her, Helena drew in a sharp breath. Rose smiled at their hostess. 'Please thank the princess. She is most kind. But we must return to our aunt.'

This was duly translated and after more smiles and curtsies, they finally escaped. Rose was eager to get back and start making sketches. She walked along behind Latife and two other Turkish ladies but in a couple of minutes, it was obvious they were going a completely different way from the one they had used to enter.

'I believe we have made a mistake,' she said, stopping.

Latife seized her arm and drew her along. 'Oh, but we are not going home.'

'We are not?' Helena looked alarmed. 'But Aunt Emily—'

'Your aunt knows all about it. Come, my dears. We ladies do not get many chances to go out. When we do, be sure that we do as much as possible.'

By now they were at the front of the vast house. A coach stood ready by the door and a group of armed guards, dressed in red and yellow, watched as the ladies climbed into the vehicle. The other guests who had left the reception at the same time, squeezed in with them now, chatting merrily. They all seemed to think it was a good adventure.

Latife called out to the guards and the coach set off, lumbering slowly on the rough road. The guards marched along beside it, some on each side. Rose spent a good few minutes observing their costumes as well. In a short time they reached a paved road and high walls shut out the view. They were passing beside one of those enormous buildings she had been looking at from the other side of the Golden Horn.

She watched the passing scene eagerly. There were plenty of people in the street. She shook her head in puzzlement. 'There is such a variety of dress,' she said, 'I cannot decide what is the general rule.'

'There is none,' Latife moved to sit next to Rose and peer out with her. 'Those men are from Kosovo. See their white trousers and those strange little hats. Over there I think they must be from Georgia. It is very mixed in Constantinople.'

Over the clop-clop of the horses' hoofs came the cries of men hawking their wares and women's voices calling down from their windows to buy the fruit and vegetables. Rose saw a merchant fill a basket with onions and then the basket was slowly pulled upwards. She was still watching the basket going up, twirling slowly on its piece of rope, when the coach turned a corner and creaked to a halt.

'Where are you taking us?' she heard Helena ask.

The ladies all laughed. Rose turned her attention back to her companions. She had to smile; there was such an atmosphere of excitement and anticipation. Everyone looked at Latife.

'Why, we are going to do some shopping,' she said, 'in the Grand Bazaar. They have copper and silver, gold and gems, spices and leather goods. And the perfumes. . . .' Her eyes sparkled. 'We shall see what is new.'

CHAPTER NINE

When the message came the following morning, that the visitor had come from the embassy for the daily report, Rose hurried downstairs. She was eager for the information she needed so she could do the military sketches quickly. She was so keen to do the task that this morning she was actually looking forward to discussing the matter with Tom. She knew he would understand all her questions and that she would clearly picture what he wanted. They could not change that insight they had into each other's minds.

She went out to the kiosk but there she checked in surprise. The gentleman standing waiting for her was not Tom. Rose was conscious of a deep disappointment. But the young man was already sweeping off his hat and bowing.

'Daresay you do not remember me, ma'am,' he said bashfully. 'Sebastian Welland, at your service.'

Rose could see that he had dressed with great care. She bit back a smile as she took in the striped waistcoat and the carefully pomaded hair. He looked very young and uncertain. His mouth was wide and sensitive. His large blue eyes were fixed anxiously on her.

'Of course I remember you, Mr Welland. You were the kind gentleman who helped us the day we arrived in Constantinople.'

His expression lightened. 'Just so – er – that is to say – it was my pleasure, ma'am.' He swallowed. 'The ambassador sends his compliments. What news of Lady Westacote? Is there any improvement?'

'Thank you, sir. She is gaining strength every day.'

He nodded. 'And – er – your sister . . . is she well?' His face was red.

'Yes. Thank you.' Rose felt a twinge of sympathy. Helena often had this effect on young men. She was so wrapped up in her language studies, she scarcely noticed. But in any case, she was now obviously attracted to Max Kendal, an attachment that seemed to have started when they discovered they shared an interest in ancient languages. But Rose could hardly tell this young man any of that.

There was a short pause. Then Sebastian cleared his throat. 'Well, better return and take the good news to our ambassador.'

Rose held up a hand to check him. 'What has happened to our usual visitor?'

'Indisposed.' stammered the young man, too hastily. He fumbled with his hat.

Rose raised her eyebrows.

Sebastian looked harassed. 'Daresay he will explain tomorrow.' He took a step back, bowed and left.

Rose gave a sigh of exasperation. What could Tom have done to render himself incapable? Was he going to disappear again just when she really needed him? The ever-present memory of his last desertion made her clench her teeth. Surely he would just not leave. After standing and staring absently at the spring blossoms on the bushes, she forced her fingers to uncurl and slowly turned back towards the house. Perhaps Aunt Emily would like her to do some drawings in preparation for the talk she was planning to give in London. Or maybe Latife would come for another portrait session.

Rose stepped into the cool, shady salon – and stood transfixed by the sight of Kerim Pasha as she had never yet seen him. He was in a towering rage. His face was a mask; his eyes cold as ice. He stood in the centre of the room, one hand on his swordhilt. His other hand chopped the air, clenching and unclenching as he launched a furious tirade at his sister. When he realized that Rose had joined them, he changed to English.

Bewildered, Rose looked from him to Latife, standing before him with her hands clasped nervously in front of her. The woman's head was bent down and her shoulders slumped. Gone was her usual graceful poise.

'I am most displeased, Mrs Charteris.' Kerim Pasha's voice was low and harsh. 'In fact, I am beside myself with rage. I learn that yesterday, my sister not only took you to visit our cousin, Princess Hulya, as agreed, but that she was then imprudent enough to take you to the Grand Bazaar.' He showed his white teeth in a snarl. 'In the *middle* of the city!'

Rose was astonished at his anger. 'We enjoyed the visit very much. It was all fascinating and . . . and we were perfectly discreet and safe all the time.'

'And did you visit many shops?'

Rose shot a glance at Latife, but she had not moved. 'Yes, we visited a number of jewellers' shops and a leather shop.'

He took a step away, smashed his fist down hard on a cupboard and said something under his breath. It did not sound very nice. Rose saw Latife wince. She transferred her gaze to Kerim Pasha and saw his broad shoulders heave as he drew in a deep, deep breath. Then he whirled round to face her. His eyes were uncomfortably fierce.

'You do not understand my anger. But my sister had you in her care and she betrayed my trust. I ordered that you were to be kept safe.'

'But we were safe,' protested Rose hotly, in defence of her kind hostess. She held his gaze, her own eyes flashing now. We had so many guards and servants with us and we were a large group of ladies. They all knew which shops to go to—' She broke off at his growl of fury.

'You have advertised their presence to the whole city,' he accused Latife. Then he threw up his hands. 'Ladies, ladies! Will I ever understand you? Now we must work even harder to keep them safe.'

He strode away. Gradually Latife raised her head. She dashed something from her cheek. Rose could see how her hand trembled but she managed a smile in her usual manner.

'I am sorry you had to see that quarrel,' she said, her voice more husky than usual.

'But what was so bad?' asked Rose, genuinely puzzled. 'In Cairo we were able to visit the markets and the baths without there being a problem.'

'Ah, but you are *Ferengi* – Europeans. You have so much more freedom than we Muslim women.'

'I am not so sure,' murmured Rose, thinking back to her marriage. What choice had she been given in that? And who had bothered about her happinness until dear Aunt Emily had offered her a home at Rivercourt? But Latife needed reassurance. It must be terrible for such a proud lady to be treated like a child.

'I am very sorry that your brother is displeased with you,' Rose said awkwardly, 'when you were doing your best to show us some of the sights of your beautiful city.'

'For pity's sake, do not mention any of the other things we did.' Latife's eyes were wide with alarm. 'My brother's role is so difficult that he fears we may also become targets. Perhaps I was to blame.' She shook her head and gave Rose a sad little smile. 'It is not often that we have the chance to go out into the city.'

'Helena and I enjoyed ourselves very much.' Rose ventured to take Latife's hand and squeeze it. 'And it perhaps masked the fact this we saw a military parade.'

Latife put a finger to her lips. Rose bit her lip, remembering that anyone could be listening behind the heavy draped curtains. Almost as if he had been there, Kerim Pasha appeared once more. She gave a guilty start. But he now looked more like his usual self. He had a book in his hand.

'Can you spare me a few minutes, Mrs Charteris?' He indicated the garden. He ignored his sister and strode outside. Latife made a slight gesture to Rose to follow him. In the kiosk he sat down opposite her, the book on his knees. For a few minutes he sat and looked at her consideringly. He ran a hand through his sleek black hair then tilted his head backwards. Rose sensed the tension flowing out of him.

She sat, hands folded in her lap, calmly watching him. Little by little, she watched the fierce light fade from his eyes to be replaced by a twinkle.

'You were able to observe the soldiers and their uniforms yesterday?' he asked without preamble.

'I suppose you sent us there especially,' said Rose. 'It all happened very smoothly. We had an excellent view of the whole procession. I remember the different uniforms very well. Foot and horse soldiers.'

'Very good,' he exclaimed. Now he was smiling.

'Well, my husband was an officer – in the navy,' she explained.

His brows drew down. 'Was?'

'I am a widow, sir.' Was it her imagination or did she hear a sharp intake of breath at that news. His eyes narrowed and he gazed at her thoughtfully, shaking his head slightly. 'I am sorry,' he said at last.

Rose nodded. She could not say that she preferred her present freedom. It was not something any man would understand, whether here or in England. As the silence stretched out, she began to wonder if he had forgotten what he wanted to tell her. She looked out at the flowers, which day by day increased in number, filling the garden with colour and scent.

Finally, Kerim Pasha picked up the book and turned to a certain page. 'These are pictures painted for our Sultan a few years ago,' he said, handing the open book to her. 'I think it will help you to have a good picture of how our soldiers dress. But we need Mr Hawkesleigh's help to decide just how to replace all these old-style garments.' He raised his hands in an apologetic gesture. 'We do not need chainmail any more.'

His embarrassment was tangible. Rose nodded and studied the

pictures in silence. She knew that he was studying her meanwhile. Her face grew hot as she realized that she was not displeased at this interest. In fact, she enjoyed his company – in spite of his imperious temper. Why not? He was achingly handsome, and his sheer masculinity would make him stand out in any group of men.

What was she thinking? Rose caught herself just in time. They belonged to such different worlds. Had she not seen how he treated his sister just now? And no doubt he could be much fiercer than that. He had absolute power over his family. She did not even know if he had a wife – or perhaps more than one. Latife had said no more about the family and she did not seem willing to take them into the harem.

'Mrs Charteris' – there was a note of amusement in his deep voice – 'is anything wrong? I have asked you three times if you need any other materials?'

Rose came back to earth. She looked down at the book then up at his amused face.

'No,' she stammered, her cheeks burning. 'I just need to discuss the new style with Mr Hawkesleigh.'

Kerim Pasha's face darkened. 'Ah, Mr Hawkesleigh. But today he cannot be found.' He raised both hands in an exasperated gesture. 'I am getting tired of people disappearing.'

'Do you think he is in danger?'

Kerim Pasha's eyes narrowed again as he caught the note of alarm. 'Of course.' He watched her face intently. 'But no more than you, if anyone had kidnapped you yesterday.'

She shook her head disbelievingly, but he insisted, 'You are valuable just because of your fair skin and hair.' He let that idea sink in. 'That is another reason why we need to keep you safe.' He stood up, and this time his voice was sharp as he added, 'I do not suppose you would care for life in the harem.'

CHAPTER TEN

Tom became aware of daylight but his eyelids were too heavy to open. He shifted his head slightly and groaned at the wave of nausea. He tried to swallow but his tongue felt too big for his mouth. He was plagued by a raging thirst. The pounding in his head made it too hard to think. For a while he just lay and waited for memory to return.

The air smelled foul and dank. Cautiously, Tom put out a hand and touched a wall. It felt slimy. His hand explored the hard surface on which he was lying. It was stone. His groping fingers reached the edge and slipped downwards. He must be on a ledge about a foot above the floor. He tried again to swallow, but his tongue seemed to be welded to the roof of his mouth.

There was no noise except for a handcart rumbling across cobblestones. The sound came from above the level of his head. Then he heard a cough. It was very close by. At that, Tom did open one eye. He was in a small room with stone walls. A faint light came from a tiny window high up. There was another man nearby, squatting in the corner with his head on his arms. Tom resolutely opened his other eye and pushed himself into a sitting position.

Something dragged at his legs. He blinked and focused slowly. There were chains on his ankles. 'What the *devil*—' He raised a hand to his throbbing skull.

'Ah, *Ingiliz*, you woke up at last. So long you sleep, like dead.' The other man lifted his head, showing a thin, dark face, shadowed by several days' growth of beard.

Tom felt his own chin. His fingers rasped over stubble. He must have been unconscious for many hours. 'Where am I?' he croaked.

The other man stared at him for a while. 'Can you not tell, *Ingiliz*?' He spat. 'This prison.'

Tom planted his feet firmly on the floor. He rested his elbows on his knees and dropped his head in his hands. He must recall what had happened to him. The last clear memory was of following Laval from the French Embassy to the baths and seeing him talk to a Turkish man as they were both scrubbed and rinsed. Tom was certain the Turk was reporting to Laval. No doubt he was the man who had sneaked into Tom's room and gone through his papers.

Hoping to get away before they noticed him, Tom had hurried to get dressed again. Then he had hidden in a coffee house by the entrance to the baths. If the two men left together, he planned to follow them. The cup of Turkish coffee had tasted quite normal. But after that, he could not remember any more. They must have other agents, who were watching him.

Tom raised his head. 'Which prison is this?'

The Turk shrugged. 'Does it matter? We all get punishment.'

'But what have I done?'

'*Ingiliz*, you have angered someone.'

Tom put his throbbing head back in his hands and shut his eyes. It was not the first time he had been thrown into gaol. As his cellmate said, for that to happen, one had only to offend someone – 'offend' meaning get in the way of their plans. Sooner or later, a guard would come in and then he could bribe the fellow to send a message to the embassy.

From the steadily growing noise outside, he judged that the day was advancing. He could hear the shouts of market traders and the clatter of carts. He rocked from side to side, tormented by thirst. At last he raised his head again and peered round in vain for a jug of water. The other man watched, his eyes narrowed in grim amusement.

It seemed an age later when the cell door opened. A massive figure came through the narrow doorway. One eye glared at Tom, the other looked evilly away at the wall. The fellow had a barrel chest and meaty bare arms. He unlocked the shackles and gestured to Tom to follow him.

'You are fortunate, *Ingiliz*,' said his cellmate softly. Not softly enough however. The gaoler swung round and swiped hard at the man's head with his club. The man flung up his arm to protect himself. There was a sickening thud and he fell back with a stifled groan. Tom grimaced and followed the brute out into a larger room and fresher air.

Sebastian was there, his eyes wide with apprehension. 'I have paid your fine,' he announced.

'Just get me some water,' croaked Tom. 'And then I need to go back to the baths.'

Later, as he consumed a large meal in his usual restaurant near the embassy, he asked Sebastian how he had found out where to find him. His assistant shook his head.

'We received a message. We have no idea who brought it. It told us which guardhouse you were in and stated that you had been arrested for improper conduct in the bazaar. The police thought you were drunk when they found you.'

'They thought no such thing!' snapped Tom. 'I was being put out of the way while that damned Hippolyte Laval and his helper go through my rooms again.' His lips curved into a harsh smile. 'Well, they can search all they like, they will not find anything.' He exchanged his empty plate for a dish of rice pilaf and set to work again.

Sebastian looked anxious. 'This business is getting more dangerous by the day. Perhaps it is as well those English ladies are in Kerim Pasha's *yali*. That is well protected.'

Tom glanced up quickly, opened his mouth then closed it again. Sebastian could not know anything about the sketches. He chewed his rice then thought of another matter.

'I want you to go back to that guardhouse,' he said. 'Pray, go right away. I should have thought of this earlier. You must pay the fine for my cellmate. Whatever he did to be put in prison, he does not deserve the treatment he is receiving.'

It took a little arguing to persuade Sebastian, but at length he gave in and set off back down the hill. Tom leaned back against the cushion and called for coffee to help complete his recovery. He still felt lethargic. Whatever drug they had put in his drink, it had completely knocked him out.

After several refills, he finally set his cup down with a sigh of repletion. He examined the other occupants of the café, wondering which ones were spying on him. His rooms had been searched again while he was in the prison. It was obvious Laval knew he was the person to watch, so he must be extra careful about his contacts.

Thank heavens Rose and her relatives were safe. He would continue his morning visits and encourage her to complete the sketches quickly. Tom devoutly hoped a British frigate would arrive soon that could take the ladies back to England before anyone could connect her to the planned military reform.

He was growing impatient when Sebastian reappeared. The younger man sank down on the bench and pulled out a handkerchief to mop his face.

Tom's thick brows drew together. 'Where is he?'

Sebastian beckoned the servant to bring him coffee. 'He would not come here. He will speak to you *in a more discreet place*. Those were his words.'

'Something odd about him,' rumbled Tom. 'Not many Turks speak English.'

'I did think of that,' said Sebastian with dignity. 'All he would tell me is that his name is Ali. Now, is there anything else? If not, perhaps I should go and report to the ambassador. He will be wondering what has happened to us.'

'I will come with you. Time to see what has been going on

there.' Tom did not add that he needed to check whether anyone had disturbed his office. In spite of all precautions, he was sure that Laval's spies could find their way into most places. Perhaps Kerim Pasha had enough guards to keep intruders away, but Tom knew he would not feel easy until he had spoken to the man himself.

CHAPTER ELEVEN

Two days later Tom made his way to Kerim Pasha's *yali* rather earlier than usual. He was impatient to see Rose's pictures. She had asked a lot of questions on his visit the previous day. It was clear that since she had seen the Turkish soldiers in that procession, she was aware of what needed to be done. Tom knew without asking that she had understood his ideas clearly. He shook his head over the mystery. Strange how their two minds saw things in exactly the same way.

Now, more than ever, he was furious that he had been forced to give her up when he had first met her and fallen so deeply in love. Tom had arrived home from that fateful ball to find his father in a dangerous rage. Tom was full of plans to ask Rose to marry him, even though he had no money of his own, but that dismal brother of hers had already complained to his father.

Tom had been treated as a scoundrel, his plans shouted down as ridiculous. In the heated argument that followed, Tom's father had had a seizure. The whole family united in blaming Tom for that. He was ordered away within the hour, never to show his face again.

He grimaced as he remembered the dark years of reckless adventure that had followed. Every dangerous mission, every hopeless scheme his commanders had hatched, Tom had volunteered for all of them. He held his life cheap, yet each time he had succeeded. His reputation for boldness and dare-devil bravery had grown until his commander-in-chief suggested that he could do far more for the war effort by resigning his commission and working as a secret agent for the Foreign Office.

Still careless of his own life, Tom had agreed. The adventures that followed were more appealing to him because they were so much more dangerous and success was therefore more satisfying. On each mission he was absolutely on his own. He did not exist officially and if he should fail and end up dead or rotting in some filthy dungeon, nobody would ever know. And all this because he had truly fallen in love with a sweet, beautiful girl who was the only woman he would ever really love.

The memory of Rose had inspired and tormented him in equal measure through the past four years. But to say that he was thunderstruck to find himself face to face with her again – and in Constantinople of all places – was a complete understatement. And so the torment continued. Just the sight of her had inflamed all the old longing. He wanted her as much as ever, but was condemned by her marriage to remain a stranger! He kicked a large stone out of the path with a muttered curse. Damn her husband, damn him!

He stopped and rubbed a hand over his face. *Find your composure!* he snarled to himself. He lifted his hat and dashed a hand through his hair. Kerim Pasha's blue-clad guards were outside the main entrance to the mansion. Tom could feel their interested gaze upon him. He settled his hat firmly on his now untidy hair and advanced towards them.

He made an effort to look calm. He must focus on the task in hand and remain coolly polite to this lady who was out of bounds. *Just view her as the artist,* he told himself. *Remember your job. It is the pictures that are all-important.*

'Welcome, Mr Hawkesleigh. You have recovered from your – er – encounter with Laval and his band of agents?' Kerim Pasha appeared in the doorway to the salon, at his most urbane.

Tom eyed him suspiciously. 'Thank you, sir. But how do you know about that?'

Kerim Pasha's lips twitched. 'I also have agents. Even if they cannot interfere in what happens to you at the time, they can alert me to help in whatever ways I can.' He turned back towards the rear of the house and signed to Tom to accompany him. 'Of course, others are watching me and my agents. It is a wearisome game of chess.'

As they stepped out of the salon, he put a hand on Tom's arm to stop him. 'Just to tell you that the written report is now translated into Turkish,' he murmured, very low, 'I hope the drawings are satisfactory. I will leave you to find out.' He nodded and turned back into the house.

Tom walked as far as the kiosk. There was nobody there. He put a hand on the rail and stood, struggling to keep his composure. Soon, very soon, an English boat would arrive and then Rose would vanish from his life once more. At this point he could not decide if he wanted that or feared it.

A light step was coming along the path. Tom turned to watch as she came towards him, her harem clothes floating around her. Those soft colours enhanced her delicate beauty. He groaned inwardly and clutched the brim of his hat so hard he nearly cracked it.

Rose smiled at him and hurried in to take her usual seat. Her face was eager and she had an air of excitement. As soon as Tom sat down, she thrust the sketchbook at him. She watched, her hands tightly clasped, while he slowly turned the pages. He nodded once or twice, sometimes flicking back to a previous page.

Tom examined each sketch thoroughly. She had done everything just as he had asked. Red jackets, blue trousers, rather full but a much closer fit than the current pantaloons, as well as boots and uniform caps with a small turban. He felt pleased and proud. It was as if Rose had seen into his mind. He looked up at last to see her biting her lip, her big blue eyes fixed anxiously on his face.

'This is marvellous,' he rumbled and was rewarded with a beaming smile that sent a slow fire flaring through him.

'Are you sure?' She looked doubtful. 'Do you think these sketches are good enough to show to His Majesty?'

'Indeed they are,' said Tom warmly. 'I should think he will be delighted with them.'

He watched as she drew in a deep breath of relief. Now she had forgotten to be so buttoned up, she was showing her natural liveliness, just as he remembered. He checked himself sternly.

'Tell me,' he said, 'did anyone see you drawing these?'

She shook her head. 'No, nobody. I sat on the balcony to work on them.' She waved a hand up to their top-floor rooms. 'There is nobody above us and I did them while everyone had their siesta.' She laughed. 'They think I am painting the view of the sea. And I have kept the book with me at all times since I finished.'

He nodded. 'That is good. But now it is absolutely vital for you to stay safely inside the house.'

Rose gave him a frosty look. 'Have you been talking to Kerim Pasha?'

'I said good morning to him. . . .' Tom raised an eyebrow. 'How does that fit in with what I am saying?'

She shrugged. 'He was furious with his sister because she took us to the covered bazaar after we made the permitted visit to a family cousin – so we could see the soldiers without making it too obvious,' she added.

Tom's dark eyes sparkled with amusement. 'Aha! What woman could ever resist shopping? Gave your guards the slip, did you?' The amusement faded. 'You know they will have had a flogging for that?'

Rose whipped a hand to her mouth. 'Oh, no! How dreadful. But why? We merely went to see the shops.'

Tom shook his head. 'You just do not understand, do you? There are Turkish officers of the old guard who will do murder rather than accept these changes.' He stabbed his forefinger against the sketchbook. 'That puts you all at risk – and I mean everyone in this household.' He leaned forward, so close she could see the golden flecks in his eyes and smell soap and lemony cologne. 'Suppose they had kidnapped you?'

The expression on his face told her how bad he thought that would be. She sat very still as the realization sank in. She was now a suspect and must avoid capture by the other side. Rose felt a shiver go down her back. But he had not finished yet.

'What's more, the French know there is a scheme afoot. They want to get the contract just as much as we do. Just think how valuable it will be – not to mention that Napoleon wants to extend his influence in this part of the world. He could cut off the British trade route to India then.' He sat back and leaned one elbow on the lattice rail. He sighed. 'We are deep in international affairs here. So, just you keep safe, Rose.'

'I am not Rose to you, sir,' she flashed, jumping up.

'*Mrs* Charteris,' snarled Tom. He unfolded his long legs and stood.

They were glaring at each other now. An amused voice said, 'It seems it was a very tiresome task, to have such an effect.' Kerim Pasha was close by, watching them.

Rose turned away, her nose in the air. 'Really, I do not need all this advice. As if I had not spent the last six months in Cairo and managed to look after myself very well.'

'Maybe so. But, my dear Mrs Charteris, please remember that while you are my guest, I hold myself responsible for your safety.' Kerim Pasha smiled at Rose. The man's voice was a caress. Tom looked from one to the other sharply. There was something more behind the words. Had the man fallen for Rose? Worse still, had she fallen for him? His face darkened.

Rose looked at Kerim Pasha for a moment before she turned to give Tom a brief nod. She swept away, her turquoise robe streaming out behind her.

Kerim Pasha laughed softly. 'I like to see a woman with spirit. She is not intimidated by our advice. But, my friend, I give you my word I will keep her safe.'

'Thank you,' ground out Tom after a lengthy pause. Then, remembering his mission, he said, 'The pictures are all here and all satisfactory. In fact, they are damned good.'

His host stepped out into the sunlight, keeping well away from him. 'Put them inside your jacket. When you get into the salon, exchange them for the book on the table by the ceramic vases as you walk past. Whatever you do, keep walking at the same pace. Do not stop. And make sure that the book can be seen under your jacket.' He clenched his jaw. 'Let us trust that there are no spies in my house.'

His tone sent a shiver down Tom's back. He waved for Tom to precede him. 'Please continue your daily visits,' he said softly, as they walked along the path. We must not do anything to arouse suspicion. Ah. . . .' He paused as they reached the salon entrance. 'I also hope you make the return journey to the embassy without incident.'

The ambassador was waiting to know if the last part of the army plan had now been safely handed over to Kerim Pasha. Tom was on his way back to the embassy but he did not feel ready to deal with all the discussions and reports just yet. He turned into his favourite coffee shop. Perhaps a cup or two of strong coffee would buck him up. Now his part of the job was done, but had he done it well enough to convince the Sultan?

He found he did not care. His head was full of Rose, her smile, the sweet scent of her and the sound of her voice, low and musical. He closed his eyes and put a hand to his forehead. Along with thoughts of Rose was the raging jealousy towards Kerim Pasha. Tom saw again the way the man's eyes glowed as he looked at her. Not to mention the honeyed tone of his voice when he assured her she was safe in his home. Tom ground his teeth.

CHAPTER TWELVE

It was with very mixed feelings that Rose climbed the three flights of stairs back to her room. She had almost treated Tom like a friend again and that was a mistake. Thank heavens Kerim Pasha had appeared, to remind her that she was simply doing a job and also that she must maintain her dignity. How could she even start to feel anything for either of them? Her hard-won freedom was more precious to her than any man's affection.

However, as the day went past, her usual occupations could not hold her attention. She spent some time talking to Aunt Emily, who kept wondering how soon they could expect to hear any news from Egypt. Helena was unusually quiet and slipped away. Rose did her best to reassure her aunt. That forced the idea back into her mind that the French really were hostile to a British presence anywhere in the eastern Mediterranean.

As soon as she could leave her aunt, Rose followed Helena out onto the balcony. She found her sister leaning against the railing, with her head down on her arms. Rose definitely heard a sniff. She made a slight noise and at once Helena jerked upright, rubbing her hand against one cheek.

'It is far too hot today,' said Rose. 'Do you think we could get Aunt Emily down to the garden? That little summerhouse is wonderfully cool but nobody ever goes there.'

'Other than you and Mr Hawkesleigh,' said Helena, still

keeping her face turned away. 'Such a pretty spot for your plotting.'

'Plotting?' flashed Rose. 'If that is what you think, you can go down each day to report on our situation for the ambassador. But oh no! You are too busy with your hieroglyphs.'

'Girls!' Lady Westacote called from inside, 'no squabbling, please.' She came out on to the balcony. 'It is true that we have been cooped up here for quite some time. I think it would be a good idea to enjoy the fresh air in the garden. Such a pretty garden, too.' She took off her spectacles. 'Well, come along, my dears. We are suitably attired for an oriental garden, are we not?'

Her mild joke restored the sisters to good humour. They giggled as they made their way downstairs, trailing scarves and muslin robes. Lady Westacote, indomitable as always, walked down without any stops.

'I am nearly back to my old self now,' she assured Rose, who kept urging her to pause and rest on each landing. 'And I am very well rewarded for the effort,' she exclaimed, as they made their way along the path to the little white kiosk. 'What a delightful garden. And the greenery makes it so much cooler down here.' She climbed the two steps into the kiosk and sat down on the cushioned bench. 'There,' she exclaimed a moment later, 'this is very pleasant. I simply must see all these sweet-smelling blooms.' And she wandered off to make a tour of the garden.

It was not very long before Fatma and a couple of other serving girls appeared with a tray of lemonade and small biscuits. Then Latife came to enquire if they were comfortable. She sat down and drank a glass of lemonade with them. It was a most agreeable spot to spend a hot afternoon. They were all comfortably settled when a serving boy ran up and knelt in front of Latife and whispered urgently. She replied and he ran off.

'It seems we must leave you ladies alone for now.' Latife rose as she spoke and adjusted her gauzy veil. 'Such a pity. I do long to meet your friends from the embassy but we ladies must keep to our customs and retire when strange men come to call.' She beckoned to the serving girls and swept them away towards the side of the house.

'Mr Hawkesleigh is here again?' exclaimed Rose, looking alarmed. 'Oh . . . I wonder—' She broke off in confusion. Surely there was nothing wrong with her drawings?

But it was Sebastian Welland who appeared first, his face breaking into a delighted smile when he saw Helena. He bowed politely to Lady Westacote and expressed his pleasure at seeing her looking so much better.

'I am quite well now, thanks to our clever hostess. Her medicine is miraculous. It is from the bark of a South American tree, I understand.' She saw Tom standing at the entrance to the kiosk. 'Ah, Mr . . . Hawkesleigh, is it not?' Her tone was less cordial.

Tom's bow was perfection. 'Delighted to see you in better health, your la'ship.'

Rose stifled a giggle. Her aunt was most unforgiving. Tom was doing his best, but as usual, his overlong hair made him look untidy.

'Ladies,' Sebastian cleared his throat. 'We have come with good news. A British frigate has arrived with dispatches from London. It will set sail to return in three days' time and the captain has agreed to give you passage.'

He beamed at them all. His smile faded when he saw no signs of joy.

'You have been most active on our behalf, sir,' said Lady Westacote slowly, 'but I did not think to leave before getting some news of my husband and the rest of our friends in Egypt.'

'As to that, I believe there could be news any day now,' put in Tom. 'But even if there is no message, you can be sure that the Turkish commander in Cairo will protect your husband's expedition with his life. They will embark for England as soon as they can. Maybe they are already on their way.'

'I will think about the matter.' said Lady Westacote.

'Are you quite certain we cannot return to Cairo?' asked Helena, turning huge, anxious eyes from Tom to Sebastian, who at once looked desperate to grant her request.

Rose bit back a sharp comment. Helena was only concerned to be with Max. As usual, it would be her job to convince them that they could not afford to lose this chance to go home.

'We must seem the most ungrateful wretches,' she said to their visitors, 'not to be thrilled at an offer of a passage home. You do see, do you not,' she looked in appeal at Sebastian, 'it is hard to travel further away from our menfolk, while we do not know if they are safe and well?'

Reluctantly, Sebastian nodded.

'Perhaps you will be good enough to inform us of your decision tomorrow,' said Tom drily. 'Come, Seb, we must not incommode the ladies any longer.'

Lady Westacote waited for the two tall figures to disappear inside before she spoke. 'I would much prefer to return to Cairo and find Philip myself.' Her voice trembled.

'It was always our plan to return to England anyway before the heat of summer, was it not?' objected Rose. 'I feel sure that Uncle Philip and the rest will stick to that. When they find us gone, they will make haste to embark as well.'

'But suppose he has taken the fever,' sniffed her aunt.

'Uncle Philip is a seasoned explorer. He can cope with a fever. It is not as if he is alone. And we cannot trespass on the hospitality of these kind people forever.'

Rose left the other two to digest that idea while she prowled around the garden. Aunt Emily was still weak and her spirits easily upset. It would not be easy to persuade her to sail for England while she feared that Uncle Philip was in any kind of danger. As far as Rose knew, this was the first time they had been apart since their marriage.

And it was plain that Helena had developed an attachment to Max Kendal. Well, that was not surprising, thought Rose. He was just as interested in ancient civilizations as she was and a handsome fellow to boot! It would be another love match, just like her uncle and aunt. But, for the present, it was going to make Rose's task even harder.

She was determined to accept this passage to England. Every day in this house was full of temptation. It was becoming harder to remember her vow to remain independent. She had become used to seeing Tom every day and indeed, she almost welcomed his visits. But she did not want to let him back into her heart.

She paced towards the boundary wall, over which she could just get a glimpse of the sea and beyond it, the hills crowned by minarets. Rose drew in a deep breath. She looked at the graceful minarets, and told herself that however kind everyone was to them, there were too many risks involved in remaining any longer. They were upsetting the household, however unknowingly. And she could sense that Kerim Pasha was more than a little interested in her as a woman. It was time to leave.

CHAPTER THIRTEEN

The following morning dawned and they had still not taken a decision. Rose knew that she would soon have to meet Tom. She had to give him a definite answer, but Lady Westacote still clung to her wish to have news of her husband before she would consent to leave.

Hoping that Tom would have some major argument that would take the decision out of her hands, Rose went out slowly to their usual meeting place. Rather to her surprise, she found Kerim Pasha in the garden. He was beaming at her as she walked towards the kiosk. He came close, eyes sparkling, took her hand and kissed it.

Rose had never seen him so demonstrative – except on the occasion he had lost his temper. She was a little wary but smiled back, her brows lifting in an unspoken question.

'Mrs Rose, I have some news for you – a lot of news, actually.'

She nodded. Really, he was like a boy this morning.

'First, my thanks for the sketches you drew. They are very clear and illustrate the report well.'

She nodded again. 'I am glad if I was of help.'

His white teeth flashed in a smile. 'Now, something even more important.'

Rose clapped her hands together, suddenly guessing. 'You have had news of my uncle?'

He nodded. 'They have left Cairo safely. They are returning to

Portsmouth on a ship of the line.'

'Oh, thank heavens,' whispered Rose. She closed her eyes, realizing just what a weight was rolling off her shoulders.

She was recalled to the present by his velvet voice, saying softly, 'But I am sad, because it means that we will lose your charming company here.'

The sound of boots striking on the stones of the path made them both turn. Tom was approaching. His face was set and he did not smile as he bowed.

Kerim Pasha repeated his news.

Tom's expression lightened. 'I was certain you would manage to get information almost as fast as a bird can fly,' he said. 'I am all admiration, Your Excellency. I wish we could communicate with the same speed.' He gave Rose an enquiring look. 'I take it this helps to settle your plans?'

Kerim Pasha waved towards the kiosk. 'I would urge you to go in, out of the sun while you discuss this. Excuse me now.'

Rose sat down, deep in thought. Eventually she raised her head and nodded. 'My aunt does not yet know about Sir Philip leaving Egypt, but I am sure she will now be in a great hurry to sail for England. When must we embark?'

'The frigate will sail in two days' time.' Tom's voice was dull.

Rose looked at him carefully. 'Have you had bad news?'

He sat in silence, rubbing his knuckles. Eventually he glanced at her briefly, then looked away. 'I received a letter from my brother Freddy.' He hesitated. 'You remember him?'

Rose nodded.

Tom heaved a sigh. 'Apparently my father died at the end of last year.'

'I am very sorry,' began Rose, but broke off when he shot her an angry look.

'Don't be!'

She stared in shock. He sat there for a while with his head bowed down. Rose waited in silence, not daring to ask any questions.

Tom seemed to be struggling to contain his anger. At last he raised his head. There was a fierce light in his eyes. His mouth twisted unpleasantly. 'My father banished me,' he growled. 'I have not seen him – in fact, I have scarcely set foot in England since that November when you and I—'

Rose jumped up and turned to face the garden She clutched the lattice rail. 'Do not talk of it,' she said breathlessly.

'No,' he said in a gloomy voice. 'You must be relieved that soon you will be reunited with your husband.'

Rose went very pale. She swallowed hard. 'You did not know?' she whispered at last. 'My husband was killed in action over two years ago.' Slowly she turned to face him again.

Tom was sitting staring up at her. His face was white, his dark eyes wide.

Two days later, Rose and Helena watched from the bridge as their ship slowly cast off from its mooring near the mouth of the Golden Horn. They had said their farewells to Latife and Kerim Pasha and all his household earlier. It had been an emotional parting. Latife had clung to Rose. Kerim Pasha had been urbane and charming, but Rose knew he was reluctant to see her leave.

Already, as the ship turned southwards and the wind caught the sails, Helena's adoring slave was answering her eager questions about the many buildings along the shores. Sebastian was obviously walking on air. The ambassador had decided to send him to London with dispatches, and as an escort for the ladies on the voyage.

On the quayside Tom stood ramrod straight, watching them depart. Rose clung to the rail, her eyes on his steadily receding figure. She thought of his face, so white and shocked when he had learned that she was a widow. And of his anger against the father who had banished him.

She drew in a shaky breath. No doubt George and Augusta had gone rushing to inform the old man about his son 'seducing' her at the ball where his older son was getting engaged. They had truly poisoned that occasion for all concerned. Perhaps Tom had

had no more choice than she had at that time.

So this chance encounter in Constantinople had been for the best. Now she understood *why* he had kept away from her, all those years ago, she could forgive him and face the future without the burden of resentment.

She gazed towards the quay but already it was just a blur as the frigate picked up speed, rising and dipping to the waves. How different their lives might have been. Rose blinked away a tear. 'Goodbye, Constantinople,' she whispered. 'Goodbye, Tom.'

Tom watched until the ship was just a dot on the edge of his vision. 'Goodbye, Rose,' he muttered. Now she had gone, he knew he would have preferred to carry on enduring the agony of seeing her each day even when she was out of reach. At last he turned away and began to walk slowly in the direction of the embassy.

He was feeling more lonely than for many years. He tried to focus on the next task he would be called on to carry out. Perhaps he could find something more actively dangerous than this current job, a mission that would occupy his thoughts and tax all his ingenuity. But his thoughts kept returning to the great hole that had opened up in his life.

Suddenly, he heard a shout and the next moment there was an almighty crash just as someone hurtled into him, pushing him sideways into a doorway.

'What the—?' Winded and bruised, Tom scrambled to his feet, clenching his fists ready to defend himself. But the man who had cannoned into him did not move. In fact, Tom saw he had one arm in a sling and he was rubbing it as if it hurt badly.

'You always in trouble, *Ingiliz*,' said his ex-cellmate. 'Take more care.'

'What happened?' Tom looked at the chunks of masonry so very close by. He brushed his coat down, retrieved his hat and made an attempt to smooth his hair.

'You have enemies in this city. That stone meant for you. *Kismet* I near. I go now.' He stepped back.

'No, wait. You just saved my life. Your name is Ali, isn't it?'

91

The man frowned. 'Better forget my name.'

Tom gestured at the broken arm. 'Do you need any help?'

The man gave a twisted smile. 'You get me out of gaol. Take care *Ingiliz*.' He slipped away before Tom could say any more.

It was a very sober Tom who arrived at the embassy soon afterwards. He sat down to take stock of his life. Whatever the outcome of his report, his work in Constantinople was done. And maybe, just maybe, it was time for him to visit England again.

You're a fool, he warned himself. *She did not want any further contact with you. And what about Kerim Pasha?* He shrugged all these doubts away, something deep inside told him it was worth a try.

CHAPTER FOURTEEN

London, October 1804

'Taffeta!' said Lady Westacote firmly. 'That was what our ball gowns were made from when I was a girl.' She gave a reminiscent sigh. 'Ah, my first formal gown . . . blue taffeta, tight waisted and with panniers. It was so delightful. I remember I had long lace ruffles at the elbow and satin ribbons to fasten the front over a slip of white silk.'

Helena rolled her eyes at Madame Lisette, the modiste. 'Yes, Aunt, we have seen your portrait where you are wearing that gown, at Rivercourt.'

'It is a charming picture,' said Rose hastily, 'but fashions have changed. The line of the dress is completely different now, Aunt Emily. And as for lace ruffles . . . they do not go with these new puff sleeves.'

'Hmph!' Aunt Emily twitched her shoulders. 'I really cannot wear those.'

'But, milady, we 'ave made your gown wiz long sleeves.' protested Madame Lisette, 'and added a pleat at ze back so you will not find ze skirt too narrow.' She turned the lavender crepe dress to demonstrate. Lady Westacote nodded reluctantly. 'I will do ze same for your walking dress also,' the dressmaker promised her.

By now the assistants had helped Rose into her new evening

gown, a slender column of jonquil silk. She looked at her reflection and bit her lower lip. 'The bosom is cut *very* low.'

'But zis is ze classical line, ze very latest mode. See 'ow well you look, madame. Wiz your figure, zis style is made for you,' she urged, 'and we can add different trimmings to ze neckline.'

'Indeed, Rose, it looks delightful' Helena assured her. 'See, here is my gown.' She took the amber silk from the assistant. 'I warrant it is as low cut as yours.'

Madame Lisette clasped her hands. 'You 'ave excellent taste, *mademoiselle*. You will be *ravissante* in zat colour.' She raised a finger and the assistants scurried to bring out the day dresses that had been ordered and which were now ready for approval.

Helena's eyes lit up. 'Oh, how delightful. The line is so simple and elegant.' She seized a sprigged muslin dress from an assistant, admiring the pleating on the sleeves and neckline.

Both sisters bent over the dresses, well satisfied with their choices. Rose had selected a moss-green walking dress in fine cambric. The front was made high, ornamented with darker green velvet frogging across the bodice and on the sleeves. Helena was gloating over a cherry-red day dress with several rows of pintucks at the hem.

Watching the sparkle of triumph in her sister's eyes, Rose was certain that Helena was planning to charm Max Kendal. She liked fashion and had a good eye for colour, but had never shown interest in such dashing gowns before. When Helena then picked up a pale-pink muslin with delicate ruching at the hem and round the neckline, Rose was sure of it. Her sister would look stunning in these gowns. But it would not do to say anything yet.

They had finally been reunited with their uncle and Max at Portsmouth, where the men had waited for them to arrive back in England after an uneventful voyage from Constantinople. News of their journey had been signalled from their frigate to any other British boats they met, so both sides had gleaned a little news of the others during the weeks it took to reach England.

The two men were in good health if rather baked from their

time in the hot desert sunshine. They explained that they had prolonged their stay at Saqqara to study the layout of the massive temple complex there and look for the entrance to the pyramid. They had collected a large quantity of papyri and figurines, as well as stone tablets and pots.

When they had eventually returned to Cairo to find the ladies driven out, unprotected, there had been the devil to pay, rumbled Sir Philip, his normally cheerful face darkening, but that was all he was prepared to tell them. Helena had pressed Max for more details, but he told her that he had sorted out the matter with the consul. When she insisted, he simply gave her his famous impression of being a statue.

At Portsmouth, they bade farewell to Sebastian, and thanked him for looking after them so carefully all the way from Constantinople. He had orders to make all haste to London with letters from the ambassador for various ministers. During the voyage he had become like a member of the family and they abandoned any formality. They were on first-name terms and teased him mercilessly about his fashionable aspirations.

The ladies waved him off with fond promises to meet again in London at the beginning of October. Max made no comment on this, or on Sebastian's obvious infatuation with Helena. He watched from under his craggy brows, his grey eyes piercing and his face impassive. Lean and handsome in a brooding kind of way, Max was always a law unto himself. His restless energy sometimes made him a tiring companion, but he was an old friend and they were used to his ways.

He had accompanied them as far as Sir Philip and Lady Westacote's charming old house on the banks of the Thames at Caversham near Reading. They spent a couple of days planning an exhibition they would set up at the British Museum in October. Leaving the Westacotes to write their papers and Rose to complete the drawings required by everyone, Max had then travelled on to Warwickshire to assist his elderly father, Lord Fennington, with matters of business on his estates. Now, after several weeks in the country to rest and prepare all their materials, the antiquaries were in London to deliver lectures and set out their treasures.

It was Uncle Philip who insisted that the ladies must all have new clothes. 'I feel it is important for people to see we can be bang up to the latest fashion. Demme! We cannot have these gals turning out in those harem garments they brought back from Constantinople.'

And so they were in Madame Lisette's shop in Rumbold Street, following their uncle's orders to the letter. Lady Westacote, having made her choice of dresses rapidly, had lost interest now.

'But, Aunt, you need a new wrap to go with the lavender dress,' Rose coaxed her. Lady Westacote shrugged and sniffed but Madame Lisette speedily drew her attention to a three-quarter length coat of a deeper shade of lavender, and with a wide shawl collar in velvet. It was most attractive and Rose was not surprised when her aunt took a second, more interested, look, then smiled and nodded agreement.

Now their aunt was equipped, both sisters made haste to find coats for themselves. Rose selected green to tone with her new walking dress and Helena decided on a deep-blue velvet spencer.

'Girls, have you finished yet?' Lady Westacote clapped her hands together in a fever of impatience. 'There is scarcely time for luncheon before we must set off for the exhibition.'

They took their leave, Madame Lisette promising to have the made-up dresses delivered to the house at once.

'Is there anything else?' asked Lady Westacote fretfully as soon as they were out of the shop.

'Shoes, scarves, gloves and muffs, hats. . . .' Rose gave a peal of laughter at her aunt's horrified face. 'Not today. We will leave all those items for tomorrow.'

They quickly covered the short distance to Sir Philip's fine house in Half Moon Street. The clock in the entrance hall was striking twelve when Hudson, the white-haired butler, admitted them. Shedding their outdoor wraps in haste, the ladies trooped into the dining-room. Here they found Sir Philip, standing at the window, a glass of wine in his hand.

'Ah, there you are, my dears,' he beamed, 'and mighty punctual – especially for ladies who have been shopping for clothes.' He chuckled and set his glass down on the table just as the door opened again to admit the butler.

'Come, everyone, make haste.' Lady Westacote was already pulling out her chair. 'Here is Hudson all ready to serve our meal.'

'But I thought Max was to join us here?' Helena frowned, hesitating.

'He said we were on no account to wait for him,' replied her uncle. 'He is no doubt still arranging the exhibits to his taste.'

'And anyway, he scarcely ever spends much time at the table,' said Lady Westacote, 'it is no wonder he is so lean.'

Helena sighed and came to join them. There was silence as they ate. Helena was decidedly cross and Rose glanced at her from time to time. Her sister was just picking at the food on her plate. Rose found the meal excellent and ate with a good appetite. She was looking forward to the promised round of social events. This was the kind of life she had dreamt of for so long. She promised herself she would accept each and every invitation.

The door opened and Hudson came in. 'The items from the dressmaker have been delivered, your ladyship.' As he turned to go out, there was a loud knock at the front door. Helena brightened. A minute later, Max walked in. He was impeccably dressed in a dark-blue jacket and buckskins. His linen was sparkling white and he looked extremely handsome. His usual restless energy was transformed into eager anticipation today.

'My apologies,' he said, striding to the table and seating himself. 'I am sure you will excuse me for being late when I tell you that everything is set out now exactly as you wished at the British Museum.' He raised his quizzing glass and inspected the remains of the sirloin. 'Ah, that is just what I need at present.'

Lady Westacote beamed at him. 'I knew we could rely on you, dear Max. While you eat, we ladies will change our clothes and then we can set off. Come girls, let us hurry.'

The gentlemen stood as the ladies left the table. Max grinned at Sir Philip and reached for the mustard. 'That means I have time to make a good meal.'

Sir Philip winked. 'And I can enjoy a glass of port.'

Rose heard them laughing as she sped up the stairs. Both she and Helena dressed quickly in their new walking dresses and coats. Snatching up their bonnets, they went to see how their aunt was getting on with her new dress.

'You look very well, dear Aunt Emily,' Rose assured her. 'With this clever pleat down the back you will not feel constricted at all. And the colour suits your fair complexion perfectly.'

'Even without lace ruffles and panniers,' muttered Helena, but Rose frowned at her to be quiet. This was an important occasion and she wanted her aunt to feel both comfortable and smart. They trooped back downstairs. The men appeared in the doorway and inspected them thoroughly.

'Charming,' said Max. His gaze swept all three, but then lingered on Helena. Her cherry-red dress emphasized her shining dark hair and big brown eyes. There was a distinct gleam in Max's eyes and a suspicion of a smile crossed his face.

Sir Philip raised his quizzing glass to inspect his wife's appearance. 'You look er . . . different, my dear. But very smart,' he added hastily, as she began to bridle. 'All the crack. Makes a change from the old style and we must move with the times, eh?'

Max shrugged into his caped greatcoat and took his hat from Hudson. 'Sir Philip, with your permission, I shall take Helena in my curricle. You will wish to escort Lady Westacote and Rose in the carriage.'

Helena had already run down the steps. She looked absolutely edible in her new red dress.

Rose heard Max saying, 'I doubt if the visitors will even notice the exhibits,' as he followed her sister out into the street. Rose suppressed a sigh and walked sedately behind her aunt and uncle to the carriage. Nobody was showing any interest in her new clothes. She thought back to the weeks in Kerim Pasha's mansion and the interest shown in her appearance by both the Pasha and Tom.

The memory brought a wistful smile to her face. She passed the journey in recalling all the sunny afternoons spent in discussions in that charming little white kiosk in the sweet-scented garden overlooking the Golden Horn. She was feeling a certain regret at the change of scene when she realized the coach had stopped. Well, she was smartly dressed and perhaps she would make a few agreeable acquaintances. Rose pasted a smile on her face as she prepared to alight from the coach. Now she must give all her attention to supporting her aunt and uncle with their exhibition – if anyone was interested in this ancient civilization.

CHAPTER FIFTEEN

The exhibition was a success. Visitors had crowded in from the moment it opened. Two hours later, Rose could see her aunt and Helena still talking busily to a crowd gathered round the table where they had set out the papyri, together with sheets of paper showing some of the symbols. Judging by the noise in that part of the hall, everyone was excited by this ancient writing.

She glanced over to where her uncle and Max were escorting a group of gentlemen round the vast hall. She could hear animated talk and much laughter so it seemed they were enjoying their tour. All the artefacts found by the expedition had been set out, together with a number of statues and stone plaques brought back a few years earlier.

Rose's task was to explain facts about the pots and figurines. She had a constant stream of young ladies and their mamas attracted to these fascinating items. She also kept an eye on the table where all her drawings of the pyramids at Giza were displayed. It made her smile to hear the exclamations of wonder at the grand scale of these buildings. To Rose's secret surprise, Ancient Egyptian civilization seemed set to become a fashion.

When at last there was a lull in the crowd, Rose wandered over to the Rosetta Stone with its perfectly chiselled lines of text in three languages. One day, perhaps, her aunt and Helena would work out the meaning of the hieroglyphs. She stroked a finger over the carved symbols, smiling a little as she wondered what that language would sound like.

Then a voice spoke behind her. She went rigid with shock, her finger still on the line of hieroglyphic text. Surely it was not possible . . . and yet, she knew that deep and mellow tone. Her heart began to beat faster. She could not turn round, not yet. It could not be *him*; she had bade him farewell in his sunlit garden on the banks of the Golden Horn, over four months ago. She recalled his lean face, austere but softened by a warm smile as she had thanked him and wished him well with his plans.

It had been hard to say goodbye. Rose had felt secure in that house – although she realized that she was staying there under very unusual circumstances. The women in the harem did not have the freedom that had been given to the English guests and Rose knew she could not accept the restricted way of life they lived.

The voice spoke again. She must be mistaken, but it was just too intriguing. Very slowly, she turned round until she was facing the direction the voice had come from. Max and his group of visitors were standing around her drawings. She immediately focused on one tall figure. He was the right height, but this gentleman bore no resemblance to Kerim Pasha.

For a start he was clean shaven. His glossy black hair was brushed into a fashionable style. He had magnificent side whiskers. His clothes had obviously come from a top tailor and fitted him perfectly. Jacket, buckskins, gleaming boots, impeccable linen, top hat and gloves, everything of the best and everything undeniably in the English style.

Rose blinked. She looked again. Were her eyes functioning properly? Before she could decide, Max was ushering the group towards her. She dragged her eyes away reluctantly from the mystery gentleman and turned towards Max. He flashed her a brilliant smile. That meant he was pleased with his success this afternoon. He came up and took her hand, pulling her a little way forward.

'Gentlemen, you were admiring these fine sketches. Allow me

to present our artist, Mrs Charteris. It is thanks to her patient work that you can see where all these treasures come from – as well as how much work is left for us to do when we return to Egypt.'

The gentlemen murmured compliments. One or two of them clapped. Rose attempted a general smile. She stood with her hands clasped together tightly. This was a moment of triumph for her, but she was more concerned to solve the mystery. Could she ask Max who his guest was? The gentleman she was interested in made no sign that he recognized her. She watched as they all followed Max back to the table. He was talking eagerly and from time to time he indicated something and the others bent over the drawings, nodding and murmuring.

Rose went slowly back to her figurines. She was rearranging them idly when she heard a step behind her. It was Max. And beside him was the mysterious gentleman.

'May I present a colleague from Hungary? Count Varoshenyi has come to London especially for this exhibition. He is most impressed by your artistic talent.'

Rose looked from Max to the 'count' and caught the warning in his eyes as he inclined his head.

'My compliments, madam,' he said loudly. 'Such fine work. I had to express my admiration.'

'I say, Kendal, can you spare a minute to explain this?' came a call from one of the group. With a murmur of apology, Max turned away. Rose was left face to face with Kerim Pasha. She drew in a deep breath. Her heart quickened its beat.

'It is you!' she whispered, leaning forward. Her very blue eyes were wide with amazement.

His hawklike face betrayed nothing. Only his eyes gleamed a message. He took a step back, executed a sharp little bow and rejoined the group of men, already moving away down the hall. Rose stood rooted to the spot, the unspoken questions trembling on the tip of her tongue. Before she had time even to turn back to her place, Lady Benson and her two fat daughters rushed up to her.

'Oh, Mrs Charteris, do tell us what he is like. We could not but see how very handsome he is. *Such* a distinguished air!' Lady Benson clasped her hands to her bosom and stared soulfully at Kerim Pasha's straight back as he walked away.

'How fortunate you are to speak with the most handsome man in the room. Pray what is his name? Where is he from? Is he staying in Town?' The daughters were breathless with eagerness.

Rose dealt with their vulgar curiosity as best she could, realizing how wise Kerim Pasha had been to pretend he was a stranger. In a very few minutes, she was surrounded by a crowd of young ladies, all agog to find out what they could about the newcomer. The words *Hungarian* and *count* echoed round until Rose felt her cheeks burn with embarrassment.

At last it was time to leave the exhibition for a rest and tea at a nearby hotel. Rose sipped her drink in silence. She could not attend to any of the conversation. Her mind was full of questions about what Kerim Pasha was doing in London and why he was in disguise. It must be the next step in those plans for army reform. So it was very urgent and it gratified her that she had played a part – even if a very small one – in the scheme.

It had been a long and eventful day. Rose smoothed down the skirt of her new green dress. She had noticed Lady Benson examining it closely and felt pleased that it was so very stylish. It was still fresh and uncreased, which was good since there was no time to go home and change. In another hour her aunt was going to give a talk about her discoveries and her first attempts at unlocking the secrets of the hieroglyphs.

It was not quite the evening entertainment Rose dreamed of, but she owed her uncle and aunt so much that she wanted to assist them in any way possible. This exhibition was so important to them. With the discipline of long practice, Rose schooled her face into a calm expression. She had learnt the skill during that tormented year when she was a prisoner at home, with Augusta's sneers and taunts forever in her ears.

Later, she had needed it when living with her husband's family, where she soon found that her parents-in-law considered her to be a burden on their housekeeping. Hugh's wages had not been sufficient for the young couple to set up their own home.

It seemed to Rose that she would never have the means to enjoy the kind of life she longed for, with lively entertainment and friends who enjoyed social gatherings and smart clothes. Time was passing. But thanks to her drawings, she made enough money to have some choices. And for the present, they were fixed in London, so there would be some social events to attend.

The conference room was crowded. Rose took a quick survey. She noticed Lady Benson and her daughters in the audience and bit back a smile.

'Goodness!' exclaimed her aunt, pleased. 'I did not expect to see so many people here. And most of them are ladies. Now that is promising.' Lady Westacote bustled up to the front of the room to arrange her notes and illustrations.

Max strolled in and consulted with Lady Westacote. Helena joined in and the three of them seemed launched in a private discussion that had them all eager faced and animated. Rose smiled to herself that such matters could be so enthralling. At last Max seized Helena by the arm.

'Enough.' he said firmly, 'let your aunt decide. Come, I have kept seats for us all down here.' He led them to the seats near the back of the room. Sir Philip joined them a moment later. Rose noticed how fondly he was smiling as he watched his wife.

Helena leaned forward to address her three companions. 'Look at this crowd,' she whispered, 'It does seem we have set off a new interest,'

Max gave a low laugh. 'So you can find more enthusiasts for your work?'

Rose kept silent. In her opinion the large number of ladies in the audience had come in the hope of seeing Kerim Pasha again. Her aunt and Helena must be the only two females in London who were unaware of his arrival and who were not scheming to invite this handsome and eligible 'count' to a party or a dinner.

Lady Westacote had finished her main talk and was taking questions when Rose became aware of a tall figure lounging against the wall nearby. He had certainly not been there when the talk began. She felt a strange sensation along her spine. She glanced under her lashes at this latecomer. In disbelief she registered the long muscled legs, the powerful shoulders, the handsome profile – and the blond-streaked brown hair, waving wildly as usual.

Still watching from the corners of her eyes, she saw him turn his head, searching the audience. His gaze was just coming up to her row when she bent her head down, pretending to pick a thread of lint from the skirt of her new gown. At last she straightened up again and glanced cautiously to her left. Tom Hawkesleigh kept cropping up in her life. Rose was not sure whether she felt more pleased or alarmed about it.

As she looked, yet again she felt a shock of disbelief. Next to Tom was Sebastian, but a Sebastian with his arm in a sling and with a livid scar on his cheek. Rose stared in horror. When they had waved goodbye to him in Portsmouth, he had been in good health and cheerful. Now he looked pale and ill.

He saw her looking at him and nodded in greeting. The question session was over and people were beginning to talk generally. Rose hastily made her way to his side, looking her concern.

'Oh, Sebastian, whatever has happened? When we last saw you, all was well.'

'Highwaymen,' he said briefly. 'They broke my arm, but I am all right now.' When she would have asked for more details, he broke in abruptly, 'What about you?' He smiled at her. 'But I can see you are well. And your aunt and Helena?'

Rose gestured towards her sister, standing beside Lady Westacote now and talking animatedly. 'As you see. She is well and happy, thank you. But they will be very sorry to see you like this.'

She had not yet acknowledged Tom although she was acutely aware of him standing so close beside her. Now he cleared his throat. 'Your aunt seems to be fully recovered from her fever,' he rumbled. 'Deuced sharp mind she has. Amazing ideas. And nobody went to sleep. I was watching to see.'

In spite of herself, Rose had to laugh. She looked up into Tom's dark eyes and saw how they lit up in response to her smile. He looked thinner than when she had last seen him. There were lines beside his mouth. In spite of her determination never to forget how he had made her suffer, Rose felt a pang. Something stirred inside her that felt very like tenderness.

He was still watching her, a wry smile on his face now. 'Seb here has told me that your journey home was uneventful, thank heaven. Are you quite settled in London now?'

'For the present; we are busy with the exhibition and these talks. My uncle and his friend are trying to raise funds for another expedition to Egypt.'

Tom raised an eyebrow. 'So they want to go back?'

Rose nodded and gave a reluctant smile.

'Well, it cannot be done overnight,' rumbled Tom. 'I think you will have time to catch your breath.'

She wanted to ask him about Kerim Pasha,but he was looking towards Lady Westacote. 'Excuse me, I must pay my compliments to your aunt.' He bowed and strolled away.

Rose watched her aunt receive him with a formal dignity. She soon thawed, however as Tom continued talking. Sebastian chuckled. 'He is the most complete hand, is he not? Able to charm the birds off the trees.'

'That is my aunt you are talking about!'

His face changed. 'Oh, I beg your pardon.' His apologetic look changed to a grin as she burst out laughing.

'Yes, my aunt has not forgotten his initial hostility. But if she had not pardoned him before, she certainly has now. Come, let us join them.'

As they walked towards the group at the front of the room, she noticed Sebastian limping. Rose put a hand on his arm. 'You were really badly treated by those ruffians.'

He grimaced and nodded but said nothing.

Sir Philip was inviting Tom to dine with them the following day. He insisted on including Sebastian in the invitation.

'And now, my dear,' he said to his wife, 'I do think it is time to call it a day here. It has been a capital success, capital. But now we are all exhausted.'

At once, Rose found Tom by her side. 'May I have the honour of driving you home?'

She opened her mouth to refuse. Then she saw Max offering his arm to Helena. She took a deep breath. 'Thank you. That would be delightful.'

They set off behind Max's curricle, but soon lost it in the evening traffic. Rose waited until Tom had negotiated his team through the busy crossing into Piccadilly. He seemed to be in a good mood.

'I wanted to ask you about Sebastian,' she said.

'Sebastian, is it?' His voice was a growl. 'You are mighty friendly with him, then?'

'Who could resist him?' she replied calmly. 'I do believe Aunt Emily thinks of him as a son.'

The only response from Tom was a sniff.

'He was always helpful to us. And *you* were very unwelcoming when we first arrived in Constantinople,' she pointed out.

Tom shot her a sideways glance. 'I had less than an hour to do those cursed sketches.'

'Is that why you and Kerim Pasha are here in London?'

The horses broke into a canter as Tom's hands slackened on the reins. He got his team back under control and demanded in a thunderous tone, 'Who told you he is in London?'

When Rose explained about the exhibition he sighed. 'Trouble!' He said no more until he drew up in Half Moon Street. Then he glanced at her again, taking in her new green gown. 'Pity you're so damned beautiful.'

'I did not ask for insults!' she snapped, preparing to get down from the curricle. 'Thank you for the delightful drive, Mr Hawkesleigh.' Rose swept away with her nose in the air. Behind her she heard a muffled curse.

CHAPTER SIXTEEN

The sound of the door-knocker came quite clearly into the sitting-room. Rose and Helena looked at each other in dismay.

'I declare, I cannot face any more visitors,' grumbled Helena. 'It has been an endless succession of mamas and daughters all morning. I wonder if they are truly interested in Egyptian antiquities or if their real purpose is to show their daughters off to Max – who, of course, is not here.' She stood up and smoothed down her dress. 'I suppose he is rather good-looking.' she added thoughtfully.

Rose coughed to hide a smile. It would be no bad thing if Helena did feel a little jealous. But, while she agreed that Max was very handsome, in her opinion, the mamas were hoping for a glimpse of the mysterious 'count'. She went to peep in the mirror over the fireplace to tidy her curls. As she turned back she saw her sister whisking towards the door at the back of the room.

'Helena! What are you doing?'

Her sister shook her head as she pulled open the door. 'Sorry, but I cannot endure any more false admiration for our intrepid adventures in Egypt,' she whispered. 'That was not what they were saying before we set off last year!' She blew a kiss and gently closed the door behind her. At the same moment, Hudson appeared in the other doorway.

Rose assumed a social smile and braced herself. She turned to meet the next bunch of curious ladies.

'Count Varow-shenyee,' announced Hudson.

The surprise rooted Rose to the spot. She wavered for a second, then resolutely stepped forward to welcome him. He was devastatingly handsome in his claret jacket and impeccable buckskins. She saw him smile as he moved towards her. He bowed over her hand. When he straightened up he gave her a keen look. Rose knew he had felt her hand tremble in his grasp. She was still too astonished to do more than stare at him.

'You must pardon this intrusion,' he said smoothly, his voice a delight to her ears, even in her flustered state. 'I met Sir Philip earlier and he insisted I should call. And I owe you an apology for yesterday. It seemed better to appear to be strangers.'

Rose was still breathless. There was so much to understand. She opened her mouth but could not get a word out.

'What?' he asked, amusement in his voice. 'Did you think I could not dress differently? You did it, after all, while you were in my country.'

'Yes, yes . . . of course,' she stammered. 'If I seem astonished, it is because I had no idea you meant to come to London.'

He nodded and smiled again. He seemed very ready to smile today. 'It is not my first visit. I must thank you for not betraying my identity yesterday.'

'I was astonished that you had become Hungarian.'

His white teeth showed in a grin. 'Ah, that is not untrue. There was a Hungarian in my family. Many generations ago,' he added, 'but we still remember her name.'

She indicated a seat. 'Please, let us be comfortable.'

He hesitated. 'Are you expecting any other visitors?'

For answer, Rose went to the fireplace and tugged the bellrope. The door opened. 'Hudson, if anyone else calls, we are not at home. And please send in some tea.' She took a seat and gestured to him to take the chair opposite. 'We have had a lot of callers today – compliments and enquiries about the exhibition.'

He nodded. 'Ah yes. Strange how these ancient civilizations fascinate people.'

Rose raised her brows. 'From your tone, it seems that you do not share that interest?'

He gave a short laugh. 'As you know, my interest is the future.' His face sobered. 'My energies are all taken up with that task.' He paused as Hudson brought in the tea tray.

While Hudson lit the candles in their sconces around the room and Rose busied herself with the cups, Kerim Pasha walked over to the window. He peered out into the darkening street. He came back towards the tea table and accepted the cup she offered him. 'Thank you. Now, tell me, if you please, is your aunt fully recovered from her fever?'

'She is very well now. We can never be grateful enough to you and to dear Latife for your kindness.'

'But it was our pleasure. My sister sends all kinds of messages. She misses your company.'

Was it her imagination, or was there a hidden meaning in his words? His voice sounded very earnest. His keen eyes watched her closely. Rose was still thinking how to reply when the door opened. In walked her uncle, followed by Max.

Sir Philip strode forward and shook hands very heartily. 'My dear sir, I am most honoured that you could call. We are so much obliged to you.' He cleared his throat. 'In fact, impossible to put into words—'

Kerim Pasha held up both hands. 'Dear sir, please do not speak of it again. It was fortunate I could be of help.'

'Do you make a long stay in England, Count?' Max drew him aside and they talked together easily. Sir Philip interrupted to insist that Kerim Pasha must stay to dine. The invitation was accepted and the men withdrew to the library until it was time for dinner.

When they assembled again in the drawing-room, Rose found that Tom and Sebastian had arrived, both very smart in their evening attire. Tom bowed but said nothing. Rose was conscious of him watching keenly as she greeted Sebastian. Helena, who had followed Rose into the room, checked at the sight of the extra

111

guest. She tilted her head to one side, studying him. Rose saw a muscle quiver in his cheek as he waited.

At last Helena's face broke into a smile. 'Now I recognize you,' she said. 'You look very well in western dress.'

She held out her hand. Kerim Pasha bowed over it with exquisite grace. 'I am honoured that you remember me. But I would be in your debt if you would think of me as Count Varoshenyi while I am in London.'

Helena looked puzzled. 'If that is your wish, sir.'

'Oh, most definitely.' His face was stern. Rose thought he must be considering the consequences of discovery. She remembered the warnings of danger he had given her in Constantinople. A shiver ran down her spine. It was indeed a very sinister business if his enemies had followed him even to London. However, to look at him, nobody would guess that he felt any apprehension.

Kerim Pasha made polite conversation throughout the meal, praising the exhibition and offering suggestions about sites for future exploration, putting Max in a fever of enthusiasm to return to Egypt.

Even if he is not an antiquarian, he knows the history of all those lands, thought Rose. She directed a brief look at Tom. He was adding his comments to Kerim Pasha's descriptions. So he had also travelled widely in the Levant. That must be where he had been for the past four years. He was describing a remote village where he had once taken refuge. Rose looked at him again and felt another pang for what might have been. As if he felt her gaze he turned and met her eyes. His smile faded. Then he raised his brows. Rose hastily bent her head over her plate.

When the ladies withdrew, Kerim Pasha looked from Tom to Sebastian. 'I had not been informed of your injuries,' he said. 'Can you explain what happened and when?'

Sebastian fortified himself with a large gulp of port and choked. Wiping his eyes, he said, 'When we reached Portsmouth, I saw the ladies safely reunited with Sir Philip and Mr Kendal. The ambassador had instructed me to waste no time in delivering his letters, so I set off for London by coach. We had not gone many miles when three ruffians held us up. They put a bullet through the driver's shoulder and they hauled me out and ... and ... demanded the letters I was carrying. I refused.' He stopped, his face twisted and he swallowed hard. He indicated his broken arm. 'They insisted. In the end they found the letters for the minister. . . .' He shook his bent head. 'I just hope they could not decipher the code.'

'Enough!' put in Sir Philip. His face was grave. He turned to Kerim Pasha. 'I apprehend we are dealing with affairs of the highest importance?'

Kerim Pasha nodded. 'I regret that you and your family have been drawn into this. It is always the case that such matters become intertwined with what seems to be a completely different affair.'

'Demme, sir.' Sir Philip banged his fist on the table, making the glasses jump. 'This young man travelled from Constantinople with my wife and her nieces. They thought he was providing a safe escort!'

'And so he was, sir,' Tom reassured him.

Sir Philip stared at him very hard from under his eyebrows, his mouth working. 'But all the time he was bearing secret letters so important that his enemies would attack and torture him to discover them.' Sir Philip's face was red and angry.

'There was no possible risk while they were all on a British frigate,' insisted Tom. 'Indeed, sir, they were safer there than when you left them in Cairo while you went on your expedition up the Nile.' It was his turn to give a stern look. 'And we are indebted to the count, here, for getting help to you so that you were able to return without being attacked yourselves – although that was for different reasons,' he added, when Sir Philip's face turned an unhealthy shade of purple.

'We were at fault to leave them,' put in Max quietly. 'We relied on the consular staff, but we stayed away longer than intended and the consul was called away to an emergency in Alexandria.

The situation can change so rapidly out there. However' – he gave Sir Philip a warning look – 'let us be thankful that the ladies were so resourceful and that they escaped to the safe haven provided by our guest.' He waited for Sir Philip to nod agreement, then turned back to look keenly from Tom to Kerim Pasha. 'And now, it is our turn to offer what help we can for your . . . er . . . business.' He raised his brows.

Kerim Pasha put his hand on his heart. 'My thanks for your offer. It is much appreciated. And I agree with all my heart – your ladies are most valiant.' He glanced at Tom and raised one eyebrow. 'When I first saw them, I was filled with admiration. Why' – his eyes narrowed as he looked round the table – 'even I would not care to face the thugs of Cairo without an army at my back.' His hand curled into a fist.

Tom looked down to hide the sudden flare in his eyes. He had already seen how Kerim Pasha's face softened when he looked at Rose. The man would like to carry her off to his own land. Tom frowned into the ruby liquid in his glass. He knew she admired Kerim Pasha and, dammit, the man was handsome, charming and wealthy enough to indulge any female's whims. If she was still serious about her projects for helping poor children, she could do far more with his backing than she could ever dream of here in England.

Tom's hand trembled slightly as he raised his glass to his lips. How ironic that he had received the strictest orders to protect Kerim Pasha's life with his own while the man was here to negotiate this treaty. Then it occurred to him that Rose was less frosty now towards himself. But could that be because she was more interested in Kerim Pasha? He frowned over this, not heeding the conversation around the table.

Then the port reached him again, rousing him. He pushed the bottle on and forced himself to listen. Max was urging Kerim Pasha to maintain his pose as a wealthy antiquarian. So the fellow would be haunting the house then. And as if that was not torment enough for him, his conscience lashed him over poor Seb. The young man was calm again since they had turned the conversation into other channels. The letters given to Seb had been a blind. They had used the young man shamefully, but it proved what they had suspected. Their opponents were working in England as well as in Constantinople. Tom straightened up and flexed his shoulders. His instinct told him there was dire trouble ahead. Well, he could handle *that* kind of trouble!

CHAPTER SEVENTEEN

'Do you miss your Turkish clothes?' asked Helena. She was sitting at the dressing-table, pinning up her hair and twisting a red ribbon into it. Rose was sorting through the filmy garments she had brought back from Constantinople. She stopped to watch her sister's skilful fingers at work.

'I wish I could achieve such a result. You make it look so simple, but I have to rely on Prue's help.'

Helena grimaced. 'Prue is rather heavy handed. And she scolds too much. Sometimes I wonder if she remembers how long it is since I left the nursery.'

'Yes, but she looks after us well. And,' added Rose, folding a pale-turquoise robe and laying it carefully on the bed, 'she is more comfortable with us than with George and Augusta and Papa.' She came to peer at her own reflection over Helena's shoulder. She adjusted a curl that was falling over her forehead and added, 'I did write just after we reached Rivercourt, to inform Papa of our safe return from Egypt.'

'And you have not had any reply.' Helena jabbed the last pin into her hair. 'Well, it is a long time since we thought of our father's house as our home. Prue as well.' She cast a quick glance towards her sister. 'No doubt Augusta has decided we are beyond the pale.'

'She is happy to know that we are overseas, but I think she will be concerned that we do not disgrace her while we are in England.'

Helena made a disgusted sound and tossed the hairbrush down with a thud.

'Why did you ask about the Turkish clothes?' said Rose hastily.

Helena picked up the hand-mirror and surveyed her reflection from the back and side. 'Oh, the *count'* – she stressed the word – 'in his new role put me in mind of appearance. It makes me wonder if we are all able to change our identity with our dress.'

Rose took a peep down into the street. 'He certainly looked every inch a western gentleman last night.' She pulled on her coat and set her bonnet on her head. 'I feel like my normal self dressed in these clothes,' she said at last. 'I cannot recall that I felt any different in those gauzy trousers and silken tunics. They were just suitable in that house and for that climate. They are not much use here. Still, I like to keep them. It reminds me of our kind friends and the haven they offered us after our awful flight from Cairo – and dear Aunt Emily being so ill.'

'So unlike her,' nodded Helena. 'And just look at her now.'

'Yes, it is such a relief. That fever seems to have gone for good. Mr Hawkesleigh assures me that it is not something that recurs.' She adjusted the pots and brushes on the dressing-table idly, frowning a little. 'I wonder what the gentlemen were discussing last night. They stayed in the dining-room for ages.'

'And they were not in a very good mood when they did join us,' agreed Helena, buttoning up her new spencer. 'Even Max showed no interest in the exhibition, or in discussing Aunt Emily's theory about two of the hieroglyphs. Really, I think she has made a most important discovery.'

'Yes, certainly, but pray leave it for the moment,' begged Rose hastily. 'We really must visit Madame Lisette's and see if our other gowns are finished. And then we need to search for bonnets and shawls, gloves, shoes, oh, so many things.'

'My practical sister Rosalind,' sighed Helena. 'What a pity you did not marry some sprig of fashion. You were so excited when you first went to Town.' She rummaged in a drawer for her gloves. 'But then you came back home and meekly accepted Papa's choice of husband. I would have said that Hugh Charteris was much too dull for you.' She pushed the drawer shut and looked up. 'Why, Rose, how white you are. What did I say?'

Dumbly, Rose shook her head. She turned away and picked up her reticule and gloves. Still without speaking, she opened the door and they set off down two flights of stairs. By the time she reached the entrance hall, Rose had overcome the stab of sorrow at the way her life had been shaped by others. She reminded herself that she was now mistress of her own destiny. And today was going to be an enjoyable shopping day, full of ribbons and scents and the pleasures of trying on new clothes.

Lady Emily was ready, but her attitude was that of a lamb being led to the slaughter. The girls spent the short carriage drive in coaxing her into a better mood. At length she accepted that she had to have new clothes in order to impress on society that she was not some fusty recluse with no idea of life in the modern world.

'And if you just let Madame Lisette advise you, dear ma'am, she will turn you out in bang-up style,' urged Helena.

Aunt Emily sat up at that. 'Really, Helena. You must not talk like Max. That young man must guard his tongue in front of you.'

Helena giggled. 'Perhaps I heard it from Sebastian, ma'am. And he can do no wrong where you are concerned.'

'Impertinent girl!' But Lady Westacote was smiling as she descended from the carriage and entered the shop.

When they emerged, the shop boy was staggering under a pile of bandboxes that were tenderly loaded into the carriage. Rose persuaded the others to walk round the corner into Bond Street in search of new bonnets and shoes. They had not been in more than two milliners' however, when they found a number of ladies coming up and greeting them very warmly.

It became a struggle to excuse themselves in order to complete their shopping. So many matrons insisted on issuing invitations to musical evenings, dancing parties and impromptu suppers.

'Bring *all* your party, dear Lady Westacote,' beamed Lady Benson, 'we shall be charmed to meet them all.' She gave Rose a rather calculating stare as she turned away. Rose stifled a fit of giggles. Lady Benson had set her sights on Count Varoshenyi. Well, if she had judged him by the quality of his tailoring, no doubt she assumed that he was a wealthy landowner. That was indeed true but when Rose thought of Lady Benson's plump daughters in harem clothes, she could not help a choke of laughter.

Her aunt frowned. 'Really, whatever has got into you girls this morning? What a sad lack of conduct.' She darted into the next milliner's shop, adding, 'This time I shall take any hat that fits so we can get back home quickly. I cannot wait any longer to test my theory about the pharaoh's cartouche.'

Eventually, they all found bonnets to match their new coats. Rose was very tempted by an enormous sable muff and decided she could afford it. It was just the thing to set off her green coat. As Lady Westacote had now lost patience with shopping, it was agreed that the two girls would return another day with Prue to buy such items as linen, silk stockings and shawls.

'How I like this new dress,' said Rose, when they were back in their bedroom. She held up a powder-blue muslin dress with white trimming on the neckline and sleeves. 'But I need a stole to go with it.' Her eyes brightened. 'I wonder. . . .' She bent over the pile of Turkish clothes again. A few minutes later she gave an exclamation of triumph and draped a beaded and tasselled white silk scarf over the gown. 'What do you think, Helena? It is a harem item,' she added, her blue eyes sparkling with mischief.

'So, are you setting out to entice the count?' Helena dodged away with. a peal of laughter as Rose flicked the scarf at her. 'You think I am lost in my lexicons, but I can see what is under my nose.' She came and put an arm round her surprised sister. 'I saw how he looked at you last night. And it is time you had a bit of enjoyment in life. Poor Rose.'

'What do you mean by "enjoyment"?' asked Rose suspiciously.

Helena smiled and opened her hands. 'Why, the things that give you pleasure . . . or do I mean the people?' She tilted her head and fixed a keen gaze on Rose.

Rose's eyes flashed. 'You surely do not think I am encouraging him – or any gentleman—'

'No, no, but you have been too busy looking after us, it is time to enjoy your passions now, while you can. I know you like being part of society life in London.'

'Well, so I do, poor feather-headed female that I am. And pretty dresses and smart accessories do fascinate me. But you are already finding me admirers. And what of yourself?' Rose looked meaningfully at her sister and saw the colour creep into her cheeks.

Helena forced a little laugh. 'Oh, I have my passions as you well know. I mean heiroglyphs of course.' She gestured at the new muff. 'That could be useful to me. It is large enough to keep a couple of lexicons in. Or even the Rosetta Stone.' She kept a straight face as she watched Rose's look of horror at the idea. Then she gave an exaggerated sigh and shook her head, 'But my fashion obsessed sister merely wants to parade in Bond Street and Hyde Park and send the gentlemen wild.' Her eyes were twinkling wickedly.

Rose stroked the soft fur of the muff. Then she fluttered her eyelids and sighed like a bored debutante. 'You are right. I am going to take part in society life. It seems we are now famous enough to be on everybody's guest list.' She waggled a stern finger at Helena. 'And *you* are going to accompany me to all these events, starting with Lady Benson's dinner party this evening.'

CHAPTER EIGHTEEN

Tom was in a good mood. He did not often try his luck at the gaming tables, but this evening he was winning steadily. He endured some sarcastic comments from his fellow players. They were old friends he had not seen in several years. Now they remarked that they wished he had not been in such a hurry to return to England if he was going to win all their money.

Tom accepted another glass of claret and picked up his cards. He was concentrating on making his choice when a discreet voice coughed insistently at his elbow. 'Ahem. Sir?'

Irritated, Tom looked up. 'Dash it, man, do you not know better than to interrupt the game?' He glared down his formidable nose.

'Yes, sir, but if you please, this is urgent.'

Reluctantly, Tom took the note, broke the seal and frowned over the contents before stuffing it in his inside pocket. 'Excuse me, gentlemen,' He unfolded his long legs from under the table and tossed his cards back into the pile in the middle of the cloth. 'I am unable to continue.' He scooped up his winnings.

'Dash it, Hawkesleigh,' protested a very eager card player, 'you have broken the game, sir.'

There was a chorus of protest from the others. 'No, let him go before we lose our shirts. Good riddance!'

Tom laughed. 'I'll win your shirts another evening.' He left the overheated card room and ran lightly down the stairs to the entrance hall. The young man who had handed him the note came forward and ushered Tom out of White's Club. There was a plain coach drawn up close by. Both men got in and at once the vehicle moved off.

'Did it have to be this evening?' grumbled Tom. 'Just when the cards were in my favour for once.'

'Sorry, sir, but it is Lord Bethany,' said the messenger in hushed tones.

Tom grunted but said no more. They soon arrived at the elegant house in Ryder Street where Kerim Pasha was staying. Tom disappeared inside and shortly afterwards reappeared followed by the tall figure of Kerim Pasha, settling his top hat on his dark head.

Now the coach rumbled over cobblestones as they travelled westwards. The three men sat in silence. At length the coach swung off the road onto a gravelled drive and pulled up in front of a tall building.

'If you could wait here for a moment, gentlemen?' The young man jumped down. Tom felt in his pocket discreetly. His fingers closed round the familiar smooth form of his pistol. He hoped he would not have to use it.

'Do you anticipate trouble, Mr Hawkesleigh?' Kerim Pasha sounded amused.

Tom looked out of the window again. 'I do not know, sir. Considering what they did to Sebastian Welland, it is obvious they mean to get the information they want.'

'Ah . . . and who exactly are *they*?'

Tom shook his head slowly. 'So many people have a stake in this. Our people, your people, the Hapsburgs, and the French, obviously!' After another pause, he added gloomily, 'It could even be the Russians. They would not want your army to be more efficient.'

'Now that is interesting.' Tom could hear the smile in his companion's voice. 'Maybe they are all in a grand alliance against the Ottoman Empire.'

'We know they have enlisted the help of a very sinister

gangmaster here in London.' Tom continued, 'Silas Browne is so powerful he acts as he pleases. If they sought his help, it indicates that your opponents are utterly determined to thwart your plans.'

'They can try,' said Kerim Pasha in a harsh tone. 'The sooner I get these improvements started, the better. And I trust that tonight we can get the process agreed.'

Their messenger now reappeared and invited them inside. Tom followed Kerim Pasha, who walked into the house in a lithe, unhurried manner as if he was about to enjoy an agreeable evening's entertainment. The villa was luxuriously furnished and well lit. They were shown into a large library where two men were seated at a long table. Both surveyed their visitors keenly. At length, the older man rose to his feet and bowed.

'Welcome, sir,' he said in a languid voice. He was plainly dressed yet he had a commanding presence. Tom knew that Lord Bethany, the minister who dealt with difficult secret enterprises, was an old fox. It was whispered by those who dealt with him that he always made the other side weep.

He was attended by Witherson, his private secretary. Tom grimaced. Witherson was even more ruthless than his master. Tom had met him on a previous occasion when dealing with another mission and he had not enjoyed the encounter. Witherson was a pale, balding man, with stooping shoulders and large, spiderlike hands. If he noticed any mistake or weak point in an argument, he would stop the discussion just by raising a finger. Such was his capacity for weighing up every minute detail that even Lord Bethany accepted correction from his secretary.

No doubt they intended to make a deal with Kerim Pasha which would involve a massive payment to the Treasury without committing very much to the Turk's requirements for his training programme. However, to Tom's secret enjoyment, this evening they were not able to organize things all their own way. His eyes crinkled with amusement at Kerim Pasha's ability to argue them down without heat but with a steely determination.

'If I am to train an elite corps of young officers, I require the best you have in terms of equipment, as well as engineers and officers in sufficient numbers.' Kerim Pasha held up a warning hand. 'The best, gentlemen. My officers will know. I will know.'

'If we send you our best officers and engineers, we need to be certain that they will be safe,' put in Lord Bethany. 'This business is sure to cause fierce opposition.'

'Very fierce, I do not deny it. That is why everyone will go to my country estates in Anatolia. They will be far from any threats there. Your men will remain there, I swear to you. The officers they train will gradually be placed in key posts in Constantinople.' He indicated Tom. 'This gentleman has already made a very detailed plan of each stage.'

All eyes turned towards Tom. He nodded. 'It is a very discreet plan. It should work well.'

By four o'clock in the morning the hours of hard bargaining had taken their toll on everyone except Kerim Pasha. He sat, keen eyed and alert, his energy dominating the room. Tom lounged in his chair, a glass of brandy by his hand, his long legs stretched out under the table. He contemplated this man whose ruthless determination he admired wholeheartedly. It took a lot of courage to undertake such a task, but Kerim Pasha would succeed if anyone could. In that endeavour Tom was proud to work with him and wished him every success.

But when it came Rose . . . Tom's mouth set in a grim line. He could not bear the idea of another man touching her. Each time he saw Kerim Pasha speak to her in that way he reserved just for her, Tom wanted to smash his fist into that darkly handsome face. He scowled into his glass, brooding. He was no nearer winning back her trust. He took a sip of his brandy and brought his attention back to the business in hand.

There was silence now apart from the scratching of the quill as Witherson noted down the terms of the agreement. From time to time he looked over his spectacles at one or other of the men around the table, brushing the quill against his large jaw. Then he would nod and carry on with his writing. When he had finished and sanded the paper, he passed it to Lord Bethany, who frowned over it for some time. He sighed several times but nodded. The secretary at once began to copy the text on to a second sheet of paper. At length, both copies of the agreement were ready.

Lord Bethany took up the quill and scrawled a signature on the page. 'These will be the only two copies,' said the minister in a low voice. 'I am authorized to sign on behalf of the chief of staff. And you, sir' – he looked over his spectacles at Kerim Pasha – 'do you have authority from the highest level?'

Kerim Pasha inclined his head. 'His Majesty, Sultan Selim has given me full powers to act on his behalf in this matter.' He picked up the quill and added his signature.

The minister rubbed a hand across his face. 'Do you require a translation, Your Excellency? For the Sultan,' he added when Kerim Pasha's brows rose in a question.

'God forbid! His Majesty understands enough English to read this – and the fewer people to see it the better. Until we start work, of course.' His eyes met Tom's across the table.

Tom's eyes glowed as he returned that look. They had done it! The sense of pride surged up that his plan was about to be put in operation. He had to restrain himself; he wanted to jump up and down. Then he thought how many difficulties lay ahead. The proud soldiers of the Ottoman Empire would cling to their old ways. They would do murder rather than accept these changes. And enemies were already stalking them. So now it was a matter of honour to see that Kerim Pasha remained safe for the rest of his time in London.

CHAPTER NINETEEN

'Is this *all* your party?' Lady Benson's eyes raced from Rose and Helena to Sir Philip and Lady Westacote and finally Max. 'I am sure I made it plain that all your antiquarian group would be welcome.' She looked accusingly at Rose. 'My daughters were so looking forward to making the acquaintance of your Hungarian friend.'

Rose opened her blue eyes innocently. 'Are you referring to the gentleman who was at the Egyptian exhibition, ma'am? I believe he was part of the group that Mr Kendal took round to explain all the latest discoveries.'

Max heard his name and turned towards them. 'Are you talking of Count Varoshenyi?'

The older daughter whirled around from greeting Helena. 'Did I hear you mention the count?' she exclaimed in a breathy voice. 'Is he coming this evening, Mama?'

'Apparently not,' said Lady Benson, snapping her fan shut. 'Such a disappointment to my dear girls.' Her ample bosom swelled under its barely adequate covering of purple satin. After a tight-lipped moment she recollected herself and gave Max a hard smile. 'They are both so interested in everything to do with antiquities. But let me make my daughters known to you, Mr Kendal. Clarissa and Clorinda.'

The two girls curtsied and pressed in close, eager-eyed. Max, known for his *sangfroid* in many a dangerous situation in desert and jungle, seemed to Rose to have gone pale. She watched in growing amusement as the two sisters bombarded him with seemingly artless questions about his adventures and the interesting people he had met.

When they showed no sign of ending their interrogation, Helena made an attempt to join in the conversation. Clarissa pointedly turned her shoulder and Clorinda drew Max towards the painting over the fireplace, talking non-stop as she indicated various details. Before Helena could manage to break in on their remarks dinner was announced.

Rose was claimed by a pleasant-looking gentleman with grey hair. When they were all seated at the long table, she was not surprised to see that Clarissa was sitting next to Max, while Helena was placed further down, next to an amiable youth who obviously admired her beauty, but Rose doubted he had ever heard of Egypt or ancient languages.

It was the start of a long and boring dinner. Rose kept a social smile on her face and did her best to convince the gentlemen on either side of her that foreign travel was quite acceptable for young ladies in the modern world. They looked very disapproving of such ideas, but smiled at her nevertheless. She supposed she had her smart new gown to thank for that.

Rose saw that, as usual, Helena was attracting admiring glances from the men. Her amber silk robe shimmered and seemed to enhance the light of those glorious brown eyes and the shining coils of her dark hair. The string of turquoises round her neck set off her appearance delightfully.

On more than one occasion Rose caught Lady Benson examining Helena with narrowed eyes. She also found her hostess's gaze on herself. She was certain that nothing could be amiss, however. Her jonquil silk dress was very stylish and she had added some lace to make the neckline more demure. Her hair was dressed in a simple topknot with a few curls falling over her ears. Perhaps Lady Benson was examining her pearl necklace. Rose gave a tiny sigh. It had been her mother's and was her most precious possession.

In her turn, Rose looked at Lady Benson's two daughters. They had unremarkable features and hair that was more mousy than brown. Both had round faces and looked as if they would benefit from more regular exercise. Yet both were very self-assured and their voices could be heard over everyone else's conversation. Their white silk dresses were cut in the latest fashion. At one point she caught Max's eye and had to suppress a smile. He was obviously desperate for the ladies to finish their meal and withdraw.

At last Lady Benson stood up and the ladies followed her out of the room. Helena caught up with her sister and pinched her arm. 'I cannot endure much more of this,' she hissed, 'they are all so boring!'

Before Rose could reply, she found Clarissa standing in front of her.

'Do pray come and sit with me where we can have a little quiet conversation,' she said, drawing Rose towards a sofa in the window embrasure. She sat down and smoothed her skirts. Then she gave Rose a sideways look. 'I must ask you about the mysterious count, Mrs Charteris. He has made such an impression on my sister and myself that we are in a fever to know all about him.' She adjusted the many bangles on her plump arms, darting her eyes towards Rose's face every few seconds.

Rose shook her head. 'But I really cannot help you. I spoke two words to him about the pictures at the exhibition. That is all. I agree that he is very handsome,' she added as an afterthought.

'Oh surely, Mrs Charteris. If he is interested in your antiquities, he must be attending some of those boring lectures about old languages.' pouted Clarissa.

'Perhaps he was only in London for a few days.' Rose tried to keep her tone disinterested. This fever of interest was not going to please Tom. The 'count' was on a secret mission, after all. A large shadow came between her and the light from the candelabra. It was Clorinda. She was grinning, her eyes alight with curiosity.

'Have you found out all about him?' she asked her sister.

Clarissa shook her head. Both of them turned a calculating look on Rose. She maintained a gently innocent air. What a pair of man-eaters! Then she noticed another girl, hovering behind Clorinda. She also had an eager expression, as if ready for some tasty morsels of gossip. Clorinda introduced her as Miss Julia Delamere.

'Julia is our *particular* friend,' she informed Rose. 'She is quite the most fashionable debutante this season.'

'Are you enjoying all the events?' Rose asked politely.

Julia made a dismissive gesture. 'Oh, it is all very well. I like to have new gowns and spend my time at parties and balls. But I did it all last year as well.'

'Oh, I see.' Rose looked more closely. Julia was small and reasonably pretty but her manner indicated that she considered herself superior to everyone else. She inspected Rose from head to foot, her eyes narrowing as she noticed the lustrous pearl necklace.

'What do you use on your hair to achieve that shade of blonde?' she drawled.

Rose smiled sweetly. 'It is my natural colour,' she said. She could not resist a glance at Julia's unremarkable light-brown hair, elaborately dressed with ribbons and flowers.

Julia's pale-blue eyes flashed. 'Is it true that you have been travelling in foreign lands?' she asked with a slight titter. She peered at Rose's face. 'Mama would never dream of letting me damage my complexion in such a way.' She patted her cheek and simpered, then twirled round and minced off. The effect was rather spoiled as she dropped her fan and had to stop and retrieve it.

'Dear Julia is rather overwrought at present,' confided Clarissa. 'She nearly caught a viscount last year but somehow it all came to nothing.'

'Yes, but now her mama is planning to marry her to Mr Hawkesleigh,' put in Clorinda.

Rose nearly dropped her own fan at this pronouncement. She was itching for the sisters to continue with their confidences, but the door was opening and Clarissa beamed as the men entered the drawing-room.

'At last!' she said. 'Now we can make the tea.' She jumped up and walked away without another glance. For once, Rose would have been glad to hear a little more gossip. Was Tom aware of this proposed match? What did he think of Miss Julia Delamere. She found it distressing to consider the idea of Tom with another woman. Yet only a few months ago she would have said that she never wanted to see him again. Something had changed and Rose was not sure she liked the feeling. It threatened to be painful.

Helena roused her. 'Let us take a cup of tea,' she murmured. 'I do believe those two girls will serve it all to the men if we are not quick.'

Rose stood up. 'Those girls are taking a great deal of interest in Max this evening. More converts to ancient civilizations.'

Her reply was a snort. 'Flummery! Their interests lie quite elsewhere. But I will be astonished if they get a second chance to chase after him. If I know Max, he has decided to set off on an urgent expedition to the Greek Islands, starting tomorrow.'

They laughed and went towards the tea table. Rose recollected her aunt's instructions. 'After this, we must circulate and discuss our exhibition as much as possible.'

At last the evening was over and they were in the carriage to return to Half Moon Street.

'Detestable,' yawned Helena. 'I feel that we wasted our time entirely. The Bensons are not a family I wish to meet again.' She kicked Rose's ankle. 'What do they suspect about you and Count Varoshenyi?'

Rose glared. 'That hurt. Do not take your ill-humour out on me!'

'Surely you are not going to quarrel again!' Lady Westacote stifled a yawn. 'I am very grateful to you for spreading the word about my lectures and the prospect of deciphering the hieroglyphs. Most of the ladies showed a definite curiosity in the subject.'

'There is certainly a growing interest in the ancient civilization of Egypt,' put in Sir Philip. 'That will help us to raise funds for our next expedition. It is a costly business, and any help is welcome.' He nodded. 'I found a couple of possible backers this evening, so do not say the evening was wasted, young Helena.'

Helena merely shrugged.

'At least you were much admired in your new finery,' said Rose.

'I do not care for that,' muttered Helena, then, realizing how ungracious she sounded, she looked towards her uncle. 'That is to say, Uncle Philip, I am very happy with my new dress and if it helps your cause for me to look fashionable, so much the better.'

'Was that a thank you, miss?' he chuckled. 'Never mind, you can get back to your studies in the morning.'

'Unless we have more visitors!' she muttered.

CHAPTER TWENTY

The only visitor to call the following morning was Max. He arrived while they were still at the breakfast table, but he was so much part of the family that he simply sat down and Lady Westacote poured him a cup of coffee.

'I met young Welland as I came through Piccadilly,' he remarked. 'He seems to be recovering from that beating now.' He sipped his coffee. 'Of course, his arm needs time to mend. He told me he must return to Constantinople and plans to set off within the month.'

Sir Philip merely grunted without raising his head from the letter he was reading. The ladies all looked at each other.

'We cannot let Sebastian go away without holding a dinner for him,' said Lady Westacote.

'Dear Seb, he deserves that at least,' said Helena warmly.

There was a crash as Max's cup hit the saucer. 'Upon my word,' he said, 'you are mighty fond of this young fellow.'

'Of course,' murmured Helena provocatively. 'Do not forget how well he looked after us on the journey home from Constantinople.'

Max's eyes narrowed. Helena gave him a stare. 'We can have our own friends,' she said cheekily. 'We are not young ladies on the catch for a husband, like your new friends last night.'

At that, Max threw back his head and gave a bark of laughter.

'I began to wonder if they would drag me away to their lair. A pair of Gorgons.'

'Were they interested in Egypt or in you?' Rose asked him, her face innocent.

He gave her his rare smile. 'Well, they were certainly not interested in Egypt.'

At the general laughter that followed, Sir Philip raised his head. He took off his spectacles and held out his coffee cup for a refill. 'A busy day ahead, eh?' he said, spooning sugar liberally into his cup. He looked at Max. 'We must call on Lord Teyworth; he told me last night that he will help us set up a fund for a further expedition.'

'Splendid!' Max's face lit up. 'The sooner the better. I cannot wait to get back to explore further. And next time, we will take the ladies with us when we travel up the Nile.'

Helena and Lady Westacote beamed at each other. 'We could study hieroglyphs so much better if we can get more papyri,' said Lady Westacote eagerly.

Rose felt her heart sink right down to her toes. It was hard not to utter a protest, but she knew they would not understand her feelings. She forced her lips into a smile, but nobody was looking at her anyway. For something to do, she took another slice of bread and spread butter over it slowly and precisely. Her chest swelled with a silent sigh while she cut the bread into tiny morsels. She was thinking of the heat and discomfort of another long spell in Egypt.

Rose had always been fascinated by London. Even this present short stay in Town was providing her with a taste of the life she enjoyed so much. She loved the bustle of the city streets, the wide avenues with splendid buildings, smart carriages bowling along, fine ladies and gentlemen out shopping or walking and riding in Hyde Park. There were so many famous places to visit, as well as all the theatres, art galleries and libraries. And she loved to browse in the smart shops and study the latest fashions.

From her previous visit, she remembered the busy round of

entertainment: dinner parties, balls, concerts and outings to more distant places of entertainment. She had been starved of these things for so long. She did not want to go back to the heat and difficulties of life on expedition. Unlike her aunt and sister she was not interested in ancient civilizations.

Aunt Emily had always been such a bluestocking that the family had despaired of her ever settling down. And then she was lucky enough to meet and fall in love with Uncle Philip. She sometimes said she had accepted him so that she could travel more freely. They were a happy couple, both kind and generous, but completely absorbed in their expeditions and studies.

Helena had shown the same scholarly interests at a very young age, which was why their father had consented to allow her to join Aunt Emily on that first expedition to India. That experience settled Helena in a determination to follow a life of travel and study, which she claimed was freedom for her. No wonder she was looking so radiant as she planned a return to Cairo. Rose darted a glance round the table. They were eagerly discussing what monuments they would visit and what type of boat to hire for a long trip up the Nile.

Oh, no! thought Rose. *How can I submit to live on a poky little boat for months? Sand in everything . . . and there will be snakes and scorpions . . . and crocodiles!* She clenched her teeth and pushed her plate away. The mangled slice of bread looked how she felt. There was a dark cloud looming over her.

When she raised her head, Max was watching her. He said nothing, merely raising his eyebrows with a slight smile. *He knows,* she thought, but she could see how his face was so much more animated than usual. He would prefer to be out there with the crocodiles, just so long as there were ruins to explore.

'Would you care for a visit to the opera this evening?' he said, including the other ladies in his question. 'Young Welland told me that the great Signora Bertina will be singing.' He looked at Rose. 'I know you enjoy music.'

It was a bribe, and a poor one at that. However, it was one

outing she would enjoy so she nodded and thanked him. It helped her to forget the horrors ahead of her to think about the evening's treat as she accompanied her aunt and sister on a visit to Hatchard's Bookshop. While they searched for books on Egypt, Rose slipped away to browse the shelves for the latest novels and books of poetry.

She selected three books and went to pay for them. She tucked her purchases in her muff, smiling at the difference in her choice of books from those lexicons that were making Helena talk excitedly to Aunt Emily. The rest of the day was spent at a lecture hall where Lady Westacote gave another talk on the importance of the discoveries being made in Egypt. It was well attended. Rose sat at the back of the room and discreetly read some of the poems in one of her new books. But even she sensed the interest in the room. Apparently Egypt was coming into fashion.

When they reached the opera house that evening, the ladies found a smiling Sebastian waiting for them in the foyer. They all greeted him warmly, with praise for his fashionable appearance and enquiries about his arm.

'By Heaven, you must tell me your secret,' growled Max. 'I have known these ladies for years, but they have never made such a fuss of me.'

'Would you care for it if we did?' Helena laughed at him. He shook his head at her, then took her hand and laid it on his arm. They set off up the stairs together. Rose did not hear what he said in reply, but she saw them laughing together, heads close.

Sebastian walked up the stairs between Lady Westacote and Rose. 'May I say how charming you both look in your elegant gowns?' he said. He walked up another step, then went red and stuttered, 'That is to say I have never seen you at such a grand event before. For all I know, you often dress like this.'

'It is the first time I have been to the opera,' whispered Rose in reply, 'and you are looking very smart as well.'

He glanced at her gratefully. He did indeed look very fine in his wine-red jacket and ivory satin breeches. His fair hair was cut in the latest fashion and his cologne smelt expensive. Rose wondered if he still cherished hopes of winning Helena's heart. She decided it must be obvious that Helena and Max were growing closer ever since the start of their visit to London.

The music was all that Rose could wish. She enjoyed the first act and was only sorry when it was time for the interval. From all around came the hum of conversation and the flashes of colour as people moved from one box to another to see friends. Rose sat in a dream, thinking over the fine singing.

Gradually she came back to earth and realized that there was a visitor in their box. Although his back was turned towards her, she knew at once that it was Tom Hawkesleigh. He was talking to her uncle and aunt. Then he turned to speak to Max. Rose examined his face. Tom's features had always been finely chiselled, but she felt certain that he was thinner than before. There were dark circles under his eyes that added to his gaunt appearance.

She heard her aunt mention Sebastian's name and then realized that Lady Westacote was inviting Tom to the dinner she was planning to give before Sebastian left. 'And I would wish to invite Count Varoshenyi. . . .' Rose heard her aunt say. Her own thoughts whirled. Why was fate pushing her into contact with these men who caused her heart to beat faster? She had established a stable, emotion-free pattern to her life and after the crises she had endured, that was all she wanted now.

She puzzled over the perversity of fate, looking vaguely round the large theatre. A face in a box opposite caught her eye. It was that young lady who was friends with the Benson girls. Rose studied Julia's appearance. Overdressed, as usual. Then she realized that Julia was staring at her, her face decidedly angry.

Whatever have I done? wondered Rose. She turned her head and saw Tom giving her a slight bow. She nodded to him and he turned away and left the box. He had not approached her, not said a single word, not even smiled! All at once the magic was gone from her evening and she felt bereft.

136

She looked back towards Julia, but the girl was now talking to another member of her party. Rose took a deep breath. Did Julia consider Tom to be her property? Well, Rose could not tell her that she was determined not to marry again. She clutched her fan. Why then did it hurt that Tom was now aloof? This was ridiculous! She straightened her shoulders. She would enjoy the rest of the opera!

Yet, somehow, the second act was less enthralling than the first as images of endless sand dunes and vast pyramids drifted across her mind and could not be entirely banished. From time to time she cast a discreet glance at Julia's box, but not once did she see Tom there. That was a comfort of sorts. Then she was angry with herself. She must not be a dog in the manger.

'Will you be happy to return to Constantinople?' Rose asked Sebastian at the end of the evening, while they were waiting for their carriage.

He pursed his lips. 'It is a very good posting,' he said. 'If I have to work abroad, I am very lucky to be in that city.'

'Yes, but do you want to go abroad?' she insisted.

He gave her a curious look. 'I enjoy travelling to other lands,' he said. 'and it is my work to learn about diplomacy.' He shrugged. 'I have three older brothers. I am obliged to make my own way in life.'

She smiled warmly at him. 'You are already doing very well. One day, you will be a distinguished member of the government.'

He gave a short laugh. 'Maybe, but meanwhile, it is my diplomatic duty to inform you that your aunt is beckoning. Your carriage is here.'

CHAPTER TWENTY-ONE

'Rose, are you still busy?' Helena put her head round the drawing-room door.

Rose placed the last flower in the vase and stood back to admire the effect. 'There, I have finished everything now. And I have completed all the sketches Aunt Emily required. She does not wish to be disturbed. She is going over her notes for the speech she will deliver this evening.'

Helena slipped an arm through her sister's as they mounted the stairs. 'It is a fine, dry day. Come with me for a walk in the park.'

This was unusual. Rose wondered what her sister wanted to discuss that needed to be said so privately. In a very short time, they had pulled on their boots and coats. Rose tied the strings of her bonnet and picked up her new muff. Helena was adjusting the collar of her deep-blue velvet spencer. She set her little bonnet over her dark hair and tied the ribbons under one ear.

'For a scholar, you are very fashionable,' said Rose.

'For a widow, you are very young and pretty,' retorted Helena, pushing her sister out of the door and hurrying her down the stairs. 'We shall not be gone long,' she informed Hudson airily, as he opened the front door for them. 'Any visitors can be asked to wait.'

Rose frowned at this, but already Helena was pulling her across Piccadilly and along to the wide gates that led into the park. They walked under the trees in silence for a while. Rose looked around at the greenery.

'Shall you not miss this when we are back in Cairo?' she asked.

Helena shook her head. 'Not really. There are many green areas along the Nile, you know. My chief interest is in unlocking that hidden language – and, of course, I want to do so before any French scholar manages it. That is most important to me.'

'So are we walking out here while you attempt to convince me to return to Egypt with a light heart?'

Helena gave her sister's arm a squeeze. 'I know it is not a passion for you as it is for the rest of us. Poor Rose, what choice do you have? Your dowry was taken by your husband and his family and Papa will not make you an allowance.' They paced on, each thinking of their father.

Rose sighed. 'If only our dear mother had lived. Papa was not so . . . so narrow-minded when she was there to run the household.'

Helena nodded agreement. 'All this is Augusta's doing. She is such a nip-farthing. There is plenty of money, but she is not willing for us to have a penny.'

Rose held up her hand. 'We should not speak of her. She is our sister-in-law after all.'

'And so full of family feeling that she denies you a home or even a penny of income.' Helena's voice shook with rage. 'I think she is ashamed of us both and likes to pretend we do not exist.'

'Well, thank goodness for dear Aunt Emily and Uncle Philip. They have been more like our real parents. They pay me a handsome amount for my drawings and they even provide most of my clothes.' Rose looked thoughtfully at Helena. 'And you have been with them for several more years than I have. You really are the daughter they never had.'

'Fortunately, we are all passionate about the same things. I could never submit to live in this cramped and restrictive society here.' Helena gestured in the direction of the city. 'Oh, I know you enjoy being in society – the dinners and the dances and the outings and new clothes—'

'I have not noticed you refusing to be interested in pretty new clothes,' retorted Rose, stung.

'Yes, well, of course I like nice clothes, but I like ancient languages and I enjoy the freedom of my chosen way of life. I could not bear to be dependent on having a good reputation, or never going out alone for fear of being gossiped about.'

At the mention of reputation, Rose bit her lip. How she had suffered from Augusta's narrow ideas on that subject. That brought her thoughts back to Tom. In spite of her resolve to keep her distance, Rose could not help wondering why he was looking so grim and worn. Was it something to do with his work and with Kerim Pasha?

They had come out into an open space and a rather feeble sun was shining. It lit the grass and the russet leaves on the trees. Rose slowed and looked at the view with pleasure.

'Are you planning another picture?'

Rose shook her head. 'Not now. I am waiting to learn what it is you want to discuss.'

Helena bit her lip. 'Can you not guess?'

Rose looked at her. 'I might have an idea. But you must tell me.'

Helena returned her look very steadily. Her eyes glowed. 'Max and I have agreed to marry. I hope you will not dislike it.'

Rose put her arms round her blushing younger sister. 'I like it very much. It has seemed more and more likely to me as I have observed you both recently. He is such a self-contained man, but I could see he has been seeking your company more and more. And getting jealous,' she added, remembering certain episodes over the previous weeks.

Helena hugged her back. 'I am so happy. It took me a while to realize how my feelings had changed. I used to be in awe of Max, he seemed such an independent man, so intrepid and focused on his adventures. After we arrived in Cairo, I began to feel differently about him. And he showed more interest in me.'

'I should hope so.' Rose pushed back a lock of her sister's hair that had fallen across her forehead. 'You are a beautiful girl,

140

especially when you are talking about ancient carvings and hieroglyphs. How could one dedicated explorer fail to be attracted to another?' She smiled, a little wistfully. 'You were meant for each other. It is just like Aunt Emily and Uncle Philip. You are right, Helena, you could never submit to the usual restricted life of a woman in society.'

'But you are going to come back to Egypt with us?' urged Helena, a note of anxiety in her voice.

Rose nodded. 'If it is a choice of Cairo or returning to live with Augusta, George and Papa, I have to say I prefer Cairo.'

'That takes such a weight off my mind.' Helena beamed. 'Of course, it would be wonderful if you should find someone you really wished to marry. Then you could stay in London and go to concerts to your heart's content. And I would accept that, although I should miss you dreadfully.'

Rose blinked rapidly. How Helena had softened in this last year. She looked up and smiled . . . and froze. Her attention had been caught by a man on a black horse. He was riding a large, raking animal and he had the best seat on horseback that she had ever seen. Man and horse moved as fluidly and elegantly as if they were one creature.

'Oh!' she said impulsively. 'How I wish I could paint that. But I could never catch that grace.'

Helena looked up. She shaded her eyes against the sun. 'I think. . . .' she said, 'no, I am certain, that it is our Count Varoshenyi. And yes, he is magnificent on a horse. Woe betide him if the Benson sisters see him now.'

The rider came closer, raised his hand in greeting and came up beside them. He raised his hat and smiled, his teeth white in his tanned face. His grey eyes gleamed.

'I am very happy to see you again,' said Kerim Pasha.

His deep, rich voice sounded very comforting, especially at this moment. Helena's news was not an unmixed joy for Rose. Her sister was inevitably going to be less close to her in future.

'We were just admiring your prowess on a horse,' said Helena.

His brows rose. He looked from one to the other. 'Do you ride?'

'Of course. If we had not learnt, we would have been completely cut off. Our home was a long way from the nearest village.' Helena laughed. 'But in Egypt, we had to make do with donkeys.'

He leaned forward. His eyes were on Rose. 'Would you care to ride with me now?'

She gasped. 'I – er – we do not have any riding horses in Town.'

'That is not what I asked.' His tone was suddenly that of the great lord. 'I can be at your uncle's home within an hour, with a suitable mount for you. Both of you,' he added, turning his head to acknowledge Helena.

'Not I, thank you,' she said, 'I am expecting a visitor shortly. But I am sure Rose would love to ride. It is a pleasure that does not often come her way.'

He wheeled his horse around. 'In one hour then.'

'Now what have you done?' said Rose, torn between embarrassment and the longing to ride. 'And my riding habit is old – it is the one I had when I married Hugh.'

Helena pulled her along the path back towards Piccadilly. 'We must hurry then and see what we can do to make it smart.'

CHAPTER TWENTY-TWO

Precisely one hour later Rose stood ready in the hall. She peeped in the pier glass at her reflection. The riding costume, fortunately, was of a severe cut and its dark grey twill showed no sign of wear. Her hat was a small pink bonnet with a turned back brim. Helena had dressed it up with a pink ostrich plume and a knot of ribbon. Rose worked her fingers into her leather gloves. She dropped her whip and bent to retrieve it. Her heart was beating uncomfortably fast. She was getting into deep waters.

Her sister was pushing her at Kerim Pasha! Perhaps because she herself was in love, she wanted Rose to be in love also. Rose frowned. Any kind of relationship with this man was impossible, but . . . it was also impossible to resist his charm. He made her forget how lonely her life was.

There was a knock at the door. Rose caught her breath. She almost turned and fled, but Hudson had appeared and seen her. He trod across the wide hall in his usual stately way and opened the door. Rose swallowed down a flurry of nerves. Hudson turned towards her. Slowly she walked forwards. Kerim Pasha's tall figure was outlined against the light.

'Delightful,' he said, taking her hand. He gestured to where a groom stood holding the two horses. 'I trust you will enjoy riding this fine lady.'

The grey was indeed a beautiful, spirited mare. Rose looked at Kerim Pasha, her deep blue eyes shining. He nodded, satisfaction evident in his face. 'Yes,' he said, 'I think she is worthy of you.'

They rode back into the park and for a while simply let their horses have their heads. The quiet surroundings and the easy stride of her mount made Rose laugh out loud with pleasure. This was a rare treat indeed! After a while, however, Kerim Pasha slowed his pace to a walk.

'I am enjoying this very much,' Rose smiled at him. 'You must have selected the very finest mount at the livery stables.'

He shook his head. 'Ah, if only we were on my country estate. There I have some truly magnificent horses. Do you hunt?'

'No,' she said, 'that was not possible.'

He smiled. 'It is one of my favourite pastimes – a swift horse, a fine hawk and the wide, rolling plains of Anatolia under a blue sky – but not as blue as your eyes, Rose.'

She did not know how to reply to this. After a slight pause, she asked, 'Are you making a long stay in Town, Count?'

He raised his brows.

'I ask,' she hurried on, 'because I would like to send a little gift for your sister when you do return home.'

'You are too kind,' he said. 'I will certainly call before I leave. I do not think it will be many more days now.'

'Oh!' She checked any other questions. His business was too delicate to be discussed. Here was yet another man whose life was spent in travelling. All the men in her life, except for her father and brother, were people whose work sent them far from their homes and lands. Even Hugh, her late husband, who had joined the navy at the age of sixteen, had spent more time away from home than on dry land during the last ten years of his life.

'Have you nothing to say?' Kerim Pasha asked, after watching her with a strange little smile on his handsome face. 'I did hope that you would feel sorry to lose my company.'

She brought her thoughts back to the present. 'Oh yes, I-I am very sorry. It has been delightful . . . b-but I know you have much work to deal with. And I always knew you could not stay here.' She stared ahead, between her horse's ears.

She heard him heave a sigh. They proceeded for some minutes in this heavy silence, then, 'Come, one last gallop,' he said.

She saw the flash of his white teeth, the gleam of his eyes and she kicked her horse to urge it alongside his.

They raced along the tracks, fortunately meeting nobody this time. However hard she tried, Kerim Pasha always kept his horse just ahead. At the end of the circuit, Rose was laughing, her hair blowing in little tendrils around her face and her cheeks flushed with the speed of their ride.

He gave her a long look. Finally, he raised his brows. 'That is how I shall remember you. You are a lady of great spirit. Oh yes,' he went on, as she shook her head and murmured a protest, 'I saw how you held your family together when you arrived in my city. What a pity that your role is so – so restricted in this society. You could have a much greater destiny.'

Rose held her breath. What was he implying? Then there was a shout and another pair of riders came close and rode past, looking at them curiously. Kerim Pasha was still watching her. 'You are very pensive all at once. Are you tired?'

Rose forced a little laugh. 'No, of course not. I could never be tired of riding this beautiful horse. I am most grateful to you.'

'Do not be!' His voice was harsh. 'It is a such a little thing to do and the pleasure is all mine. I do not often have such agreeable company.' His horse sensed the change of mood. Tossing his head, he broke into a canter. Rose urged her mount forward and they made one more circuit of the park in silence. As they approached the entrance gate again, Rose said, reluctantly, 'I think it is time for me to return home. I have to assist my aunt in her preparations for this evening's lecture.'

He grinned. 'She is a most determined woman. A lady of great spirit and culture in her chosen field.'

'But you prefer to work for the future,' Rose reminded him with a smile.

He threw up a hand. 'You are right. It is my destiny to do this work.' His eyes grew unfocused, as if he were seeing something

145

terrible. Then he shook his head and gave her a smile again. 'It is vital for my people. And I will never forget that you helped us.'

Did he . . . did the Sultan look at my sketches?' she asked shyly.

'Certainly. He studied them carefully.'

Rose wished she could have seen the moment. She knew that people generally liked her drawings, but they had never before been done for such an exalted personage. She felt a warm glow of achievement and gratitude towards this proud man beside her who had had faith in her ability. But she must also remember that it was thanks to Tom that she had been given the opportunity in the first place.

Her lips quirked in a smile, thinking of Tom. What would he say if he could see her now. She led the way out of the park and across Piccadilly. They turned into Half Moon Street in silence, both invigorated by the fresh air and exercise. Outside her uncle's house, Kerim Pasha dismounted with his usual fluid grace. He handed his reins to the waiting groom and came to Rose's side.

She felt the strength of his arms as he lifted her down smoothly and set her lightly on her feet. He did not release her immediately but stood looking at her with a fierce light in his eyes. She heard his sharp intake of breath. Then he took a step back and offered his arm, very correctly. She laid her fingers on it and felt the tension in him. As they crossed the pavement and he knocked on the door, she glanced at him from under her lashes. His face was impassive.

Hudson opened the door wide and Kerim Pasha was bowing over her hand. He waved aside her thanks. Rose lingered in the doorway to watch him mount and ride away, looking every inch as though he belonged in the saddle. She continued to admire the sight until Hudson cleared his throat loudly.

'The family is waiting for you in the study, ma'am,' he announced in a tone of gloom.

Rose opened her blue eyes wide. 'Problems, Hudson?'

He cast his eyes upwards. 'You could say that.' He trod over to the study door and opened it for her.

'—and if you do that I shall not marry you!' Helena's words came clearly as Rose, casting Hudson a startled glance, walked into the room.

Sir Philip was standing by the fire, his normally pleasant expression wiped away by a thunderous frown. Lady Westacote sat at her desk, pen in hand, looking utterly distracted. Max stood with his feet apart, hands on his hips. Helena whirled round and flung herself at Rose. She cast her arms round her sister's neck.

'I mean it!' she said and burst into angry sobs against Rose's shoulder.

Automatically, Rose stroked her sister's head, soothing her as she had done when they were children. The storm was soon over. Helena straightened up and dashed the tears away. The others had not moved.

Rose looked round in bewilderment. 'Whatever is wrong?'

Her uncle's mouth was a thin line and he merely shook his head. Aunt Emily shrugged as if to say that the matter was beyond her. Rose looked at Helena but she shook her head. The tears were still threatening.

The memory of her delightful morning faded. As so often, she would have to deal with the situation. She fixed a calm gaze on Max. 'Please can you enlighten me?'

He shrugged his shoulders irritably and thrust his hands into his pockets. 'I merely wished to do things properly. While Philip and Emily have been as parents to both of you, I feel it is proper to write to your father, informing him that Helena and I are getting married.'

'I won't have it,' burst out Helena, 'I could not bear them to make the kind of fuss they always do make. Augusta with her sour face and George calculating every penny of expense.' She choked. 'And after the way they treated Rose . . . refusing her an allowance when she was left widowed with no income of her own. They are not my family.' She flung her arms round her sister again and choked back another sob.

'Money is not an issue,' said Max, in clipped tones. 'But you are going to be my wife and eventually you will be a viscountess. I want everything to be done correctly for your sake.'

'You are being very noble, dear Max,' said Rose, 'but let the matter rest for now.' She glanced down at Helena's tumbled hair. 'Today should be a day of happiness for us all. I am so pleased that you have made up your minds at last.' She looked at her uncle and mouthed, 'Champagne?'

He stared for a moment, then a smile replaced his tight-lipped expression. He nodded and went to pull the bellrope.

'While you organize that, Helena and I will retire for a few moments to tidy ourselves up.'

She ruthlessly bundled Helena upstairs, and in a very short space of time had her changed into the new pink dress and her hair freshly pinned up. Rose then dragged her back downstairs again, even though her cheeks were still rather pink from the crying.

'This is all nerves,' whispered Rose, as they reached the study door. 'Poor Max deserves a rather better reaction to his proposal. If you are not careful, he will change his mind and offer for Clarissa Benson instead.'

They both giggled and so entered the room smiling, to find the others seated and looking more at ease now. Hudson followed them in and served the champagne.

'You have a glass as well, Hudson,' said Sir Philip. 'Demme, this is splendid. Our little Helena and my young friend, Max Kendal are making a match of it.' He turned towards his wife and raised his glass to her. This reminds me of old times, my dear.'

She gave him a misty smile. 'Oh, *Philip*!' She sipped her champagne and added, 'Now we must make our dinner party extra special.'

'Yes, but pray let us keep it small,' begged Helena, 'just for our close friends.'

CHAPTER TWENTY-THREE

The champagne lightened the atmosphere. The whole family was delighted at the news of the engagement. As they laughed and toasted each other, harmony was restored between the newly engaged young couple. Then lunch provided an opportunity for discussing wedding plans and the prospect of a speedy return to Egypt.

Rose was satisfied as she looked round at them all. It was wonderful to see them united by their common interests and their genuine affection for each other. She left them still making plans and slipped away to the room she shared with Helena. She rummaged in a drawer for her sketchbook and charcoal sticks. Then she cast herself down on the window seat and stared out at the racing clouds over the rooftops, conjuring up the image she wanted to draw.

She was smiling at the finished picture when Helena burst into the room.

'There you are,' she said, 'we are waiting for you. Honestly, Rose, of all the times to start a new picture! Just look at your hands.'

Rose shut the book hastily and put it away in her drawer. She had forgotten about going to Somerset House, where Lady Westacote was giving another talk. Quickly she washed her hands and made ready to go out. After all the events of the morning she felt really tired. But, beside her, Helena was dancing along, so happy that Rose was obliged to smile and listen to all her confidences and praise of Max.

At Somerset House, in the room allotted to Lady Westacote, Rose was impressed to see yet another large audience, mainly of ladies. Helena whispered to her that Lady Benson was there with both her daughters.

'Guard Max with your life!' Rose whispered back with a mischievous grin.

'I do not need to,' said Helena in a lofty tone. She took another look down the room. 'What puzzles me is the way they are looking at *you*.'

'They seem to be trying to freeze me.' Rose whispered, after a short interval of peeping at them discreetly. She shrugged. 'Perhaps we are still in disgrace after their dinner party.' She moved towards the door. 'This time, it is my turn to slip away,' she told Helena. 'I am going to view the pictures in the main gallery. I shall not be long.'

It was a rare opportunity to view the collection of pictures and Rose was determined to make the most of it. She wished that she could stay longer in London and study the techniques of the portrait painters in more detail. But today she would take a general look around so that on her next visit she could concentrate on the paintings that most interested her. She thought of how once upon a time, she would have asked Tom to accompany her. They would have enjoyed the visit together, sharing opinions and jokes.

Thinking of Tom was becoming a habit. She must break it, especially if he was to marry that silly girl . . . but Rose suddenly knew that she did not want Tom to marry anyone. She gulped and resolutely fixed her gaze on the next painting.

The main gallery was hung from floor to ceiling with a variety of work; portraits, groups, landscapes, animal paintings. Rose moved slowly round, noting several that she would return to examine more fully. There was a second room and she turned into that, wandering slowly from one picture to the next, admiring the fine compositions and the skilful brushwork that produced such delicate effects in the skin tones and fine clothes of the newer portraits.

Entranced by such a feast for her eyes, Rose wandered here and there around the room. Standing close to a group of ladies, she became aware that one of them was telling her companions that the light was beginning to fade. Rose gave a guilty start and wondered how long she had been here.

The ladies were leaving by the main door and now Rose was quite alone. She walked back through the main room and into the corridor leading to a side staircase. Lady Westacote was giving her talk in one of the rooms belonging to the Antiquarian Society, on the ground floor.

Rose stood at the top of the steps and looked back. The light was definitely too poor now for her to study any pictures. She gave a tiny shrug and set her hand on the banisters. Before she could move, however, she heard a man's voice below her.

'Are you certain this is the place?'

'Aye, the general is here.'

'Yes, never mind that but is *he* here yet?'

'Ain't seen him yet.'

Rose held her breath. There was a grunt. Then she heard the chink of coins. The first voice spoke again. This time she noticed the trace of French accent.

'When you see him 'ere you must be quick, you understand. No mess. And afterwards you get the rest of the money.'

Rose clutched her throat. She was rigid with horror. Then she heard heavy steps starting up the stairs. She backed away, then turned and tiptoed along the corridor. She reached the door of the now deserted salon, where the dim figures in the paintings stared down at her. She picked up her skirts and fled across the wide room and into the second, smaller chamber. She was panting hard now with the fear of pursuit. She dived for the door at the far end and let out a screech as she bumped into a tall, very hard body.

Tom watched his two helpers return from checking the top floor of Somerset House.

'All clear, sir,' whispered one.

'This side as well. Ain't nobody up here,' nodded the other.

Tom raised his brows and let out a sigh of relief. 'Let's keep it that way,' he said in a low voice. 'Jessup, you keep watch up here on this landing. Timms, we'll take the next floor.' He led the way down the elegant staircase and watched as Timms set off along the west wing.

Tom began to inspect each room of the east wing. It did not help that some rooms were still unfinished. There were piles of sand, plaster and tools, with heaps of rags, buckets and trestle tables. Easy places for a determined man to hide, thought Tom grimly. But search as he might, he could find no trace of anyone.

Today's meeting between Kerim Pasha and General Lord Talbot was to agree which officers and what equipment would be sent out to Constantinople with the Pasha on his return journey. And until the day that boat set sail with its precious cargo, Tom knew that his careful plan would not be fulfilled. The Foreign Office had given him the task of keeping Kerim Pasha safe while he was on English soil. For Tom it was a matter of pride to succeed in that.

However, thanks to Kerim Pasha's desire to sample the English way of life, it was proving to be a nerve-racking job. Completely impervious to all risks, he slipped off to see the life of the city. Tom's agents had complained bitterly of the risks he took but there seemed no way to stop him. And Tom admired the man's zest for life. But when he discovered the Pasha had been out riding with Rose in the Park, he had to control an impulse to throttle the man himself.

No matter how difficult his duties, Tom was constantly preoccupied with thoughts of Rose. He understood why she felt so bitter towards himself. That arranged marriage had been distasteful to her and she still blamed him for abandoning her. Someone must have intercepted all those letters he had sent her. And yet, thought Tom, as he cautiously opened another door and slid through into a wide room, he could sense that from time to time she warmed to him. He was certain she still understood how his mind worked, just as when they had been so young and so much in love. But each time she quickly shut it off, turned away, smiled at other men, especially at Kerim Pasha, damn him!

At that moment he stiffened and listened intently. He could hear footsteps racing towards him. He stood firmly in the doorway to block whoever it was. The next moment a female figure flitted into view, looking over her shoulder as she ran. She crashed smack against him and gave an ear-splitting shriek.

'Steady!' he said, and grasped her by the upper arms. She was gasping with fright and clutched at his driving coat. 'Are you all right, ma'am?' he said as he felt her trying to pull away. 'There is no need to be in such a taking; assure you.' He held her slightly back from him. Then he frowned and jerked his head forwards. 'Rose?' His voice was incredulous. She looked up into his face, gave a gasp of relief and melted against his broad chest. He tightened his hold. This was heaven! But her bonnet was blocking his view of her.

'What the deuce are you doing up here on your own?' he rumbled, 'It is growing dark. No wonder you were frightened.'

Rose had got her breath back now. She pushed away from him, but kept one hand firmly on his arm. 'Oh, Tom. Thank heavens you are here. There are two men at the bottom of the stairs. I heard them talking. Then one of them started coming up the stairs.'

'Why should that frighten you so much?'

She let go of his arm and put up her hands to straighten her bonnet. 'You do not understand! They were saying' – she broke off and glanced around. She gestured to Tom to bend his head down and she whispered in his ear, 'I heard a French accent. The French man asked the other to watch out for someone and . . . and kill him.'

'What?' With an effort Tom kept his voice quiet. 'You must have misunderstood.'

'Oh no, no, I definitely heard him say: "No mess" and I heard the chink of coins. . . .' She looked at him anxiously. 'Oh, Tom, I immediately thought of-of Count Varoshenyi. I know his b-business is most important.'

So all this was concern for Kerim Pasha. Tom drew himself up and offered his arm with a frigid bow. 'Allow me to escort you back to your friends, ma'am.'

'Yes, but won't you warn him?' Rose wrung her hands. 'Why should this make you so angry?'

'What were you doing up here all alone?' he snapped.

She gestured vaguely towards the walls. 'The pictures. . . .'

'Ah!' Through the freezing anger he dimly remembered that she was an artist. 'Come.' He drew her hand through his arm.

His search was ruined. In any case, he now knew that the spies were here and what they intended. He strode along towards the main staircase so that by his side Rose was forced to trot in order to keep pace. Thank heavens, Timms was nowhere in sight. He hastened on, Rose stiff and tight-lipped now. They descended the staircase into the main entrance hall.

'Thank you,' said Rose coldly. 'I recognize this part of the building. My aunt is giving a talk in a room around that corner.'

'I will do myself the honour of restoring you to her,' said Tom through gritted teeth. He looked down his impressive nose at her. They moved on. There was the sound of a door opening just before they turned the corner. Voices sounded and people began to come out. The talk was over.

Rose still had her hand through Tom's arm when they came face to face with Lady Benson. Clarissa and Clorinda were one step behind their mother, gossiping and giggling. All three stopped dead when they saw Rose.

'Well!' exclaimed Lady Benson. She swept an icy glare from Tom to Rose and back again. 'Come, girls.'

They swept past as if Rose did not exist. Clorinda muttered something in which the word 'Julia' was quite clear.

Tom raised his brows. 'What was all that about?'

'Pray do not regard them. They have taken a dislike to me, I fear.'

He gave a snort. 'I should say that was a piece of luck.' There was something of the old warmth back in his dark eyes. 'Well, you are safe now.'

She withdrew her arm reluctantly. 'Yes. Thank you. But what about those men?'

Tom's face became distant. 'Pray do not think of it any more.' He bowed sharply and walked off.

CHAPTER TWENTY-FOUR

Tom stalked round the corner and took up a brooding pose, leaning against a pillar with his arms folded. He watched the people leaving Lady Westacote's lecture. They drifted across the hallway and out to their carriages. At length a smile flitted across Tom's lean face. When she was frightened up in the gallery, Rose had called him Tom and clung to him in a very pleasing way. She had been very glad to keep hold of his arm all the way downstairs as well.

Perhaps he still had a chance to win back her affections. His face brightened. At this point he remembered what he was supposed to be doing and he strode through the hall to meet Sebastian coming from the other wing of the building.

'No sign of anyone on this side,' said the younger man, 'but it is impossible to check every room on every floor.'

'They are here anyway,' said Tom. 'We just have to be vigilant. I have men posted.' He noticed Sebastian staring at his cravat and put up a hand to discover that it was partly untied. He quickly reknotted it and smoothed back a lock of hair that had fallen over his forehead. It was true that Rose had bumped into him quite hard and then she had grabbed hold of him. Perhaps his dishevelled appearance was the reason why Lady Benson had stared at him so coldly. She had jumped to conclusions. Tom only wished that what she suspected had really happened.

With an effort he brought his attention back to Sebastian. 'Is everything ready for afterwards?'

Sebastian nodded. 'The decoy carriage at the front and a double to get into it.'

There was the sound of conversation and footsteps coming along from the opposite end of the hall. Lady Westacote's voice was clearly audible, commenting on the talk she had just given. Tom pulled Sebastian back into the nearest doorway. He did not want Rose to see him again and start asking awkward questions. He had too much to deal with at present.

Thanks to Rose, he now knew that the French were closely involved in the plot to have Kerim Pasha murdered. If that happened, it would create a major international scandal. The Ottoman Empire would be insulted and immediately cut all links with Britain. Of course, the French wanted to regain their influence in the eastern Mediterranean.

In fact they were so determined that they had joined forces with the infamous Gripper Browne. Tom's agents had discovered that much, although scarcely anyone would mention Browne's name. His thugs were ruthless and exacted total silence from anyone involved with them. It was quite likely that he even had people placed in the government offices. But Tom was absolutely resolved to see his mission through to a successful conclusion.

He checked discreetly. The main hall was empty again. Signalling to Sebastian to follow, Tom led the way past the room just vacated by the antiquarian group. He opened the next door, which revealed an anteroom, well lit. A large man stood by the inner door. He nodded at Tom.

'All in order, sir.'

'Good. Wait outside now, Timms.'

The man's eyes darted from Tom to Sebastian and then towards the inner room. Timms raised his eyebrows meaningfully and moved heavily to the outer doorway.

Tom walked into the larger room. He bowed with great formality towards the dark-clad gentleman seated at the table. The gentleman made no sign he had noticed Tom's arrival. He merely flicked open his snuffbox. Very deliberately he raised a tiny pinch of snuff to his nose. As he inhaled, his hooded eyes lifted to survey Tom. His narrow face was deeply lined and impossible to read.

The silence stretched out. Tom watched as General Lord Talbot dusted his fingers on a lace edged handkerchief and put the snuffbox away in an inside pocket. Sebastian shifted from one foot to another. My lord's gaze transferred to him and inspected his arm, still in a sling.

At last the door opened. Kerim Pasha appeared, immaculate in his superbly tailored clothes. My lord's eyes widened. Lithe as a panther, Kerim Pasha walked up to the table and bowed. He took a seat opposite the general.

'It is a great pleasure to meet you, sir,' he said courteously, 'as one general to another, I trust we can cut straight to the heart of the matter.'

General Talbot's expression changed slightly. Tom thought he registered surprise.

'I was told you were a Turk, sir.' His voice was rusty and cold.

Kerim Pasha looked down his nose. 'Indeed, I am. What proof do you require?'

The general raised his hand in a slight negative gesture. 'I confess, sir, that I am surprised. But let us proceed. I have heard of your business from Witherson here.'

The spider-like adviser to the Foreign Secretary rose from his seat in the corner and advanced to the table.

'Gentlemen,' he said, surveying them both over his spectacles, 'you are authorized to make a mutually satisfactory agreement concerning the number and rank of officers for this mission. And for the necessary supplies,' he added, consulting a paper in his hand. He walked away from them, stopped to glare at Tom and slowly resumed his way to his own chair.

There was a short silence. When the general made no attempt to speak, Kerim Pasha placed his hands on the table and began. He listed the number of officers he required to train his elite staff in the handling of new weapons. He wanted supplies of guns and ammunition. Rifles, he said, not muskets. He needed gunsmiths and engineers to teach the latest theories on siege breaking and on handling the new cannon being made already at the French-built gun foundry in Constantinople.

At the mention of the French, General Talbot stirred. 'They have been your allies?' he grated.

Kerim Pasha inclined his head. 'Twenty years ago,' he replied. 'And, believe me, sir, they are trying very hard now to regain that position. You will appreciate that I am in great haste to conclude this deal and avoid my country becoming the ally of Napoleon's France.'

'Hah! Bad business, very bad,' nodded General Talbot. He had almost thawed, thought Tom, watching the statuelike figure. How unfortunate that he was the senior general and only he could authorize this type of task. He was such an inflexible man and had not seen active service for a number of years. But it seemed that Kerim Pasha was getting a positive response now.

It did not take much more discussion before the general summoned Witherson to make a note of the meeting.

'And I require everything to be ready within the week.' Kerim Pasha looked down his nose at the two men.

Witherson bent his icy gaze on Tom. 'You must deal with that, Mr Hawkesleigh.'

'Yes sir,' said Tom, wondering how he was to find a full cargo of guns and ammunition in such a short space of time, never mind choosing officers and getting them on board a ship bound for Constantinople.

'The officers will travel with me,' said Kerim Pasha.

'That is very short notice, sir,' said Witherson.

'Less time for anyone to talk,' smiled the Pasha, at his most regal. 'Secrecy is needed, both here and in Turkey. I will sail to one of our southern ports so these experts can reach my estates without anyone in Constantinople knowing they have arrived in the country.'

At last the agreement was made. The general and Witherson departed. Kerim Pasha rose and glanced round at Tom. 'Thank you, my esteemed helper,' he said with a smile. 'Now what do you plan to do with me?'

Tom gestured towards Sebastian. 'We have arranged a new house for you, Your Excellency.'

'And you plan to escort me there and guard me?' When Tom nodded, he laughed. 'But how dull. My stay in your country is almost at an end. I would see something of your entertainments while I have the chance.'

'Well, I do believe a group of villains are trying to murder you, sir.' He grinned when Kerim Pasha shrugged as if to say that was nothing new.

'First we must get out of this building without anyone knowing which way we went. And then we will decide on an entertainment for this evening.'

Some hours later, the three men were sitting in a private gaming hell, the only three people there, thought Tom sourly, who were still entirely sober and not focused on the gaming. He and Seb were playing a desultory game of piquet while Kerim Pasha strolled about, watching the play at different tables with keen interest.

From time to time he came back to Tom with another question.

'Why is it that some men play on even when all their money is gone? They are writing notes to cover their debts.'

'We call those "vowels",' put in Sebastian.

'I have been invited to join in at some tables,' said Kerim Pasha, resuming his seat at their small table. 'What happens when they have spent more than they possess?' he asked.

'Then they are ruined.' Tom said shortly.

Kerim Pasha shook his head slightly. 'In every land there are quick ways to ruin.' His dark eyes suddenly pierced Tom. 'Do you play these games of chance.'

Tom gave a short laugh and gestured at the cards on the table.

'As you see, I have little skill. I learned to play just to entertain my grandmother. The cards have no fascination for me.'

Kerim Pasha looked satisfied. He gave both. of them a gleaming smile. 'Tomorrow, gentlemen, we will go to Tattersalls. I wish to see your finest horses.' He shot Tom a keen glance. 'Our villains do not appear to like cards, but maybe they are interested in horseflesh.'

CHAPTER TWENTY-FIVE

Something was not right. Tom leaned his head against the high back of the chair in the study and frowned in concentration. They had taken the Pasha to Tattersalls at Hyde Park Corner and returned without mishap. As well as Tom's own agents, they had been accompanied by Kerim Pasha's personal bodyguard, Ferdi. He was a silent and rather sinister individual, dressed in a frogged green jacket and breeches in the Hungarian style.

They came back to a narrow house in Bolton Street, the third change of dwelling for Kerim Pasha. Tom had assembled a good team of watchmen, mainly former soldiers and comrades from his army days. Old Hanley, acting as the butler, was more at home on the battlefield than receiving polite guests. Only, there were no guests. Hanley's job was to keep strangers out. He could smell an enemy at fifty paces and he would not hesitate to use force if he suspected a caller was a threat to 'Count Varoshenyi'.

When they arrived, Hanley gave a nod to say that all was well. Tom left the others to go inside, while he checked the street one more time. There were plenty of people passing through so it took him some time to be satisfied that they were all going about their own business.

As he returned he saw a man in rough clothes, with a bonnet pulled down over his ears, looking up at the first floor of the house. When he saw Tom, the man turned his head away sharply and set off down the street, disappearing into the nearest crowd of people. It was not the fact that they already had a spy following them that worried Tom, but the fact he was sure he knew that man.

He was still trying to recall who it could be when the door opened and Sebastian came in. He looked at Tom and raised his brows. 'Opera,' he said.

Tom raised his brows. 'He is not going to enjoy that, surely.'

Sebastian threw himself down in the chair opposite Tom's. 'Says he wants to see the English version of dancing girls.'

Tom shook his head gloomily. 'We must hope he just wants to look at them. What a nightmare if he takes a fancy to one of them. . . .' He grinned briefly at the expression on Sebastian's face as he digested this remark.

'Oh, *Lord*!' said the younger man, aghast.

Tom nodded. 'Just so.' Reluctantly he unfolded himself from his chair, stretched, then shrugged his jacket back on. 'I must talk with Timms about security for this expedition.'

Tom found Timms in the kitchen with his feet up on a chair. There was a large flagon of homebrewed on the table beside him and a saucy kitchen maid had brought her bowl of potatoes close by so she could talk to him while she peeled them. When she saw Tom's scowl, she bobbed a curtsy, picked up her bowl and fled.

'Now don't go agetting agitated, guv'nor,' said Timms in his rich drawl. 'We all be in need of a rest. Bless me if ever I met such a restless gent as the count there. So cool he was, yesterday, every inch the fine lord . . . an' then, well, I ask you, guv'nor, what came over him?' He shook his head solemnly and took a long pull of his beer. 'An' here's us, all atrying to keep him safe. Fair worn out I am.'

'Just save your strength for this evening,' growled Tom. 'We have to organize security for a visit to the opera.'

Timms groaned and looked longingly towards the range, from where came the savoury smell of roasting meat, mingled with the scent of fresh baked bread. 'I hope we'll have time for our dinner first. Need our strength, we do.'

'Have you got anyone outside?' asked Tom.

' 'Course I have,' said Timms indignantly. 'We're safe enough in here. But all this running around the town, that's when we must look out for trouble.' He straightened up. 'Never fear, guv'nor, the boys 'n me, we won't let you down.'

Tom nodded. He felt the tension in his shoulders ease slightly. 'Thank you, Timms. We just have to make sure nobody can get a clear shot at him.'

'Nobody's going to shoot a gun at the opera, so you just rest easy, guv'nor. An' when we're in the street, we'll take care of things.' Timms picked up his flagon again, then caught Tom looking at it. 'You want one o' these?'

Tom decided he could spare five minutes.

Count Varoshenyi drew all eyes that evening. Seated in a first-floor box at the theatre, he appeared unaware of the glances constantly cast his way. His dark blue jacket and cream brocade waistcoat set off his starkly handsome features. A diamond pin winked among the folds of his snowy cravat. His hair shone blue-black in the candlelight. He sat still and calm but Tom could see that he was examining every detail of the theatre and the audience as well as the performers on the stage.

Tom, smartly dressed himself in a close-fitting jacket of his favourite claret colour and with linen to rival Kerim Pasha's for dazzling whiteness, sat on one side of him and Sebastian on the other. Timms was stationed outside the box. Even so, Tom felt uneasy.

It was all very well to try and tempt the spies to show themselves. That was what Kerim Pasha wanted, but Tom's chief concern was to make sure the Pasha stayed alive. That was going to be the tricky part of the evening. In such a public place, it would not take long for word to spread. It would be easy for Gripper Browne's villains to ambush them as they left after the performance. And who was that individual who had been looking up at the house? Again, something stirred in Tom's memory but he had to give it up.

He made an effort to follow the plot, in case Kerim Pasha wanted to discuss it later. The man lost no opportunity to study the customs and interests of English society. No doubt it was all useful material for when he was planning future policy back home. Tom was willing enough to humour his charge – except where Rose was concerned.

Of course Sir Philip was full of gratitude to the man who had taken in his wife and nieces, so he had offered an open invitation to Kerim Pasha to visit the house. Tom glowered. Rose had gone riding with him. It was clear that Kerim Pasha wanted her. Tom felt the usual blaze of anger and forced himself to uncurl his fists. When the lights went up for the interval, Kerim Pasha stood up. Tom and Sebastian rose also.

'I believe it is the custom to visit friends during this pause,' smiled Kerim Pasha. 'I can see Lady Westacote and her family over there.' He gestured at a box on the other side of the theatre. 'I wish to do everything properly.' He gave Tom a shrewd glance. 'We will all go together.'

Tom was sure that the corridor outside the boxes had never been so crowded. He and Seb managed to keep either side of Kerim Pasha as they made their way through the throng of staring, gossiping people. It was with profound relief that he followed his charge into the Westacotes' box. But his relief was short lived. He stifled a groan even as he admired Lady Benson's strategy!

She had guessed where the count would go. She was already in the box, talking to Lady Westacote. She glanced up triumphantly when she saw Count Varoshenyi at last where she could be introduced to him. A stealthy glance round showed Tom that she had brought those two bouncing girls with her. Horror of horrors, one of them had her eye on him! Tom felt an urge to back out of the box and leave everyone to sort themselves out. But then he looked again and saw Rose looking at him. When she met his eye, she smiled. Tom brightened. He edged forward towards her.

165

He was struck, as always, by her sweet expression. Those deep-blue eyes were smiling at him in just the way he remembered from that long ago time when they had been the best of friends and trusted each other with all their secrets. The noise, the other people filling the cramped box, everything faded away and Tom saw only Rose, smiling at him and lifting her face towards his with that little tilt he loved to see.

He smiled at her, unaware of how tender his expression had become.

'You have not had any problems, then?' she whispered.

'Problems. . . ?' he stammered. He was drowning in those blue eyes and could not remember ever having any problems.

'You know – in the gallery. And I see he is still safe.' She nodded towards Kerim Pasha.

'Oh . . . er . . . no problems,' gulped Tom, coming back to earth. 'What about you? Have you recovered from the scare?'

'Thank you for helping me.'

Tom grinned at her. 'That was a pleasure.'

Her eyes opened even wider. She hastily unfurled her fan and wafted it in front of her heated cheeks. She looked away. Tom wanted to keep her talking, but a tall figure appeared by their side. Kerim Pasha was greeting her.

Rose smiled at him. 'Are you enjoying the performance, Count Varoshenyi?'

He gave a low laugh. 'I am not sure that enjoy is the correct word. I find it very interesting. So different from our own music, of course.'

Lady Benson pushed in between Tom and Kerim Pasha. Her elbow dug into Tom's side and he glared indignantly, but she was intent on her prey and ignored him, merely edging her bulk forward into the small gap.

'Are you fond of music, dear Count?' She gave him no chance to reply. 'You positively *must* come to my musicale on Thursday evening. My husband will be so pleased to make your acquaintance – and my daughters perform so well on the

166

pianoforte and the harp.' She beamed at him, darted a cold glare at Rose and Tom and reluctantly moved back.

Kerim Pasha's gaze went from Rose to Tom. 'What kind of event is a musicale? From your faces, I guess it is not very interesting.'

'That would depend,' said Rose carefully, 'on who is performing.'

He nodded, eyes dancing. 'I understand you.' He turned his head to survey Lady Benson and her daughters, then shot a quick glance at Tom. His eyes gleamed with mirth and he nodded again. Tom's lips quivered but he kept a straight face. The next moment he lost all desire to laugh as he heard the Pasha say to Rose, 'It is an age since I saw you.'

She laughed and protested, 'Two days cannot be called an age.'

Tom felt a searing flash of anger. Just how friendly were they? He did his best to keep his expression neutral. 'It is time to return to our seats, sir.' His voice was deeper than usual with suppressed anger. He squared his shoulders and led the way back, just remembering to watch out for possible villains.

When the lights were dimmed, Tom sat, frowning and fuming inwardly. No less a personage than the Foreign Secretary had ordered him to keep a close guard on Kerim Pasha. But at present, Tom was struggling to repress a strong urge to smash his left fist into the man's jaw. He sat with hands clenched at the irony of his current situation. He must protect his rival. That meant he was obliged to watch the same rival trying to woo Rose.

Lately she seemed more friendly towards him, but now she was showing a warm attachment to this man he was sworn to defend, but who he would happily toss out of the box. Tom made himself recall how Rose had smiled at him. He did not think she had been quite so welcoming to Kerim Pasha – had she?

Tom's gaze slid sideways. Kerim Pasha was still sitting upright, intently studying the action onstage. Good! He was not looking at Rose. Then Tom saw him raise his chin a little and lean slightly forward. The chorus girls had come on stage. Tom could see

Sebastian's head turn towards Kerim Pasha as well.

There was some clapping and whistling from the spectators, especially those in the parterre. The girls danced and sang and when they reached the end of their song the applause was tumultuous. One or two of the girls blew kisses at certain gentlemen in the boxes close to the stage.

Kerim Pasha turned to Tom. 'This is so strange to me. I did not find their dancing enticing. And yet' – he glanced down at the frenzied audience – 'they have caused so much excitement.'

Eventually above the din came shouts of 'Encore' until the music started again and the girls performed another verse of their song and danced even more enthusiastically than before. The whistling and shouting continued. Yet the three of them heard the thud at the back of their box. Timms was sprawling on the floor in the open doorway. Two black-clad figures darted inside. One stood over Timms, the other advanced towards Kerim Pasha.

'No noise,' he grated out. 'Just come quietly.' He gestured with the knife in his hand.

The girls were still singing and the audience was intent on them, cheering and clapping. Kerim Pasha stood up and took a step towards the intruder. Sebastian held his breath. Tom jumped up with his fists clenched. The man snarled and glanced at Tom. In that instant Kerim Pasha sprang, grabbing the intruder's right arm with one hand and his throat with the other.

Tom reached them in one stride and gripped the man's upper arms to hamper him. He jabbed his knee into the man's legs, forcing him down. The second intruder now lunged at Kerim Pasha. The next moment he shrank back. The Pasha now held the knife and there was murder in his face.

For a second the villain wavered, arms hanging, his eyes swivelling from the knife to his mate, held down by Tom's iron grasp. Sebastian took a step towards him and the man turned to flee. He checked again when he saw that Timms was back on his feet. The angry Timms drove his fist hard into the thug's stomach. When he doubled up Timms kicked his legs out from under him and sat on him.

Kerim Pasha turned his furious gaze back to the first villain. He drew the knife across the skin of the man's throat. 'Shall I kill him now?'

'You cannot do that here.' It was Sebastian who spoke. 'I will go for help to have them arrested.'

'Young fool!' Kerim Pasha spat the words out. 'Do you think you will get as far as the street?' He flashed a glance at Tom. 'I kill this one, yes?'

'No! He is more use to us alive.'

The noise in the auditorium was subsiding. Tom used the man's neckcloth to tie his hands then helped Timms to do the same with the other brute.

'How are we going to get away?' whispered Sebastian.

'We must wait.' Tom pulled out his handkerchief and mopped the blood from his cut hand. He looked at Kerim Pasha, whose hands were also bleeding.

The Turk shrugged. 'A small price to pay,' he murmured, 'but when a man wounds me, I always kill him.' His eyes burned.

CHAPTER TWENTY-SIX

The final bow had been taken and the curtains closed for the last time. Rose still leaned forward, her arm resting on the rail as she gradually came back to reality after the stirring last scenes of the drama. She had enjoyed the fine singing and the lively dance of the chorus girls. What a pleasure to spend an evening in this way. It was so agreeable to be dressed in her new evening gown and with her hair swept up in a sophisticated style ornamented with a jewelled clip and a silk flower.

A smile touched her lips as she heard behind her the less than melodious sound of Uncle Philip snoring. He always claimed that music was just a lullaby. Aunt Emily was tut-tutting and trying to rouse him discreetly. Helena sat beside Rose, who was talking in a low voice to Max. These days, Helena and Max never seemed to have enough time to discuss everything. They were so happy in each other's company.

Rose felt very glad for them but their closeness meant she was going to be lonely again. Now there were two pairs of antiquarians in the family and she was isolated. True, she was necessary to them all because of her drawing skills. But she did not share their passion for the objects they dug out of the sand. She was not looking forward to leaving this town life behind to return to the heat and dust of Cairo, where the others would search happily for ancient remains and spend whole days seeking clues to the lost language of Egypt.

And so she sat on, watching the people in the theatre and wishing her life could be like theirs. She smiled at the kaleidoscope of colours and the sparkle of jewels as the other spectators gradually stood and moved around in preparation for leaving. She watched the gentlemen holding the elegant and expensive opera cloaks for their female companions. Rose had always loved listening to her mother's tales about when she and Aunt Emily had been girls enjoying a London season with its entertainments and splendid fashions. It had always been her dream to live that life also.

A shadow crossed her face. When they returned to Cairo, there would be no events of this kind. She liked going to the play or to picture galleries. And she liked being part of polite society. It had been another source of pleasure to receive visitors during the interval. True, Lady Benson had been cold and hostile again, but Rose was not going to let that spoil her evening.

Their other visitors had been most welcome, especially Tom. Rose wondered why she felt so very pleased to see him. Perhaps it was because the sight of his tall, strong figure made her feel safe, especially after the fright she had experienced the day before. And this evening he looked very smart and handsome, and then he had smiled at her just as he used to do when—

Rose pulled herself up. It was not wise to think of that. But instinctively she turned her gaze towards the box where he and his companions had been sitting. To her surprise, they were all still there. In fact, Tom was watching her intently. Rose looked again, more closely. Tom stood up. He was definitely trying to attract her attention. Now he was signalling to her to come, then holding up his hands as if pleading. And he had a white cloth wrapped round one hand.

'Helena,' Rose pulled her sister closer. 'Look over there. I do not know why but they want us to help.'

'It does seem so.' Helena turned to Max.

He was checking discreetly that Sir Philip had woken up. Max gave Rose a wink. 'I think we are ready to leave now.'

'Yes, but pray can you tell what Mr Hawkesleigh wants?' Helena indicated the box opposite.

After one glance, Max jumped to his feet. 'I will go ahead.'

When the rest of the party reached the box, there was no sign of Max, the door was firmly closed and Sebastian was standing in front of it. He greeted them with studied politeness and engaged Sir Philip and Lady Westacote in conversation. Somehow they were all walking down the stairs together. Rose was surprised but she supposed that the others had already gone on.

A moment after they reached the vestibule, Sebastian disappeared. Rose suddenly knew that something bad had happened. She thought of the conversation she had overheard at Somerset House. She put a hand to her mouth to stifle her gasp of fear. *You fool! Tom's hand was bandaged.* She whirled round, scarcely conscious of what she was doing. She must help him. She flew up the stairs, but at the top she collided with Tom. He gripped her arm, none too gently.

'I was afraid you would do that,' he rumbled, obliging her to turn round and walk down the steps again. 'Just act normally. We need you to stay with us for the moment.'

'You are hurt?' she whispered.

'It is nothing. We are all fine but we must get away before—' He broke off.

Rose shook her arm free. 'You were asking for help. I saw you.'

He nodded. 'And you sent it. Mr Kendal is assisting us.'

She gave a huff of exasperation. 'I do not understand this. But I must clean your hand. How it bleeds. It needs stitching.'

Tom muttered something and pulled the sodden cloth tighter. Rose fumbled in her cloak pocket. 'Here.' She handed him her own handkerchief. She then noticed Kerim Pasha walking behind them. His face was harsh, his gaze cold and keen, darting from left to right as if watching for a would-be attacker. Then she saw that he also had a bloodstained cloth wrapped round his right hand. It was partly concealed by the folds of his greatcoat but there were smears of blood on the skirts of the buff coloured fabric.

172

Rose swallowed hard. She wanted to know what other injuries they had sustained. But they had reached her waiting uncle and aunt.

'Come, my dear,' said Sir Philip, still sleepy. 'Our carriage is waiting.' He nodded at Tom. 'We shall see you gentlemen at dinner tomorrow.'

'Is Mr Kendal not with you?' asked Helena.

'He is kindly helping us with some business.' said Tom grandly.

Helena shrugged. 'Very well.' She followed her uncle and aunt towards the door.

Rose still hesitated. She looked from Kerim Pasha to Tom. Then Sebastian appeared. Following him were several tough-looking men. Rose could sense Tom's relief at the sight of them. By now, she was imagining all kinds of dreadful events. Still, they were all here and Max had only joined them five minutes ago, so he must be all right. But she wanted an explanation. She raised her eyes to Tom's face.

He gave her a half smile. 'Thank you. Please go! We shall be fine now.'

Kerim Pasha did not speak. He seemed hardly to see her. After an instant's wavering, she nodded and followed Lady Westacote outside.

CHAPTER TWENTY-SEVEN

Tom winced as old Hanley stitched the torn flesh together. 'Are you sure that is a proper needle you are using?' he growled between clenched teeth. 'It feels like a fork.'

'All done,' Hanley surveyed his work with pride. 'That'll heal all proper, that will, Cap'n. But as for your clothes—' He broke off and shook his head. 'In a proper mess, ain't they?'

'It was a price worth paying,' put in Kerim Pasha. 'We can always get new clothes. Now we have drawn the villains out into the open, I think they will keep coming. They are desperate to spoil my mission.' His eyes gleamed and he threw back his head and laughed.

Hanley rolled his eyes and muttered, 'Well, I never! His hands is all cut to ribbons an' he can laugh like a boy.'

Kerim Pasha held up his stitched and bandaged hand. 'I am an old soldier, like you, Hanley. In times of war, such minor injuries are less than nothing, as you know.'

Tom sat up straight. He wished he had not made that remark about the fork but borne the pain in silence. He looked at the suddenly smiling Pasha.

'So what do we do now, sir?'

'We keep offering them a chance to get close. Then we can pick them off one at a time, or we send them for interrogation.' His eyes narrowed. 'There are some of them I would want to take back with me. . . .'

'The French ones?' asked Tom, wondering what the Pasha intended.

'If we can find them, yes.' Kerim Pasha's teeth showed.

Tom felt just a little sorry for any French spy on that ship. Then he remembered how the thugs had beaten poor Seb and he shrugged.

'By morning we should have some news of the two we caught this evening,' went on the Pasha. 'I wish I had my own men here to interrogate them.'

'Oh, our fellows will do a good job, never fear.' Tom exchanged a glance with Hanley. The former soldier was from a unit that now specialized in undercover work. Hanley winked and nodded agreement.

They left the kitchen and Kerim Pasha indicated the library. 'There is another matter I wish to discuss with you before we retire.'

Once settled in chairs either side of the fire, he gave a sigh. Tom waited. Kerim Pasha stared into the flames for a long time. The silence stretched out. Tom began to wonder if he had offended in some way. He racked his brains. It had been a long day and he was sure the next day was going to be just as hard. A few hours' sleep would be welcome. Then he noticed that Kerim Pasha was considering him earnestly.

'I wish to talk about Rose,' he announced.

Tom frowned forbiddingly and shook his head. His thoughts on this subject were absolutely private. But Kerim Pasha was not deterred.

'It is clear to me that you and Rose are attached to each other,' he continued.

'*Were* attached,' croaked Tom, 'a long time ago.' He scowled and looked away. What business was it of this man's?

A soft chuckle made him look up. 'I am not blind, Tom. And I sense your anger when I get a smile from her.' He raised his eyebrows. 'Yes, I am very attracted to her, but I see that she likes her life here and I also see how she looks at you.' He held up a hand. 'Do not frown at me for desiring her. She is beautiful in her character as well as her face. And she has such spirit. A man could search all his life and never find such a woman.' He paused and rubbed his chin, smiling absently into the flames.

Tom watched him, torn between anger at such an open avowal of desire and wonder at why the man wanted to discuss the matter. He bit back the angry retort that rose to his lips. Yet it was ridiculous to fight over her when he was the one who had caused all her misfortunes. But she should have been his.

The anger surged again as he recalled how she smiled at Kerim Pasha. It was plain that she enjoyed the man's company. Yet she was not willing to give up her freedom even for all that he could offer. Poor Tom was not sure that made matters any less difficult to bear. He stole a look at his rival and was astounded to see that Kerim Pasha was watching him with a sympathetic smile on his face.

'It is not a matter for discussion!' snapped Tom, glaring at something clenched in his good hand.

'Oh, but I think it is,' responded his tormentor. 'You look as if you wish to fight a duel with me. Believe me, that is not necessary. In a few days I shall be just a memory for both of you.' He placed a hand on his heart as he added, 'For Rose I am just an exotic man who appreciated her courageous spirit. Surely you will allow me that much?'

Tom looked at him and Kerim Pasha held his gaze. At length Tom nodded reluctantly. 'She is so beautiful,' he said hoarsely, 'I have never managed to forget her.' He dashed a hand through his hair. 'God knows I tried.' He jumped up and strode restlessly round the room.

Kerim Pasha waited patiently. At last Tom came to a halt, facing him. 'It is not just because she is lovely to look at.' Tom gestured despairingly. 'We just seemed to fit together right from our first meeting.' He turned away again and resumed his pacing. 'But we were both so young. I had no money and my father was not willing. . . .' He struck his fist hard against the wall.

'So you lost her.' Kerim Pasha's voice was thoughtful. He glanced at Tom's broad back. 'And now. . . .'

Tom swung round. 'And now,' he said, 'she appears to prefer her independence.' He glared at Kerim Pasha. 'Or maybe—' He bit off the rest of what he had been going to say.

The other man shook his head slowly. 'No!' He got to his feet and put a hand on Tom's shoulder. 'You will find your way through this. I know it.'

The door closed silently behind him. Tom stood rigid for a while. Then he went to the bureau and poured himself a measure of brandy. He took the glass back to his chair and sat down again. After a few sips, he shook his head and uncurled his fingers from the object he had been clutching. It was Rose's handkerchief, spoiled now with bloodstains but still it was hers. His mouth twisted in a mocking smile. 'You fool,' he said, and picked up his drink.

The sky was growing light and still Tom could not sleep. He went over the conversation for clues. Kerim Pasha had noticed something in Rose's behaviour that told him she preferred Tom to himself. Tom was sure he looked like a lovelorn idiot whenever she appeared. And even if she did prefer him, it did not mean she was willing to give up her independence.

She had developed an icy shell and he could find no way to crack it. She had made it plain that anything between them was in the past. Without a word being said, Tom knew her marriage had not been a happy one. That appalling sister-in-law had no doubt forced Rose into a speedy marriage for fear of scandal. How quick the harridan was to assume the worst.

At last, he drifted into an exhausted sleep, into which came images of Rose riding away from him on a swift horse, or else smiling her beautiful smile, but never for him.

Rose was also lying awake, wondering what had caused the wounds on the men's hands. They did not want any mention of the matter and Max was likely to be just as taciturn. However, maybe she could get Sebastian to tell her what was happening. Rose did not like to feel so helpless. Moreover, she was uneasy that villains were stalking them all even into places of entertainment. Who knew where they would strike next?

She stifled a sigh and resisted the urge to get up and pace about. Beside her, Helena slept peacefully. Although she was cross that Max had not returned at the end of the opera, she was not particularly interested in the undercurrent of intrigue that now enveloped them all.

Lucky Helena, thought Rose. She sighed again, more loudly this time. If she was to look her best at the party, she must get some sleep. She turned over and determinedly set herself to imagine painting a gentle landscape. It pushed more alarming thoughts out of her mind, and gradually she relaxed.

CHAPTER TWENTY-EIGHT

When they all assembled at breakfast, Aunt Emily expressed her hopes that the forthcoming dinner party would be a fitting occasion to mark Helena's engagement.

'It is wonderful to see another marriage of two like-minded people, my love,' she told Helena. 'Together with dear Max, you will make a formidable team and advance our understanding of ancient cultures.' She beamed fondly, while pouring out the coffee. Then she looked at Rose. 'Such a pity you never had a grand celebration to mark your wedding. Really, your father hardly made any effort at the time.'

'I expect Augusta wanted to economize,' put in Helena drily.

'It did not signify, Aunt,' said Rose hastily, with a frown at her sister. 'Today I shall enjoy myself very much, seeing my sister so happy.'

'Well, for someone so pleased with life you look very heavy-eyed to me,' objected her aunt. Rose wished she would not be so sharp at times, when usually she was lost in her studies. 'But I am afraid,' went on Lady Westacote, 'that I shall have to leave the preparations in your hands, Rose. I am going with Philip to meet the committee about funding our next expedition. And Helena will come with me, of course.'

'Everything is organized,' Rose assured her aunt. 'It only remains for Uncle Philip to agree with Hudson about the wine.'

'Eh?' Sir Philip looked over his spectacles at her. He folded away the letter he was reading. 'We will have champagne, of course! Demme, Helena is getting engaged – and to my trusted colleague, Max.'

Helena's eyes were sparkling. 'You are all very kind to me,' she was saying when Hudson came into the breakfast parlour bearing two large bouquets. He presented them to the girls, who were silent as they looked at the message on the cards.

'Count Varoshenyi,' said Helena in a mystified tone. She looked at her sister, who nodded. Helena shook her head. 'Why?'

'It is your engagement party' Rose almost snapped. 'No doubt he feels it is the correct way to compliment you.'

Helena pulled a face and glanced at Rose's flowers. 'And you?'

Rose shrugged. 'Of course he would not leave me out.' She stared back fiercely as Helena looked at her, then she shook her head. 'I assure you, it is only that.' And she knew that while she was pleased to receive his flowers, she felt nothing more than a warm admiration for the man himself, however handsome he was and however much he made it plain that he admired her.

By the early afternoon, everything was ready for the dinner party. Rose and Mrs Phelps, the housekeeper, had agreed on all the details. Rose had arranged the flowers in the drawing-room and dining-room, and now her head was aching so badly she decided that it was time for some fresh air and exercise.

She sent for Prue, who grumbled but nevertheless accompanied her mistress on a walk to Bond Street to look for new gloves and silk stockings. The day was overcast and the light poor, but still it was an outing.

They had just passed the entrance to Bolton Street when Prue muttered 'Good for nothings.'

'What did you say?' Rose had been preoccupied with her own thoughts.

'Them two cheeky fellows.' Prue jerked her head to indicate the general direction. 'They stared at you real hard an' then they come along the street. They're still walkin' along behind us. I don' like it one bit.'

Rose glanced back. 'I cannot see who you mean. There are lots of people going about their business.' But she quickened her step.

The two ladies carried on and in the throng of people, Prue could no longer tell if the men were still there. Having selected several pairs of stockings and a charming pair of gloves, not without Prue objecting to the price, Rose thought she had still enough time to call in at Hookham's Circulating Library. Eventually Prue came to fetch her while she was still hesitating between several exciting looking novels. With a sigh, Rose realized that she must indeed return to oversee the last minute preparations for the evening.

They hurried out into the dim afternoon and walked briskly along the busy streets. Carriages rolled past and a few men on horseback trotted by, making Rose think of her ride in the park with Kerim Pasha. However, she was recalled from her pleasant daydream by Prue's voice. The maid sounded uneasy.

'Miss Rose, them two men is still followin' us. I don' like it. They must be plannin' to steal your purse.'

Rose tried to tell herself that it was just a coincidence. She felt a little chill creep across her shoulders, but refused to allow herself to look round.

'Do not look again, Prue. We shall be home in less than ten minutes. And there are lots of passers-by. Nothing will happen.' She gave a giggle. 'Maybe it is you they are following. One of them is smitten by your beauty.'

Prue gave a snort. 'Give over, Miss Rose, do!' She marched on purposefully, the parcel under one arm, her other hand clenched into a fist and her face forbidding. They got as far as Berkeley Square and Prue confirmed that the two men were still following them. They hurried across the road then Rose heard somebody call out, 'One moment, please.'

Her heart leapt as she recognized Tom's voice. His deep rumble was infinitely reassuring. At the same time it sent a shiver of awareness down her spine. She turned gladly towards the two men approaching them. Kerim Pasha and Tom raised their hats and smiled. Rose greeted them with more warmth than she usually allowed to appear.

'We are returning from Davies Street,' said Tom.

The name meant nothing to Rose and her bewilderment must have shown in her face.

'Manton's Shooting Gallery,' he explained. 'We have been trying out our marksmanship.'

'And selecting a fine pair of pistols,' said Kerim Pasha.

At that, Rose became alarmed. 'So you can defend yourself against villains?' she was asking, when an exclamation from Prue made her break off and turn to see what was wrong.

'They've gone now, ma'am.' Prue only used 'ma'am' for Rose in front of visitors.

Rose turned back to the gentlemen. 'Prue says two men have been following us all the time we have been out,' Rose told them. She raised her brows as she saw them exchange a meaningful glance. 'So,' she exclaimed, 'you also believe that to be true.' She looked at them intently.

Tom's face was inscrutable. His dark eyes met hers in a bland look that somehow infuriated her. There had been too many mysterious incidents and Rose felt it was time for an explanation. Her temper snapped.

'Well?' she pressed him. 'Why are these men following us? Surely they are interested in you?'

'But this is not acceptable,' said Kerim Pasha smoothly. 'It is uncomfortable for you. We will escort you home.'

'Do you consider that we are unable to protect ourselves,' said Rose, still watching Tom's face. 'Prue is quite formidable, I assure you.'

'Not enough to deal with two of 'em, though,' replied Tom. 'Let us take you home at once.'

Rose's eyes flashed. They were hurrying her and still not offering any explanation. 'I do believe you know something,' she challenged Tom.

He frowned and indicated that they should move along the

street. Rose pinched her lips together, but she walked on between the two men. Prue, as eager to move on as Tom was to make her, followed hastily, scarcely the correct step or two behind.

'Are you going to tell me what is wrong?' insisted Rose, glaring at Tom in frustration.

He shook his head and kept walking. On her other side, Kerim Pasha was aloof. His gaze was directed towards the other side of the street. Rose had the impression he was scouting for a possible attack. She tried again. 'How are your hands today?'

'Healing.' Tom shot her a quick glance. 'Nearly there now.'

'Yes,' snapped Rose, 'but I wish to know why this unseemly haste and what we are hurrying from.'

There was no answer. She made a little growling noise. 'Why can you not tell me what these men want?'

They turned into Half Moon Street. Tom looked over his shoulder. He exchanged a glance with Kerim Pasha, then gave Rose a half rueful grin. 'Well, whatever it was, you are safe now.'

She was furious. 'The minute you have gone, I shall go out again.'

Tom's expression changed. 'That would be foolish.'

'It would be dangerous,' came the Pasha's softer tone.

Rose whipped her head round to face him. 'But *why*?'

'My dear ma'am, are you fishing for compliments? They are perhaps looking for a pretty girl to kidnap.'

'Give over arguing, ma'am,' urged Prue. 'Just thank the gentlemen and let's go in. Plenty to do afore this evenin'.'

Rose hesitated for an instant. She was not going to get any answers but obviously, they considered that there was a danger. She gave an exasperated huff. 'Thank you, gentlemen,' she snapped and flounced up the steps and in through the door that Hudson was holding open for her.

'Our pleasure,' said Tom drily, but she was not looking. He raised his hat. 'We look forward to seeing you this evening,' he added, but he was addressing the closed door.

CHAPTER TWENTY-NINE

She had heard him though. That much was clear to Tom when he arrived at the house in Half Moon Street later that evening. Rose was carefully avoiding him. Why did she have to be so damned independent? He watched her discreetly as she moved among the guests, smiling and chatting easily. Tom liked the way her corn-coloured hair was arranged in a classic Greek knot bound up with a ribbon the same colour as her gown. And the slim, simply cut gown enhanced her tall, elegant figure. It was in a silver pink material that shone and changed colour slightly as she moved.

Tom suppressed a sigh. She occupied his thoughts to an alarming degree these days. It did not help to see her looking so very beautiful when he seemed to be forever kept at a distance. She had reached Kerim Pasha now. Tom's eyes sparked as he watched the Pasha take both Rose's hands in his and kiss them, his eyes on her face, while she smiled at him in the friendliest manner.

Abruptly, Tom turned on his heel and stalked out of the drawing-room. He found himself walking along the hall and made for the pier glass, where he stared at his reflection moodily. He realized there were a couple of footmen in the hall, so he pretended to adjust the diamond pin in his cravat, twitched the sleeves of his jacket down and then, with another sigh, turned to make his way back to the drawing-room.

Hudson was admitting another guest. Tom brightened a little

on seeing Sebastian. He strode forward to shake hands.

'You have left off your sling, I see.'

Sebastian grinned. 'Thank the Lord, I no longer need it.' He made a fist. 'The strength is coming back. I want to be hale and hearty before I set off on that deuced long sea voyage back to Constantinople.'

'Speaking of which.' Tom took him by the arm and looked for a quiet corner. He led his unresisting assistant over to a spot near the study and muttered, 'We have to be sure you do not take any of Gripper Browne's thugs on board with you. Count – er – Varoshenyi must get home in one piece.'

'How can we flush them all out?' asked Sebastian in frustration. 'There are always more of them. Besides, he has his own bodyguards.'

Tom nodded gloomily. 'It will still be a challenge to keep him safe.'

'Y'know what I think? He is quite capable of looking after himself.' Sebastian grimaced. 'Last night in the opera box, he took the knife from that ugly brute and he did not regard the pain. It was amazing!'

Tom nodded. He cast a swift glance around to be sure there was nobody within earshot. They re-entered the drawing-room, where Rose was obliged to come forward to welcome Sebastian. As Tom remained close to him, she was forced to acknowledge him as well. He kept a sardonic gaze on her as she dropped him a neat little curtsy, to which he replied with a magnificent bow.

'Such a pleasure,' he said drily, looking at her down his long nose.

Rose cast a sharp glance up at him then smiled at Sebastian. 'Your arm is better!' she said, 'I am so glad.'

Hudson appeared to announce that dinner was served. Tom found he was to sit at Lady Westacote's left hand. To his joy, Rose was placed next to him. When the soup was removed, footmen quickly placed the first course on the table and then Hudson and his assistant filled everyone's glass with sparkling champagne.

185

Sir Philip rose to his feet. 'This is a very special occasion,' he announced, beaming round at his guests. 'You must know that Helena and Max have settled it between them to marry. Tonight we drink to their engagement.' He raised his glass and everyone followed suit.

'And to a speedy marriage!' said Max, with a gleaming look at Helena, who smiled charmingly. 'Before we return to Egypt,' she said.

There was a chorus of congratulations and some kisses and handshakes. When they had all settled down again, Tom glanced at Rose. She was occupied in cutting up the slice of roast pheasant on her plate. Tom thought she was not quite happy. After all, she was going to lose her sister after they had become so close. He wanted to say something comforting but felt she preferred to keep silent for the moment.

Then she laid down her knife and fork and picked up her glass. Tom was suddenly reminded of the last time they had drunk champagne together. He picked up his own glass and took a sip. Rose glanced at him sideways and he knew she was thinking of the same occasion. Opposite them, seated at Lady Westacote's right hand, Kerim Pasha observed both of them, his face impassive.

Sebastian, seated on the other side of the table to Rose, had long accepted that Helena was never going to be more than a friend. He had shown no surprise when the engagement was announced. Now he was eating his dinner while occasionally adding a comment into the general conversation. The topic was all about how soon they could return to Egypt and continue the search for more ancient sites and objects.

Tom, alert as he was for any response from Rose, noticed that she did not join in at all. He also noticed that she ate scarcely anything.

'May I pass you this dish of sweetbreads?' he murmured eventually, hoping to get some response from her.

She shook her head without looking directly at him. 'No, I

186

thank you.' She saw Kerim Pasha's eyes regarding her thoughtfully and blushed. After that, she made the effort to address a few remarks to her sister and to Sebastian.

It was not long before Lady Westacote rose to leave the room.

'We have more guests arriving shortly,' she reminded her husband. 'But you can take your time. The girls and I will be there if anyone comes early.'

As Tom had expected, the other visitors were the people willing to sponsor another expedition. He stifled a yawn. This family was totally single-minded in its aims. Helena and Max were obviously made for each other. However, Rose was not happy to be leaving London, that was clear to him. She was busy serving tea to the guests and in any case, she was still avoiding him.

It was a dilemma. If he told her she was being targeted by vicious thugs who would use her as a bargaining counter to get hold of Kerim Pasha, she might well want to confront them. She was brave, but she could not win against such people. Tom's fingers curled when he thought of what they would do to her.

He wandered out into the hallway to think. How could he keep Rose safe? The devil of it was that they had no idea when Gripper Browne's men would strike. Maybe the two fellows they had captured at the opera would talk, but he doubted it. Gripper Browne had such power over his world that anyone who revealed anything would be killed anyway.

After a quiet glass of brandy in the study, Tom was no nearer a solution but felt he must return to the company. In the drawing-room doorway he stopped as if turned to stone. Rose was sitting on a sofa in an alcove by the window. Kerim Pasha was also seated on the sofa, talking to her very earnestly. Neither of them realized that Tom was watching them.

Struck to the heart, Tom saw her nod her head. She was following every word he said with painful attention. Then she raised her hand and dashed away a tear. She leaned closer towards him and said something. Kerim Pasha seized both her hands and pressed kisses on them.

Tom swung round and strode back out. He was so furious, he was halfway along the street when he realized he must have walked out of the house. He let out a huge groan. After everything that man had said yesterday, he was still making up to Rose. How was he to endure seeing Kerim Pasha again, never mind continuing to organize protection for him? What was going on? No doubt the Pasha had simply melted in the face of so much beauty. When he heard that the younger sister was getting married, he must have decided that Rose would be more easily persuaded to accept him. And he had admitted that he loved her.

Tom smashed his fist against the wall.

'What's the problem, sir? Sir. . . ?'

'Eh?' Tom slowly raised his head.

Timms was there, solid as ever. There was a shrewd expression on his face. 'All's well out here so far. Best go back inside, eh, sir?'

Tom was ushered back towards the house with Timms by his side. He nodded and went up the steps again. Behind him, Timms raised his eyebrows and pursed his lips.

In the hall Tom paused to straighten his cravat. The next instant Rose came rushing out from the drawing-room, her head down. She bumped into him.

'Steady,' said Tom. He gripped her arms, resisting with difficulty the urge to clasp her tight against him. She raised her face and Tom stared down into those deep blue eyes. He bent his head towards them and saw the shine of tears on her cheeks. He caught her hand. Such a dainty little hand, swallowed up in his large, strong fist.

'What has happened to upset you?'

She sniffed. 'Oh, Tom. Ker— Count Varoshenyi has made me so happy. . . .'

Tom dropped her hand as if it were a hot coal. A sort of red haze blurred his vision. But Rose was still talking and at last the words began to make sense.

'. . . wherever my family goes in Egypt, they will have the

protection of the Turkish soldiers. It is *such* a relief to me.' She stopped and frowned. 'Tom? Are you quite well?'

There was something in Tom's throat that prevented him from speaking. He nodded and managed a smile. Rose flitted over to the pier glass.

'Heavens! I do look a fright! I must tidy myself.' She smoothed back a stray curl then pulled out a tiny lace handkerchief and dabbed at her eyes.

'You look perfect.' Tom had found his voice now. His heart had steadied. He feasted his eyes on Rose; her elegant silhouette, her smooth, shining hair and the lovely face, turned towards him. Those blue, blue eyes were staring at him. Tom continued to smile at her. He could not help himself, the relief had made him light-headed. He saw her gaze widen, then the dark lashes veiled her eyes.

'Come,' he said, 'we should not linger out here.'

'Oh, no, indeed!' She raised her eyes at that and darted him a shy smile but the colour had come into her cheeks. Then she laughed and walked back into the drawing-room at his side.

189

CHAPTER THIRTY

Rose slipped on the robe that Prue handed her and picked up the hairbrush.

'Thank you,' she said to the weary maid.' You help Miss Helena now.'

Prue stifled a yawn and turned Helena around so she could undo the tiny buttons on her pink evening gown.

'So, miss, you and Mr Kendal are betrothed now. Hudson announced the news and we all had a glass of champagne to toast you and your future husband.'

Helena extended her left hand. 'Thank you, dear Prue. Yes, and we have settled that we will be married very soon.'

Prue exclaimed over the opulent ring. She shook out the evening dress as Helena stepped out of it. 'Well, we must start to think of wedding clothes at once.'

Rose drifted away to the window seat, leaving Prue to ask shrewd questions about materials and styles. Helena laughed and agreed or suggested other possibilities in a very girlish and frivolous way. Rose smiled to herself. What a change these last months had wrought in the earnest scholar of the family. How fortunate Helena was to have found a man who could not only understand but share her passion for history.

Helena, like Aunt Emily before her, was going to have a full and interesting life with a true soulmate. Rose was delighted for her sister but it was not easy to know that she was now the odd one out in this family. They were all going to be so happy in Egypt, whereas she was going to hate the sand, the heat, the enclosed life so far from London society.

Well, no good to worry yet. They would still have some time in London and another trip down to Rivercourt before they sailed. Rose brushed her hair steadily and considered her own evening. Her aunt and uncle were happy to welcome Max into the family. Rose's lips twitched as she imagined the gossip when the announcement of the engagement appeared in the newspapers. Polite society would consider that this match had been deliberately engineered by Sir Philip and Lady Emily. Mr Kendal, son of Viscount Pennington, was an extremely wealthy man and overseas expeditions were expensive.

They would whisper that Helena had been deliberately placed in his way. But those who had lived through the tempest of feelings and who knew Helena's dedication to her studies, knew that this was a love that had grown gradually and truly from a very inauspicious start.

Rose gave a little sigh and turned to look outside. Clouds raced across a sky lit by a fitful moon. She watched for a few moments then directed her eyes down to the darkness of the street. She blinked hard and looked again. There was someone standing on the pavement opposite. She could see the pale shape of his face, staring up at her window.

It must be close on two o'clock, not the time for people to be abroad, unless they were up to no good. She thought about Tom's concern and how he had rushed her home so swiftly, that afternoon. Suddenly, Rose felt really worried. 'Prue,' she interrupted, 'are all the doors secured and the windows shut downstairs?'

'Of course, Miss Rose. Getting fanciful are you, thinking of them two fellows chasing after us?'

'There is a man down there now. He has not moved and he is staring up at this window.'

Prue and Helena rushed forward so fast that they collided and banged their heads together.

'Ouch! Miss Helena, your head is hard.' Rubbing her face, Prue peered out. She looked where Rose indicated and drew in a long breath. 'Lawks, miss, there sure is summat going on!' She stared at Rose.

'I do hope the doors are secure,' said Rose again.

'Nay, miss, that's no crook out there. That's a watchman. That Mr Hawkesleigh, he wanted to be sure you're safe, you mark my words. I saw how he looked at you.'

Rose frowned at her but Helena was smiling. 'Do tell me, Prue, how did he look?'

'It is of no consequence,' snapped Rose.' Do not invent things.'

'I know what I saw,' said Prue with a little nod. 'He ain't going to let anyone harm Miss Rose. Come on,' she added, folding down the blankets and indicating that they were to get into bed, 'you both look fair hagged and we shall have lots o' visitors in the morning, so get some sleep now.'

When at last Helena's slow breathing betrayed that she slept, Rose sat up against her pillows and rested her arms on her knees. She stared at the endless succession of fast moving clouds across the sky. She was glad there was a sturdy man out there to keep watch. Being followed by rogues was not a pleasant experience. And obviously Tom felt she needed protection.

All evening she had been aware of Tom. Although she was still annoyed during dinner because he would not explain what the danger was, now she felt she understood his motives. 'It is better if you know nothing about the matter,' he had said. Well, she was not a child and could make her own decisions, but sometimes it did feel good to be cared for. It occurred to her that Tom was not good at explaining why he did things, he just did the job.

Rose frowned and dipped her face down onto her clasped hands. During that time they were in the hall alone together, she had seen Tom's expression when he thought she was not looking. She sighed. Could she bear to sacrifice her present freedom for a what might be just a brief moment of pleasure?

Hugh had seemed handsome and agreeable before their wedding. But he had never shown any consideration for her as a person. Upon their marriage, she had just become his possession. And if Hugh was capable of loving, it was certainly not with her. She cringed at the memory of the embarrassing and humiliating sessions that were the only conjugal contact they ever had. Thankfully, they were not together for long before he was recalled to his ship.

She was sure that with Tom it would be different. She lifted her head to stare at the clouds again. Even after all this time, the memory of Tom's kisses was potent; she still recalled the effect on her body of being in his arms and craving every sensation he could give her. After seeing the softened look on his face this evening, Rose at last admitted to herself that she wanted to recapture that delightful sense of pleasure. Tom would not treat her like Hugh had done. She knew *that*. A little smile curved her lips. She slid down into the bed and almost at once fell asleep.

CHAPTER THIRTY-ONE

Early the following afternoon Rose made her way down to the library. Everyone else was out and she intended to use the time to complete some sketches for her uncle's next public conference. Before starting on that task, she flicked through her own small sketchbook, smiling at some of the views and portraits of the past few months. A pencil profile of Sebastian, taken during the voyage home, a view of Gibraltar – not very good, she grimaced to herself; there had not been enough time there – other quick sketches of Helena and her aunt and so on. Then she turned to her latest picture and tilted her head to one side. Yes, it was a good likeness.

The picture was of Kerim Pasha but dressed as Count Varoshenyi. He stared out from the page with his regal look, the hawklike features emphasized by the stylish clothes. Western dress suited his tall figure better than the eastern pantaloons with their loose folds. Rose turned back to a painting she had made in Constantinople, of the Pasha in his blue tunic and pantaloons, with his neat little beard and white turban on his proud head.

A smile lit her face as she remembered his kindness and his very evident admiration. She admitted that he was a fascinating man, but there was no comparison in what she felt for him and the way she felt about Tom. On an impulse she picked up the charcoal and quickly drew Tom's head in profile. She outlined his broad forehead, his proud nose and the firm yet full lips. She shaded in the hollows beneath his high cheekbones. Then she started on the unruly hair and chuckled as she drew in the tangles. No matter what he did, it curled and twisted its own way.

Rose was still thinking of Tom and still smiling later, while completing the painting of a mummy for Sir Philip. She did not notice the tap on the door. It was not until Billy, the new footman, coughed discreetly just behind her, that she jumped and came back to reality.

'Sorry to disturb you, ma'am,' he said. 'Cor, ma'am, that looks real, that does.' He nodded at the picture of the mummy, brightly coloured now.

Rose wiped her fingers on a rag. 'Thank you. But did you come in just to admire my work?'

'No, ma'am, sorry, ma'am. There's a visitor here and only you at home.'

Rose frowned at him. 'I am working. Could you not say there is no one at home? Where is Hudson?'

Billy shook his head. 'Hudson's in the wine cellar, doing the new order. It looks like a real important gentleman, ma'am. He's asking about the new expedition.'

'Oh, very well.' She examined her hands for any trace of paint and went out to the front drawing-room.

The visitor did not stay long. Rose smiled and said all the correct things about his interest in the forthcoming expedition to Cairo. As soon as she had seen him off, she returned to the study. She glanced at the bureau where she had propped up her picture of Tom. It was not there. Rose shook her head. Had she become absent-minded? Where had she put it? Her irritation with herself quickly turned to alarm as it became obvious the sketchbook was missing.

Rushing out into the hall, she called for Billy. At last, another footman appeared. Billy was sent for but he could not be found anywhere. By now Rose's heart was beating uncomfortably. The pictures in that sketchbook could be dangerous if they fell into the wrong hands. She must tell Tom at once. He had men working for him, he would know what to do. She darted into Hudson's little cupboard and pulled down an old cloak kept there for rainy days.

'I will not b-be long,' she informed the footman, who was staring at her in shock. 'I must just go to Bolton Street.' She gestured to him to open the door. Even as he hesitated, there came a loud thud on the knocker. The footman gulped and turned the handle. He swung the door open and Kerim Pasha stepped inside.

He looked towards Rose and smiled. He held up her sketchbook.

She gaped at him. 'Thank heavens! But how—?' Then, pulling herself together, she ushered her guest into the drawing-room.

'How did you find that so quickly?' Even as she asked the question, her face flamed. He must have seen all the sketches. She found she could not meet his eyes.

There was a pause. Then Rose heard his soft chuckle. 'I am very flattered, Rose. Not one but *two* pictures of me. And both very like,' he added in a thoughtful tone.

'I should hope so,' she said abruptly, 'If I did them at all.'

'Oh, everything is very good. But in the wrong hands it could be a problem.'

She did look up at that. 'However did you get it?'

For answer, he walked over to the window and beckoned her to join him. He indicated the street. 'Do you not think there are a lot of people out there today? I mean crossing sweepers, grooms, delivery boys, strangers passing by?'

She nodded, comprehension dawning. 'They are all watching this house?'

'Precisely! And when your footman was seen hurrying away to a certain tavern, he was, er' – he made a slicing motion with his hand – 'stopped before he could hand this over.'

'I should have kept it hidden,' she said, holding out her hand to take the book.

He smiled. 'Well, it has been very useful. And may I say, I am flattered.' He kept hold of the book and moved back to the centre of the room. 'This is my farewell visit, Rose. What do you say to the ceremony of tea in your fashion?'

She had to laugh. 'Very well. But I am so sorry we are going to lose you.' She rang to order the tea. 'By the way, there is a package for dear Latife. It is here, ready to be sent round to your address.'

He looked at the large crate standing near the door. 'But that is almost as much as my own personal luggage. Whatever is in it?'

She shrugged. 'Oh, porcelain, a picture . . . some jewellery. My aunt and my sister also wanted to send gifts.'

He shook his head. 'As I said before, I will never understand women. But you are all very kind. I am sure Latife will write to you.'

'I should like that,' she said eagerly, indicating to Hudson where to place the tray.

'Hudson, is it not?' said Kerim Pasha, 'I fear you will not see the young footman again.'

Hudson looked pained. 'Billy, do you mean, sir? I hear as how he's run off.' He looked at Rose for confirmation.

'It seems he is not trustworthy,' nodded Rose.

'Only took him on when you all came up from the country, ma'am. He had good references, but you never can tell, these days.' He shook his head sadly and padded out.

They drank their tea. At last Kerim Pasha gave up the sketchbook. He stood to take his leave. 'I thank you for your gift to my little sister,' he said in his soft velvet voice, 'but the best gift I could take her would be you, Rose.' He took a deep breath as she whitened. 'No, I know very well that you would not come – not as I wish – I am not blind. I see how you look at Hawkesleigh. I just wanted to tell you.' He looked at her, infinite sadness in his eyes.

Rose looked back steadily. She could feel the tears gathering in her eyes and blinked hard, willing them back.

'No tears,' he said, 'but may I be presumptuous and steal a kiss?'

She nodded and turned her cheek towards him. But he pulled her to him with strong hands and planted a sweet, strong kiss on her pretty lips. There was a sudden noise at the door. Kerim Pasha raised his head just as Lady Benson marched into the room.

'Upon my word!' exclaimed that lady in a tone of outrage. She swelled with indignant wrath. Rose and Kerim Pasha exchanged a glance. Whatever embarrassment she had felt at such a kiss was lost when he winked at her. She bit her lip to hide her smile. He seized her hand and bowed over it. Rose clung onto his fingers but at length he let her go and turned to the goggling newcomer.

'Madam, you see me taking my farewells. Excuse me, I must speak to Sir Philip about that footman.' He inclined his head, reached the door and turned, raising his eyebrows expressively to Rose as he went out. She turned away from her unwelcome visitor and picked up the teacups. It was a mistake. They rattled in their saucers as she restored them to the tray.

Lady Benson was torn between outrage and disappointment. 'Well for you if he *is* going away. I never saw such conduct. It does you no credit. How long does he go for? He will miss my musicale.' This last was almost a wail.

Rose bit back a sharp retort. She was in no mood for Lady Benson's impertinent questions.

'Such a distinguished air,' continued that lady, clasping her hands to her bosom, 'even if his manners are somewhat forward.' She eyed Rose malevolently. 'Perhaps I should give you a hint, Mrs Charteris. A young widow cannot be too careful in today's censorious world.'

'Pray do not give yourself the trouble,' flashed Rose. 'My aunt is all the chaperon I need.'

Lady Benson gave an angry titter. 'All she sees is her ancient scripts.'

Rose strode to the bellrope and pulled hard. To her relief, Hudson appeared speedily.

'Lady Benson is just leaving,' she stated coldly. 'Good afternoon, ma'am.'

'Foolish girl,' spluttered the angry matron, 'do you think that the matter ends like this?'

Rose shrugged. When she heard the door close behind the older woman, she grabbed her sketchbook and raced upstairs to her room. She opened the page with the portrait of Kerim Pasha in his western clothes. She swallowed hard and turned back to look at him as an Oriental potentate. A tear spilled out. Rose blinked it away. She was only sad for him and his obvious pain.

CHAPTER THIRTY-TWO

The following morning Aunt Emily announced that she urgently required a certain lexicon but had no time to go out and buy it.

'I wonder, Rose dear, if you would be willing? I know you always welcome a chance to visit the bookshops. Take Prue with you. Helena is assisting your uncle and Max and they have already gone out in the coach.' She rustled the papers in her hand, frowned with an effort of memory and looked up again. 'Oh, while you are in that direction perhaps you could call in at Hardings. I absolutely must have another pair of gloves. Mine are all so dirty. It must be the dust and the charcoal when I show the pictures. And now, if you will excuse me, I simply must finish my paper for the talk this afternoon.'

So Rose set off on foot with Prue, not at all sorry for a chance to visit the magnificent drapers' shop, as interesting to her as the hieroglyphs to her aunt and sister. In her haste, she forgot about taking one of the footmen for protection. They dealt with the lexicon first then arrived at Hardings in Pall Mall. The shop was busy, but it did not take long to find the new gloves.

'Is that everything, then?' said Prue, tucking the neatly wrapped parcel under one arm. But Rose was in no hurry to leave this vast store so she made the excuse that she wanted new ribbons for her blue morning gown. On the way to find ribbons, Rose trailed from counter to counter, entranced by Indian muslins here, silks and gauzes there and exclaiming aloud over the range of attractive scarves and stoles. She looked longingly but reminded herself that she had sufficient items for the present.

'Everything is very tempting, Prue,' she coaxed the frowning maid, 'We don't often get the chance to come here, so please be patient. Oh, look at that beautiful lace – I could trim my evening dress with that, it would be so charming.'

'Give over, Miss Rose,' Prue objected out of habit, but then she sighed and followed her mistress, who had already darted to the counter. Rose was happily debating between two delicate patterns when she heard someone speak her name. Turning to look, her heart sank. What bad luck! She had not realized the person next to her was Miss Delamere. Julia had one gloved hand on a huge tangle of ribbons strewn across the counter.

'Are you in hopes of receiving an invitation to another ball, Mrs Charteris?' said Julia Delamere with a titter. 'It is so hard, is it not, when one must strive to disguise the fact that the dress is the same one yet again.' She glanced at the lace patterns and sniffed, raising her sharp little nose in the air. Rose did not trouble to reply to this spite. She turned her attention back to the lace in her hands, deciding on which one would go best with the jonquil silk.

'We are here to select trimmings for my new gowns,' continued Julia, with emphasis on the new. 'Mama wishes me to look my very best.' She waited hopefully, but Rose merely inclined her head and tried to catch the salesman's eye to make her purchase.

'It is very important, you see,' went on Julia in a confidential tone. 'Mama is certain that I can expect a proposal from Mr Hawkesleigh very shortly.'

This had the desired effect. Rose opened her eyes very wide and looked her interest.

Julia nodded. 'Mr Hawkesleigh is very much the prodigal son. There was some quarrel in the family a few years back and he was sent abroad. His grandmother left him a snug estate but while Mr Hawkesleigh's father was alive, he would not allow his son to have the property. Luckily, Sir Frederick is more generous.'

Rose could not help wanting to know more. 'You seem very well informed on this matter,' she ventured.

Julia gave a shrill laugh. 'Oh, we have known the Hawkesleighs for ever. Now he has come into his inheritance, he will be looking to settle down, Mama says. And, of course, we are neighbours down at Southercombe. She says if I look my best, he cannot *fail* to be attracted.' She gave another irritating titter and indicated the handful of ribbons in front of her. 'So here I am, buying a few fripperies.' She cast Rose a sidelong glance. 'Mama is planning a party to welcome him back to England.'

'But he has been back for some time,' observed Rose, in a sharper tone than she meant to use.

Julia waved her hand, setting her bangles jingling. 'Of course, it would not have been proper while he was still in disgrace with his family. Everything is different now he is established in his property, Mama says.' She plucked a roll of red ribbon from the pile and thrust it at the shop assistant. 'This one! Be quick, man.'

Prue muttered something uncomplimentary, but Rose merely dug an elbow in her ribs to silence her. Let Julia pay and go. She did not want any more of her confidences. It definitely felt that she was being warned off. She glanced at Julia. How much did she know of Tom's old links with herself? If they really were neighbours at Southercombe, Julia could have heard something from Rose's old schoolfriend.

She decided to try. 'Is Lady Hawkesleigh well?' she asked Julia, who was drumming her fingers on the counter while the assistant painstakingly rolled the length of ribbon and wrapped it in tissue paper.

Julia opened her pale eyes wide. 'I was not aware you knew the Dowager Lady Hawkesleigh?'

Rose shook her head. 'No, I have never met her. I am asking about Jane; she was at school with me.'

It was obvious Julia did not know that. Rose felt relief. So Julia was just warning her not to get in the way of her planned conquest of Tom. But as she paid for her purchase, it struck her that she would very much dislike seeing Tom married to Julia Delamere – or in fact to anyone. She stopped short, her mind in a whirl. Surely she was not seriously contemplating giving up her freedom?

'Come on, Miss Rose. We haven't got all day.' Prue's impatient tones penetrated the tumult in her mind. Rose followed the maid out into the street, her head bent down as she accepted the inevitable conclusion. Was that why she had felt nothing more than admiration for Kerim Pasha? Was that why she had taken pleasure in donning her best dresses for evening dinners and outings? Surely, she, Rose Charteris had learned the lesson that no man was to be allowed close again!

And yet. . . .

They were walking along Piccadilly by the edge of the park, when a man approached Rose. He was dressed in clothes that marked him as a foreigner, probably a seaman. He had a bonnet pulled down over his ears. His thin face was swarthy and his eyes were as dark as olives.

'You Mrs Charteris?' he asked, keeping pace as Rose kept walking.

She glanced at him but did not respond. He fell into step with her.

'Please, Mrs Charteris, I come with message from Kerim Pasha.'

At that Rose turned her head towards him. The man did look Turkish and she knew the Pasha had some Turkish servants with him. But surely he had dressed them all in Hungarian style clothing? She felt suspicious, yet, if Kerim Pasha was in need. . . .

'What is your message?' she asked coldly.

He gestured towards the park. 'Please, you come . . . help him.'

Rose glanced at Prue.

'Don't go, Miss Rose,' urged the cautious Prue.

'Yes, but. . . .' Rose frowned in distress. 'If he really is in trouble, I must help.'

'Why you, Miss Rose? He has all them other men to watch over him.'

The man was beckoning urgently. 'Help,' he said again. 'Here.' He pointed towards the gate that she had ridden through in Kerim Pasha's company not so many days ago. With all these villains following him, perhaps he did need help.

'Let us at least look through the gate,' she told Prue and walked the few steps to do so. At once her arm was seized by the man. He pulled her towards two other men who were waiting just inside the gate.

She had walked into a trap! The men grinned and swaggered as they approached. They had reckoned without Prue, however. She launched herself at them, kicking and scratching and yelling loudly for help. Cursing her for the blows she landed, the men took a few minutes to overpower her.

But in that time other men came running. One of them was Tom. Puffing behind him was a rather portly fellow. Tom came racing towards Rose but he stopped short when he saw the curved dagger her captor was holding to her breast.

'Ali?' Tom sounded incredulous. 'It *is* you!' His face darkened. He took a wary step forward. Ali moved the knife to Rose's throat.

Tom stopped. 'Let her go.'

Ali spat. 'You tell Pasha I have woman. He must stop his plans. My country not want your new weapons, *Ingiliz*!' He looked round for his two helpers but they had run off when Tom's men appeared. Ali pulled at Rose's arm to move her. She resisted. Sensing that he was outnumbered, Ali looked wildly round again and turned to flee.

He had not gone very far before Tom launched himself on him. Rose had an impression of long legs powering across the grass and a whirl of arms as they grappled each other. Then two more of Tom's men reached them and she saw Ali's hands being bound behind his back. Tom gave some hasty instructions and rushed back to Rose.

He was an almost unrecognizable Tom. His eyes were blazing and his face was hard with fury. Rose stared up into his grim face, still too bewildered by the rapid pace of events to be afraid. At last she drew in a deep breath.

'You saved me.'

He grasped her by the upper arms. 'Thank God we were watching.'

'What were they going to do?' she asked.

'Use you as bait to get Kerim Pasha.'

'So he is not in danger?' she quavered.

Tom's eyes flashed. 'Not as much as you. Let me escort you home.' He pulled her arm through his. Suddenly Rose felt weak. The reality was sinking in that she had almost been kidnapped. She waited while Prue gathered up their parcels. They walked slowly and in silence.

'Please come inside,' she managed to say, as they waited for Hudson to open the door.

Tom shook his head. 'Not now. I must sort out the aftermath.' He looked at her, his face grim. 'Please do not go out without a couple of footmen as escort.'

Rose nodded. She swallowed hard. 'I have understood now. I am sorry to be so troublesome to you.'

Tom gave her the ghost of a smile. 'You are never a trouble.' He bowed and turned back towards the park.

The next two days dragged past. It was so dull without visits from Tom or Kerim Pasha. Sebastian came to call. He made both sisters promise they would stay indoors until he gave them the all-clear. At last he came to visit, together with Max, and they spent a long time talking to Sir Philip in his study, to Helena's fury.

'It cannot be anything to do with our marriage,' she complained to Rose, 'because why would he bring Sebastian to discuss that?'

Rose, busy at her easel, merely shrugged and continued with

her work. She was painting a copy of an illustrated manuscript for her aunt. Helena paced up and down the room, nibbling a fingertip as she considered.

'If you ask me—' she began, just as Rose opened her mouth and said, 'I suppose it is to do with—'

They stopped and laughed. Then Rose continued, 'Obviously, they are still watching out for spies in the house. If Billy was so easy to bribe, there may be others who would sell information.'

'Billy was new to the household,' replied Helena. 'Even so, it is not very comfortable. And now they keep us as close as when we were at school.'

Rose nodded. She painted in a priest's tall hat and considered the effect. 'We have scarcely been out of the house in three days.'

'And not at all in the evenings,' nodded Helena. 'I would really like to go to the theatre.'

'We have not had any visitors either.' Rose raised her delicate brows, suddenly struck. 'Hmm, I wonder. . . .' She rubbed her cheek thoughtfully. 'I hope that obnoxious Lady Benson has not been spreading tales.'

There was a tap at the door and Max put his head round.

'Would you ladies be willing to risk your lives by going for a walk in Hyde Park?'

'We are so bored in here that the prospect of risking our lives seems a welcome diversion,' said Helena, rushing over to greet him affectionately.

He smiled at her fondly and moved aside to allow Sebastian to come into the room.

'We do have bodyguards or we would not suggest this,' he said in his earnest way. He grinned at Rose. 'It may just be a way of getting yet another villain to reveal himself. If we catch enough of them we must surely find one who will talk.'

Shortly afterwards, the four young people were approaching the Stanhope Gate. At this time of day the park was crowded. Both sisters were very glad of the exercise and the prospect of seeing some other people. Helena was in front, her arm linked in

Max's. Rose slowed her steps a fraction to allow a slight distance. When she judged that they were out of earshot she pressed Sebastian's arm and said, 'Where are the others?'

He gave her a sidelong glance. 'Can't talk about that.'

She shook his arm. 'Do you think I would tell anyone?'

'Of course not. But supposing those ruffians did get hold of you! Far better if you know nothing. Besides,' he added in a rueful voice, 'Tom would shoot me at dawn if I gave anything away. Worried about you, y'know!'

They walked on in silence while she considered this. 'First in Constantinople, now here, this web stretches *everywhere*.'

'Just so.' Sebastian sounded rueful. 'But eventually it will go back to Constantinople and you will be safe again. You would be better off in the country though. Just for a while,' he added, when he saw the dismay on her face.

Helena turned round. 'Keep a firm hold of Seb's arm. Those Benson girls are coming this way.'

'If you were not holding me so firmly, I confess I might run away,' said Max in a low voice. 'They are more fearsome than any bandits I ever met with on my travels.'

But although the two sisters looked at them all closely as they passed by, they did not speak. Lady Benson gave a cold nod in passing. Of course, it would have been a different matter if Kerim Pasha had been with them. Rose wondered if he was already aboard ship and on his way back to his own land. But no, surely Sebastian was supposed to be returning with him.

'When do you leave?'

He gave an exasperated sigh. 'Rose, that is another question I cannot answer.'

'Well,' she said, 'I can see that you are already becoming a splendid diplomat. Let us hope things go well and that you rise very rapidly in your profession. Constantinople is a great centre for diplomacy, so you are well placed to succeed. You are very discreet nowadays. I am impressed.'

He placed his free hand on his heart and smiled. 'You do me too much honour, ma'am.'

'I am not jesting.' They walked a little further, then she added, 'We shall miss you.'

He gave a wry smile and glanced at Helena, leaning on Max's arm as she walked ahead of them.

'She was in love with Max long before she met you,' Rose reminded him, 'and indeed, he is the only husband for a girl like my sister. Seb, let me take this opportunity to thank you.'

At that, he jerked his head towards her again. He lifted his eyebrows in a question.

'For doing your utmost to take care of us,' she explained. 'In fact, since we first met you, you have had the task of looking after us. You will be glad to finish with this duty.'

'Not at all,' he smiled warmly at her. 'It has been a pleasure.'

'What have you learnt from all those villains you have caught?'

His manner changed. 'Rose! You will destroy my career.'

'But I want to know,' she argued. 'Surely you discovered who their leader is and what he wants?'

Sebastian shook his head. 'We know the leader's name, but he rules like a medieval despot. They are more afraid of him than of us. Of course,' he added gloomily, 'he only operates for money. It is thanks to what you overheard in Somerset House that we know the French are behind all this.' He glanced at her in sudden alarm. 'Please do not even tell Helena I said any of that.'

She nodded. It was almost crushing to realize that she was caught up in an international plot. And if they were after her, what about—?

'Tom!' she said, stopping short and pulling her arm free. 'Is he in danger?'

'Tom can take care of himself. I assure you! They are both fine. Just a couple more days. Then I shall take my leave.'

'Oh, Seb,' she said remorsefully, 'and you had such a horrid journey when you arrived. I hope you will get to your ship safely.'

Now she had three gentlemen to worry about. They were all involved in the same vast scheme and attracting so much hostility.

Why was politics always such a dirty business? She looked at Max's lanky form as he strolled ahead with Helena, his head bent to listen to what she was telling him. Even Max had been drawn into this affair. How safe were they now?

CHAPTER THIRTY-THREE

Tom was in the reading room of White's Club. He sat frowning and drumming his fingers on the polished table next to his deep armchair. He looked so forbidding that another gentleman, who had turned to request him to stop the irritating noise, thought better of it. The glass of brandy stood forgotten on the same table, its golden contents untouched. At length, Tom heaved a sigh and dashed a hand through his hair.

He had come here to seek refuge after attending the dinner party at the Delamere's house. His brother Freddy was also invited and he had insisted that Tom attend with him. Tom had assumed that the Delameres were inviting him just as a mark of respect to Freddy, now he had inherited the title. But it was obvious from the moment the brothers arrived that Mrs Delamere had Tom in her sights. She cooed her delight at seeing him again for the first time in so many years and reminded him of how they were all neighbours down at Southercombe.

Tom bowed politely and looked at her down his impressive nose.

'And, of course, you will scarcely remember my little Julia,' she purred, drawing that sharp-faced damsel forward.

Tom bowed again and murmured that No, he did not remember her. At all!

'Oh, how ridiculous,' trilled Mrs Delamere, 'we must give you both the chance to become acquainted.' She fluttered her fan, smiling a determined smile. 'Perhaps, Mr Hawkesleigh, you will take Julia in to dinner.'

'Nobbled, old boy!' breathed Freddy in Tom's ear as he went past. Tom shot him a burning glance. It was not that the girl was ugly, but he felt not the slightest interest in her. And like every other red-blooded male, he resented being pushed into a trap in this way.

They had not proceeded very far through the meal when he was heartily bored. Miss Delamere's conversation was limited to the parties she had attended and the gentlemen who admired her. Moreover, she had a very irritating titter. Tom contemplated the dish of ragout set just in front of him. He was tempted to upend it over the girl's head if she made that shrill noise once again. And here was her mother, leaning forward and beaming at them, saying how pleased she was that they were becoming such good friends. Everyone round the table must be expecting an announcement before the end of the week, thought Tom savagely. *Save me!* he pleaded silently on catching Freddy's eye. But Freddy merely gave an evil grin.

It was coming it a bit rich, thought Tom indignantly, when Mrs Delamere, whom he remembered as a cold, calculating woman not at all fond of small boys, had ignored him until she learned about the property his grandmother had left him. Tom sipped his wine, schooled his face into a politely neutral expression and waited impatiently for the ladies to withdraw. But even when they did at last retire, the relief was only temporary. Scarcely twenty minutes later Mr Delamere led the gentlemen through to the drawing-room.

'I hope there will not be music,' Tom muttered to Freddy. His brother shook his head and chuckled. With a sinking heart, Tom saw that Mrs Delamere was already urging Julia towards the pianoforte.

'And perhaps, Mr Hawkesleigh, you would be so kind as to turn the pages for her . . .' she cooed in that syrupy voice he had taken in deep dislike.

Tom closed his eyes in anguish at the recollection. The evening had been torture from beginning to end. It seemed an age before he had escaped and he was in no mood to talk to anyone, least of all Freddy. His unsympathetic brother was now upstairs in the gaming-rooms.

Now Tom was attempting to let the tension flow out of his body. He was disgusted by the Delameres' blatant interest in him only because of his new status as a landowner. Especially, he recalled indignantly, when contrasted with the determined way the whole Delamere family had ignored him these last weeks in London! It was even more sickening because they had always been neighbours down in Oxfordshire, on visiting terms with his family. Tom drummed his fingers even faster.

His eye lit on the brandy and he picked up his glass at last, much to the relief of the nervous gentleman, who could now return to his newspaper. A couple of sips of the excellent brandy helped Tom to calm down. He set his head against the back of his chair and closed his eyes. His mind turned to more important matters. How was Sebastian coping with Kerim Pasha on the sea voyage? By now they must be heading down the English Channel and safe from pursuit by Browne and his gang of thugs.

Poor Seb, he would be somewhat in awe of the Pasha, but he had support from the team of handpicked young officers also on the ship. They were to start training Kerim Pasha's own elite officers in modern techniques of warfare as soon as they arrived. Another team would follow in three months' time. Tom grimaced. It was going to be a long and dangerous enterprise. He raised his glass in a silent toast to the determined and forceful Kerim Pasha and the massive job ahead of him.

From there it was a small jump to the reason he was still in England. A smile grew as Tom contemplated Rose, her character, so fiercely independent and proud. She was brave, enduring a way of life that he could see was none of her choosing. Yet for all she obviously preferred life in London to the erratic wanderings of her uncle and aunt, she clung to what she deemed to be her freedom. Tom sat upright, clenching his fists against the wide arms of his chair. Her marriage must have been a bad one.

A crease formed between his thick brows. Most girls had only a very limited choice of who they married. But he knew that four years previously, Rose was in love with him as intensely as he was with her. If only they had not been so young and powerless. And if that damned sister-in-law had not interfered, maybe he would have been allowed to become engaged to her, even if they had to wait a while before they could marry.

But that miserable pair – Rose's brother and sister-in-law – had run straight to his father to complain about him seducing Rose at the ball. It had spoiled the evening for Freddy and Jane and, as for himself . . . he had been banished from England on the spot. His father, in spite of his weak heart, flew into a violent rage and ordered Tom never to darken his door again.

No, reflected Tom, taking a large sip from his glass, with his whole family accusing him of putting his father's health in danger, he had done the only thing possible and set off on a life of adventure overseas. But during those years, even though he had tried to be angry with Rose, he had never managed to forget her. Every girl he had met – and he had met plenty – had always been compared unfavourably to her.

By the time his glass was empty, Tom had made up his mind. Unlike his younger self he now had plenty of money, earned by his work for the government. And thanks to his grandmother, he owned a prosperous estate. He was certainly in a position to support a wife. He grimaced again. In fact he was obviously considered a good bargain, witness the ordeal he had been through this evening.

But whether he settled down in his new home, or whether he set off abroad for more adventures would depend entirely on Rose. It was time to speak. Here, he checked. She would not be persuaded easily. At length, however, Tom snapped his fingers and grinned. Surely his plan would work.

CHAPTER THIRTY-FOUR

The ladies had been out paying morning visits. It was a crisp, dry day with a wind blowing, enough to make Rose long to be in the countryside. She thought wistfully that she would like to ride for miles and enjoy the last of the autumn colours in the fields and hedges.

Perhaps they would go down to Rivercourt soon. Surely everyone must be tired of this endless round of social visits and exhibitions by now? She smiled at the thought of returning to the dear old house with its striped frontage of black beams and white plaster. Such a pretty house but sadly in need of repair.

Now her uncle and aunt were home for a while, there would be a chance to undertake the maintenance. Inside as well, it was time for some redecoration. She followed Lady Westacote out of the carriage and into the hall, dreaming of fresh hangings for the drawing-room at Rivercourt. She untied her bonnet and placed it on a side table.

Hudson was close by, holding out a silver tray. 'Letter for you, ma'am.' He was almost smiling.

Rose broke open the seal and unfolded the single sheet. She nodded and smiled as she read. 'Sebastian,' she said in answer to an enquiry from Helena. 'All is well. By now they are already well down the Channel.' She glanced at the letter again. 'Aunt Emily, he sends his respectful greetings and says be sure to call on him if you happen to be in Constantinople.'

'Indeed I will,' said her aunt warmly. 'That boy is such a treasure. Not that we plan to return to Constantinople but one never knows.'

'What is that about Constantinople?' Sir Philip had come out from his study. He was looking very cheerful. 'No, never mind, I have such good news for everyone.' He laughed as they all exclaimed. 'Come into the drawing-room.'

They skipped inside in anticipation.

He laughed again and looked fondly at them all. 'My dear ladies. How pretty you all are. My news?' His eyes shone with excitement. 'Why, I refer of course to our next expedition.' He took a deep breath and waved his arms excitedly, 'we have another sponsor, Mr Pounteney, no less. He will make a very handsome donation on condition that all our finds are displayed in the British Museum. With this amount of money, we can return to Egypt very soon.'

His wife cast herself into his arms and Helena squealed with excitement. Rose felt her heart thud into her boots. She tried to keep a smile on her face. They were not looking at her anyway. She told herself that it was a great honour for Sir Philip to be entrusted with this mission. Her own drawings would also be part of the display and that was a matter of great pride to her. After all, she wanted to be independent. Yes, she did. It was just that—

Someone was speaking her name. She raised her head.

'It will be a splendid opportunity,' said Aunt Emily, 'my dear Rose, you know we depend on you for so many things.'

They were all looking at her enquiringly. She swallowed. 'I do congratulate you, Uncle Philip,' she croaked. It was difficult to speak. She cleared her throat. 'I am sensible of the great importance of this mission. Of course you are delighted.'

'But you are not.' Helena came to put an arm round her sister's shoulders. 'This time we will be better organied in Cairo – more servants, good protection.'

Rose nodded, remembering Kerim Pasha's promise. 'Yes.' She

215

forced a smile. 'I am sure it will be safer this time.'

Hudson brought in the tea tray. Behind him Max appeared in the doorway. There was a chorus of voices as they all told him together of the new plans. Rose drifted quietly towards the window. She heard Sir Philip declare that tea would not do. He told Hudson to bring champagne.

The doorknocker sounded again. Shortly afterwards, Tom was shown into the room. He shook hands with Sir Philip, listened to the news and offered his congratulations.

'Have you come with news of Count Varoshenyi?' asked Helena saucily. 'Sebastian was before you. We know all about them.'

Tom looked at her down his nose. 'I know you know.' He grinned at her surprise. 'Seb left that letter with me to deliver when he and the count were safely on their way.'

'And are *you* going abroad again, Mr Hawkesleigh?' Lady Westacote asked him smilingly.

Tom looked grave. 'I do not know, ma'am.' He glanced at Sir Philip. 'I have come at the wrong time. I will not presume to stay now.'

'Oh, please do,' she urged him, as the doorknocker sounded again. 'If I am not mistaken, we are going to celebrate. You really must join in.'

A couple of the gentlemen sponsors and their wives were ushered into the drawing-room. The atmosphere became very partylike especially when the champagne began to flow. Everyone seemed to be rejoicing. Rose felt stifled. She had hoped it would take much longer to raise the necessary funds for another journey to Egypt. Unfortunately for her, the Orient seemed to be immensely popular. Wealthy people were almost queuing up to participate in some way in the thirst for more exhibits and more knowledge of this ancient culture. And in this new fashion, her aunt and uncle were celebrities. Certainly this afternoon, half the *ton* were calling to offer congratulations.

Nobody would notice if she slipped out for a few moments. She needed a place to scream. Just as she reached the hall the footman was admitting some more visitors. Rose simply could not make polite conversation at this moment. She darted into the study and closed the door with a sigh of relief. At once she gave vent to her feelings in a long growl then stamped over to the sofa and pummelled the cushions with all her strength.

'No winter at Rivercourt' – thump, thump – 'just more sand' – thump – 'scorpions' – thump, thump – 'and heat.' She gave another exasperated growl and flung the cushion across the room.

'If you need a fight, I will oblige you,' said a deep voice behind her. She whirled round. Tom was lounging against the door, grinning at her. 'I promise I will fight back,' he added, a definite laugh in his voice.

Rose drew herself up, quivering with temper. 'Is it not obvious I wish to be alone?' she demanded. 'Please leave, sir.'

'I was Tom last time,' he reminded her. He was still grinning.

Rose felt the rage and frustration overwhelming her. 'Out!' She indicated the door.

Without a word he turned and went out. She gulped. Why did she feel disappointed? But her misery overtook her again. And now, when she had finally accepted that she loved him, Tom had gone! Maybe he was already engaged to Julia Delamere. Her nostrils flared and she turned back to the sofa cushions. She drove her fists into them – one-two! One-two!

'I have a better use for them than that.' Tom had come back without her realizing. 'Besides,' he added, 'you are creasing that charming pink gown you are wearing. And your hair is. . . .' He looked at it admiringly, coming loose from its pins and falling over her shoulders. 'Mmm, delicious. It is as tidy as mine.'

Rose glared. 'I told you to—' She broke off. He was holding a bottle of champagne and two glasses. 'Where did you get those?'

'Hudson. A good butler always understands these things.' He set them down on the desk and began to open the bottle. He whistled.

'I cannot see what you have to be so merry about,' she snapped.

He glanced at her, raised his eyebrows and eased the cork out of the bottle. There was a loud pop. 'Ah!' His voice betrayed satisfaction.

'You can join the rest of the party if you wish to drink champagne.' Her voice sounded pettish, even to herself.

He held out a brimming glass. Rose shook her head. There was a silence. The sound of voices and laughter came from the other side of the hall. Tom looked at her steadily. Rose held his gaze. Whatever she saw there brought the colour to her cheeks. She put up a hand to smooth her hair. A smile curved Tom's lips. Then his face changed as he watched her.

'I know why you are in such distress.' His voice was deep and gentle. 'I understand, Rose. You are not drawn to a wandering way of life.' He held out a hand to her. 'Let us say no more about the events that separated us when we were young and powerless. I know we have both suffered in the years since. But now, Rose, I beg you to do me the honour of accepting my hand in marriage.'

She felt the blood drain from her cheeks. He was *sorry* for her. That had to be the reason for this declaration. Or else he still felt guilty. Despair flooded in and made her shake uncontrollably. She stood there, clasping and unclasping her hands. There was a muffled noise in her ears as if she were underwater. No coherent ideas would form in her mind, other than the one thought that Tom did not love her.

Tom watched with his head on one side. His expression went from puzzled to exasperated to alarmed. Suddenly she felt his big hands taking hold of her arms, guiding her to sit on the sofa. Her knees were shaking so much that she was glad to obey.

'Here, drink this.'

A glass was thrust into her hand and obediently she swallowed. The sensation of bubbles in her throat broke the spell. She frowned. 'Tom, this is champagne.'

He refilled the glass. 'Yes, sweetheart. You need something at once and it is all I have to give you. Come on, drink up. You are still very white.'

Rose put a hand to her head. 'Tom, I- I thank you for your kind offer but I cannot accept.'

Silence. She held her breath. He did not move. At last she looked up. He was standing just in front of her, watching intently.

'That is not good enough,' he said when her eyes met his. 'Dash it, Rose, why not?'

CHAPTER THIRTY-FIVE

Rose bent her head down hastily. 'I have no desire to be married again,' she mumbled to her shoes. Her jaw was clenched. Tom was a kind man but that was not a good enough reason to accept. It would be intolerable to love him as she did when he was only offering marriage to help her out of her difficulties. It would be as bad as her dismal marriage to Hugh. She gripped the edge of the sofa so tightly her knuckles went white.

Tom said nothing. Rose kept her head down but gave him a hasty glance under her lashes. He was such a splendid figure of a man and, as always, she was acutely sensitive to the unspoken pull of attraction between them. Yet it was just his kind heart that made him want to help her. Her pride told her it was better to go back to Egypt and make her own way in life. She gulped.

Then a hand came down in front of her face, slid under her chin and gently tilted up her head.

'At least look at a man when you refuse his offer of marriage.'

His dark eyes were glowing, his face was softened. As usual, she noticed, his hair was lifting into curls and falling over his forehead. A lump grew in her throat. She loved him so much, not because he was dashing and handsome and strong but because he was Tom, the man she had loved since she first saw him. The man she felt was the other half of herself.

His eyes widened and he bent his head closer. 'Rose. . . ?' His voice was the veriest murmur, whispering over her nerves like velvet.

She jerked back as if scalded. Tom's hand dropped. He straightened up. There was another silence while he studied her face. 'Are you too proud to accept my offer?'

She shook her head vehemently.

Silence.

'What then?'

She felt rather than saw Tom dash a hand through his hair. She heard the angry intake of his breath. She saw his glossy boots move away. He strode over to the window, thumped his fist into the wall and strode back.

'I cannot, I cannot. . . .' The words burst from her. She jumped to her feet and twisted round towards him. 'You do not know. . . . I-I . . . I prefer my freedom to anything.' She hid her face in her hands.

A second later, she felt Tom's arms go round her. He guided her head against his shoulder and pressed his lips against her hair. Rose let out a shuddering sigh. Her hands were clenched by her sides and she was as rigid as a board.

'I understand,' murmured Tom. 'Your marriage was not the marriage you wanted; your husband was not the *man* you wanted.'

A tremor ran through her. Tom rubbed his large hand gently across her shoulders. 'You should not judge all marriage by that unhappy one, sweetheart. When the love is mutual, it can be so very wonderful.' He was still caressing her back. She could hear the beat of his heart, firm and steady, and feel his mighty chest rise and fall gently.

Gradually Rose relaxed. Her hands unclenched, she leaned against him, moulding herself against his powerful torso.

'I would never harm you or force myself upon you,' he said at length. 'But I want you, Rose. I always have. It is not just for your beauty, although that enchants me. We belong together and I know you feel that too.'

He pulled back and looked earnestly at her. She gazed at him in wonder. A smile trembled on her lips. He *did* love her. But could he not say the words? His eyelids seemed to have grown heavier. He moved close again and put his hands on her shoulders. She raised her head, ready now to be kissed.

His lips were warm and sweet against her own. He was very gentle, holding her shoulders in a light clasp and soon breaking the kiss to lean his forehead against hers. 'There,' he whispered, 'that was not so terrifying, was it?'

Rose smiled and rested her forehead against his. Taking this for agreement, Tom kissed her again. There was more pressure from his mouth this time but Rose responded eagerly.

Shortly afterwards, Tom poured more champagne and drew her to sit down beside him on the sofa. 'Do you agree with me that this is very pleasant?' he asked, his eyes sparkling. He took her free hand in his own, raised it to his lips and turned it over, pressing a long kiss on her palm. Rose reached up and ruffled his hair.

'Hey,' he protested, 'if you knew how long it takes to make it neat.'

She laughed – and laughed again with sheer delight. Her fears and doubts seemed ridiculous now. She leaned against Tom's shoulder and at once he caught her close and angled his head for another kiss.

For a while they were lost to the world. It was an unpleasant shock to realize suddenly that someone was standing over them as they lay against the sofa cushions, kissing passionately.

Tom sat up. Rose struggled onto one elbow and looked up into her sister-in-law's outraged face.

'Augusta! Whatever—'

'It is all of a piece,' announced Augusta in awful tones. 'Both you and Helena are so undutiful. Your sister gets engaged without any reference to her father and brother. I had to learn of it from my friend, Lady Benson. She also wrote that you were being very free with your favours and I see it is true.' Her bosom swelled with wrath. 'Just look at the state you are in. Your hair is tumbling down your back. Your bosom is nearly out of your dress. . . .' She choked. 'However shall I tell your father?'

'It is of no consequence what you tell him,' said Tom, rising to his feet. He scowled at her and advanced menacingly. His eyes were like flint. 'If you were a man, I would knock you down for this intrusion, you meddlesome female.'

'Oh,' Augusta quavered, quite unused to any contradiction. 'Keep your distance. I am here to defend my family honour.'

'Honour be damned!' growled Tom. He clenched his fists and took another step towards her. 'You caused us enough misery four years ago. And I wager your meddling stretched to intercepting all the letters I sent to Rose. Well, now, woman, you can go or you can stay, but we are going to proceed from where we were when you so rudely intruded.'

He gave Augusta one more burning look, then turned his back on her, bent over Rose and slid the sleeve of her dress down her shoulder. Slowly he moved until his mouth was about to touch the soft white skin he had revealed.

'How dare you!' shrieked Augusta. 'Shame on you. . . . Oh!'

Rose had tilted her head back. She drew in a slow, audible breath. At that point Augusta gave a little scream. Rose opened her heavy eyes and saw her sister-in-law rushing out of the room.

Tom looked over his shoulder. 'Good riddance!' he muttered. He pressed Rose back against the cushions and took two long strides over to the door. He turned the key.

'And now, my darling. . . .' His wonderful mouth curved in a smile.

'Tom, I have not said I will marry you.'

He walked closer. His eyes were glowing. 'Well, say it, my love. We are not going to spend any more of our lives apart.' Suddenly he became serious. He pulled her to a seated position and went down on one knee in front of her. He took both her hands and clasped them firmly.

'Rose, for four years I tried to forget you. When you did not reply to my letters I was so full of anger that I took on any dangerous mission in any dangerous foreign land. Then chance brought us face to face. When I saw you again, I knew how much I still loved you. Please, my darling, say you will share your life with me.' He kissed one hand and then the other. His unruly hair flopped forward over her hands.

Rose was caught between laughter and tears. Her heart felt as if it would burst out of her chest with love and joy. She pulled her hands free and took his face between them. She traced his cheekbones and the line of his strong nose, then smoothed back the blond-streaked hair from his forehead.

'Yes,' she said at last. The laughter bubbled up. 'Oh, Tom, yes. I have been desolate since we parted all those years ago.'

At once he clasped her to him tightly. She felt the huge sigh of relief that escaped him. He tucked her head under his chin and spread his large hands over her back. 'Thank God! If you knew how long I have been waiting to persuade you. . . .' His hand stroked through her hair, then slid round to her cheek. He leaned forward to kiss her again. And again.

'You have pulled my dress quite off my shoulder,' murmured Rose eventually.

'Mmm,' he rumbled. 'Been waiting an awfully long time to get this far. In any case, this sofa is too damned narrow, I shall make sure we have wider ones in our own home.'

Disney
MOANA

Level 4

Re-told by: Kathryn Harper
Series Editor: Rachel Wilson

Pearson Education Limited
KAO Two
KAO Park, Harlow,
Essex, CMI7 9NA, England
and Associated Companies throughout the world.

ISBN: 978-1-2923-4684-7

This edition first published by Pearson Education Ltd 2020

1 3 5 7 9 10 8 6 4 2

Set in Heinemann Roman Special, 14pt/23pt
Printed by Neografia, Slovakia

Published by Pearson Education Limited

Acknowledgments
Getty Images: Fotokia 24, Westend6I 26-27
Shutterstock.com: kdshutterman 24, mapichai 27, MiOli 24, Standard Studio 24

For a complete list of the titles available in the Pearson English Readers series, visit
www.pearsonenglishreaders.com.

Alternatively, write to your local Pearson Education office or
to Pearson English Readers Marketing Department,
Pearson Education, KAO Two, KAO Park, Harlow, Essex, CMI7 9NA

In This Book

Moana

A girl who lives on the island of Motunui

Gramma

Moana's grandmother who knows about the past

Maui

The Demi-god who uses his hook to change shape

Tamatoa

A monster crab with a lot of treasure

Te Kā

A scary fire monster who lives on Te Fiti's island

Te Fiti

The Mother Island who loses her heart

Before You Read

Introduction

Long ago, the island of Motunui was beautiful and green. There was a lot of food, and people were happy. One day, a little girl called Moana found a beautiful green stone, which her grandmother kept for her. Years later, life on the island is difficult and people are hungry. With the green stone around her neck, can Moana help her people?

Activities

1 **Read the sentences and choose the correct word. You can use the Glossary on pages 22–23.**

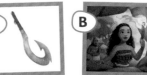

1 This white *hook* / *stone* has powers.
2 The *cave* / *boat* is dark.
3 The *pirates* / *fish* are attacking the boat.
4 There's a *reef* / *tree* in the ocean.

2 **Look at the cover. What do you think is going to happen to Moana in the story?**
Moana is going to ...

1 learn to sail   **3** save her island   **5** fight monsters
2 learn to fly   **4** live on a new island **6** make a friend

Gramma told a story from the island's past.

Te Fiti made the world. It was beautiful. Then Maui the Demi-god took her heart. He wanted the heart's power so that he could make life. Te Kā, the fire monster, also wanted her heart. The monster attacked Maui.

The heart, and Maui's hook, fell into the ocean.

From that day, darkness came into the world.

The little children were afraid.

"There *are* no monsters!" Moana's father told the children.
"But we stay inside the reef."
Little Moana wasn't scared. She went to the beach and played in the waves.
The waves gave her a shiny green stone. Her father found her and Moana dropped the stone. Gramma quietly took the stone and put it away. It was the heart of Te Fiti.

Some years later …

The island was in trouble and people were hungry. Moana thought she could help but …

"Stay inside the reef," said her father.

Gramma took Moana to a cave with boats. Long ago, their people were Wayfinders, sailing on the ocean.

"The darkness is coming," said Gramma. Then she gave the green stone to Moana. "Sail past the reef, find Maui, and take the heart back to Te Fiti," said Gramma.

"We have to take the heart back!" Moana told her father.
"There *is* no heart!" he said angrily, and he threw the green
stone away.
Moana found it. She ran to the cave, took a boat, and sailed
past the reef.
First, it was quiet. Then, large waves came. That night, there
was a terrible storm and Moana's boat hit an island.

Moana woke up on Maui's island. "A boat!" cried Maui.
"I am Moana of—" but Maui didn't listen. He put Moana in a
cave and took her boat. "Let me out!" cried Moana.
She climbed out of the cave and the waves took her to the
boat and Maui. She held up the heart.
"I am Moana of Motunui. You must take the heart to
Te Fiti!"

Maui and Moana sailed on the ocean.

"Are you afraid of the heart?" asked Moana.

"No, but I lost my hook because of it," said Maui.

PING! Suddenly, little pirates attacked their boat and jumped on it. Moana and Maui fought the pirates and pushed them off the boat.

"We did it!" shouted Moana. Quickly, they sailed away.

Moana and Maui made a plan.

"First, we're going to find my hook," said Maui. "It's in Tamatoa's cave."

"Then we're going to save the world, right?" said Moana.

Moana wanted one more thing. "Teach me to sail," she said.

Maui taught Moana to sail. She learned about the skies, the moon, the waves, and the wind.

They sailed to Tamatoa's island.

First Maui, then Moana, jumped into Tamatoa's cave. The treasure shone through the darkness.

"Maui's hook!" Moana said.

"What are you doing down here?" asked Tamatoa, a monster crab. Tamatoa held Moana up and opened his big mouth.

"No!" she cried.

"It's Maui time!" shouted Maui. He had his hook, but he couldn't change into the right animal! Tamatoa attacked him.

Moana thought quickly. "Here's a pretty stone for you!" She
pretended to drop the heart.

Tamatoa ran after it, but it was only a stone!

"It's time to go," Moana said to Maui.

"What about the heart?" asked Maui.

"I have a better one," Moana showed him the real heart and
they ran out of the cave.

Now Maui had his hook, and he practiced changing into different animals. It didn't always work, but Moana helped him.

Finally, Maui became a big, beautiful bird and flew high into the sky.

"Next stop Te Fiti," said Moana. She felt happy.

Moana sailed the boat across the ocean, with the bird above her in the sky.

Moana and Maui were nearly at the island of Te Fiti. Maui the bird took the heart and flew up to the island.

WHAM! Te Kā, the big fire monster, hit him. Maui fell into the ocean and became a man again.

Moana pulled Maui back on the boat. "I'm going to find a better way in," she said.

"Stop! Moana, STOP!" cried Maui.

Te Kā attacked the boat. Maui held up his hook.

CRACK! The hook broke a little.

"We can fix it," said Moana.

"The gods made it. You can't fix it," said Maui sadly.

"I don't want to go back there."

"Maui!" cried Moana.

"Goodbye, Moana," said Maui. He became a bird and flew away.

Moana looked sadly at the ocean. "Why did you bring me here?" she asked.

Then Moana thought of Gramma and she felt stronger again. She said, "I am Moana of Motunui. I must sail across the sea and take back the heart of Te Fiti!"

She sailed fast in her little boat to fight the terrible monster for a second time. Te Kā's hand came down to break the boat, but she sailed around it!

Moana fell into the water. She climbed back on her boat,
but Te Kā was there again …

Suddenly, a big bird stopped Te Kā before the monster broke
the boat.

"Maui!" cried Moana.

"Go save the world," said Maui.

He fought Te Kā, changing shape again and again. Te Kā
attacked him and Maui's hook hit the ground. This time it
really broke.

The waves took Moana to some rocks. She looked for the
island of Te Fiti, but it wasn't there.
"Te Fiti, where *are* you?" said Moana. "Come to me."
Moana held the heart high. "Let her come to me," she said
to the water. *ROAR!* The monster made a terrible noise. The
waves opened and Te Kā came to Moana.

Moana wasn't afraid.

"I know who you are," she sang. "This is not who you are."

The big monster was above Moana. She looked into its eyes of fire.

"You know who you are," she sang.

There was a shape on Te Kā's body—a space for the heart of Te Fiti.

"Who you truly are," Moana said quietly. She put the green stone into the space on Te Kā's body.

Suddenly, the black rocks on the monster's outside fell off. *Crack, crack, crack!* Then Moana saw the lovely face, the flowers, the green body …

It was Te Fiti! She was back! The heart brought her back!

The black island turned green and beautiful.

The waves brought Maui and Moana to a wonderful green field. It was Te Fiti's right hand. She held them up.

"Look … what I did was wrong," said Maui. "I'm sorry."

Te Fiti smiled and opened her left hand. There was Maui's hook—it was clean and new.

"Thank you," said Maui.

Moana's boat was on the beach. It was all new again.

It was time to go, but Moana didn't want to leave Maui.
"You could come with me, you know. My people are going
to need a good Wayfinder."
"They *have* one," said Maui, smiling at Moana.
"See you, Maui," said Moana.
"See you, Moana." Maui became a bird and flew away.

Moana sailed back across the ocean. Her island was
different—it was green and beautiful again.
"Moana!" her mother cried. Her family and all the people
of the village welcomed her home.
The people took the old boats from the cave. Soon, the boats
were on the ocean. The people learned to sail—past the
reef—with Moana, their Wayfinder.

After You Read

1 Choose three characters from the story and describe them with words from the box.

> good bad scared angry sad strong kind funny

2 Put the story into the correct order.

a The fire monster becomes Te Fiti.
b Pirates attack Moana and Maui.
c Moana finds Maui.
d Moana listens to Gramma's story about Te Fiti.
e Moana takes a boat from the cave.
f Moana and Maui find Maui's hook.

3 Why did these things happen? Match.

1 Gramma gave Moana the heart because …
2 Moana found Maui because …
3 Maui wanted his hook because …
4 Maui and Moana fought the crab because …

a she wanted his help.
b it helped him change shape.
c it had the hook.
d she wanted Moana to save her people.

Glossary

attack past tense **attacked** (*verb*) to try to hurt a person; *The pirates attack Moana and Maui.*

cave (*noun*) a space under the ground or in a large rock

darkness (*noun*) a place where there is no light

fix past tense **fixed** (*verb*) to make a thing work again; *"We can fix the hook," Moana said.*

heart (*noun*) a part of the body that helps you live

hook (*noun*) a thing you use to catch fish

island (*noun*) land with water around it

pirate (*noun*) a person who sails on the oceans, attacking other boats and stealing things from them

pretend past tense **pretended** (*verb*) to act as if things are true but they're not; *Moana pretends to drop the heart.*

reef (*noun*) a line of rocks or sand near the top of the ocean

rock (*noun*) a hard, dry, large stone you find on the ground

sail past tense **sailed** (*verb*) to move across the ocean in a boat; *"Sail past the reef, find Maui, and take the heart to Te Fiti," said Gramma.*

stone (*noun*) a small rock

teach past tense **taught** (*verb*) to help people learn; *"Teach me to sail," Moana said to Maui.*

treasure (*noun*) a lot of gold and silver; what pirates look for

wave (*noun*) the shape of water moving in the ocean

Phonics

Say the sounds. Read the words.

ew · flew · new

oo · food · moon

ue · blue · true

Say the poem.

Maui flew,
And the sky was blue.
No stars, no moon.

Moana knew
That the heart was true.
She could go home soon.

Values

Know your family history.

Find Out

Where did the islands of Hawaii come from?

Hawaii is a beautiful place in the Pacific Ocean. It is part of the United States of America.

Hawaii has eight big islands and many small islands. The islands came from volcanoes. The eight big islands of Hawaii first erupted about 8 million (8,000,000) years ago.

Hawaii gets bigger by about 24 soccer fields every year! The lava cools and makes new land.

This mountain is an old volcano

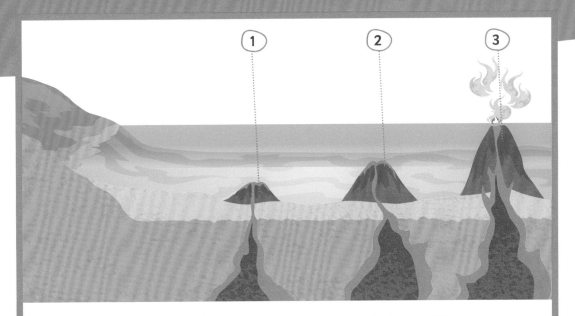

How does a volcano make an island?

1 Deep in the ground there is hot rock. It breaks through the bottom of the ocean and becomes lava.

2 The mountain grows under the ocean.

3 The lava erupts, or comes out suddenly, through the top of the ocean. Over time, this makes an island.

The Wind in the Willows

Mole and Rat become Friends

LEVEL 4

Original story by: Kenneth Grahame
Re-told by: Melanie Williams
Series Editor: Melanie Williams

Pearson Education Limited
Edinburgh Gate, Harlow,
Essex CM20 2JE, England
and Associated Companies throughout the world.

ISBN: 978-1-4082-8839-9

This edition first published by Pearson Education Ltd 2014

3 5 7 9 10 8 6 4 2

Text copyright © Pearson Education Ltd 2014

The moral rights of the author have been asserted
in accordance with the Copyright Designs and Patents Act 1988

Set in 17/21pt OT Fiendstar
Printed in China
SWTC/02

Illustrations: Cory Godbey

Published by Pearson Education Ltd

For a complete list of the titles available in the Pearson English Kids Readers series, please go to
www.pearsonenglishkidsreaders.com. Alternatively, write to your local Pearson Education office or to
Pearson English Readers Marketing Department, Pearson Education, Edinburgh Gate, Harlow, Essex CM20 2JE, England.

One spring morning, Mole was busy in his little house.

'I'm spring-cleaning, I'm spring-cleaning,' he sang.

He dusted and washed and painted.

Suddenly, he stopped. He did not want to do any more spring-cleaning. He wanted to be in the spring sunshine!

Mole put on his coat and went outside.
He ran round and jumped in the grass.

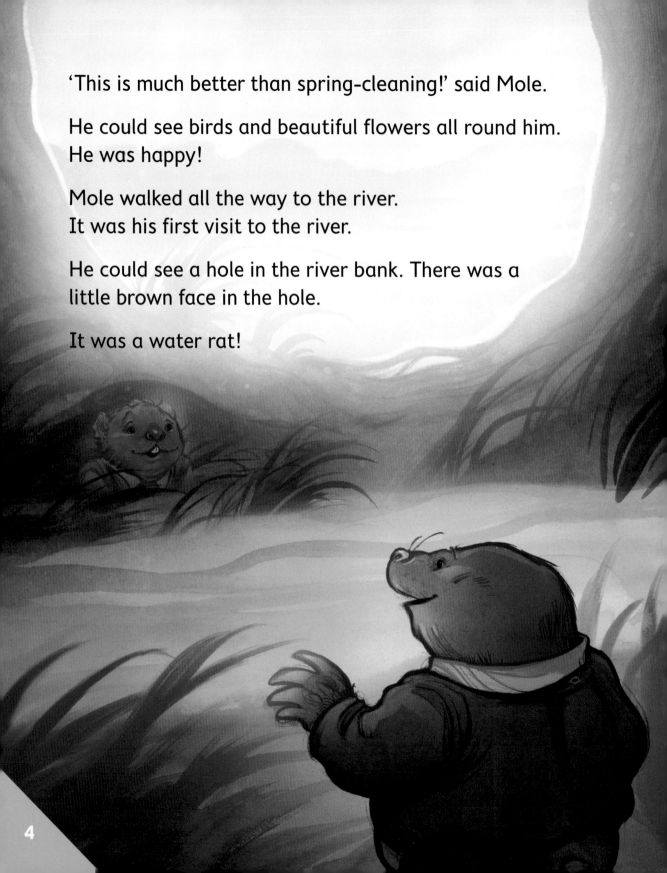

'This is much better than spring-cleaning!' said Mole.

He could see birds and beautiful flowers all round him. He was happy!

Mole walked all the way to the river.
It was his first visit to the river.

He could see a hole in the river bank. There was a little brown face in the hole.

It was a water rat!

'Hello, Mole!' said Water Rat.

'Hello, Rat!' said Mole.

Rat rowed across the river in his little boat. Mole jumped in.

'Let's take some lunch in a basket and go for a row down the river,' said Rat.

'That's a good idea!' said Mole.

Rat put some food into the basket.

Then the two new friends rowed down the river.

Rat rowed and rowed. Mole looked at the water and listened to the sounds of the river. He was very happy.

'What's that in the water?' asked Mole.

'Oh, that's my friend Otter,' Rat answered. 'Hello, Otter.'

'And WHO IS THAT in the boat?' asked Mole.

'Ah,' laughed Rat. 'That's Toad! Hello, Toad.'

Mole and Rat ate their lunch on the grass by the river bank.

Then Rat started to row again.

'I want to row now,' said Mole.

'It's not easy,' said Rat.

But Mole wanted to try. He took the oars and
... oh no! ... Mole fell into the river.

'Come home with me,'
said Rat. 'I've got
some dry clothes.'

Mole stayed in Rat's house for many weeks.

One summer day Mole said, 'Let's go and visit Toad.'

'That's a good idea,' answered Rat.

The two friends got into the boat and Mole rowed them up the river.

'There it is! There's Toad Hall,' said Rat.

'Hello my friends,' said Toad. 'Lovely to see you, yes, lovely. Follow me.'

'Look at that!' Toad said excitedly.

'Www ... what is it?' asked Mole.

'It's a gypsy caravan, my friend. It's the new thing!' answered Toad. 'Going to new places, you know.'

After lunch, they all climbed on to the caravan.

'Now we're ready.'

'Come on horse, let's go,' said Toad. 'This is the life for me!'

It was a beautiful afternoon and Mole, Rat and Toad walked and rode on the caravan in turn.

Late in the evening they stopped and ate their supper.

The horse ate its supper in the field - lovely green grass!

In the morning, after a good breakfast, they started on their journey again.

Suddenly they heard a sound behind them.

POOP POOP

Suddenly the old grey horse heard the sound. **POOP POOP**!

It was scared and ran into the field next to the road.

'Oh, no,' said Mole. 'Look at the caravan!'

Toad sat in the road. 'Poop Poop,' he said. He pointed at the car. 'THAT is the new thing.'

'Let's take Toad home,' said Rat to Mole.

Autumn arrived.

'I want to visit Badger,' Mole said to Rat one day.

'We don't go in to the Wild Wood, Mole,' answered Rat. 'Oh no.'

But Mole wanted to go. He went to the Wild Wood without Rat!

Poor Mole was very scared.

The Wild Wood was dark and then it started to snow.

Mole was lost!

Rat woke up. Mole was not there. Where was he?

Rat looked outside and saw Mole's footprints in the snow.

Rat followed the footprints into the Wild Wood.

'Mole,' he cried. 'Where are you? It's me – it's old Rat.'

'Rat, is it really you?' said a small, tired Mole.

'Yes, it's me,' answered Rat.

'We must go home now, Mole,' said Rat. 'Follow me.'

But there was a lot of snow. Rat could not see their footprints.

Suddenly Rat stopped and said, 'Look. What's that?'

'I don't know,' answered Mole.

'I do,' said Rat. He started to dig in the snow.

After ten minutes, he pointed to a door.

'We're at Badger's House,' laughed Rat.

They knocked loudly on the door.

The door opened. It was Badger.

'Come in, you two. You're cold and hungry,' said Badger.
'Come and get warm by the fire.'

Rat and Mole sat by the fire. They ate an excellent
supper, which Badger made for them.

Then it was time for bed.

The next morning, Rat and Mole came downstairs for breakfast.

There were two hedgehogs at the table!

'Good morning,' said Rat.

'Good morning,' said one of the hedgehogs. 'We got lost in the snow. We knocked on Mr Badger's door. He's very kind. He gave us some breakfast.'

'Where's Mr Badger?' asked Mole.

'He's busy,' answered one of the hedgehogs.

After breakfast, the hedgehogs went home.

Later, Badger came into the kitchen and made them an excellent lunch.

'Thank you Badger,' said Rat. 'Now, we really must go. We don't want to be in the Wild Wood at night.'

Badger took them through a tunnel which went under the Wild Wood.

It was December. Rat and Mole were on their way home. They walked through a little village. The houses were pretty in the snow. Inside, all the people were warm and happy.

Mole and Rat left the village and walked on through the snow.

Suddenly, Mole stopped. What was that smell?

It was HOME. He could smell his home.

Mole stopped. He was close to his old home!

Yes, it was small. Yes, it was untidy but it was HOME.

'Rat,' called Mole. 'Stop. We're near my old home. I can smell it. I want to go there.'

'No time,' shouted Rat. 'The snow is coming.'

Mole sat down by a tree and started to cry.

Rat sat down next to Mole.

'Oh, Mole, I'm sorry. Let's go and find your old home,' he said.

'But, it's getting dark,' answered Mole.

'Use your nose,' answered Rat. 'We're going to find it!'

Mole stood up. Yes, he could smell it.

They were near ...

MOLE END

There it was!
He could see his door.

Mole opened the door and looked inside his home.

It was dusty and untidy. The house felt sad without him.

'Oh, Rat,' said Mole. 'Why did I bring you here? It's so cold. Your house is so much nicer than mine.'

Rat dusted and cleaned … and dusted and cleaned.

Then he made a fire and some supper.

After supper, the two friends sat by the fire. They were very sleepy.

'Mole,' said Rat. 'This is a lovely home.'

After Rat was in bed, Mole sat and thought.

He liked his new life and his new friends – Rat, Otter, Toad and Badger.

But he loved his old life too.

It was wonderful to be home!

Activity page ❶

Before You Read

❶ **Match the words to the pictures.**
1 basket
2 gypsy caravan
3 oar
4 tunnel
5 footprint

 a

 b

 c

 d

 e

❷ **Look through the book. Find these characters.**
What are their names?

 a

 b

 c

 d

 e

Activity page ❷

After You Read

❶ Read and write True (T) or False (F).

1 The story begins in the winter. ☐
2 Mole meets Rat near the river. ☐
3 Mole stays in Rat's house. ☐
4 Mole learns to row. ☐
5 Toad lives in a big house in the Wild Wood. ☐
6 Toad likes Gypsy Caravans better than cars. ☐
7 Badger goes to visit Mole and Rat. ☐
8 Mole wants to go back to his old house. ☐

❷ Complete the sentences with *breakfast*, *lunch* or *supper*.

1 Rat and Mole have _____ by the river.
2 The horse ate its _____ of grass in the field.
3 After they arrived at his house, Badger made _____ for Rat and Mole.
4 The hedgehogs ate _____ in Badger's house.
5 Badger made _____ before he took Mole and Rat home through the tunnel.
6 Rat cooked _____ for Mole in his old home.

❸ Mole wanted to go back to his old home. It was small but he loved it. Describe your home. Why do you like it?

24

GWR

Principal Stations

Colin G. Maggs

LONDON

IAN ALLAN LTD

First published 1987

ISBN 0 7110 1713 1

Published by Ian Allan Ltd,
Shepperton, Surrey;
and printed by Ian Allan Printing Ltd
at their works at Coombelands in
Runnymede, England

*Photographs from the Locomotive &
General Railway Photographs
collection are reproduced courtesy of
David & Charles Ltd.*

Contents

Paddington

Paddington, almost synonymous with the Great Western Railway, is a building on a grand scale, and like the company's early locomotives, is tall and broad. This, however, is the present Paddington station, the first was different in architectural style and also in position.

When the line opened to Taplow on 4 June 1838, two temporary platforms were used at Paddington; the cancellation of the decision to use the London & Birmingham station at Euston allowing insufficient time to create a permanent building. Although a rather more final structure opened later in 1838, no attempt at ornamentation was made. The structure was purely functional, the directors having resolved that a more fitting station

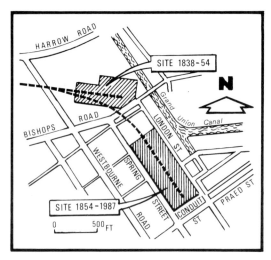

should be built at a later date. Imaginatively and economically, the entrances and booking offices of this first station were situated in some of the 26 arches under the brick-built Bishop's Road bridge, while the space to the north of the booking offices was occupied by engine and carriage sheds and a variety of workshops. The various buildings were constructed principally of timber, and practically the whole area of the passenger platforms was covered over. The two departure platforms were on the south side of the carriage approach, the two

arrival platforms being on the north side. They were of timber supported on brick walls, their dimensions being:

Departure platform No 1: 240ft×17ft 6in
Departure platform No 2: 235ft×17ft
Arrival platform No 1: 255ft×25ft
Arrival platform No 2: 340ft×34ft

A feature of the station was the number of turntables and traversers which were used rather than conventional turnouts, in order to economise in space.

By 1850 the need for improved accommodation became urgent, so early the following year the directors proposed the construction of a new 'passsenger departure shed' to the east of Bishop's Road bridge and a new 'merchandise building' north of the existing passenger station, the latter to be used as a four-platform 'arrival shed'. By February 1853 the directors decided that the best course would be to build an entirely new station east of Bishop's Road bridge.

This new station was designed and constructed under Brunel's supervision, with assistance on ornamentation from Matthew Digby Wyatt. The *Illustrated London News* of July 1854 commented: 'The principle adopted by them was to avoid any recurrence to existing styles and to make the experiment of designing everything in accordance with the structural purpose, or nature of the materials employed — iron and cement.'

Three departure and two arrival platforms were provided, with five empty carriage storage roads between. These roads in later years proved invaluable for allowing space for further platforms to be put down. The two inner platforms were used as auxiliary platforms, access being via an ingenious, hydraulically-powered drawbridge, thus avoiding passengers having to mount the steps of a conventional bridge. When both departure platform roads were clear, hydraulic power moved the drawbridge from its storage place below the

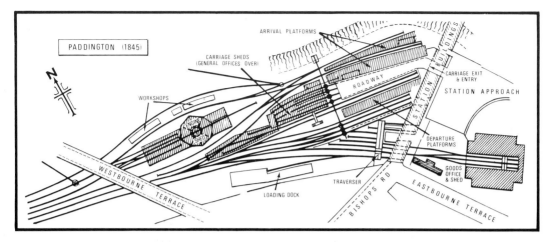

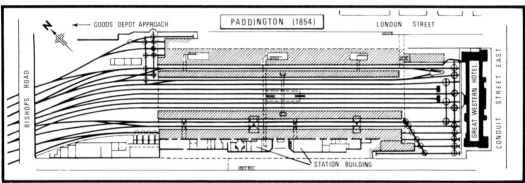

platform and raised it roughly 1ft, enabling passengers to cross from one platform to the other on the level. A narrow subway linking the arrival and departure sides was for the station staff only. As at the first Paddington station, roads were linked by space-saving turntables and traversers.

The *Railway & Travel Monthly* of June 1913, describes the traversers between Platforms 1 & 2 and 3 & 4.

'24ft 10in of the two lines or pairs of rails between these platforms are supported on a movable platform, which also extends beneath each of the platforms, and at either side carries an additional pair of rails, ie four pairs of rails in all. The traverser is held in position by two keys, and when the keys are released and the hydraulic power by which the traverser works is applied, it moves slowly in the direction of either of the platforms as

Below:
Bishop's Road bridge forming the front of the original Paddington station; the passenger platforms being situated beyond. The goods shed and sidings are in the foreground. The present Paddington station was built to the right of this view. *British Railways (WR)*

required, thereby transferring in an expeditious way the vehicles from one line of rails to the other.'

The four turntables on the siding next to the Bishop's Road end of the main departure platform were for loading private carriages in which the owners were to travel. The habit of travelling in private carriages soon died, and by 1867 these turntables had been removed. Similar tables for discharging coaches were provided on the arrival side. What is known today as the 'Lawn' was covered by lines and turntables, with a horse and carriage landing between the hotel and No 1 platform. The larger turntables, 22ft in diameter, were used principally for transferring mail vans from an arrival road to storage sidings, or the departure side. A sector table released engines of incoming trains. Armstrong, Whitworth & Co installed an hydraulic system, Paddington being the first to be so equipped on a large scale. This form of power was used for moving the sector table, larger turntables, passenger drawbridges,

and carriage traversers, in addition to lifting and traction power in the goods depot.

The chief architectural feature of the 1854 station was the splendid roof, influenced by the Crystal Palace built for the Great Exhibition in 1851. It was the first large British station to have a metal roof. *The Life of Isambard Kingdom Brunel* describes it well.

'The interior of the principal part of the station is 700ft long and 238ft wide, divided in its width by two rows of columns into three spans of 69ft 6in, 102ft 6in and 68ft, and crossed at two points by transcepts 50ft wide, which give space for large traversing frames. The roof is very light, consisting of wrought iron arched ribs, covered partly with corrugated iron and partly with the Paxton glass roofing, which Mr Brunel here adopted to a considerable extent. The columns which carry the roof are very strongly bolted down to large masses of concrete, to enable them to resist sideways pressure.

'This station may be considered to hold its own in comparison with the gigantic structures which have since been built, as well as with older stations. The appearance of size it presents is due far more to the proportions of the design than to actual largeness of dimension. The spans of the roof give a very convenient subdivision for a large terminal station, dispensing with numerous supporting columns and at the same time avoiding heavy and expensive trusses. The graceful forms of the Paddington station — the absence of

incongruous ornament and useless buildings —
may be appealed to as a striking instance of
Mr Brunel's taste in architecture and of his
practice of combining beauty of design with
economy of construction.'

The space under the roofing was 700ft×240ft 6in,
containing four platforms and 10 roads. The two
departure platforms measured 27ft and 24ft 6in in
width, those of the arrival side being 21ft and 47ft,
the latter of stone. The *Illustrated London News*
for July 1854 gives details of the roofing.

'The roofing contains 189 wrought iron ribs, or
arches, of an elliptical form, and arranged in rows
of three each, parallel to one another, with twelve
diagonal ribs at the transcepts. The height to the
under side of the ribs in the central opening is
54ft 7in from the line of rails: from the springing it
is 33ft 9in. The height in the side divisions is 46ft.
The ribs against the building are supported by
sixty-three cast-iron pilasters, or square columns,
and those to the other portion of the roofing rest
on sixty longitudinal wrought-iron girders, each
about 30ft long, and supported by sixty-nine
circular columns. The ribs over the central opening
are 1ft 8in high, formed of quarter-inch plate with
flanges top and bottom, giving a width there of
6 inches. The ribs over the side openings are 1ft 4in
high, formed in the same manner. The central half
of each of the curved roofs is glazed, and the other
portion is covered with corrugated galvanised iron.
'There are two transcepts — one a third and the
other two-thirds down the station. Facing the
length of each transcept is a balcony on the office
block.

Above:
**A crowd of passengers leave the original Paddington
station in 1843.** *Courtesy London Illustrated News*

'The execution of the design has been superin-
tended by Mr Brunel, principally through one of
his chief assistants, Mr Charles Gainsford. The
work was done by Messrs Fox, Henderson and
Co.'

The principal buildings, 580ft in length and 30-40ft
in width, were alongside the departure platform

Below:
**A view facing west in 1854, showing the vast train shed.
Bishop's Road bridge can be seen beyond.**
Courtesy London Illustrated News

Above:
The last broad gauge 'Flying Dutchman' waits to leave Paddington on 20 May 1892, headed by *Bulkeley* of Gooch's 'Iron Duke' class. Note the mixed gauge track.
Author's collection

and Spring Street, now Eastbourne Terrace, an additional storey being added in the early years of the 20th century. Management departments used the upper floors, and the traffic department the lower ones. As Queen Victoria used the GWR frequently en route to Windsor, a suite of waiting rooms was provided for her use, with the convenience of direct access from the carriage approach to the station platform. The entrance and exit passages of the suite opened into a central high-domed reception room, on either side of which were the retiring rooms decorated in creamy

white and gold. The Moorish theme in the design was echoed in the decoration of the panels above the windows of the south wall and the cross-bracing just below the roof. The station cost £650,000 and covered eight acres. Its interior was

Below left:
In this view dating from circa 1912, the movable bridge is seen emerging from Platform 1 to give a level link with Platform 2. The latter is of wooden plank construction.
Railway & Travel Monthly

Below:
Moving a van from Platform 2 across to Platform 1, circa 1912, by means of a traverser. The track slides sideways beneath the platform. Note the hydraulically powered capstan for pulling rolling stock.
Railway & Travel Monthly

Above:
Platforms 1 & 2 on the departure side of the station, photographed circa 1905. *Lens of Sutton*

originally painted red and grey. Unlike the other major London termini, Paddington has no imposing exterior facade; indeed it would have been difficult to provide one as the train sheds are fitted into a cutting.

The departure side of the new station was brought into use on 16 January 1854, up trains still terminating at the old station near Bishop's Road bridge until the arrival side opened on 29 May of the same year. Demolition of the original station was then soon completed.

The first significant addition to Paddington was the opening of the mixed gauge Metropolitan

Railway, which the Great Western supported to the tune of £175,000 in order to make a connection with the City of London some four miles distant. Bishop's Road station with a timber overall roof, opened on 10 January 1863, a connection being made with the Paddington arrival platform by means of a corridor and steps. For three years Bishop's Road was the Metropolitan Railway terminus, and for its first seven months was worked by the GWR with broad gauge stock. This

Below:
No 3009 *Flying Dutchman* **leaves Paddington with a down express. No 3009 was built as a 2-2-2 in 1892 but re-built two years later into a 4-2-2, as shown here. On the right-hand side of the photograph is the parcels platform, No 1A.** *Author's collection*

line gave rise to an interesting curiosity. In June 1866 the morning broad gauge train from Windsor through Bishop's Road to the Metropolitan Railway, slipped coaches for Paddington at Westbourne Bridge signalbox, the vehicles free-wheeling into the terminus where they were due three minutes after the main train arrived at Bishop's Road. This peculiar working continued for two years.

It was not until about 1870 that a footbridge at the west end of the main line station linked the arrival and departure platforms and also the corridor to Bishop's Road station. An extension from Bishop's Road station, the Hammersmith & City Railway, opened on 13 June 1864, becoming the joint property of the Great Western and Metropolitan companies in July 1867. Today, Bishop's Road station tends to be overlooked by many passengers who, after getting off a main line train, feel drawn eastwards to the Bakerloo and Circle lines, rather than westwards, and yet it is much closer if they have been travelling at the rear of the train. The Metropolitan Railway between Praed Street Junction and South Kensington was opened in 1868, but not until 1887 did a subway beneath the Royal Hotel offer a direct link between Paddington and Praed Street stations, avoiding the elements and road traffic. The

Above:
Queen Victoria's funeral procession approaches Paddington station on 2 February 1901 down the slope to the arrival side, which was specially chosen for the occasion as its platforms were accessible to vehicles. This view shows the station side of the Great Western Royal Hotel, and in the foreground are the buildings then located on the site of the 1932 offices.
British Railways (WR)

Bakerloo line arrived on 1 December 1913 and was extended to Willesden Junction two years later. Its booking hall is under the cab road between Platforms 8 & 9.

The first standard gauge train arrived at Paddington on 14 August 1861, a public service on this gauge commencing on 1 October giving the GWR through access to the whole of the West Midland Railway, the Taff Vale Railway and much of South Wales. From September 1870 most local trains to and from Paddington were of standard gauge stock, broad gauge expresses continuing until 21 May 1892.

By 1878 traffic had developed to such an extent that additional platform space was necessary and an arrival platform, now No 9, was added. As this cut off access to the cab road, the first overhead cab bridge was provided. In 1884 a further

platform was built on the site of the central carriage roads, the abolition of the broad gauge allowed space for another new platform in 1893. At various times existing platforms were lengthened. The extension to the 1,150ft long No 1 platform, the 960ft No 1A completed in 1908, was used for down excursion trains. As this new platform ran parallel to the down main line, services leaving Platform 1A did not interfere with trains standing at Platform 1. In 1933 Platform 1A became a double-sided parcels platform. Total platform lengths increased from a total of 3,500ft in 1854 to 8,285ft in 1911.

In the winters of the 1890s, freshly cut spring flowers from Cornwall were displayed at the station to advertise the mildness of the winter and the earliness of the spring, in order to entice out-of-season travellers to the Cornish Riviera. About 1900 a huge three-sided clock was erected, the dials of which can be seen from any part of the building.

Christmas 1880 saw the station illuminated by electric light — the second station in London to be so illuminated, the first being Liverpool Street in 1879. The generating plant at the east end of Bishop's Road down platform was supplied by the Anglo-American Brush Electric Light Co. Proving rather unreliable, it lasted less than four years, when the Telegraph Construction & Maintenance Co of which Sir Daniel Gooch was chairman, took over. This was more successful than its predecessor, and the GWR purchased the installation in 1887, but when the generating site was required for an extension of Platform 1 in 1907, current was supplied by the GWR's Park Royal generating station which also supplied power for the Great Western & Metropolitan joint Hammersmith & City lines on which electrical working commenced on 5 November 1906.

An important programme of extensions and improvements was drawn up in 1906, and from 1909 until 1916 work was continuously in progress. The most important additions were three more platforms, these requiring a new train shed of 109ft span on the arrival side, built to match the original structure and increasing the total area of the glass roof to 3½ acres. Erecting the shed involved a great deal of difficult engineering work owing to the limitations of space, ameliorated by appropriating much of the high level coal yard and part of the company's Mint stables. To compensate for the loss of the latter, an additional storey was added to what remained. The height of Platform 12 varied from 3ft to 3ft 9in, the portion at the west end being 3ft high so that it could be used for passenger traffic if required; the central portion being 3ft 4in high for parcels, and the other end 3ft 9in high for milk traffic. Each of the three platform roads was provided with an innovation as far as the Great Western was concerned, in the shape of Ransomes & Rapier hydraulic buffer stops, those at No 10 platform still being in place today. The additional platforms were brought into use between November 1913 and December 1915, with the new train shed being completed the following year. Until 'in and out' working was introduced, Platforms 8 & 9 were the main arrival platforms, having a central road for taxis. On new roadways, Durax paving was used. This consisted of small cubes of granite laid fan-shaped on a concrete foundation, the joints being filled with liquid pitch and cement and affording an excellent foothold for horses.

In 1913 a total of 1,100 parcel carts and 200 mail vans used the 'Lawn' every 24hr, but lines and turntables on the 'Lawn' right up against the hotel were removed for 180ft to make an area for loading parcels for distribution. The 'Lawn' received its name from the fact that it was a grassed area prior to the station being built.

Paddington escaped enemy damage in World War 1, but anti-aircraft shells aimed at an enemy plane fell on the station in March 1918 causing £80-worth of damage to the roof. During World War 1 troop and ambulance trains used the station, and a 24hr-a-day buffet was in operation, with tea being dispensed by female volunteers.

The cast iron columns of Brunel's original roof lasted for 70 years and then Grierson, the company's engineer, rightly felt that if one was struck by a locomotive, the consequences could be disastrous, so between 1915 and 1924 they were replaced by steel hexagonal columns, which support every third roof beam. During this period, the Bakerloo tube of the London Electric Railway was pushed westwards from Edgware Road to Paddington on 1 December 1913. Escalators connected with the main line station, and the tube was extended to Queen's Park in February 1915.

In 1925 the first instalment of the reconstructed Paddington goods station was started, while two years later the Post Office underground railway was opened. More powerful locomotives made the efficient handling of longer trains possible, so platforms were lengthened using pre-cast concrete platform walling and umbrella roofs typical of the period. The edges of the pre-cast units were shaped so that a concrete dowel dropped between two units locked them in a mortarless joint. Paving stones were then laid to form a top surface. 200ft of completed platform could be laid in the quiet hours between midnight and 6.30am.

The Development (Loans Guarantees & Grants) Act of 1929 for the relief of unemployment, provided £1 million for redevelopment work at Paddington, which was started in May 1930 and finished in 1934. This work consisted of extending Platforms 2-11 beyond Bishop's Road bridge as mentioned above; the parcels depot being moved from the 'Lawn' to Platform 1A, with a new parcels depot constructed above in Bishop's Bridge Road, thus releasing the 'Lawn' to become a passenger concourse covered by a new steel and glazed roof. A specially designed digital clock was provided, the largest in the world, with 3ft-high numerals changing every minute. Two new steel framed office blocks were built either side of the 'Lawn', that on the arrival side being in contemporary style. It carried GWR PADDING-

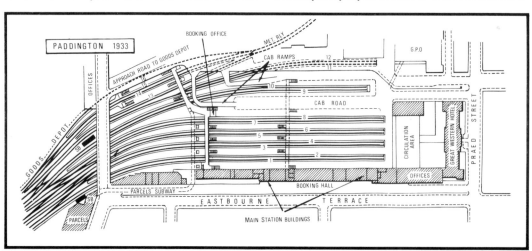

Above:
Another view of platforms 1-4 showing particularly well the detail of the roof construction. *Ian Allan Library*

Platform Number	Length in feet
1	1,150
2	1,125
3	1,125
4	1,050
5	1,050
6	1,000
7	1,035
8	1,200
9	1,200
10	980
11	980
12	750
13	600
14	600
15	600
16	600
Parcels Platform A	930
Parcels Platform A South	580
Total:	**16,555**

TON in 5ft 6in high letters which can still be seen, as well as the building date 1932 in smaller characters. The block on the departure side was constructed in classical tradition to match the earlier buildings. The permanent way was remodelled, while colour light signals and power-worked points replaced mechanical signalling, the track being reconstructed for three-quarters of a mile outside the station; works including the improvement of Ranelagh Bridge engine yard. To cope with the general increase of passenger traffic, especially that serving the fast developing outer suburbs, new platforms were made by rebuilding Bishop's Road station. The former up and down platforms were replaced by two islands and an engine siding provided in connection with changing steam for electric traction to work Great Western trains over Metropolitan lines. From 10 September 1933 the name Bishop's Road was dropped, the platforms becoming Nos 13-16. Platforms 13 and 16 were served by Hammersmith & City electric trains. Platform lengths now were:

On 22 May 1935 Paddington scored another first — the first Crown Post Office on a railway station was opened. An electrically operated train indicator was installed on the 'Lawn' in 1934 and a public address system was put into operation two years later. 1936/37 saw Platforms 5 & 6 resignalled to allow reversible working, necessary because until

'Castle' class 4-6-0 No 5040 *Stokesay Castle* after arrival at Paddington with an up Bristol express on 28 April 1957.
C. R. L. Coles

1968 Paddington arrivals and departures were signalled from separate boxes.

At the outbreak of World War 2 many trains left Paddington with young Londoners being evacuated to the safety of the West Country. In 1941 a parachute landmine demolished part of the departure side and offices, while on 22 March 1944 a V-1 flying bomb damaged the roof and Platforms 6 & 7. Headquarters staff was evacuated during the hostilities to Aldermaston, travelling down and back by special train daily. A fine war memorial by T. S. Tait stands between the doors of the royal waiting room and commemorates the 3,312 men and women of the company who gave their lives during both world wars.

The Coronation Year, 1953, saw Brunel's booking hall adjacent to No 1 platform being replaced by a modern design better able to cope with the three million annual bookings. In 1958 the vista from the 'Lawn' was obstructed across the ends of Platforms 1-8 by a barrier screen bearing the arms of counties served from Paddington. 1963 saw the roof repainted in its original colours of terra cotta and grey.

Intensive use of rolling stock was hampered by the fact that Platforms 1-4 could only be used for departures and Nos 7-11 for arrivals, while Nos 13-16 were shared with London Transport. In steam days, with the use of separate roads for incoming and outgoing empty trains and loco-motives, Paddington could despatch main line trains at 5min headways and on peak summer Saturdays in the 1950s, nine main line trains left between 10.30 and 11.15am. To avoid shunting movements at Paddington, corridor trains were made up daily at Old Oak Common and local trains at West London Carriage Sidings. To turn round main line stock from arrival to departure required a minimum of about 2½hr, whereas 40min was an adequate margin for in and out working. The new scheme allowed a 40min turn-round for locomotive-hauled trains; 20min for a locomotive-hauled train going to depot and 6-9min for a diesel multiple-unit. In and out working saved 70 coaches, two pilot locomotives and 120 staff, many of them signalmen.

Lines were shared with London Transport, because certain GWR passenger trains ran through to Liverpool Street until 15 September 1939, the trains of 10 coaches being close-coupled in order to be accommodated within the limits of the Underground platforms. Freight trains ran to Smithfield until the 1960s. Operating difficulties arose with working diesel multiple-units between the close-headway electric service, and the AWS equipment on DMUs had to be clipped up before reaching the electrified lines, so Platforms 15 & 16 were given over entirely to London Transport use and Platforms 13 & 14 converted to terminal lines.

This work was carried out as part of a £2 million modernisation programme announced in 1965 following the withdrawal of steam traction. Track re-modelling combined with resignalling allowed in and out working to all platforms; complete segregation of the electric lines and raising the speed restriction at many turnouts from 10 to 20mph. Work was planned to be carried out in nine stages between September 1967 and May 1968. The first stage in October/November 1967 saw half the station closed, with West Country and West Midlands trains diverted to Kensington (Olympia); those from Birmingham to Marylebone; some suburban services terminating at Ealing Broadway. On the arrival side, tracks were lowered by 1ft and most platforms reconstructed and raised to a standard height of 3ft. Ninety-six point heaters were installed to prevent delays during cold spells. A new signalbox controlling Paddington was situated at the extended Old Oak Common box, Paddington being the first London terminus to be controlled from a distant location. In 1970 a new ticket office was opened and a new lighter barrier screen was built across the ends of Platforms 1-8 and set 40ft westwards to increase

the passenger circulating area. This was necessary because short turn-rounds of stock meant that accommodation had to be provided for passengers who arrived early, yet could not be allowed on the platform until the train was ready to receive them. Mechanical ramps were fitted to Platforms 1 & 2 to facilitate the loading of cars.

In 1982 a bronze statue of Brunel by John Doubleday was placed on the 'Lawn' and this surveys the scene from the top of a new flight of steps to the Underground station. This new, widened entrance was made in 1986 and set back towards the 'Lawn' to make transfer simpler, smoother and quicker, eliminating congestion caused by passengers queuing at the Circle line ticket office in the subway. On 13 February 1984,

Below:
The impressive appearance of the arrival side was rather wasted as few passengers would have bothered to look back at it as they left. A Southern Railway express parcels van is calling, whilst a large number of taxi cabs stand on the rank between arrival platforms 8 & 9. The date is December 1938 and a *Daily Telegraph* poster bears the headline 'British Reply to German Trade Drive'.
Great Western Railway

BR Western Region headquarters moved from Paddington to Swindon and at the time of writing, the old offices are being gutted and refurbished. This is part of the almost continuous programme of keeping Paddington, the busiest station on the Western Region with 50,000 passengers daily, up-to-date. Since the late 1970s most main line services have been formed of InterCity 125 units, and lengthy trains are largely a thing of the past. As the full length of the platforms was rarely utilised, the buffer stops at Platforms 1-8 were moved 37m further west, increasing the size of the 'Lawn' by 35% — an additional 1,250 square metres, Platforms 9-11 remained at their former lengths to cope with any exceptionally long trains. Small shops have been installed some 15m behind the repositioned buffer stops, providing a useful facility for passengers en route to their trains, as well as brightening that part of the station. A new destination indicator is positioned prominently above the shops and visible from all parts of the concourse. Tractor-hauled trolleys of parcels and mails to Platforms 1-8 have access restricted to only two points, thus limiting their movements across the 'Lawn' to the advantage of passengers. Paddington despatches about 220 tonnes of newspapers every night, the figure rising to 550 tonnes on Saturdays.

The Great Western Royal Hotel

The Great Western Hotel, later the Great Western Royal Hotel, which forms an imposing facade to the station, was built by the GWR and when no one could be found to lease it, Brunel and a few other shareholders 'being unwilling that the hotel should remain empty and be a loss to the proprietors, formed themselves into a company to lease and work the hotel'. Brunel was soon made the hotel company's chairman and their altruistic attitude certainly paid dividends, 10 per cent in fact in the first half year.

Designed by Philip Charles Hardwick in close collaboration with Brunel, it was in the style of Louis XIV. An important structure, Pevsner in the 'Buildings of England' considers it '. . . one of the earliest buildings, if not the earliest building, in England with marked influence from the French Renaissance and Baroque'. With seven storeys high flanking towers, it contained 112 bedrooms and 15 sitting rooms in addition to various public rooms. Many of the sitting rooms were in suites; a feature which was at that period found in great hotels on the continent, but rare in Britain. Another modern touch was that the staircases and passages were fireproof.

On the pediment by John Thomas, a noted sculptor, were carvings characterising peace,

Top:
Dean 'Metro tank' 2-4-0T No 3588 with a rake of six suburban coaches adjacent to the Metropolitan Line platforms of the former Bishop's Road station in 1937. The conductor rails for underground electric stock are clearly visible. *P. F. Winding collection*

Above:
It is 10.15am on a June day in 1935. Passengers are making their way towards the stock of the 'Cornish Riviera', the famous 10.30 departure, at Platform 1. The empty stock had been brought in by the Pannier tank now standing at the buffers. Note the post office and other shops on the left, which rather detract from the grandeur of the station architecture. *Great Western Railway*

plenty, industry and science. The hotel was joined to the station by gangways and a footbridge, luggage being transferred to the departure platform by a trolley mounted on rails set at 4ft centre to centre. The hotel was officially opened by Prince Albert and the King of Portugal.

When the lease expired in 1896, the hotel was taken over by the GWR. Kept up-to-date, it has

always enjoyed every modern facility. By 1907 lifts had been introduced; each of the 165 rooms was equipped with a telephone, while pneumatic tubes also to every room enabled guests swiftly to despatch and receive telegrams, or order food from the kitchen. A 52-bedroom extension was opened in 1936, bathrooms added to most bedrooms and the hotel frontage was simplified by ironwork and window balconies being removed, together with other ornamentation in 1936-38.

Above:
With the imposing edifice of the goods station is the background, 'Castle' class 4-6-0 No 4074 *Caldicot Castle* enters Paddington with an up West of England express.
Locomotive Publishing Co (51518)

Right:
The unprepossessing entrance to Paddington on 25 July 1946. To a modern eye, the line of cars proves more interesting than the station architecture.
Great Western Railway

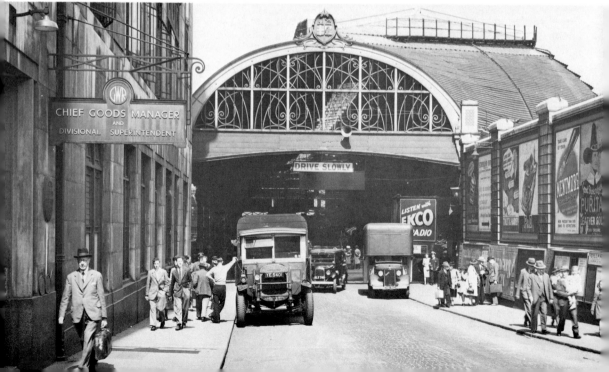

Left:
A 1946 view of the offices built in 1932 on the arrival side of the station, showing also the roof of the northwards extension to the station. The lettering on the office building is 5ft 6in in height. *Great Western Railway*

Below left:
A lively view of entrance/exit on the arrival side of the station on 25 July 1946, with the 1932 offices on the left. *Great Western Railway*

Above right:
A pair of rather grimy 'Castles', Nos 5020 *Trematon Castle* and 5081 *Lockheed Hudson*, arrive at Paddington with an up express. *P. Ransome-Wallis*

Right:
An evening view looking towards the buffers in May 1949, with a 'Modified Hall' standing at Platform 4. *D. J. Sutton*

Below:
A fine view of the station roof and platform canopies, seen from above the Bishop's Road bridge in September 1951. *M. W. Earley*

Left:
On 24 March 1951, No 4096 *Highclere Castle* stands at Platform 9 with the empty coaching stock for a Bristol express, whilst No 6005 *King George II* has arrived at Platform 9 with the 7.30am from Shrewsbury.
Brian Morrison

Below left:
'County' class 4-6-0 No 1008 *County of Cardigan* draws empty coaching stock away from the arrival side.
C. G. Pearson

Right:
On 2 May 1959 the 'Brunel Centenarian' was run by the Railway Correspondence & Travel Society to mark the centenary of the Royal Albert Bridge, Saltash. The seven-coach train is seen awaiting departure from Platform 5 at Paddington behind 'Castle' No 7001 *Sir James Milne*. Detail of the roof and its elegant support columns is well-illustrated in this view, with the large station clock visible in the background. *P. F. Winding*

Below:
A familiar sight for many years on the lines around Paddington were the '9700' class condensing Pannier tanks based at Old Oak Common. On 4 July 1959 No 9703 draws empty coaching stock out of Platform 5 past a set of colour light signals. In the background 'Modified Hall' No 6962 *Soughton Hall* awaits its departure time.
C. R. L. Coles

Above left:
'Britannia' Pacific No 70019 *Lightning* **of Cardiff Canton shed stands at Platform 8 after arrival with the up 'Red Dragon' on 10 September 1960.** *Dennis C. Ovenden*

Left:
Platform 1 at 11.40pm in the early 1960s with the Penzance sleeping car train waiting to leave.
G. F. Heiron

Above:
The old and the new at Paddington on New Year's Day 1964. On the left No 7029 *Clun Castle* **waits with the 9.15am to Worcester at Platform 4, while 'Western' class No D1039** *Western King* **leaves Platform 3 with the 9.10am to Wolverhampton.** *P. J. Lynch*

Right:
Part of the station not normally seen by the public — the lift shaft heads in July 1986. *Author*

Right:
The directors' balcony facing one of the transcepts. On either side of the war memorial are doors leading to the Royal Waiting Room, with the royal coat of arms on the left and the GWR coat of arms on the right. *Author*

Below:
The glory of former days is recreated on 16 July 1978 with the Great Western Society's Vintage Train of restored GWR carriages standing at Platform 4 prior to departure on a special train to Kingswear. *John Titlow*

Far right:
The imposing facade of the Great Western Hotel, viewed in 1854. *Author's collection*

Bottom right:
The immaculate, ornate interior of the Great Western Royal Hotel on 6 September 1922. *British Railways*

Engine Sheds and Locomotives

The first shed was a roundhouse plus four-road shed immediately west of the arrival platforms. Closed in March 1855, its site being required for the approach to the new station, it was replaced by a long four-road shed at Westbourne Park. A three-road shed was added in 1862, and another of the same size 11 years later. It closed 17 March 1906 when Old Oak Common opened three miles from Paddington. Designed by G. J. Churchward, Old Oak Common was the largest shed on the GWR and a prototype internal turntable depot and really four combined roundhouses, each with 28 radiating roads. An electric traverser gave access to the 12-road repair shed. The shed closed to steam on 22 March 1965. Old Oak Common diesel maintenance shed opened in October 1965, one of the turntables from the steam depot being retained to give access to the stabling roads. A HST depot opened 10 years later. There was also a turntable and locomotive yard at Ranelagh Bridge just outside Paddington station which engines could use when turn-round time was short.

Singles of various classes worked nearly all Paddington passenger trains until 1894 when 4-4-0 Armstrongs appeared, followed by various other 4-4-0s, and 'Saints' and 'Stars' in the next decade and by Collett's 4-6-0s. 'Britannia' Pacifics arrived at Old Oak Common in 1951, principally being used on Bristol trains. The last steam-hauled working to leave Paddington on a regular passenger service was the 16.15 to Banbury on 11 June 1965 hauled by No 7029 *Clun Castle*. Local trains were worked by 'Metro' 2-4-0Ts, 4-4-2Ts appearing in 1905 on fast services to Reading, semi-fasts to High Wycombe and on a variety of slower services. The '6100' class 2-6-2Ts, built specially to work accelerated London suburban services, appeared in 1931, lasting until dieselisation just over 26 years later. Today 110 HST services use Paddington every 24 hours.

A frequent visitor was GWR diesel railcar No 17 placed in service on 4 May 1936 to improve the punctuality of stopping passenger trains in the district, as henceforth parcels were carried by railcar instead. It worked as far as Oxford. A second car, No 34, appeared on 15 September 1941. These were the ancestors of the present Class 128 motor parcels vans W 55991/2 allocated to Reading.

The only regular 'foreign' working into Paddington was a return Paddington-Brighton by an LBSCR locomotive and rolling stock to avoid passengers having to transfer between termini. It started on 2 July 1906. Although the service was widely advertised, its popularity rapidly declined, and with the train showing a loss, it was withdrawn one year after its introduction.

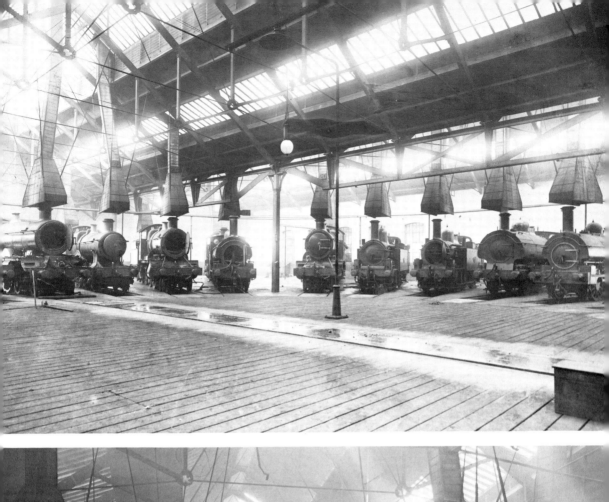

Reading

Reading was, and is, an important station and junction; the busiest station on the Western Region after Paddington and the second highest revenue earner. An average of 30,000 passengers use the station daily, with up to 4,000 people changing trains. All GWR trains to the West of England passed through, as did those to South Wales, Gloucester and Cheltenham, Worcester and Hereford, and until the opening of the Princes Risborough line in 1910, Birmingham, Shrewsbury, the Midlands and North Wales and Birkenhead trains too, in fact most GWR expresses went through Reading. Furthermore, the importance of the route from the Midlands to the South coast via Basingstoke must not be overlooked.

The railway made a poor start at Reading. Six days before the station opened, a whirlwind blew the roof off the train shed, carrying workman William West for 200ft until the roof struck an office chimney hurling him into a trench and causing fatal injury. The line from Twyford opened on 30 March 1840, the *Reading Mercury* reporting:

'At the Station House every accommodation was afforded the spectators that could be reasonably expected or desired by them, the extensive platform immediately adjoining the offices having

been thrown open to the public and seats provided, in a most handsome manner for their convenience.'

The down station house was almost complete and preparations were made for building that at the up station. Some passengers who were not used to railway procedure thought that they could arrive seconds before scheduled departure, the *Mercury* having to print the warning:

'It is highly important that the public should bear in mind the absolute necessity of passengers procuring their ticket at least five minutes before the departure of each train.'

The line was extended to Steventon on 1 June, while a branch from a junction just west of Reading station opened to Hungerford on 21 December 1847, eventually extended to become a cut-off to the West of England via Westbury. A branch from Southcote Junction to Basingstoke and the LSWR opened on 1 November 1848.

Reading was the first, and also the longest lived, of the one-sided stations which Brunel designed for towns which lay to one side of the railway. To avoid passengers having to cross the line, and enabling through trains to run clear of the station, he made the startling innovation of having

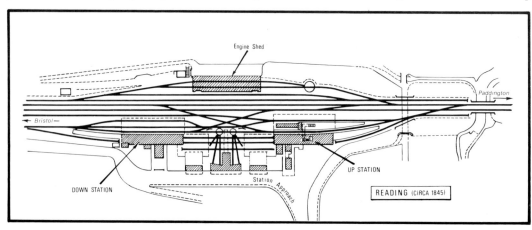

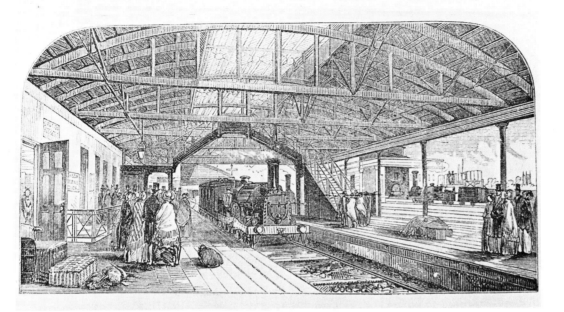

Above:
An up train arrives at Reading station circa 1850. The roof of the down station is visible in the distance, with the engine shed on the right-hand side. *George Meason/ Author's collection*

separate up and down platforms on the same length of track. Logically the up station was nearest London. Some London Directors anticipated problems with conflicting train movements quite unavoidable with the scheme and Brunel was

Below:
Double framed 4-4-0 No 3560 stands on one of the centre roads at Reading in 1922. The locomotive was originally built as a broad gauge convertible 0-4-4T, altered to standard gauge the following year, and rebuilt as a 4-4-0 in 1899. *M. W. Earley*

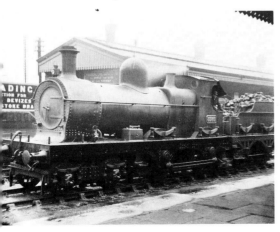

asked 'to submit another plan for Reading Station with sheds either side', but a week later they gave in to his persuasion and adopted the plan. In pre-interlocking days, conflicting movements certainly gave rise to danger, on one occasion the approaching 'Flying Dutchman', mistaken for a stopping train, was diverted to the platform road, passing through the turnout at 55mph, only the stability of the broad gauge preventing an accident. Both up and down stations had a large, square brick building in the style of a town house with unusually solid-looking chimney bases, reminiscent of a graveyard monument. An awning sheltered the south front, and a 200ft-long train shed lay to the north, supported on cast iron columns. Open on three sides, the shed had a corrugated iron roof with a very flat arch. The site being newly-made ground, the building rested on rows of wooden piles. On the night of 12 October 1853 the open iron flap of a goods van on a train from Basingstoke struck and broke each of the outer columns causing the roof of the down shed to collapse. It was replaced by a temporary structure. In 1861 up and down platforms were linked, the roof of the new section being of tarred felt on rough wooden posts.

On 1 October 1861 the line from Reading West Junction to Paddington was converted to mixed gauge; Oxford to Reading West Junction having enjoyed mixed gauge from 22 December 1856 to allow through running to the LSWR at Basingstoke. To avoid the need for additional rails through the station complex, narrow wooden platforms were erected either side of the main line

for standard gauge trains. The GWR also built a standard gauge line from West Junction, it descending the embankment on a gradient of 1 in 40 and passed under the main line to gain the South Eastern Railway tracks. Goods traffic from the Midlands and North began on 1 December 1858.

1863 saw Reading Corporation register a complaint regarding the poor condition of the station. The Great Western taking no action, the following year the subject arose in Reading Quarter Sessions, the station's inconveniences and the potential for a major accident being listed. In 1867 the directors decided to build a new facade. Of Italianate style, it was constructed of buff brick with a row of well-proportioned pedimented windows above the canopy. The central clock tower was surmounted by a finial, an enlarged copy of those used on contemporary semaphore

Above:
A view of Reading station looking east in 1919, showing the typical GWR umbrella-roofed island platforms. The information on the nameboard stresses the station's importance, announcing that it is the junction for Newbury and the Devizes line, and for the Basingstoke branch. *L&GRP (8572)*

signals. This tower, although at one time the tallest building in the vicinity, is now made insignificant by tower blocks. Work was finished in May 1868 and although cosmetically the station had a neat exterior, the working side still suffered from the cumbersome one-sided arrangement.

Below:
No 4921 *Eaton Hall* **leaves Reading with a Portsmouth-Birmingham Snow Hill express.**
Real Photographs (T5053)

In 1896 a contract was signed with Pattison of Westminster to rebuild the station in brick and stone at a cost of £6,000. J. C. Inglis, the Great Western chief engineer, introduced the policy of not building train sheds at intermediate stations as they had been found to be a costly mistake — expensive in repairs, with little or no gain in comfort in return for the outlay. When the new station finished, it took the public some time to get used to this innovation, W. J. Scott commenting in an 1899 *Railway Magazine* that '. . . even so fine a station as the new Reading, for lack of an overall roof, looks only a magnified and glorified "roadside intermediate" '. In 1897 the old platform was demolished to be replaced by no fewer than 10 new platforms.

The down main platform (No 1) 960ft in length and 30ft wide, had at its western end a double bay 400ft in length with three bay lines accommodating trains for the Berks & Hants and Basingstoke branches. Platform 2 arrival and Nos 3 & 4 departure were an island 1,150ft in length and 50ft at its broadest, its length only being exceeded on the Great Western by Taunton. This island platform was pierced at each end by a single bay from which ran local trains to London and Didcot respectively. The up relief platform, 900ft×20ft was the shortest of the three, the bay line and the two goods lines beyond transforming it into an island. A spacious well-lit subway 300ft in length gave access to the platforms, an additional booking office being sited at its Caversham end. Today there is an additional exit from the subway to the Alder Valley bus station. Hydraulic lifts dealt with luggage. One curiosity of the new layout was that an up express not calling at the station could by-pass the platform, but inconsistently, this facility was unavailable to down trains, though

Above:
At the other end of the station, No 6938 *Corndean Hall* passes the East box with an up Cheltenham service.
M. W. Earley

today's signalling system allows a non-stop down train to run through on the up main. Another problem particularly frustrating on summer Saturdays when a procession of reliefs had to be handled, was that a fast train from Newbury not stopping at Reading and an up express from Didcot booked to call, had to use the same stretch

Below:
On 29 July 1951, No 7022 *Hereford Castle* passes Reading at speed with the 4.55pm Paddington-Cardiff, and leads its 11-coach train through the complex junction at the west end of the station. *M. W. Earley*

of track for 120yd. Umbrella roofs supported on riveted iron columns sheltered the platforms, which were lit by incandescent gas lamps. Buildings on the island platforms were of red brick with blue brick around windows and doors. The roof was glazed in front of the buildings, but unlike similar roofs at Taunton and Newport, the glass is semi-opaque and hardly admits sufficient light. Two large signalboxes controlled the layout: West box, at the time of its construction the largest of the GWR, was 100ft in length, 20ft wide and contained 185 levers, needing three signalmen and a telegraphist on each shift. The East box contained 115 levers.

North-west of the station was the signal works, in 1906 covering eight acres and employing over 500 men. Four-wheel petrol locomotive No 27 shunted sidings at the works from 1926 until its withdrawal in 1960.

A shorter and better placed junction line with the SER than the old line through the goods yard, was made from the east end of the GWR station straight from the main lines, forming a double road connection, which was opened on 17 December 1899.

Passenger and parcel receipts for 1912 amounted to £128,406, the number of passengers being booked was 539,082. In 1913 the stationmaster's staff numbered 278 in summer and 276 in winter. In summer the station was provided with an extra inspector and an additional ticket collector.

As neither of the connections with the SR were ideal for through heavy World War 2 traffic, yet another connection was put in, this time further east. To avoid building a new signalbox at this junction, a miniature power frame with all-electric interlocking was installed at Reading East Main signalbox, all new points and signals being electrically operated. As Westinghouse had not previously supplied signals to the GWR and time was pressing, the posts sported Great Central pattern finials which were the closest type available. This spur was opened on 1 June 1941.

The Reading MAS scheme came into operation on 26 April 1965, the box being on the north side of the station, the lower walls of blue brick and the upper part timber. The line to the fish dock at the east end of the down main was electrified, numbered Platform 4A and brought into use for two-way working on 5 September 1965 enabling the adjacent Reading South station to be closed. On 4 May 1975 a second electrified bay, No 4B, was brought into use avoiding the difficulties resulting from Waterloo and Redhill trains having to use the same bay. Reading is one of the few

Below:
Looking in the opposite direction, 'Modified Hall' No 6977 *Grundisburgh Hall* **in British Railways mixed traffic lined black livery approaches Reading on 13 April 1952 with a Cheltenham-Paddington train.** *M. W. Earley*

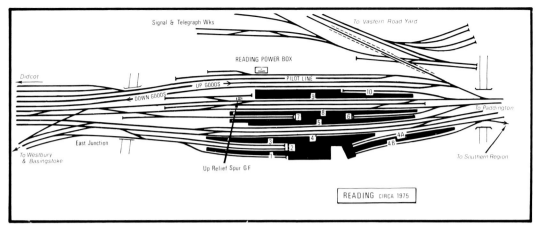

Signal & Telegraph Wks

To Vastern Road Yard

READING POWER BOX

Didcot

PILOT LINE

UP GOODS

DOWN GOODS

9

10

To Paddington

7   8   6
      5

East Junction

3   4   4A
  1 2   4B

To Westbury
& Basingstoke

Up Relief Spur GF

To Southern Region

READING CIRCA 1975

stations where all bays are still in use and none have been lifted or put to other use.

Spring 1967 saw a new feature bringing more custom to the station — the interchange with the coach link along the M4 to Heathrow Airport. By 1973 there were more than 250,000 Railair passengers annually, the station's reception lounge having to be extended to cope. Trains also run hourly to Gatwick Airport. In addition to VDU screens giving travel information, there are electrically moved slats, while manual indicators are situated at the ends of both sets of bay platforms at the end of No 4. The subway has an indicator displaying the platform from which the next fast train to Paddington departs.

Passenger traffic at Reading has grown to such an extent due to the area's buoyant business base, coupled with a frequent service to London and an increased flow of Railair passengers, that the station facilities have become inadequate. For example, queues form in the rather congested

Below:

On 4 January 1959 'Large Prairie' No 6102 storms away from Reading with the 10.12 Sundays only service to Paddington. *J. C. Beckett*

booking hall. At the time of writing, work is proceeding on a £50 million joint development of the 25 acre site, Councillor Janet Bond, Mayor of Reading, cutting the first sod with a JCB digger on 1 July 1986. Costs are being partly met by the sale of a freehold office site. The rest is borne by BR which has planned a 1,600 space multi-storey car park to the north of the station and linked to it by bridge; a 70,000sq ft retail warehouse and a mechanical letter sorting office for the Post Office with a subway link to the station; Reading being a

Left:
No 5943 *Elmdon Hall* arrives at Platform 5 on 2 August 1960 with a Weymouth-Paddington train.
Dennis C. Ovenden

Below left:
On the same day No 4082 *Windsor Castle* approaches the station with a Paddington-Hereford service. The up bay platform is visible to the left of the photograph.
Dennis C. Ovenden

Below:
No 7027 *Thornbury Castle* stands on the centre road on the north side of the station in August 1963.
J. E. MacDonald

concentration point for mail for re-sorting and despatch to Berkshire, Buckinghamshire, Greater London, Oxfordshire and Wiltshire. A new building on the site of the present car park and the former SR station will have a concourse; 10 position ticket office; travel centre; bureau de change; telephone enquiry office; Railair lounge and better catering and left luggage facilities. Completion of this is scheduled for May 1988. The present Grade II listed building will be refurbished to contain a waiting lounge, coffee bar and BR office accommodation.

The goods depot built in 1880 on the site of the former engine shed, had to be moved to make room for extending the passenger station, a new goods depot being opened north-east of the passenger station below the level of the main line. It had two platforms, each capable of accommodating 20 wagons, and the cranes were hydraulically worked. A large grain warehouse was over the shed, and the western end accommodated the offices in which worked 39 clerks. Principal traffic was biscuits from Huntley & Palmer, seeds from Messrs Sutton & Son, beer from H&G Simonds, and Elders & Fyffe bananas.

Top:
On 11 September 1961, No 5076 *Gladiator* **waits to take over from 'Schools' class 4-4-0 No 30917** *Ardingly***, which has arrived with the Margate, Ramsgate and Hastings-Wolverhampton train, which it has worked from Redhill.** *R. N. Jones*

Above:
Towards the end of steam operations, former LSWR Urie 'S15' No 30499 passes through the station with an up freight on 2 February 1963. Reading South station can be seen on the left of the picture, below the level of the GWR station. *L. Sandler*

Right:
Work in progress at the east end of Reading General on 19 April 1965 building the connection from the Southern lines into the new Platform 4A. This was in preparation for the closure in September 1965 of Reading South, situated on the right of this picture. In the foreground can be seen the remains of the former short parcels bay at the London end of Platform 4, which was replaced by Platform 4A. *L. Nicholson*

Below:
An unusual and very interesting view of Reading station on 28 April 1970 from the cab of Class 52 'Western' No 1022 *Western Sentinel* which is approaching Platform 4, the down main platform, at the head of the 'Cornish Riviera'. Another 'Western' awaits the right-away from Platform 5 with the 07.25 Plymouth-Paddington, whilst 2-BIL unit No 2025 leads a Reading-Waterloo train out of Platform 4A. The block in the background is Western Tower, the divisional manager's offices. *G. P. Cooper*

Left:
The main station building, with the buffet and bar on the left, photographed from Platform 5 during the 1970s. *C. J. Leigh*

Below:
Reading General station seen from the top of Western Tower in May 1970. A Class 52 approaches Platform 4 with a down express, whilst an electric multiple-unit climbs the bank towards Platform 4A. On the right of the picture a car park occupies the site of the former Southern Railway Reading South station. The connection from the Southern line can be seen in the distance, to the east of the station. During the 1970s a further platform, No 4B, was added adjacent to No 4A in order to accommodate Gatwick services. *D. E. Canning*

Right:
An 1890-1900 riveted canopy support pylon, photographed on 13 June 1986, showing signs of age at its base. *Author*

Engine Sheds and Locomotives

The two-road shed opposite the passenger station opened in March 1840. Closed in 1880 to make room for a goods depot, it was replaced by a roundhouse built in the apex between the Didcot and Newbury lines, a four-road carriage shed being built close by. In 1930 the turntable was repositioned and the shed converted to a straight nine-road type which closed to steam on 2 January 1965. A diesel depot was opened to the southwest of the steam shed in August 1959.

Many of the locomotive workings will be found under the heads of other stations. In 1921 the local passenger service to Didcot and Oxford was worked by older 4-4-0s and 2-4-0s; 4-4-0 'Flowers' headed Worcester expresses, with 4-4-0 'Counties' on semi-fasts to Oxford, Swindon and Weymouth. 4-4-2Ts worked most of the Reading-Paddington trains and also the Temple Meads-Paddington section of the 1.35pm ex-Taunton, often loaded to 10-12 coaches. 4-4-2 French compounds hauled Oxford and Swindon fasts and cross-country runs to Basingstoke and the LSWR. In the autumn of 1921, 2-8-0 No 4700 worked the 9.15pm Paddington-South Wales express, while Pacific No 111 *The Great Bear* headed the 9.5pm down Mail to Bristol. In the period 1924-31 older 2-4-0s and 4-4-0s were withdrawn from stopping passenger trains, being replaced by 2-6-0s. From 1930 these in turn were displaced by 'Halls', members of this class working Weymouth and Reading-Paddington fasts, Oxford and Basingstoke trains and many slow passengers and goods. '6100' class 2-6-2Ts edged out the 4-4-2Ts.

Left:
A particularly good view of Reading locomotive depot in the early years of the 20th century. A 4-4-0 'County' class locomotive and several double-framed 4-4-0s are standing in front of the shed, with an 'Aberdare' class 2-6-0 on the connecting spur to the left of the picture. *Ian Allan Library*

Above left:
'Castle' class No 5076 *Gladiator* at Reading MPD, its home shed, on 22 September 1962. *J. R. Carter*

Above:
Two former GWR 4-6-0s, Nos 6990 *Witherslack Hall* and 7817 *Garsington Manor* await their next duties at Reading depot.
J. R. Carter

— 3 —

Bristol

The first proposal to link Bristol, then the second city in the kingdom, with the Capital, was the London & Bristol Rail-Road Co put forward in 1824. In the autumn of 1832, four Bristolians met in Temple Back, on the site of the later goods depot, formed a committee and appointed the young Brunel as engineer. The GWR's Bristol Board of Directors worked independently, though in conjunction with the corresponding London Board, and the line from Temple Meads to Bath was opened on 31 August 1840, the first train leaving behind *Fireball*. That day a total of 5,880 passengers were carried in 10 trains, takings amounting to £476 and comparing very favourably with £226 when the line opened from Paddington to Maidenhead. On completion of Box Tunnel, the line was opened throughout from Bristol to London on 30 June 1841.

Meanwhile the Bristol & Exeter extended the broad gauge westwards and on 1 June 1841 *Fireball* left with the first train to Bridgwater, the line being opened to the public 13 days later. Exeter was reached on 1 May 1844. Another broad gauge company, the Bristol & Gloucester, opened on 8 July 1844, completing a chain of rail communications from Newcastle-upon-Tyne to Exeter. The Bristol & Gloucester was taken over by the Midland Railway the following year and this being a standard gauge company, for operating convenience it wished to operate only on one gauge, the standard being first brought to Bristol on 29 May 1854.

Bristol needed better communication with Cardiff — only 25 miles away as the crow flies, but 93 by rail. The Bristol & South Wales Union Railway opened from Bristol to New Passage Pier on 25 August 1863, a ferry carrying passengers to Portskewett Pier where a branch linked with the South Wales Railway. In addition to through journeys, it also generated a certain amount of local traffic since it served parts of Bristol's northern suburbs. The ferry was of little use for freight and certainly no good for mineral traffic, so the Severn Tunnel, which remains Britain's longest railway tunnel, was built and opened to passengers on 1 December 1886. Bristol was now a very

important railway centre with lines radiating to London, Birmingham, Cardiff and Exeter. Two cut-offs relieved the station of unnecessary through traffic, the opening of the Wootton Bassett-Filton line being on 1 May 1903 and Castle Cary-Cogload Junction on 11 June 1906.

Clifton Down was reached on 1 October 1874 and the line extended to Sneyd Park Junction on 24 February 1877, giving access to Avonmouth Docks over the Bristol Port Railway & Pier, a rather odd line which until that date had not been linked to the rest of the British railway system. A branch was opened from Bristol to Portishead on 18 April 1867 and to Radstock and the North Somerset coalfield on 3 September 1873, through working to Frome taking place the following June. All GWR lines in the Bristol area were mixed gauge by June 1874 and those of the Bristol & Exeter within the following year.

The terminal station at Temple Meads is one of the finest examples in the country of an early station built in an imposing style to inspire the confidence of both investors and travellers, the 184ft-long Tudor facade facing Temple Gate giving the impression of a gentleman's country seat. It has angle turrets and a central oriel, above which are the arms of the cities of London and Bristol, which were adopted by the company for its own arms. Originally there were two flanking gateways but the right hand one has been removed. The office block and train shed are built in limestone, some being from rubble extracted when Box Tunnel was being cut. The train shed has an impressive timber cantilever roof of 72ft span unsupported by any crosstie or abutment, being carried on octagonal iron piers and is without parallel elsewhere in early railway architecture, a greater achievement even than the present Paddington which was started 13 years later. Each principal was formed of two frameworks like cranes, meeting in the centre of the roof, the weight being carried on the octagonal columns and the tail ends of the frames held down by the side walls, the hammerbeams being purely decorative. As the two tail ends did not press against each other where they met, there was no outward

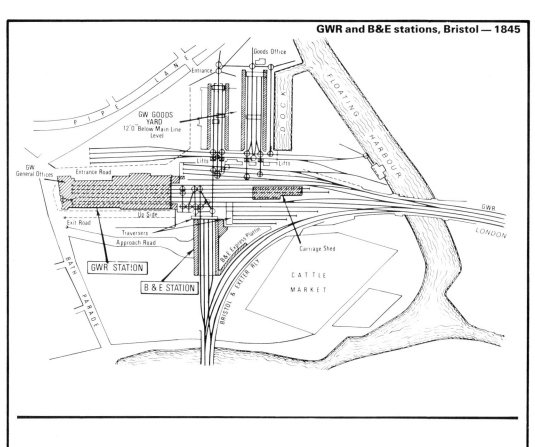

GWR and B&E stations, Bristol — 1845

Goods Office

Entrance

P I P E L A N E

GW GOODS
YARD
12'0" Below Main Line
Level

Lifts   Lifts

GW
General Offices

Entrance Road

GW
General Offices

Up Side

B & E Express Platfm

Traversers

Approach Road

Exit Road

GWR STATION

B & E STATION

Carriage Shed

C A T T L E
M A R K E T

BRISTOL & EXETER RLY

D O C K

F L O A T I N G   H A R B O U R

GWR

LONDON

B A T H   P A R A D E

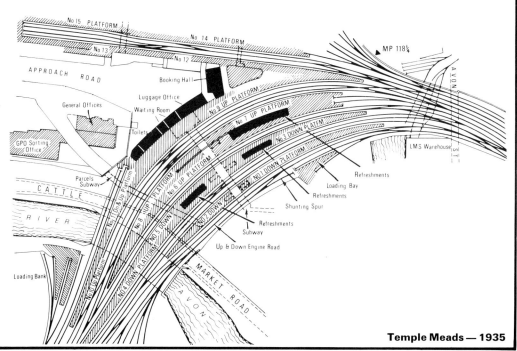

No 15 PLATFORM

No 14 PLATFORM

No 13

No 12

MP 118¼

A P P R O A C H   R O A D

Booking Hall

Luggage Office

Waiting Room

General Offices

Toilets

GPO Sorting
Office

Parcels
Subway

No 9 UP PLATFORM

No 7 UP PLATFORM

No 3 DOWN PLATFM

No 1 DOWN PLATFORM

LMS Warehouse

A V O N   S T

Refreshments

Loading Bay

Refreshments

Shunting Spur

Refreshments

Subway

Up & Down Engine Road

C A T T L E
R I V E R

A V O N

No 10 Dn & Up Platform

No 8 UP PLATFORM

No 6 UP PLATFORM

No 5 DOWN

No 2 DOWN PLATFORM

M A R K E T   R O A D

Loading Bank

No 10 Up Platform

No 4 DOWN PLATFORM

Temple Meads — 1935

47

thrust. Being set so close to the platform edge, the piers were rather an obstruction to passengers, but matters were improved when, following the abolition of broad gauge, the platforms could be widened.

The glazed roof covered the distance of 220ft, almost the whole length of the platforms. At the terminal end of the shed, the flat, low ceiling was supported by closely-spaced slender iron columns, this being an engine shed — a rare, if not unique position. Because of the necessity to give clearance to water-borne traffic, the station had to be built 15ft above ground level. The booking office was on the ground floor, passengers having to mount stairs to the platform. First and second class staircases were provided as well as separate waiting rooms.

As B&E trains had to be reversed in or out of the station, it opened a terminus at right angles to that of the GWR. A simple timber train shed, it lacked the grandeur of its GWR counterpart and because of its construction and position near the cattle market, was popularly referred to as the 'cow shed'. An 'express platform' was built on the double track curve linking the two railways and although situated on the up line, it was used by trains in either direction — in other words, it was yet another one-sided station.

In October 1854 the B&E opened a splendid office block to the south of the station approach. Designed by F. C. Fripp whose initials are carved high on its north side, the building is of symmetrical Jacobean design with shaped gables and twin towers with Ogee caps. It now contains various BR offices.

By 1865 the two platforms in the Great Western terminus were insufficient to deal with GWR and MR traffic, and a separate station for B&E trains was far from ideal. That year the three companies obtained an Act to build a new joint station, though disputes regarding the proportionate cost delayed the start for six years, and a further six were required for the actual building. The B&E terminus was demolished and a great curved train shed with a span of 125ft (23ft more than the largest span at Paddington) was built on the site of the former express platform, Vernon & Evans of the Central Iron Works, Cheltenham, being appointed contractors for the metalwork. Brunel's original train shed was doubled in length, the architect sympathetically using a similar style to Brunel's original, but with roof supports in metal and using thin ties. The office block and main entrance in Draycot stone is very pleasing and continues Brunel's Tudor style. It has a 100ft high clock tower, but the destruction of its high pitched cap by German raiders in 1941 gave it a lighter appearance. Sir Matthew Digby Wyatt, an old friend of Brunel, who had assisted with the 1854 Paddington station, was chief architect for the

extension, though Francis Fox of the B&E took a share; the green and gold exterior canopy, almost certainly his design, being virtually identical to his at Weston-super-Mare. Each company had its own booking office within the Great Hall, passengers for the respective companies entering by their own doors, a scroll above each bearing the appropriate legend. Inside the entrance doors are pinewood porters' booths, but the imposing pine entrance doors have been removed as they had to be left open, causing the hall to be cold and draughty in winter and in their place are automatic opening swing doors.

The first section of the new station opened on 6 July 1874. Platforms 1-4 were in the new train shed, No 1 (the down main) being 286yd long and Nos 2-4 each of 143yd, the island platform being mainly used by down Midland Railway trains, facilitating interchange as passengers merely had to walk across the platform to a down GWR train. Platform 4 was the GWR up main; Nos 5 and 6 were the lengthened arrival platform of the original terminus, its outer end being used for MR departures and the inner for New Passage, or later, South Wales trains. Platform 7 was for arriving and departing Clifton Down and Avonmouth trains. Refreshment rooms were built in the apex between the old and new stations.

So fast had traffic developed that even before completion, the station was inadequate. The bridge over the New Cut was widened so that the down platform could be lengthened and a down bay brought into use in October 1892, while the removal of the broad gauge lines allowed an additional island platform to be added in 1898. By the 1920s at Bank Holiday periods trains were held in block from Highbridge waiting for a platform at Temple Meads, and on summer Saturdays between 1920 and 1930 it was not unknown for local trains from Bath and Radstock to take two hours for the last mile into the station, while on at least one occasion it was 3hr 20min. At all times the shortness of some of the platforms added to the delay, since trains had to draw forward and stop in order to bring the last vehicles to a platform. As at Paddington, in 1929 the Loans & Guarantees Act gave an opportunity to improve the situation. P. E. Culverhouse more than doubled the station's size by building on the site of the down approach road. Shanks & McEwan of Glasgow, the main contractors, began work in November 1930. The roofs of the new platforms were of the usual umbrella type, buildings being of white or brown carrara bricks on a grey concrete plinth. The enlargement was completed in December 1935, the new layout having five up and five down platforms, a bay for Portishead trains and four platforms in the old terminus. In three places scissors crossings were provided between a

SOUTH EAST VIEW OF THE GREAT WESTERN RAILWAY TERMINUS, BRISTOL.

Left:
The imposing frontage of the Great Western Railway terminus at Temple Meads, viewed from the south-east circa 1840 is an engraving by J. Harris.
Author's collection

Below:
The interior of Brunel's train shed in broad gauge days with some 'hand shunting' in progress.
L&GRP (19851)

platform and an adjacent through road so that two trains could be accommodated simultaneously along one platform face. Platforms 3 and 4 were 1,300ft in length, 7 and 8 were 1,050ft and 9 and 10 were 1,370ft. Passengers reached their platform via a 300ft long and 30ft wide subway, this also giving access to hairdressing salons and baths. Parcels had a specially dedicated subway. Rather surprisingly in view of the fact that Paddington had been electrically lit since 1880, gas lighting was used for the new platforms and remained in use until 1960 when it was replaced by fluorescent tubes.

The signalling was renewed in 1935, Bristol Temple Meads East power box being the largest on the GWR and had 368 'levers' which were actually slides. It had 23 block bells, each having a different tone. The building still looked modern when replaced by an MAS box 35 years later. Bristol West box had 328 levers and was also

Above:
A close-up of the previous illustration, showing the elegant construction of the train shed roof, and the inconvenient columns originally close to the platform edge. *L&GRP*

Right:
Brunel's train shed in the background, viewed in October 1965 from beneath Wyatt's extension of 1878. *Author*

manned by three men and a boy. The MAS scheme allowed platforms to have two-way working, while through programming of locomotives largely obviated engine changes at Temple Meads, reducing the number of movements required and also cutting the time spent at a platform from 18min in 1938 to 4min in 1976.

In 1940/41 the station received several hits by German bombs, one burning out the booking office, which was temporarily replaced by army

huts in the station approach. Cellars below the station were used as an emergency centre for key rail personnel and as an air raid shelter for passengers and staff.

Contraction of traffic in the 1960s caused Brunel's train shed to become redundant for railway purposes and it was closed on 12 September 1965, becoming a car park. The Grade I listed building was handed by BR to the Brunel Engineering Centre Trust on a 99-year peppercorn lease on 29 September 1981. The Trust is engaged in a 10-year work programmed to restore the station and create a new exhibition centre for civil engineering of all kinds.

Left:
2-4-0 No 73 *Isis* leaving the new Temple Meads station with a down stopping train. *M. J. Tozer collection*

Below left:
An early view of the new GWR Temple Meads station of 1878. *Author's collection*

Below:
An up royal train leaves Brunel's terminus in the early 1920s hauled by No 4082 *Windsor Castle*.
M. J. Tozer collection

Temple Meads had a superintendent in place of a stationmaster, the position being filled alternately by the GWR and LMS. He was only responsible for operation and the station fabric, the guards' inspector, parcel agent and passenger manager all enjoying autonomy. W. Orton (LMS) was succeeded by W. Thick (GWR). The first time that platform timetables were needed in Thick's day, the clerk made the necessary alterations to the old timetable, deleted the name Orton, and replaced it with Thick. The printer in response reproduced Orton in wide letters! Maintenance of the permanent way and the station generally, together with signalling and telegraph apparatus was undertaken by the GWR on behalf of the Joint Committee. Except in the early days, porters were all GWR appointments. There was always a shortage of shunters at the station, because porters received about £1 a day in tips and had no wish to take up shunting as they only received basic porters' rates and missed the tips. An LMS train was allowed to be delayed for a certain number of minutes in the event of a GW connection being late. Passengers complaining of a missed connection were allowed to phone or telegraph at the railway's expense, giving the person at their destination the new time of arrival.

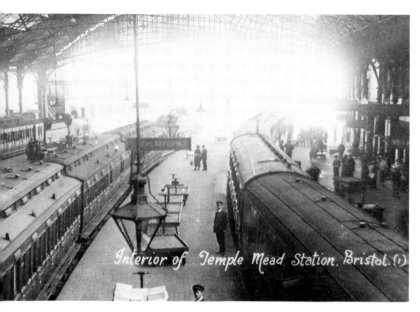

Interior of Temple Mead Station, Bristol. (1)

Top:
Different roof styles: Digby Wyatt's train shed of the 1870s and 'umbrella' platform canopies of the 1930s. 'Slar' class No 4019 *Knight Templar*, with its tender lettered British Railways in Great Western lettering heads an up express soon after Nationalisation. *L&GRP (15386)*

Above:
Collett '1400' class 0-4-2T No 1415 adds a four-wheel parcels van to the rear of a South Wales train at Platforms 7 & 8 on 15 September 1951. In this view three years after nationalisation, the locomotive has received its smokebox numberplate but still carries GWR paintwork.
Ian Allan Library

56

Top:
No 5000 *Launceston Castle* in pristine condition stands next to Bristol Old Station signalbox, within the 1870s extension to Brunel's train shed.
Real Photographs (6440)

Above:
Class 3MT No 82041 heads the 12.12pm stopping train to Bath Green Park on 3 October 1964. The details of Wyatt's extension to the original Brunel train shed show clearly in this view. *B. J. Ashworth*

Left:
There is just one minute until departure time according to the clock on Platform 14 as the 12.12pm Temple Meads-Bath Green Park waits with No 82041 at its head on 3 October 1964. A wealth of detail is visible in this photograph, including the wooden plank platform. *B. J. Ashworth*

Right:
An excellent illustration of the original Brunel train shed and the Wyatt extension, showing how the roof styles of roof construction blended together. BR Standard 5MT 73030 has arrived at Platforms 12 & 13 with the empty stock for a northbound express, whilst the British Railways exhibition train is stabled at Platform 15. *B. J. Ashworth*

Below:
Stanier 'Black 5' No 44841 leaves the straight train shed on 23 August 1952 with the 8.20am Bristol-Bournemouth. *J. G. Hutback*

Top:
The approaches to Temple Meads are seen from the window of a westbound train after passing Bath Road depot in April 1956. *C. R. L. Coles*

Above:
A view in the late 1950s from the road bridge seen in the previous photograph. No 6814 *Enborne Grange* arrives with a train from Weston-super-Mare, as another 'Grange' departs with the 5.30am Paddington-Penzance. It is of interest that several years after nationalisation the tender of No 6814 is still in postwar Great Western livery. *G. F. Heiron*

Top:
**A view from the London end of the station on
28 September 1959 with '5600' class 0-6-2T No 6630
trundling through on a southbound freight.** *M. Mensing*

Above:
**On 14 June 1954 the 'Bristolian' was returned to its
prewar 105min timing, non-stop in both directions
between Paddington and Temple Meads. Although the
train was not normally a 'King' duty, on the first day of
the accelerated timing it was worked by No 6000** *King
George V*, **which had hauled the very first 'Bristolian' on
9 September 1935. The return working awaits departure
at the London end of Temple Meads.**
P. F. Winding

Left:
BR Standard '2MT' tank No 82043 stands beside a water column on 28 September 1959 with the empty stock of the 8.22am arrival from Witham and Yatton. *M. Mensing*

Below:
'Castle' No 5082 *Swordfish*, fitted with a straight-sided Hawksworth tender, strides away from Platform 6 with the 12 noon express to Paddington in October 1956. *G. F. Heiron*

Right:
No 1014 *County of Glamorgan* in shining British Railways mixed traffic livery stands at Temple Meads on 24 September 1951 with the 8.20am from Weston-super-Mare to Paddington. *Ian Allan Library*

Below right:
A fine view of the station approach road in August 1957, with the old station on the left and the main buildings of the 1870s station in the background. *G. F. Heiron*

Above left:
Platform 5 of Temple Meads in 1959, seen from the 12 noon departure for Paddington, which is pulling out of Platform 6.
G. F. Heiron

Left:
No 5052 *Earl of Radnor* stands at Temple Meads with an evening departure in December 1960.
J. R. Smith

Above:
An excellent view of the frontage of the original station as it was in 1979. *British Rail*

Right:
Migrant birds decorate the station tower in October 1967. The original spire was destroyed by German bombing in 1941.
P. J. Fowler

Above:
The Bristol & Exeter Railway office building at Temple Meads, photographed in May 1980. *Author*

Right:
The entrance hall with its ornate windows. The flat Tudor arches leading to the newsagent's on the right are echoed in the booking hall. The kink allows a passenger approaching the platforms to see more of the walls, and leads to a feeling of anticipation as to what is round the corner. The date is 4 September 1986. *Author*

Below:
Great Western Railway coaches stand beneath the roof of Temple Meads once again in July 1978 in the shape of the Great Western Society's Vintage Train on the 'Torbay Express' special from Paddington to Kingswear.

Engine Sheds and Locomotives

The first GWR engine shed at Bristol was situated east of the station, near the site of the later South Wales Junction. Originally consisting of three roads, a four-road standard gauge building was added. Bath Road shed was originally a six-road B&E depot beside the locomotive works. In 1877 a two-turntable roundhouse took in the works site. Rebuilt in 1934 as part of the Bristol reconstruction scheme, the main shed had 10 roads with a three-road repair shop alongside. The depot principally stabled passenger engines, those for freight being dealt with at St Philips Marsh on the Avoiding Line. Closed to steam on 12 September 1960, the depot was rebuilt and opened on 18 June 1962 as a six-road diesel depot. HSTs are dealt with at a maintenance depot opened at St Philips Marsh in September 1975.

Temple Meads was interesting in its early days for the variety of locomotives seen, it being the junction of three railways. Apart from Great Western engines detailed elsewhere, were Stothert, Slaughter & Co's 2-2-2s of the Bristol & Gloucester Railway with inside frames and D-shaped fireboxes; while in 1848 Kirtley built broad gauge convertible 2-2-2s Nos 66-69, which were altered to run on the standard gauge in 1854. The 2-4-0s appeared in 1870, and in 1892 4-2-0s worked the line, being replaced by 4-4-0s a few years later. 4-4-0 Compounds and the '999' class did not penetrate to Bristol before Grouping and the heaviest duties were performed by Class 3 4-4-0s. Compounds appeared in 1924 and 'Jubilees' 10 years later. 'Crabs', 'Patriots' and 'Black Fives' also worked passenger trains as well as the occasional 'Royal Scot'. During World War 2, SR 'F1' and 'K10' 4-4-0s appeared on loan to the LMS. ER 'B1' 4-6-0s appeared from 1958. Local passenger trains were hauled by Johnson '1P' 0-4-4Ts, while in later LMS days a '3P' 2-6-2T was carriage shunter.

The B&E tended to use tank engines, the most impressive examples being 4-2-4T express locomotives designed by James Pearson with 9ft driving wheels. 4-4-0STs were also used for main line passenger duties.

In the 1930s Drummond 'D15' class 4-4-0s and 'U' Class 2-6-0s worked through trains from the SR, while Bulleid Pacifics were seen on postwar football specials. GWR diesel railcars appeared on Bristol-Weymouth and Salisbury services on 17 February 1936 causing a Temple Meads porter to remark 'Here comes the dismal'. Diesel railcars also worked to Portishead; Wells, Radstock and Frome; and Severn Beach. BR diesel multiple-units were first used at Bristol on 18 August 1958 and by September the Bristol allocation of Derby-built three-car units of today's Class 116 began to arrive. April 1959 saw dieselisation of stopping services from Bristol well nigh complete, except those to Bath Green Park. The 'Bristolian' was dieselised in 1959 and steam locomotives ousted from express passenger duties by 'Warships', 'Westerns', 'Hymeks' and Brush Type 4s. Class 50s made redundant by London Midland electrification superseded Class 47s and 'Westerns' on Paddington trains from May 1974.

Prototype HST No 252001 appeared in 1975, a regular service beginning in the spring of 1977. From 1 October 1981, HSTs were introduced on North East-South West services through Bristol.

Below:
Bath Road shed viewed from the station on 7 June 1952, with the water tower and coaling stage on the left. No fewer than 15 locomotives are visible outside the shed, including a Pannier, Prairies, 'Castles', a 'Hall' and a 'County'. *R. E. Toop*

Bottom:
'Castles' Nos 4000 *North Star* and 4091 *Dudley Castle* at Bath Road, await their next duties in the 1950s. *Ian Allan Library*

– 4 –

Taunton

The Bristol & Exeter Railway opened to Taunton on 1 July 1842. As the town was only one side of the line, like Reading it was constructed on Brunel's one-sided principle. The offices were in a domestic style building. On 1 October 1853 Taunton began to develop as a rail centre for on that date the branch was opened from Durston, 5½ miles east of Taunton, to Yeovil. 31 March 1862 saw the line from Norton Fitzwarren opened to Watchet and extended to Minehead on 16 July 1874. On 11 September 1866 the branch opened from Creech Junction to Chard and 8 June from Norton Fitzwarren to Wiveliscombe, being completed to Barnstaple on 1 November 1873, this branch being marked on GWR maps as a main line. The new shortened route from Paddington to the West of England was opened to passengers on 2 July 1906, making Taunton the focus of four main lines and three branches. It is interesting and a little unusual that although it was a junction station, the actual junctions were several miles distant. Mixed gauge was extended to Taunton in May 1875 allowing machinery for the Royal Agricultural Society's show to be brought through from the Midlands without transshipment.

The development of Taunton as a rail centre had its effect on the station. Extra traffic generated by the branches, coupled with the demand for faster main line services, forced the abolition of the one-sided layout to a conventional pattern. On 17 August 1868 the lengthened down platform remained and the down booking office too, while an up platform was added on the opposite track, both being covered by a train shed. Door and window openings to the new structures had rounded tops.

Further development of traffic proved that just two platforms were insufficient, so in 1895 the platforms were extended, using the site of the goods shed at the east end of the station and giving Taunton the honour of having the longest platforms on the GWR system. Bays were added on each side at both ends. Platform awnings were supported by pylon-type columns typical of the 1890s, and the ends of the awnings curved, much more pleasing to the eye than the later triangular type. As at Reading, rainwater is brought neatly from gutters on the platform canopy, through the centre of alternate roof supports. The adequate accommodation now allowed trains from Yeovil to run through to Taunton instead of terminating at Durston. A goods avoiding line south of the station opened on 1 November 1896 proved advantageous, and it was used by some Saturdays-only trains not scheduled to stop at a platform, thus overtaking a train discharging passengers.

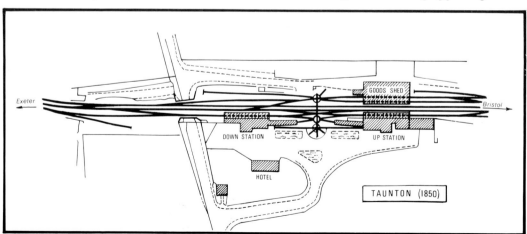

By the late 1920s Taunton was something of a bottleneck, particularly on summer Saturdays. The majority of trains stopped, many having through carriages for Ilfracombe and Minehead to be detached and when trains were following each other closely block by block, a small delay in station with a coupling or corridor connection, could cause hold-ups to snowball. As at Paddington and Bristol, the opportunity given by the Development (Loan Guarantees & Grants) Act of 1929 was taken for reconstruction. This involved passenger and goods stations, the enlargement of the locomotive depot and quadrupling tracks from Cogload Junction to Norton Fitzwarren, a distance of eight miles. The task involved Scott & Middleton in rebuilding 16 bridges and removing 140,000 cubic yards of earth. Improvements

commenced in September 1930, the passenger station being almost completely rebuilt.

The new station consisted of four main line, and seven bay line, platforms, the former varying from 1,400ft to 1,200ft in length, the alterations involving the widening and lengthening by 50ft of the bridge carrying the railway over Kingston Road. The flying junction at Cogload placed Paddington lines in the centre, so trains to and

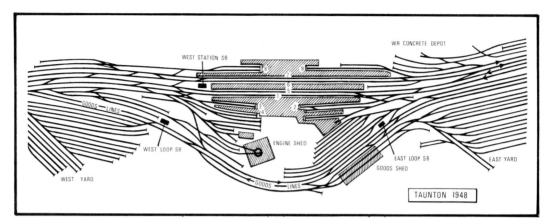

from the Capital used the island platforms, Bristol trains using the outside roads. The down arrival bay, No 2, was used mainly by Chard trains in both directions, a departing Chard train blocking both down lines and if routed on the relief line, the up main line as well. The up arrival bay, No 8 (also signalled for departures) was almost exclusively for arrivals from Barnstaple and Minehead. The two down departure bays, Nos 3 & 4, were for Barnstaple, Minehead and some Exeter stopping trains, up departure bay No 9 serving Bristol and Yeovil trains.

The train shed was demolished, individual platform canopies being cheaper and easier to maintain. The arcade on the up platform is similar to that towards the west end of Platforms 2 & 3 at Newport. The footbridge was replaced by a subway 140ft in length and 15ft wide. The pleasant 1930s-style bronze hoods over the lamps at the foot of the stairs are still extant. A new booking hall was built on the level of the approach road at the

Below:
'Rover' class 4-2-2 *Dragon* heads a down broad gauge express at Taunton circa 1891. Note the canopy to the platform extension, and the mixed gauge track.
J. F. King collection

north end of the subway adjoining the up main line platform, while on the down side the booking hall and parcels office were enlarged. The new station opened on 20 December 1931.

On 20 February 1932 the brick-built goods shed was almost doubled in size and the two platforms connected by movable bridges. A warehouse 150ft×60ft was erected over the west end of the shed while more cattle pens were provided, Taunton handling an exceptional amount of livestock. The west end of the shed is now used by a seed merchant and the other by National Carriers. The coal concentration depot opened on 1 June 1964 and closed on 31 July 1982.

As branch services were withdrawn, the last one being Minehead on 4 January 1971, some platforms proved surplus to requirements, the island platforms being taken out of use on 31 March 1976 and henceforth the lines were used by through trains. The island platform buildings were subsequently demolished, and advertisement hoardings were erected facing the seats on Platforms 1 & 2, but elsewhere trees have been planted. Stairs from the subway still remain to give access, but the exit is blocked by a large sliding roof which can be opened should the platform ever be required in an emergency. A stone-built booking office and travel centre which opened on 16 March 1983 were built in front of the 1931 booking office, almost totally obscuring it. There is an entrance/exit on the south side facing the town, but no ticket office. Buildings on both platforms are of brick and have recently been cleaned. The refreshment room's exterior on the platform side is in stone, and flower boxes have been set on the window sills. The glazed roof of the platform canopy in front of the buildings gives a very light and attractive appearance. VDU screens give train information to passengers. Three platforms are in use: No 1 down; No 2 up, and No 3 the up bay, the latter used for the departure of trains for Bristol which have previously terminated at the station. The bay at the east end of the down platform is screened off to make a warehouse area for Homestar Rapid Delivery Service, NPV vans in the siding also being used for storage. As part of the major resignalling operation based on the new panel signalbox at Exeter, the four-track section from Taunton station to Cogload Junction was reduced to two lines, although four lines remain through the station.

c.1905.

Above left:
An up view of Taunton station circa 1905 with the West signalbox on the right-hand side, and the overall roof visible in the background. *Lens of Sutton*

Left:
The interior of the station in 1931, showing the overall roof. A slip coach stands at Platform 1. Note the gas lamp on the left, suspended from the roof.
Great Western Railway

Above:
A 1921 view in the up direction from platform 5, the down main. Bay platform No 2 and platform 1, the up main are to the left of the picture. *L&GRP (8585)*

Right:
The 1931 up side booking hall viewed from the station approach road. *Author's collection*

Above:
0-6-0PT No 9671 stands at Taunton circa 1950. Of interest are the attractive moulding on the canopy, and the comprehensive nameboard, stating 'junction, for Chard, Minehead and Barnstaple branches'. *Lens of Sutton*

Right:
On a sunny 12 May 1958, 'Castle' No 5024 *Carew Castle* heads the 8am Plymouth-Crewe, which conveys coaches for Liverpool, Manchester and Glasgow. No 4098 *Kidwelly Castle* stands in the background with an up local. *Brian Morrison*

Left:
The west end of Taunton on 15 April 1956 with No 7004
***Eastnor Castle* leaving on a short down stopping service.**
R. E. Vincent

Below left:
Collett '2251' class 0-6-0 No 3215 leaves Taunton on
15 July 1957 with the five-coach 3.25pm to Minehead.
R. E. Vincent

Right:
The 2.05pm Taunton-Yeovil departs Taunton behind
'Small Prairie' No 5504. *J. Davenport*

Below:
The eastern approaches to Taunton are shown in this
photograph of No 5554 leaving with the 11.50am to Castle
Cary on 12 May 1958. Taunton East box is visible on the
far left. *Brian Morrison*

Left:
The bays at the west end of the down platform with a standard 350hp diesel shunter on pilot duties. Mogul No 7337 and an unidentified 'Hall' stand next to the locomotive depot. *Lens of Sutton*

Below left:
The original down booking office on 6 May 1986. *Author*

Above:
Original brickwork on the down side building, seen in May 1986. *Author*

Above right:
The present-day Platform 2, the up main, with the buffet and waiting room in the foreground. The glazed canopy makes the platform beneath comparatively bright.
Author

Engine Sheds and Locomotives

The two-road temporary engine shed at Bridgwater was moved to Taunton and opened in June 1842. Moved some 120ft nearer the station to allow track alterations, it was closed in April 1896 and replaced by a roundhouse with 28 radiating roads, a repair shop being added in 1932. The walls of the locomotive shed still stand and the land lies derelict. The 13 drivers at Taunton finished on 9 May 1986, the only crews boarding locomotives at Taunton now are from other depots working home. A crew room is located on Platform 1.

Early passenger trains at Taunton were worked by 2-2-2s of the 'Fire Fly' class, while from 1847 the 4-2-2 Gooch '8ft singles' appeared, but with locomotive working taken over by the B&E on 1 May 1849, that company's 7ft 6in version of Gooch's singles was used, while from 1853 the speedy Pearson 4-2-4Ts with their 9ft driving wheels were in evidence. With the amalgamation of the B&E with the GWR In 1876 the '8ft singles'

resumed working until displaced by the gauge conversion in 1892. 4-4-0STs worked broad gauge branch and main line traffic. Six 'Avonside' or 'Acheron' class 2 4-0s were stabled at Taunton in late broad gauge days to pilot trains to Whiteball Siding and also to work trains on the Chard branch.

On the standard gauge, there were '2201' class 2-4-0s, 'Sir Daniel' 2-2-2s and 'Standard Goods' class 0-6-0s, with branch services worked by 'Metro' class 2-4-0Ts and 0-6-0STs. Dean's 7ft 8in singles and various 4-4-0s, French Compound Atlantics and the GWR standard classes appeared in due course. Locomotives at Taunton were for use as pilots in case of main line failures; for local goods and passenger traffic on both branch and main line; banking duties to Whiteball and for use as local shunters in the three Taunton goods yards, shunted for the greater part of 24hr.

Great Western four-wheel petrol shunting locomotive No 24 was occupied in the railway's concrete works sidings at Taunton from 1926 until its withdrawal in 1960.

Plymouth

The Bristol & Exeter Railway extended the broad gauge from Bristol to Exeter, the South Devon Railway carrying the line on to Plymouth, Laira Green being reached on 5 May 1848 and Millbay on 2 April 1849. The broad gauge was extended from Millbay (Cornwall Junction) to Truro on 2 May 1859, with a branch to Tavistock opening on 22 June the same year. In 1872 the Devon & Cornwall Railway put forward a bill for making various lines in the Plymouth area and to avoid an expensive Parliamentary battle, an agreement was reached with the SDR on 24 March 1873 whereby, among other things, the SDR was to build a mixed gauge station at North Road offering equal facilities to the D&C; an Act being passed on 7 July 1873 ratifying the agreement. In the event, before North Road was opened the LSWR took over the D&C, reaching Plymouth on 18 May 1876 via the SDR from Lydford, and continued to its

own magnificent terminus at Devonport. In the process, the direct Cornwall loop avoiding Millbay was completed. Plans for North Road station were drawn by P. J. Margary, the SDR's resident engineer, and the building contract was let to W. G. Jenkin in 1875, both railway companies sharing the cost of extra land required for the station. When completed, a dispute between the GWR, which worked the SDR, and the Board of Trade over an engine siding, delayed opening. The GWR was in no haste to complete North Road and as a delaying tactic it installed an engine neck at the west end of the down platform, allegedly for LSWR use, but the latter had no need for this

Below:
Plymouth North Road in 1876. Note the roofs supported on metal columns extending over the lines.
Devon Library Services

facility with its own terminus just over a mile away and the GWR had no use for it either with Millbay so close.

The signalling was such that if a down train came in and overran the platform, it would traverse the offending spur and end up in the road below. The Board of Trade insisted that the signalling be altered so that if a train overran the platform, it would run out on the main line. Only when the GWR agreed to alter the signalling did the station open, without ceremony, on 28 March 1877.

The *Western Daily Mercury* of Thursday 29 March 1877 gave the following account:

'The North Road Station. This station was opened yesterday morning for the traffic, both of the Great Western and LSW Companies. The station has a very handsome appearance, and will, no doubt, be a valuable addition for the accommodation of the traffic of the largely increasing population of the neighbourhood. Twelve jobs have been assigned to the station to work the passenger traffic under proper arrangements. A great many people throughout the day visited the station, and a general expression of satisfaction was evinced at this additional railway facility for the Three Towns.'

The LSWR declared its strength by offering on 'The Shorter Route to London' a return excursion fare to Waterloo of 35-first class, 21-second class for travel by the 7.20am from Devonport and the 7.25am Plymouth, the day after North Road opened.

The station at North Road consisted of two train sheds, each with a 46ft span covering the main up or down platform for two-thirds of its length, with two through roads between the sheds. Construction was of timber due to the fact that the line was on an embankment at this point and anything heavier than wood was liable to subside. Each platform was 553ft in length and 26ft wide. A refreshment room was opened in 1888 and two years later an interesting feature was the change in direction of the LSWR trains. At first trains from Waterloo entered the station in the same direction as those from Paddington, but with the completion of the independent route from Lydford to Devonport via the Tamar Valley on 2 June 1890, the situation was reversed. Devonport (LSWR) became a through station and LSWR trains terminated at North Road until the South Western terminus at Friary was ready on 1 July 1891. Thus, as at Exeter St David's, there was the curious situation of trains for Waterloo leaving in the opposite direction from those for Paddington.

Below:
The first standard gauge up 'Flying Dutchman' leaves North Road on 23 May 1892 behind an outside-framed 4-4-0T amidst debris associated with the gauge conversion. The goods shed is visible on the right of this photograph. *Courtesy Engineering*

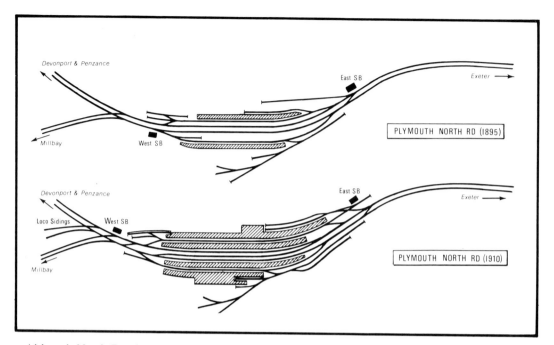

Although North Road was a GWR and LSWR (later Southern Railway) joint station, the approaches on either side were pure GWR metals. The GWR also retained exclusive ownership of the tracks through the station which represented the original route of the South Devon Railway. The station buildings, being joint property, were maintained at joint expense. In 1909 the station staff numbered 45. Outdoor work was performed by GWR men alone, but both railways employed their own office staff. In the post-Grouping period, cash taken for Southern ticket sales was remitted to that company's cashier at Exeter Central, whilst GWR receipts were merely passed down the platform to the District Cashier based at North Road. This arrangement lasted beyond Nationalisation until 1953.

Gradually the GWR expresses by-passed Millbay, and North Road assumed greater importance. Rapidly increasing passenger traffic, helped by the new boom in suburban services on both systems, resulted in the station being enlarged in 1908 when two island platforms were added. As the train shed only covered half the width of an island platform, the remainder was sheltered by a canopy erected in 1909. At the same time, steel girders were erected linking up and down sheds to give greater rigidity. The down island was 750ft long and at its widest, 25ft across. The up island's dimensions were 600ft × 24ft. The two outer faces of each island were used for each company's principal trains, with the middle faces generally reserved for local traffic. At the same time, the up main platform was extended east to give a length of 790ft and

maximum 24ft width. The roofed area on the up side was 2,383 square yards and on the down side it was 2,540 square yards, the extra space being due to the cab park on that side. A fine, ornate, cast iron footbridge extended across the centre of the station, steps down to the island being double on account of roof supports. Each flight was 4ft in width.

The last GWR express to reverse at Millbay was the overnight Penzance-Paddington train in 1929, the importance of North Road being confirmed. As part of the government-assisted New Works scheme, in 1935 it was planned to rebuild North Road with seven platforms, all bi-directional except that Platform 4 was to have been solely for down trains and Platform 5 for up trains only. It was intended to concentrate all GWR main line traffic on North Road, enabling Millbay and Mutley to be closed. Mutley, opened on 1 August 1871 to serve the expanding east end of Plymouth and only 600yd up the line from North Road, was closed on 2 July 1939. Work on rebuilding North Road began in 1938 when the present island platform Nos 7 and 8, 1,085ft in length, was built. The west end of this island was built over some former stables, which were discovered in the summer of 1985 when digging new drains. These were a relic of the early days when there was a station entrance on the up side from the former Bird Cage Road and horse-drawn cabs fed traffic to and from the trains. Platform 8 was brought into use on 27 November 1938, allowing the up side train shed and associated buildings to be removed to make way for Platform 7.

Above:
An atmospheric view of North Road in 1913 with a 'Duke of Cornwall' class 4-4-0 on an up train. *L&GRP (7825)*

The design of the steelwork for the platform coverings was a departure from previous GWR practice. Steel members, instead of being connected by plates and rivets, were joined by electric welding — quite an innovation as previous electric welding had been confined to repairing bridges and worn permanent way fittings. A considerable saving was made in the weight of steel required, since connection plates were almost eliminated and lighter rolled steel sections could be used. The cost of fabrication was higher than for riveted work, but brought a net result of a slight saving in initial cost in favour of the new method. It allowed the design to be simpler, leading to fewer crevices at joints where corrosion was invariably common and often rapid, and there was also a reduction in the time spent scraping and painting. Roofs were of corrugated iron except in front of the platform buildings where construction was of patent glazing. A subway was constructed with two parallel corridors, one for passengers and one for parcels and mail. It opened early in 1939, allowing the footbridge to be demolished.

Rebuilding work ceased on the outbreak of hostilities in September 1939, subsequent events hastening the process whereby North Road assumed its role of being the main GWR station for Plymouth. Millbay, with its short platforms, closed to passengers on 23 April 1941, the bombing of the adjoining goods station making it necessary to use the passenger platforms for goods traffic. Many trains originating at North Road continued to be formed at Millbay, which remained in use for empty stock workings until October 1969 when these were transferred to Laira.

In the immediate postwar period North Road presented a somewhat untidy appearance, looking as if the enemy had been as successful here as it had been at Millbay. The old wooden buildings were life-expired, and booking clerks of the 1950s tell of rats running over their feet. Work on rebuilding started again in 1956 as part of the 15-year Modernisation Plan of 1955. The closing of Friary station to passengers on 15 September 1958 meant that Southern trains again terminated at North Road, although trains continued running to Friary for empty stock purposes until 1962 when these were transferred to new sidings at Laira. Since North Road was now the only principal station in Plymouth, the suffix was dropped. Rebuilding was completed four years later, the new station being opened by Dr Richard Beeching on 26 March 1962. With its Brunel Bar, fully mechanised ticket office and new parcels concentration depot, Plymouth now possessed a far superior station.

There were two additions to the prewar plan. The first of these was a power signalbox, one of the first on the Western Region, which was built on the site of the old parcels offices, and which opened on 26 November 1960, working with fringe boxes on

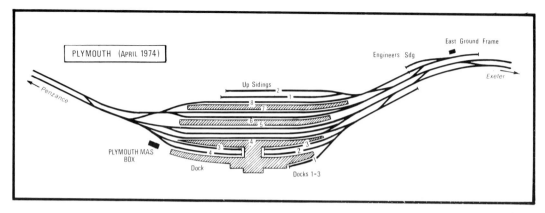

the main line at Laira Junction and Keyham. 1973 saw its district extended to cover an area bounded by Totnes and St Germans. The second addition was the 10-storey office block, now a prominent city landmark, known as Inter-City House, built at a cost of £1½ million to accommodate the offices of the Plymouth Division, allowing outdated offices at Millbay, Newton Abbot, Exeter St David's and Exeter Central, to be vacated. Sadly this impressive building, described by Beeching as 'a great mistake' before he opened it, was only in partial use by 1967 and today, British Rail uses only three floors, much of the remainder being commercially let to such diverse occupants as a firm of architects and the Manpower Services Commission.

In the spring of 1974 the whole station area track layout was drastically altered, with Platforms 2 and 3 losing their through line status. A portion of the space between these platforms was filled in, creating two sets of bay lines and direct access from the concourse to Platform 4, and in addition the through road between Platforms 4 and 5 remains in use. However, as all through lines are signalled for traffic in either direction, there is little operating inconvenience. Use of the remaining through platforms tends to be:

4 Down main; up through trains from Cornwall with parcel vans; some up services starting from Plymouth.
5 Down main relief; normally trains with detachments and some stopping trains.
6 Some down terminating trains which form up re-starting services; some local trains.
7 Up main.
8 Up main relief; some terminating and re-starting services; stabling of sleeping car attached/detached to the overnight London train.

Of the bay platforms created from the former Platforms 2 and 3, those at the east end, now correspondingly known as Docks 2 and 3, are for

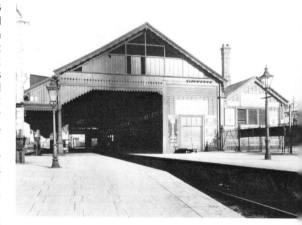

Top:
The west end of the down train shed, photographed on 28 February 1928. *British Railways (WR)*

Above:
A view in the up direction in February 1928, showing the platform canopies which were added on to the train sheds in order to shelter the central platforms. Of particular interest is the steel bracing linking the two train sheds. *British Railways (WR)*

parcels use and the 14.15 Plymouth-Leeds starts here. Platform 3 west end is for the exclusive use of the Gunnislake branch and the west end of Platform 2, now Bay 4, was the Motorail terminal, but now has no particular use except for stabling the van detached from the 22.25 Paddington-Penzance Postal, until its attachment to the corresponding up train. The bay is also used for stabling locomotives. A curiosity of the 1962 North Road station is the absence of a Platform 1. A bay platform was constructed alongside the east end of Platform 2, intended for use by the Tavistock branch trains. This was never used as such, the branch being closed at the end of 1962, when the bay was turned over to parcel use. Track was

removed on 20 July 1975 when the intended Platform 1 became part of the road area of the parcels yard.

North Road station is set just over half a mile from the centre of Plymouth, and its approach road and offices have always been on the down side. The station is single storey, apart from the concourse with its deep clerestory windows on all four sides giving an unusually light and airy interior. In appearance it is very much in the postwar style, exceptions being the lift-head shafts which are in keeping with the 1938 work and conflict with the rest of the station. The asbestos roof on the canopies makes the platforms rather dark, a notable exception being the glass roof over the bays created from Platforms 2 and 3, though the effect is spoilt by the supporting thick, ugly pillars, looking substantial enough to support a main line bridge. Flower beds towards the ends of the platforms add colour to the scene, the station in the years 1984 and 1985 winning the commercial section of the 'Plymouth in Bloom' competition.

When the new station was opened in 1962, it was proudly announced that parking was available for 50 cars, but such has been the change in the pattern of travel, that 15 years later in September 1977, a multi-storey car park built on the site of the former Engineer's Yard, was opened giving approximately 250 spaces. A travel centre was inaugurated on 7 June 1971 and extended two years later. Currently plans are in hand to rebuild it together with a commercial development of the concourse to suit the needs of both modern travel and the growth of technology.

Above:
Southern Railway 'O2' No 232 leaves North Road for Friary station circa 1936. *Lens of Sutton*

Above right:
Part of the unattractive exterior of North Road station on 9 March 1953, showing the unusual detached enquiry office. A No 93 bus to Dartmouth stands on the approach road to the left. *British Railways (WR)*

Right:
The equally unprepossessing interior of the station is shown by this photograph of the west end of the down shed, taken on the same day. One single running line is still served by two platforms, Nos 2 & 3, but since the 1928 photograph the footbridge has been replaced by the subway visible on the right. *British Railways (WR)*

Above:
A fascinating selection of period advertisements are displayed on the wooden buildings of Platform 3 in this 1953 view, looking towards Penzance. *British Railways (WR)*

Left:
Mogul No 6388 enters North Road in the 1950s with a down stopping service. *Lens of Sutton*

Below left:
Push-pull fitted '6400' class 0-6-0PT No 6421 stands at North Road on 19 August 1954 with a down local formed of two vintage auto-trailers. *H. C. Casserley*

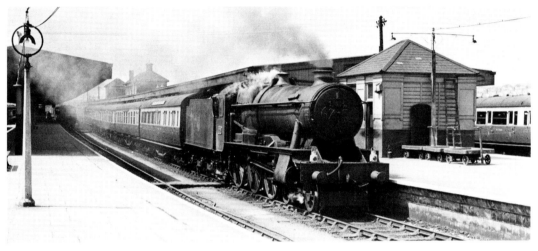

Top:
**A dramatic photograph of No 6400 and a pair of more
modern auto-coaches in Platform 6 with the Saltash
push-pull service at midnight during December 1959.**
J. R. Smith

Above:
**No 1006 *County of Cornwall* provides appropriate power
for the 10.15am Penzance-Manchester, seen arriving at
Platform 7 on 16 May 1954.** *R. E. Vincent*

Right:
**A few weeks after the closure of Friary station to
passenger traffic, 'Battle of Britain' Pacific No 34058 *Sir
Frederick Pile* pulls out of North Road with an up stopping
train on the Southern line on 5 November 1958.**
B. A. Butt

Top left:
The bright but nevertheless rather austere waiting and refreshment rooms on Platforms 3 & 4, seen on 30 October 1957. *British Railways (WR)*

Top right:
The new Plymouth North Road station on 16 March 1962. *British Railways (WR)*

Above:
An excellent general view of North Road after rebuilding. On 30 April 1962 a pair of 'Warship' class diesel-hydraulics arrive with the Manchester-Penzance train, whilst another 'Warship' waits with an up train in Platform 7. In the carriage stabling sidings can be seen a 'Small Prairie' and prototype 'Western' No D1000 *Western Enterprise* in its original 'Desert Sand' livery.
Brian Haresnape

Left:
The now closed 1930s refreshment room on Platform 7, seen in June 1986. *Author*

Engine Sheds and Locomotives

The SDR opened a four-road shed at Millbay in June 1849, this being augmented by a roundhouse at Laira opened in 1906, the design similar to that at Taunton. A turntable and coaling point was installed at the west end of North Road in the Cornwall loop triangle in 1913 and removed on 13 October 1963. Millbay shed finally closed in 1931 when Laira was extended with the addition of the Long (or New) Shed. Simultaneously with the station's renewal, two diesel depots were constructed. Belmont diesel depot, approximately on the site of Millbay Shed was opened for DMUs in 1960, closing on 5 October 1964. At Laira a new diesel depot was built on the site of the former Laira Goods Yard beside the steam shed, opening on 13 March 1962, the steam depot closing on 4 October 1964. In 1979 a £3.5 million contract was awarded to Messrs E. Thomas & Co Ltd of Truro for the construction of an HST shed 786ft × 72ft. This was opened on 30 September 1981 by R. Morrell, the Lord Mayor of Plymouth, a toppling crane marring the dignity of the proceedings.

At first passenger traffic was worked by saddle tanks of the 4-4-0 and 2-4-0 variety, 0-6-0STs coping with goods traffic. One interesting feature of SDR locomotives was that almost all passenger engines carried sand boxes on top of their saddle tanks, while goods engines carried them in front of the smokebox. Introduction of 'Duke' class 4-4-0s in 1895 meant that for the first time engines could run through from Paddington to Plymouth. In the early years of this century the 'Cities' became famous for their speed exploits between Plymouth and Paddington. They were soon followed by two-cylinder 'Saints' and four-cylinder 'Stars', later to be outshone by 'Castles' and 'Kings', although the latter were not allowed west of Keyham. 4-4-0s, mostly of the 'Bulldog' variety, worked much of the other traffic and acted as pilots over the South Devon banks, duties shared as 'Halls' came on the scene in the late 1920s and 'Granges' in the following decade. In the post-World War 2 years, 'Manors' finally replaced the last of the 4-4-0s and Hawksworth's 'County' class also arrived on the scene.

Steam railmotors appeared on local services to Tavistock, Yealmpton, Saltash and Plympton in 1904, the cars being of the suburban rather than branch variety, with extra seating in place of luggage accommodation. As problems were experienced with hauling trailers over gradients, the railmotors ran at times in pairs, back to back, with one driver and two firemen. From 1914 onwards they were replaced by 0-6-0PTs and auto coaches. A couple of '48XX' (later '14XX') series 0-4-2Ts were based at Laira, as were from 1957 some auto-fitted '4575' 2-6-2Ts displaced from the South Wales valleys. The auto-trains are best remembered around Plymouth for the '64XX' class 0-6-0PTs introduced in 1932, the locomotives often being sandwiched between two coaches at each end — mainly for the Saltash rush hour workings and Bank Holiday specials to the Tavistock branch.

'Britannia' Pacifics arrived at Laira in 1951, working mainly into Cornwall. Their reign was short, Laira crews taking a dislike to them. Standard Class 5s and Class 4s subsequently appeared, together with the magnificent '9Fs' which could be seen at times on passenger duties such as the summer Saturday Newquay-Newcastle train forward from Plymouth, sometimes unassisted. Diesel multiple-units were introduced to the area on 13 June 1960, taking over the Saltash suburban service. The first set to arrive at Laira in February 1960 for crew training was still based there 25 years later, now No P460 and famed for its unique British Telecom yellow livery.

'Warship' diesel-hydraulics first appeared early in 1958, the 'Westerns' in 1962 and Brush Type 4 (Class 47) in the form of D1500 on 20 February 1963. By then, steam turns over the former GWR lines were very few, and non existent by the autumn. On 4 June 1965 a pair of Class 37s were used in an unsuccessful experiment for powering expresses. The first 'Peak' was seen in 1970 and Class 50s four years later. HSTs entered service in August 1979, the full service starting May 1980.

Gloucester

The ink was hardly dry on the GWR Act before some enterprising citizens of Cheltenham produced a broad gauge scheme for linking their spa with the main line at Swindon, the barrier of the Cotswolds compelling the line to pass through Gloucester. The Cheltenham & Great Western Union Railway taken over by the GWR on 10 May 1844, was eventually opened on 12 May 1845. Great Western trains at Gloucester were forced to use a temporary station because the Midland Railway, owners of the land on which the station was to be built, refused to give permission, though this dog-in-the-manger attitude was hardly unexpected as the GWR had prevented the Midland laying standard gauge rails on the line south of Gloucester over which it had running powers.

In 1844 Brunel intended building a branch from the C&GWUR at Standish, seven miles south of Gloucester, across the Severn to South Wales and Fishguard, thus capturing traffic to and from Southern Ireland. Gloucester businessmen successfully employed all the influence they could muster to oppose the scheme, realising that their pockets would suffer if trade short-circuited the city. Although the South Wales Railway was nominally independent, it was entirely a GWR project. 26½ miles of broad gauge line from Gloucester to Chepstow were opened on 19 September 1851, through running from Gloucester to South Wales beginning on 19 July 1852 when Chepstow Bridge was complete.

The broad gauge Hereford & Gloucester Railway linked the two cities in its title, joining the South Wales line at Grange Court and was opened on 2 June 1855. In 1862 the GWR absorbed the Hereford, Ross & Gloucester Railway, as it had become, and seven years later converted it to standard gauge, learning many lessons that were to

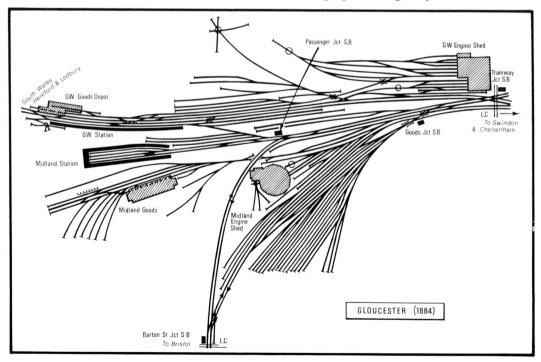

GLOUCESTER (1884)

prove useful in later conversion programmes elsewhere. The first step was the addition of standard gauge rails in the extensive Gloucester station yard, a most difficult undertaking in consequence of all trains arriving and departing from a single platform. The last GWR branch from Gloucester was the line to Ledbury built by the Ross & Ledbury Railway and the Newent Railway, opened on 27 July 1885, leaving the South Wales line at Over Junction.

Because of the inconvenience at the break of gauge, the South Wales Railway and the Gloucester-Swindon line were converted in 1872. The opening of the Severn Bridge on 17 October 1879 made little difference to Gloucester as lack of a triangular junction at Standish did not allow through running of trains from South Wales over the Severn Bridge to Swindon, but the opening of the Severn Tunnel in 1886 did affect the city, South Wales expresses being diverted through the tunnel instead of via Gloucester from 1 July 1887. The opening of the Badminton cut-off in 1903 also affected Gloucester as it meant that trains using the tunnel could run directly to Wootton Bassett and not have to use the heavily trafficked Bristol-Bath section, so from that date, more South Wales trains could be diverted through the Severn Tunnel instead of via Gloucester. Another new line which affected Gloucester was that from Cheltenham to Stratford-upon-Avon, which opened 1 August 1906, permitting through running from Birmingham to Gloucester and South Wales.

As work on the Birmingham & Gloucester Railway was more advanced than that of the C&GWUR, it was agreed that the Birmingham company should buy a site for Gloucester station and sell to the Cheltenham company three acres on the north side of its station at cost price when the C&GWUR required them. The C&GWUR station, just south of today's station, had two platforms with a centre siding for stabling coaches, the three lines being linked at the terminal end by a turntable as was contemporary practice.

To avoid reversal at Gloucester, 'T station' opened on 23 October 1847 was situated at the point where a short single-tracked line from Gloucester crossed the Avoiding Line. A shuttle service was run over the 'T Line' to connect with trains running to and from Cheltenham, Gloucester vehicles being transferred by turntable. This unusual method of working Gloucester traffic continued until the South Wales Railway opened in 1851, when a curve was built to a new through station situated north of the C&GWUR station and on the site of the present one. At first the South Wales station had one train-length platform on the down side used by trains in both directions. It was lengthened and rebuilt by Lancaster Owen in the years 1887-89, taking in part of the site of the former C&GWUR terminus which by now had been closed. As at other one-sided stations it now had a crossover mid-way along the platform to allow up trains to regain their correct road, and as at the other stations, it held to the convention of

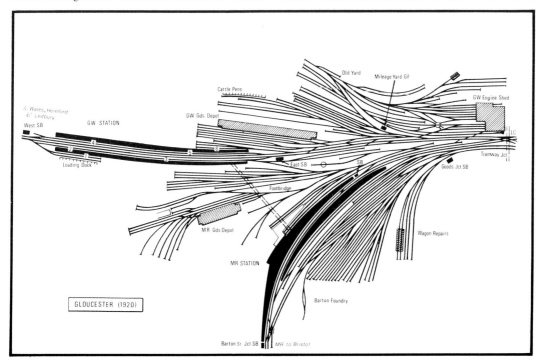

GLOUCESTER (1920)

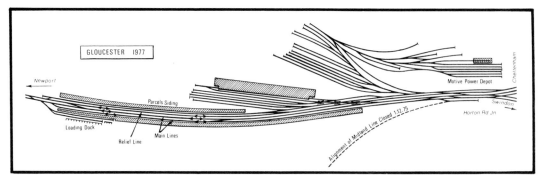

up trains using the up end, and down trains the down end. Eventually to ease working problems, a separate up platform was built on the up side in 1899. This new platform has a canopy supported on attractive cast iron pillars with a daffodil motif on their capitals the same as those at Kemble, but unlike them, the columns are painted just one colour, the relief not being picked out and much of their delight lost. The roof beams supporting the canopy are attractive. Platform walls are of brick relieved by courses of limestone and dark brick. The roof in front of the station building is glazed giving the platform a light and airy appearance. A glass screen at its west end protects passengers from the prevailing westerly winds.

When eventually the Midland terminus was replaced by an MR through station at Eastgate, a long footbridge was built connecting the GWR and MR stations. In 1919 Gloucester stations became

'closed', passengers requiring a ticket to gain admission. This led to criticism as inhabitants on the north side of Gloucester were now unable to use the bridge to reach the MR station, or those on the south to reach the GWR station.

In November 1964 new crossovers were installed at Standish Junction to allow Paddington and Cheltenham trains a through run to the former MR Eastgate station and it was envisaged that Central (as the former GWR station had become in BR terminology), would be converted into a parcels depot, South Wales trains being accommodated at Eastgate by constructing a new curved platform

Below:
The South Wales station at Gloucester depicted in an engraving circa 1850, looking east. *George Measom/ author's collection*

94

THE CHANGE OF GAUGE AT GLOUCESTER.

link to the Central tracks. Eventually it was resolved to close Eastgate and develop Central, the decision being weighted by the fact that abolishing Eastgate also did away with the trouble and expense of several busy level crossings.

Buildings at the Central station were demolished and temporarily replaced by those of a portable pattern, the insipid, flat-roofed rebuilt Central station, now just 'Gloucester', being officially opened by the Mayor, Councillor Terry Wathen, on 8 March 1977. It cost £1½ million, of which £1 million was the cost of track layout and signalling. The wheel had come full circle and traffic was once again concentrated on the down platform which had been lengthened to 1,600ft, becoming the second longest in the country, Platform 1, the extension, being mostly uncovered. The former up platform was relegated to parcels use. In 1984 this platform, still with its GWR ironwork, was brought back into passenger use and numbered 4, a new metal footbridge linking it with Nos 1-3. Platform 4 is almost ¼ mile in length, milepost 114 being at its up end and post 114¼ only a few yards beyond the down end. Platform 4 and the up through road both have chaired and keyed track — unusual today on a through line at a principal

Above:
Queen Victoria experiences the change of gauge at Gloucester on 29 September 1849, having to walk from the Birmingham & Gloucester train across to Great Western railway vehicles.
Courtesy Illustrated London News

station. Platform 2 is the west end of the former down platform and No 3 the Newport bay. Until the 1960s Platform 1 was the bay at the west end of the down platform, used for South Wales and Hereford trains; Platforms 2 & 3 were the west and east end of the down platform; 4 & 5 were the west and east ends of the up platform, and Platform 6, the bay at the east end of the up platform was used for Chalford trains. Scissors crossovers in the centre of the up and down platforms allowed a rear train to overtake a front train or facilitate the addition or removal of rolling stock or locomotives. Today all through lines are bi-directional, but platforms tend to be used as follows:

     1 & 2: HSTs and DMUs
       3: Cardiff-Gloucester shuttle
       4: locomotive-hauled trains and HSTs

95

Left:
Gloucester 'T' station house in April 1954. Passengers from Gloucester would have stepped out of their coach stopped in front of the two windows on the left, after crossing the line in the foreground. *Dr A. J. G. Dickens/ Author's collection*

Centre left:
A view from the up platform looking east around the turn of the century. *Author's collection*

Below:
'Star' class No 4050 *Princess Alice* stands at the head of a South Wales train at Gloucester Central Platform 2 on 9 June 1951. *W. Potter*

Right:
BR Standard '2MT' No 78009 heads a down freight through the station on 6 June 1953. A splendid array of banner repeater signals can be seen on the footbridge. *Ian Allan Library*

Below right:
In fine weather on 21 May 1952, '4300' class Mogul No 4381 takes the down through line with a westbound freight, whilst '2884' class 2-8-0 No 3824 stands on the up through line. The Western Region carriage sidings are visible beyond, whilst the spur to the LMR yards diverges to the right of the signalbox. *N. Ewart Mitchell*

Left:
No 5094 *Tretower Castle* waits to leave Gloucester with the 7.12pm stopping service to Swindon. *G. F. Heiron*

Below left:
A view looking west in the 1950s showing the crossover between the down main platform and the down through line. A former GWR diesel railcar stands at Platform 4. *G. F. Heiron*

Right:
No 6359 stands at Platform 2 with a down stopping train on 15 July 1959. *N. Caplan*

Below:
Another Churchward Mogul, No 4358, stands at Platform 1, the down bay, on 13 April 1957 with a Hereford train. No 4358 has just been outshopped from Caerphilly Works in lined green livery. Note the decorative ironwork on the roof of the building in the background. *W. Potter*

Left:

The operational flexibility derived from the division of the down main platform, with its crossover connections linking it to the through line is clearly demonstrated in this view dating from 12 August 1959. '5101' class 2-6-2T No 4115 stands at Platform 2 with a Gloucester-Hereford train, whilst in the background a Pannier tank stands at Platform 3 with two auto-coaches.   *S. Rickard*

Left:

No 7035 *Ogmore Castle* passes Tramway Junction in August 1960 with the up 'Cheltenham Spa Express'. The former Midland Railway Eastgate station is situated on the curve to the left of this picture, whilst Gloucester Central lies in the background beyond the departing train.   *J. R. Smith*

Below:

The east end of Gloucester Central on Saturday 1 December 1962. '1400' class No 1424 stands at Platform 3 after arrival with the 11.40am from Chalford, whilst Mogul No 6365 heads the 12.35 departure for Cheltenham at Platform 5. In the distance can be seen the 12.25 Gloucester-Hereford in the charge of a '2251' class 0-6-0. *B. J. Ashworth*

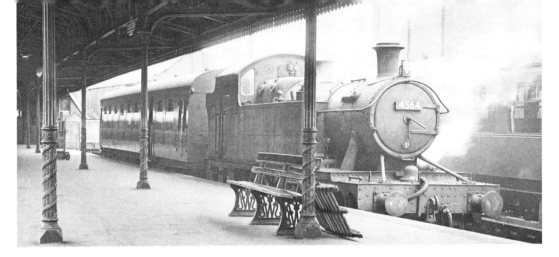

Above:

The rarely photographed up bay, Platform 6, is seen in this view of '4500' No 4564 on the 10.20am to Chalford on 14 September 1964. *B. J. Ashworth*

Right:

On 15 September a 'Grange' passes Horton Road depot and approaches Tramway Junction crossing with a lengthy freight from South Wales. The lines in the foreground passing beneath the signal gantry lead to Gloucester Eastgate station. *B. J. Ashworth*

Below:

The east end of Gloucester Central in 1964. 2-8-2T No 7205 heads a freight on the up through line, 'Hymek' No D7053 stands at Platform 6 with a train for Swindon and another 'Hymek', No D7019, is on empty coaching stock duties. *R. E. Toop*

Engine Sheds and Locomotives

The shed at Gloucester originally opened in May 1845 just east of the C&GWUR terminus. With the extension of the line to Cheltenham in October 1847, the Gloucester allocation of passenger engines was transferred, Gloucester being left with goods and ballast locomotives. Following the increased allocation required by the opening of the South Wales Railway, a new four-road, brick-built shed was opened at Horton Road in 1854 and in 1872 a further six-road shed was added. Closed to steam in December 1965, several of its engines found their way to preservation societies. The depot is still in use for stabling, signing on, fuelling and giving minor attention to diesel locomotives and multiple-units. Trains reversing at Gloucester normally have a fresh engine on the other end.

The first broad gauge locomotives were 2-2-2s for passenger trains and 0-6-0s on goods. Gooch's standard gauge 2-2-2s Nos 69-76 built 1855-56 were transferred to working Gloucester-London trains after being renewed by Armstrong and for their size were, according to Ahrons, about the best single driving wheel express engines which ever ran. 'Queen' class engines of the same wheel arrangement, No 1122 *Beaconsfield* and No 1123 *Salisbury* worked the up and down New Milford boat express between Gloucester and Paddington 1875-87, leaving Gloucester at 8am and arriving back at 8.37pm, making a long day for the footplate crew. 'Barnum' class 2-4-0s came out in 1889 with four coupled wheels being a great improvement on the single drivers for the hilly road to Swindon. A couple of unusual 2-4-0s working the Swindon section were Dean's essays into compounding, Nos 7 & 8. Churchward standard engines gradually appeared on the line, followed by those of Collett, the only locomotives not being allowed were those of the 'King' class. Until GWR diesel railcars took over most of the workings, engines using the Ledbury branch were fitted with specially small tenders to allow them to use the short turntable there.

Above right:
Churchward 'Saint' No 2906 *Lady of Lynn* at Gloucester shed on 18 April 1938. *P. F. Winding collection*

Top right:
A general view of Horton Road shed looking east in 1937. A variety of locomotives can be seen, including a double framed 'Aberdare' class 2-6-0 on the far left-hand shed road. *L&GRP (2058)*

Right:
Work-stained '2884' class No 3824 passes Tramway Junction on 30 January 1964 with a Class 6 freight for Worcester. Horton Road depot looms large behind the locomotive and Tramway Junction signalbox.
P. J. Lynch

Newport

The broad gauge South Wales Railway from Chepstow to Swansea was opened on 18 June 1850, through rail communication to London via Gloucester beginning on 19 July 1852 when the bridge over the Wye opened at Chepstow. High Street station is situated within 100 yards of Newport's main street and between a bridge over the River Usk to the east and a tunnel through Stow Hill to the west. Originally the station consisted of up and down platforms with a central non-platform road. The SWR amalgamated with the GWR in 1862 and 10 years later the gauge converted to standard. The Pontypool, Caerleon & Newport Railway promoted by the GWR, opened to goods on 17 September 1874 and to passengers on 21 December, linked the Newport, Abergavenny & Hereford Railway with High Street station. In 1879 another connecting line permitted Western Valley trains to run into High Street, while a further link gave a similar facility to those from the Eastern Valley. The now inadequate station was enlarged in 1875-78, the architects Lancaster Owen and J. E. Danks incorporating the original buildings on the down side into the new station, the rest being necessarily demolished to allow room for northwards expansion. The down platform was lengthened, an up island platform provided, and into this enlarged station all trains from both valleys, the Brecon & Merthyr Railway and the LNWR Sirhowy trains were run, allowing closure of four other stations. Scissors crossovers allowed each of the two main line platforms to hold two trains, the two central roads allowing through trains to overtake.

In 1912 the tunnel west of High Street had a double-track bore added north of the original and in 1925 the Usk Bridge was widened to take four tracks. Power signalling arrived at Newport on 29 May 1927 when the new East box with 96 levers (17 spare) replaced two former boxes. It was the first large-scale installation of the Ferreira-Insell system (R. J. Insell was the GWR signal engineer), whereby miniature four-position levers were used to set the route and work standard GWR semaphore signals. Its principal feature was that a single lever combined as many operations as were necessary to set the route and to work signals for the route required. On 24 June 1928, West box with a similar installation was brought into use with 125 working levers and 19 spares.

This was part of a reconstruction of the station by E. Turner & Sons Ltd of Cardiff which commenced early in 1923. More than 100 men were employed on rebuilding the station at a cost of more than £120,000.

Newport was one of the first Great Western stations to have a skeleton of steel stanchions and girders so that the walls merely kept out the weather, rather than supporting the building, this method leading to economy when making a tall structure, as the base of the walls did not have to be sufficiently strong to carry the whole weight of the building. The premises were practically fire-proof, the floors being a series of reinforced

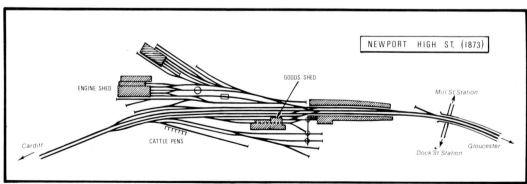

NEWPORT HIGH ST. (1873)

ENGINE SHED

GOODS SHED

Mill St Station

Cardiff

CATTLE PENS

Gloucester

Dock St Station

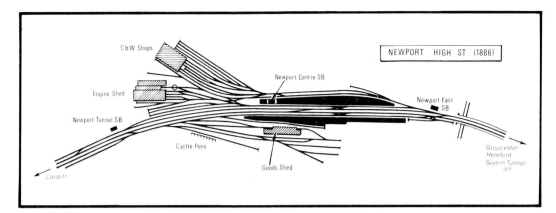

C & W Shops

Newport Centre SB

Engine Shed

Newport East SB

Newport Tunnel SB

Cattle Pens

Goods Shed

Gloucester
Hereford
Severn Tunnel
Jct

Cardiff

beams, the spaces between the beams being filled with specially made twin tubes or pots. The foundations were on rock, and the plinth of the main station block of axed-faced Cornish granite, the same material also forming a dado in the booking hall as it was well able to withstand rough usage. The main buildings on the down side have an impressive façade of multi-coloured Cattybrook bricks with Portland stone dressings, five storeys and almost 80ft high. The arches to the windows and also the panels and string course are of red sand brick.

The ground floor contained the booking hall, enquiry office, refreshment room and various platform offices. The refreshment room was panelled in oak and had a beautiful tessellated floor, while the booking office had a circular screen, the plinth of which was granite surmounted by a bronze and wrought iron grill pierced with six ticket-issuing windows. The booking hall was decorated with large photographs of beauty spots, these photographs being encased in bronze frames surrounded by marble.

The walls of the main staircase were faced with French stucco lined to represent Bath stone and had a marble dado, with fossil skirting and bands. On the first floor were the public dining room and kitchen, smoking room and writing room, together with lavatory and cloakroom accommodation. The dining room capable of seating 200, was panelled in Japanese oak, while the gas range was claimed to be the largest in Wales. The whole of the second floor, purpose-designed as a gentleman's club premises, was occupied by the County & Monmouth Club, woodwork throughout being mahogany. The third and fourth floor were equipped as offices for the divisional superintendent and district manager. The flat roof was composed of patent Diespeker Flooring covered with ¾in of asphalt, making it perfectly watertight.

Owing to the large consumption of electricity in the building and the rest of the company's property in the immediate neighbourhood, it was necessary for Newport Corporation, which supplied the power, to erect a sub-station for the purpose of receiving a supply at high tension, transforming it and then controlling it through circuit switches. The high tension supply at 6,600V was transformed to 400V for power and 230V for lighting. In the event of the AC supply failing, a DC emergency source for a limited number of lights in the booking hall and more important parts of the station came from a Corporation battery. Electricity worked three lifts: a 15cwt passenger lift serving all floors; a 10cwt staff lift also serving all floors and a small lift serving cellar, refreshment room and dining room floor. Even at this relatively early date, platforms and all important rooms were fitted with electric slave clocks controlled by a master in the stationmaster's office. The station had an automatic telephone installation and as at Paddington, the various departments were connected to the telegraph office by pneumatic message tube, the carrier taking communications at a rate of 80ft/sec. When working at full demand, the small bore heating system consumed approximately a ton of coke daily.

In addition to the platforms being extended, a new one, No 8, was provided to the north of the loading dock. A splendid glazed double colonnade lights the wide west end of Platforms 2 & 3, and is similar to one at the west end of Platforms 8 & 9 at Paddington. A single version of this colonnade later appeared at Taunton and Temple Meads. The total cost of the various improvements at Newport came to almost £½ million.

Track alterations were made in connection with the new Spencer Steelworks at Llanwern four miles east of Newport. This was because west of Newport, the up and down goods lines were on the south side of the main lines, whereas east of the station they were on each side. To obviate many conflicting movements, reorganisation was necessary in order to place both goods lines on the south side. The most important alteration at the station was adapting the former up main platform for use

105

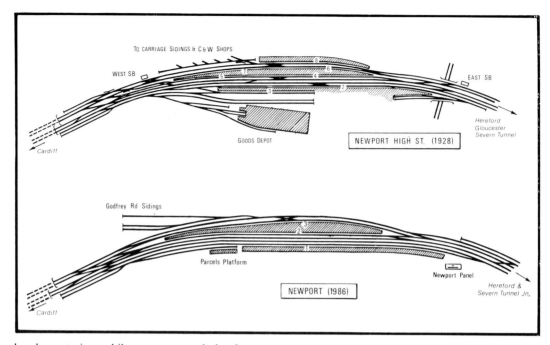

To Carriage Sidings & C & W Shops

WEST SB

Cardiff

GOODS DEPOT

NEWPORT HIGH ST. (1928)

EAST SB

Hereford
Gloucester
Severn Tunnel

Godfrey Rd Sidings

Parcels Platform

Newport Panel

NEWPORT (1986)

Cardiff

Hereford &
Severn Tunnel Jn.

by down trains, while up ones used the former down relief platform, but at times of peak traffic, down trains could be diverted to the former down main platform, which continued to be used by down parcels trains. Platforms were renumbered from the north on 16 April 1961, though subsequently have been renumbered starting from the south. A new panel signalbox at the east end of the down parcels platform opened on 9 December 1962 and is of the standard WR mosaic type based on the Integra design with entrance switches and exit buttons. Main lines are signalled for a 2½-minute headway for express trains, while the relief lines which had a maximum limit of 40mph were arranged for a 5-minute headway between freight trains.

In 1973 a modern ticket office and travel centre opened, leading on to the down platform. Most trains today use the island platform, reached via the footbridge. The goods agent's offices adjacent to the down platform have recently been demolished and a new station approach road and short-stay car park have been built on their site, a new canopy being constructed to give shelter from the weather. The carriageway approach is enlivened with the sculpture 'Archform'. Harvey Hook was commissioned by BR with a grant from the Welsh Arts Council to create this 18ft high arch of steel plate symbolising features of the city's industrial and railway heritage.

Newport was the first place on the GWR to be adapted for train control. Six controllers could communicate with all places in the division, and with other divisional controlling offices, thereby

Above right:
A 1922 view of Newport station in the up direction before rebuilding. The stone-built Newport Middle signalbox in the foreground closed six years later on 26 June 1928. *L&GRP (8849)*

Right:
Another 1922 view of Newport before reconstruction, photographed from the east end of the down platform. Note the curved lower edge of the canopy, typical of the earlier designs. *L&GRP (8850)*

keeping freight trains working under review and arranging clearances from docks, collieries and factories as required; some 550 goods and passenger trains being dealt with every 24 hours.

In the late 1930s, seven road vehicles dealt with a daily traffic of 2,500 items forwarded and a similar number of items received, while additionally there was a very considerable transfer traffic in connection with the Valley stations. The goods depot was alongside the passenger station with bridges between the goods platforms. A total of 47 wagons could be held under cover. For warehousing purposes there was a cellar covering 781 square yards, and an upper floor of equal area served by both chute and electric lift. A cartage fleet of no less than 97 vehicles was employed in the business of collection and delivery over an area of 2½ miles from the station.

Left:
Reconstruction work has started in this photograph of the island platform, taken on 14 June 1926. *Great Western Railway*

Below left:
A close-up of the same view on 23 February 1927 with work well advanced. Note the modified signalling arrangements controlling the crossover between the up platform line and the up through. *Great Western Railway*

Right:
The work completed on 16 May 1927. The old building has altered and an extra storey added. The notice board in the left-hand window advises passengers of the running of trains; the train from Badminton is four minutes late. *Great Western Railway*

Below right:
On a misty, wet 4 May 1951, ex-LNWR Webb 'Coal Tank' No 58915 stands at Platform 7 with a stopping train, as an ROD 2-8-0 struggles through the rain with a westbound freight. *H. C. Casserley*

Top:
A view of Platforms 1 & 2 in the up direction in the early 1960s, following the renumbering of the platforms.
Lens of Sutton

Above:
This 1960s view shows clearly the triangular mouldings on the down side platform canopy. *Lens of Sutton*

Above right:
'2251' class 0-6-0 No 2287 shunts empty coaching stock for a Brecon train on 18 July 1959. *R. E. Toop*

Right:
'3100' class Prairie No 3103 passes through the station with a transfer freight on 30 May 1959. The great length of the island platform is readily apparent. *J. Hodge*

111

Top:
No 5066 *Wardour Castle* **stands at the down main platform on 25 August 1952 with the 11.55am from Paddington. This picture shows clearly the down bay platform, No 3, and it can be seen that the platform itself is much wider than in the 1922 view.** *P. Ransome-Wallis*

Above:
No 6916 *Misterton Hall* **heads a Hereford-Cardiff stopping train on 25 June 1956. The massive station block built in the 1920s towers above the 1870s structure.** *P. J. Sharpe*

Top:
'8750' class 0-6-0PT No 3685 leaves the east end of
Newport with the 11.50am SO to Abergavenny, whilst a
three-car DMU on the left forms the 12.15 departure to
Blaenavon circa 1960.   *R. E. Toop*

Above:
BR Standard '9F' No 92207 leaves Newport with the
9.20am Swansea-Brockenhurst on 27 June 1959.
J. Hodge

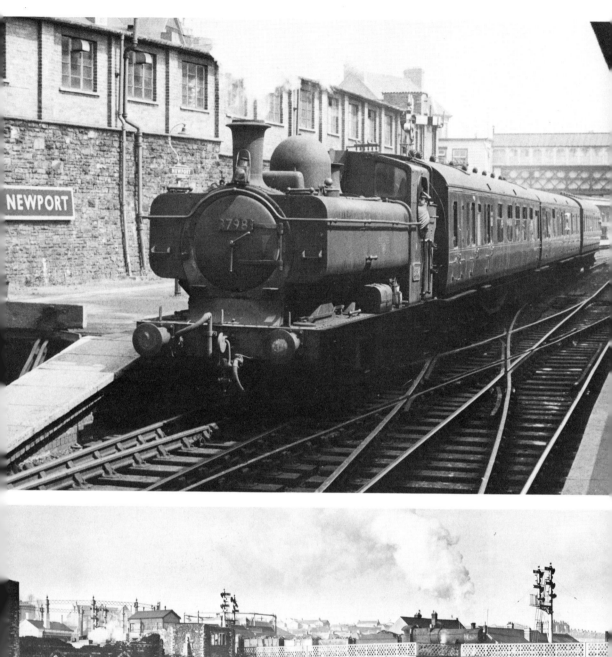

Above left:
The 11.15am Newport-Brecon leaves the new Platform 1 on 9 June 1962 behind '8750' class Pannier No 3798. This platform was used in order not to obstruct other lines when branching off at Gaer Junction. *W. A. Manship*

Left:
An up coal train crosses the River Usk at the east end of Newport station on 6 January 1957, hauled by a Churchward '2800' class 2-8-0. *S. Rickard*

Above:
A 'Castle' enters Newport from the west with a Swansea-Paddington express. *G. F. Heiron*

Right:
A view looking east from Platform 5 in the 1950s. No 5084 *Reading Abbey* has arrived at Platforms 1 & 2 with a down passenger service. The crossover connecting Platforms 4 & 5 with the up through line is prominent in this picture, together with the associated signalling which includes calling on (CO) signals. *G. F. Heiron*

Left:
The subway entrance on the present-day Platforms 2 & 3, beneath the colonnade. A similar canopy design was used on the up platform at Taunton, and a wider version at the west end of Platforms 8 & 9 at Paddington. Note the benefit of the transparent canopy roof. *Author*

Below:
An excellent view of the handsome exterior of Newport station in 1955, with considerable activity in the approach road. *G. F. Heiron*

Right:
'Britannia' Pacific No 70025 *Western Star* pulls into Platforms 4 & 5 with the heavily loaded 8.00am Swansea-Paddington in the late 1950s. The train consists largely of BR Mk 1 vehicles, but the third and fourth coaches are ex-GWR restaurant cars. *G. F. Heiron*

Below right:
WD Austerity 2-8-0 No 90676 of Ebbw Junction shed (86A) passes through Newport with a down freight in May 1957. To the right of the picture can be seen the station goods yard. *P. F. Winding*

Engine Sheds and Locomotives

The four-road Newport High Street shed opened by the SWR in August 1854 was demolished in 1916 as it had been replaced by Ebbw Junction depot at the other end of the tunnel. This opened on 17 July 1915 and was of a similar design to the depot at Tyseley.

Throughout the years the usual range of GWR standard engines appeared on trains, with 0-6-2T, 2-8-0T and 2-8-2T classes being favoured for goods work. Ex-LNWR 'Coal Tank' 0-6-2Ts still worked Sirhowy Valley passenger trains in the 1950s. In 1954 Class 9F 2-10-0s appeared on freight workings, and from 1959 engines of this class handled passenger expresses on summer Saturdays. In 1957 all Western Region 'Britannias' were transferred to Cardiff and worked Paddington expresses, thus displacing 'Castles'. GWR diesel railcars worked trains from Newport up the Wye Valley branch to Monmouth at least as early as 1942.

Birmingham

The London & Birmingham Railway opened in 1838 and enjoying a traffic monopoly, did not always provide a satisfactory service. The Grand Junction Railway, opened from Birmingham to Warrington in 1837, planned an extension southwards in 1845 to join the Oxford branch of the Great Western Railway. However the following year the Grand Junction amalgamated with both the Manchester & Birmingham Railway and the London & Birmingham Railway to form the London & North Western Railway. The need for a competing line still existed and Parliament passed the Birmingham & Oxford Junction Railway Act authorising a line from Fenny Compton on the Oxford & Rugby, to a junction with the LNWR at Birmingham. The Birmingham Extension Act provided for a projection to Great Charles Street. On 3 August 1846 the same date as these two Acts were passed, a further Act allowed the Birmingham, Wolverhampton & Dudley Railway to build a line from Monmouth Street (later Colmore Row) between Livery Street and Snow Hill, to a junction

with the Oxford, Worcester & Wolverhampton Railway near Priestfield Furnaces, Wolverhampton. As the two lines overlapped between Monmouth Street and Great Charles Street, each company had equal rights over the proposed station at Snow Hill. Before construction started both companies were absorbed by the GWR on 31 August 1848, so that the broad gauge could be extended northwards from Fenny Compton to Wolverhampton. Snow Hill station, designed by W. G. Owen, was literally on the hill; as approached from London the railway passed under Colmore Row in a tunnel, but at the other end, platforms crossed over Great Charles Street.

The 66 miles of mixed gauge line opened from Oxford to Snow Hill on 1 October 1852, though only the broad gauge lines were used. The name Snow Hill was not officially adopted until February 1858, local timetables referring to it as Livery Street or Great Charles Street, Osborne's timetable as late as 1868 still using the name Livery Street to indicate which entrance should be used —

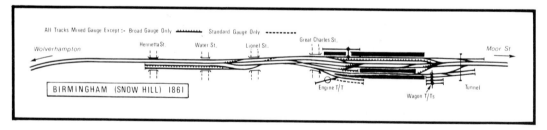

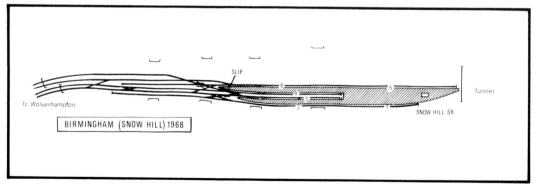

Snow Hill for up and Livery Street for down trains. Owing to difficulties in securing possession of existing slum buildings on the site, it was not possible to commence work on the station until the end of January 1852. This did not allow sufficient time to build a permanent station, and therefore a large timber train shed was provided for the opening. It covered three platforms and two through roads and did duty until 1871 when it was dismantled and removed to Didcot where it became a carriage shed on the site of the later locomotive shed.

The 1871 replacement station, although an improvement on its predecessor, left something to be desired. Reginald H. Cocks commented in the *Railway Magazine* in 1901 that '. . . it cannot be said to constitute an architectural erection worthy of the Great Western Railway Company's best efforts'. The approach to the station from public roads was very awkward, the turning into either of the station yards through the narrow entrance gates both in Snow Hill and Livery Street being far too cramped. The station consisted of up and down main platforms, each about 600ft in length with double scissors crossovers in the centre giving access to and from the two through roads. There were two departure bay platforms at the down end of the down platform, and an arrival bay at the down end of the up.

Below:
The wooden structure of the original Snow Hill station, after re-erection as Didcot carriage shed, circa 1896.
Author's collection

The Snow Hill, or up side platform contained the following offices: lavatory, telegraph, cloakroom, dining room (leased by Messrs Browning), first class refreshment room, second class refreshment room, first class waiting room, first class ladies' room, third class ladies' room, third class waiting room, stationmaster's office, booking hall, coach working offices, outward parcels office and guards' and porters' rooms. The order on the Livery Street side was similar.

The two main platforms were linked by a footbridge and enclosing everything was a cresent-shaped truss roof of 92ft span glazed in the centre, the remainder had timber cladding sealed with a waterproof compound. A smaller edition of this roof covered the bay platforms at the north end of the station. Steelwork was supplied by the Patent Shaft & Axletree Co Ltd of Old Park Ironworks, Wednesbury.

Snow Hill Tunnel originally only extended to Temple Row, but in 1874 the space above the retaining walls was roofed by brick arches carried on piers of the same material. These formed the foundation for the Great Western Arcade built at a cost of £70,000, the shops following the line of the tunnel. A ventilating system was installed to disperse fumes in the 550yd-long tunnel on a gradient of 1 in 45 rising towards the station. Air circulated from a pipe below rail level and blew smoke out through the tunnel mouths.

In 1863 the Great Western Hotel was opened above the line at the south end of the station, steps leading to the platforms. Of Italianate design, the building had flanking towers with balconies sheltered by round pediments supported on pairs

Above:
The demolition of the old station roof in 1906 during the rebuilding of the station. The Great Western Hotel can be seen in the background. *Courtesy Engineering*

Above right:
A view inside the impressive booking hall concourse in 1913. Road vehicles entered on the right-hand side of the gateway, set down passengers in front of the book office, continued around the perimeter of the concourse and drove out on the left-hand side. *Courtesy Engineering*

Right:
The sector table at the end of Platforms 3 & 4, seen in 1913. The locomotive is 2-6-2T No 3907, rebuilt in 1907 from '2301' class 'Dean Goods' No 2508.
Courtesy Engineering

of columns. Faced with white brick, it contained 126 rooms and was one of the finest Victorian buildings in Birmingham.

Train services developed to such an extent that the new station was no longer sufficient to deal adequately with the traffic, some 350-400 trains being handled daily. Extension was not easy, lateral expansion being out of the question due to the enormous expense of purchasing property in Snow Hill and Livery Street, while the tunnel to the south prevented expansion in that direction. The only answer was to develop to the north, though Moor Street station at the other end of Snow Hill Tunnel was opened on 1 July 1909 to deal with commuter traffic to and from the south, relieving pressure through the tunnel. In October and November 1902 the sum of £341,693 was authorised for rebuilding Snow Hill station. Later an additional £10,150 was provided for installing electric light throughout the hotel, station and sidings to the north, while in 1911 an extra £10,035 was required for additional items.

Work on the new station began in September 1906 being carried out by Walter Y. Armstrong, the GWR's newly appointed works engineer, C. E. Shackle being the resident engineer. The contractors were Henry Lovatt Ltd, E. C. & J. Keay supplying the steelwork and Mellowes & Co the 'Eclipse' roof glazing.

As the luxury station hotel had not proved a great success, due to potential visitors being put off by the sound and smell of locomotives at close quarters, in 1909 it was closed and converted to an office block for the divisional traffic superintendent and district goods manager and their staffs who had been transferred from the old

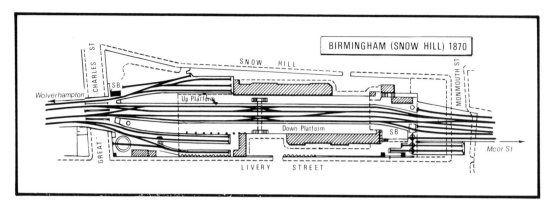

Above:
A view of the up line platform looking south in 1913.
Courtesy Engineering

Below:
A driver's-eye view of the approach to the station from Snow Hill Tunnel. *Ian Allan Library*

station. A public restaurant was provided on the ground floor. A new way into the station was cut through the former hotel from Colmore Row making a new principal entrance for foot passengers. This led into an extensive booking hall 22ft above rail level. The hall's 94ft-span roof was of glass supported by latticework steel ribs while the booking windows were set in an arcade faced with glazed tiles, each window having a classical style pediment. Either side of the long booking office a ramp paved with 'Victorite' artificial stone slabs with a carborundum composition to render them non-slipping, took passengers and luggage to the footbridge across the lines. Lifts carried baggage to the platforms while passengers descended staircases 20ft in width to cope with intense traffic. Beside the footways were inclined cab roads with entrances from both Livery Street and Snow Hill, rising by an easy gradient to the level of the footbridge.

From the two-track Snow Hill Tunnel, turnouts gave access to the four roads between the main island platforms with a relief line on either side. Each of the four through platform roads was capable of accommodating two trains at once. Between the two main platforms the two up lines

were together and the two down lines together, but on leaving the station at the north end, the up and down main and up and down relief roads were respectively side by side. This layout in the station meant that, for example, when two trains were together at the down platform, the rear could start first and passing through the scissors crossing, take precedence over the train standing in front. Platforms were numbered across from the down side. The new station had three times the platform length of the old: Nos 1 & 2, down relief, 1,180ft; 5 & 6, down main, 1,188ft; 7 & 8, up main, 1,197ft; 11 & 12, up relief, 971ft. They were about 80ft wide while the bay platforms were Nos 3 & 4, 511ft and 509ft respectively and Nos 9 & 10 of 550ft and 305ft. They were 20-30ft wide, the minimum width from the platform building to the edge being 14ft. One of the scissors crossovers was worked from the North box and the other from the South, but neither was in view of the respective controlling signalman. A 'gantry signalman' by the crossovers informed the signalmen by telephone whether it was safe to shift the crossover, or whether a train was standing foul. Another of his duties was to inform the North box when it was safe to run an engine from Platform 3 or 4 road to the electrically-worked sector table built and installed by Ransomes & Rapier, which released an engine, being more economical on space than a crossover. Disused by 1929, it was removed in 1938. Following the installation of track circuiting, the gantry signalman was abolished about 1957.

On the main platforms were various waiting rooms and a large buffet, which, like its counterpart on the up platform was decorated with panelled oak with *art nouveau* coloured glass over the doors. Extensive kitchens were below as were the booking and telegraph offices for the Livery Street subway entrance, cloakroom, bookstall, lavatories and parcels lift. The subway, 20ft in width, had 12ft devoted to passengers, the

Above:
The view looking north through the station in the period between the two world wars. *L&GRP (9018)*

remainder enclosed by a railing being reserved for luggage and parcels. The third booking office was also found on the low level and approached by subway from Great Charles Street. The design of the platform buildings used dark, salt-glazed brick on projecting plinths about 1ft 6in high of blue pressed Staffordshire bricks. The walls were relieved by buff terra cotta dressings. The glazed bricks and sanitary ware were made by Doulton & Co. The glass roof gave a cheerful appearance and tended to heighten the station's appearance. The platforms were chiefly paved with patent Victoria stone. The completed station was always bright and sparkling as the walls received a weekly wash down. Snow Hill was considered the GWR's third-best major station, ranking only after

Below:
'3521' class 4-4-0 No 3555 enters Snow Hill with a four-coach up train circa 1928. *W. Potter*

Paddington and Brunel's terminus at Temple Meads.

From the bridge over Great Charles Street the lines of rails through the station towards Paddington were on an incline of 1 in 250 and the courses of brickwork to the walls of the platform buildings facing them were laid to the same gradient, a fact not apparent to the ordinary observer.

Advantage was taken of the station's hillside site to construct a commodious parcels depot, 13,000 cubic yards of soil being excavated to make a large yard containing 11,000 sq ft of roadway and pathway 24ft below rail level, carts entering from Snow Hill. The walls were faced with cream glazed bricks, the object being to make the place lighter seeing that both yard and offices were underneath the station. Above the yard were the two parcels platforms, 500 tons of steel being used in the girders, flooring and columns of the decking, while the cross-sleeper road above was laid on ballast over asphalt and concrete. The main girders, 89ft 8in in length, were brought complete from the James Bridge Works of Messrs Keay at Darlaston 10 miles distant on a special train, each girder being carried on a pair of GWR 'Pollen' trucks. These wagons also brought girders for other parts of the station, almost 6,000 tons in total. On the same level as the parcels yard was staff accommodation, one room being assigned to each grade with lockers for personal belongings. Here guards, porters and others took their meals, gas stove and cooking utensils being provided. Fronting Livery Street and Snow Hill, shop sites and warehouses were let by the GWR to various traders, shop sites bring an unusual feature to a principal GWR station elevation. Cellarage between Great Charles Street and Lionel Street was mostly let, but some was used for the accommodation of parcels cars, horses and motor lorries.

Due to the variation in levels, roofs were of three types:

1 That covering the high level booking hall and sloping footways

Above:
'Large Prairie' No 3104 stands below a smoke trough on 15 September 1956. *H. C. Casserley*

2 The main roof
3 The umbrella roofing to the bay platforms.

The first type was a 93ft 9½in span arch with windscreen at each end, light being admitted through ¼in rough cast glass. The sloping footways and bridge were covered with glass, but the space bounded by the footways, booking hall and footbridge respectively was left uncovered in order to allow smoke to escape from the nearby tunnel mouth. The main roof covered a length of 500ft. Having a superficial area of 12,000 square yards it was of the ridge and furrow type running

Below:
'5101' class 2-6-2T No 5106 and 'Castle' No 7002 *Devizes Castle* **brings a rake of empty coaching stock into Snow Hill station on Sunday 13 September 1953, passing the highly distinctive North box whose peculiar design was dictated by the very limited amount of space available.** *E. D. Bruton*

transversely across the main line. The curved elliptical soffits of the roof trusses, the valance boarding and the cast iron ornamental casings to the columns combined to produce a graceful design, a cast iron and glass windscreen enclosing each end. The handrail over the eave's gutters cleverly doubled as a water main for roof cleaning purposes. The centre of the roof over the main lines and throughout its length was left open for a space of 22ft to allow smoke to dissipate and to admit fresh air and sunlight. It also had the advantage of saving much glass cleaning. Messrs Keay built a travelling erecting stage carrying a 7-ton crane, this stage being used to support girders and trusses prior to riveting and to give protection to traffic passing beneath while the roof was under construction. The stage consisted of three girders, making a span across two platforms and four lines of rails and travelling from one windscreen to the other.

The sides of the station were completely glazed, the upper portion of each panel suspended from handsome elliptical cast iron work which supported the bold cornice and eaves gutter. The portions below this were partially suspended and partially supported. All glazing was of ⅜in glass held securely by clips to vertical T-bars, a strip of felt being inserted between glass and steel.

Points and signals on the Siemens all-electric system were worked from two boxes, the station having one of the first electrical signalling systems on the GWR. The North box, opened 31 October 1909, contained 224 levers and because of the limited area, stood high on braced steel stanchions. The 5,000V power supply from Birmingham Corporation was converted by the GWR's sub-station to 140V. Two motor generators installed in a room beneath the station charged two batteries of accumulators to supply current to the signalling system. The furthest signal was 620 yards distant, and the furthest points 243 yards away. The South box, opened in 1913, controlled 96 levers.

The booking office contained two Regina automatic ticket printing machines, the first to be installed in Britain and only requiring blank cards to be stocked. Issuing a ticket required the clerk to

Above:
Platform 5 at Snow Hill at 5.26pm on 12 June 1958. Two three-car diesel multiple-units form the 5.40pm departure for Cardiff and Hereford, with additional corridor third coach attached at the rear. *M. Mensing*

take a blank card, slip it through a slot in a small sliding carriage which he moved along until a pointer was opposite the name of the station to which the passenger wished to book. Then by depressing a handle, the ticket dropped out imprinted with the names of the departure and arrival stations, price, date, consecutive number and class of carriage. An automatic duplicate was made on a strip of paper so that at the end of the day the clerk had only to total the strip and balance his cash. Another interesting facility was the 'shop parcels office' to which people who had been shopping in the city could request their purchases to be sent, to await their arrival at the station.

Leading off the tunnel was a blacksmith's shop and stable for the four shunting horses. When not actually at work shunting wagons in the up and down fish docks but still on duty, they were tethered to pillars between the running lines. An entrance led from the tunnel sidings to the Bank of England vaults and eased transit from bullion trains. Another interesting feature was a clapper

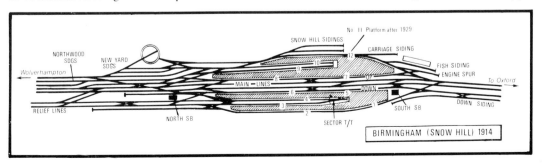

gong situated several yards to the rear of the down main home signal, its purpose being to warn drivers of the vicinity of this colour light signal, often difficult to observe in the smoke and steam in the tunnel. Snow Hill was one of the first GWR stations to be equipped with public address, the experimental system being made permanent in 1937.

World War 2 saw bomb damage on the night of 19/20 November 1940 when almost all the glass roof of the booking hall was destroyed, while on the night of 8/9 April 1941 a high explosive bomb demolished the ladies' waiting room and bookstall on Platform 5. A second bomb penetrated the down side cab road approach, exploding in the fish dock below, a third bomb piercing its way to the parcels yard. Much of the station's glass was replaced under a 1946 reglazing programme. The station was repainted every five years, a special formula paint being needed to withstand the sulphurous conditions, about 20 tons being required for a complete re-paint.

A Western Region prototype four-character train-describing panel signalbox was opened on 11 September 1960. Reversible working introduced on down platforms Nos 1, 2, 5 & 6 allowed the up side to be closed at night and later, also on Sundays. In 1961 BR announced plans to rebuild the station with platforms at street level, refreshment rooms, ticket offices and car park above, and with a shopping arcade on the third level, but the electrification from Euston to New Street meant that on 6 March 1967 Paddington-Snow Hill, Wolverhampton Low Level and Birkenhead expresses were discontinued, Snow Hill ceasing to be a main line station. Only Platforms 1-6 remained in use, the up side being declared redundant, the number of staff employed greatly reduced and goods trains diverted from the station. From August 1968 only Platforms 3 & 4 were utilised by the remaining Wolverhampton and Langley Green services. The circulating area became a car park and the station entrance was transferred to a gap in the Livery Street wall, a raised boarded crossing leading to Platform 1 past a makeshift booking office to down bays 3 & 4 where all traffic was concentrated. When unstaffed on 5 May 1969 it became the largest unstaffed halt in the country. Closed on 6 March 1972, BR demolished the derelict station in 1978 after cracks had appeared in the walls.

Below:
Seen from the window of an up train on 16 August 1958, No 7821 *Ditcheat Manor* stands at Platforms 5 & 6 with the 11am for Pwllheli. This view shows clearly how the central part of the roof was left open, and the glazing was removed from the end screen in order to allow smoke and steam to escape. *Brian Morrison*

Above right:
'Hall' No 5917 *Westminster Hall* waits to leave with the 6.00pm local to Wolverhampton on 17 September 1958. *M. Mensing*

Right:
The 4.35pm from Stourbridge Junction via Dudley has arrived at Platform 9 on 30 August 1958 behind 2-6-2T No 5101 in clean lined green livery. The stock then formed the 6.05pm departure to Leamington. *M. Mensing*

Below right:
A view looking south in the 1960s. Note the attractive curved design to the canopy end. *Lens of Sutton*

Above left:
No 4964 *Rodwell Hall* stands beneath the smoke trough at Platform 12 in the 1950s. The glazed screen can be seen clearly to the right of the train. *W. Flowers*

Left:
Snow Hill North signalbox gave an excellent view of the northern end of the station. On 21 March 1960 No 6001 *King Edward VII* departs with the 1.10pm Paddington-Wolverhampton. *R. C. Riley*

Above:
4-6-0 No 5962 *Wantage Hall* in a filthy condition passes Snow Hill North signalbox with a lengthy up freight on 21 March 1960. *R. C. Riley*

Right:
The classic view of Platform 7 from the staircase on 18 August 1962. No 6002 *King William IV* arrives with the 6.30am Birkenhead-Paddington. The bright, attractive interior of the station on a sunny day, is readily apparent. The diagrams for the 'Kings' finished shortly afterwards with the start of the winter timetable in September 1962. *B. J. Ashworth*

Left:
The 'Kings' were replaced by Type 4 'Western' class diesel-hydraulics, but the end of through Paddington services was to come in March 1967 with the inauguration of the LMR electrification from Euston. No D1000 *Western Enterprise* arrives with an up train, still carrying its distinctive 'Desert Sand' livery, but with the addition of yellow warning panels. *Ian Allan Library*

Below left:
The special character of Snow Hill is captured well by this photograph of Platform 7 on the morning of Sunday 20 March 1966. With sunlight streaming in through the roof glazing and the open central section, a Brush Type 4 diesel waits to leave with a Paddington train. *A. J. Dewis*

Below:
A plethora of porters' trucks populate an otherwise deserted Platform 5 on 17 July 1967 after the end of through main line services. *P. Weir*

Above right:
At 2.04pm by the station clock a three-car Metro-Cammell diesel multiple-unit on the up through road is dwarfed by the vastness of Snow Hill on 1 March 1967. *C. C. Thorburn*

Right:
Grimy and uncared-for, the front of Snow Hill station stands locked and gated after the start of the LMR electrified service from New Street. Passengers for the remaining few local services were obliged to use the side entrance in Great Charles Street. *D. R. Bickley*

Engine Sheds and Locomotives

Bordesley Junction, a four-road shed, opened in 1855 and closed in June 1908 when it was replaced by Tyseley, a standard two-turntable unit round-house shed with adjacent large repair shop, similar in design and construction to Old Oak Common. It closed in November 1966. At first standard gauge trains were worked by 2-2-2s Nos 69-76 and Nos 157-166. Around 1880 trains of five or six eight-wheel coaches were usually headed by a 2-2-2 of the 'Queen' class which continued to operate on this route until a larger turntable was installed at Wolverhampton about 1900 when 4-2-2s of the 'Achilles' class took over. The Oxford-Wolverhampton service was generally worked by 2-2-2s of the 'Sir Daniel' class. The

Left:
A trackless Snow Hill stands gaunt and decaying in 1977 shortly before final demolition took place.
L. E. Jones (Demolition) Ltd

Below left:
This view of the derelict Snow Hill looking north in 1977 shows how the station was adapted to the sloping site. Both the hotel and the booking hall concourse had been demolished several years earlier in 1969 due to their dangerous structural condition.
L. E. Jones (Demolition) Ltd

Below:
The interior of Tyseley roundhouse in December 1964, with 'Modified Hall' No 7908 *Henshall Hall*, 'Hall' No 5988 *Bostock Hall* and '5600' class 0-6-2T No 5684 ranged around the turntable. *R. A. Garland*

Birkenhead line saw 2-4-0s of the '56' class which also ran to Hereford. Six of the '717' class 2-4-0s were for many years the only passenger tender engines shedded at Bordesley Junction and together with others, worked turns to Cardiff. Local passenger trips were handled by Wolverhampton-built 0-4-2Ts. In the early 1900s a demand arose for more powerful tank engines and as the works was busy, '2301' class 0-6-0 tender engines were converted to 2-6-2Ts, but these were eventually displaced in 1929 by new engines of this wheel arrangement. 4-4-0s of the 'Atbara' and 'City' classes worked between Paddington and Wolverhampton, while from 1912 'Atbaras' worked Birmingham-Swansea services. Dean's 4-4-0s were replaced by the 'County' class and until the weight restrictions over the Stonehouse Viaduct, Gloucestershire, was lifted in 1927, were the heaviest engines permitted on expresses to Bristol started in 1910. 'Saint' and 'Star' 4-6-0s gradually took over work of the 4-4-0s. 'Castles' did not appear regularly on Wolverhampton services until about 1935, though 'Kings' were used from 1928. While 9 July 1934 saw the inauguration of a Snow Hill-Gloucester-Cardiff (General) diesel railcar service, in the summer of 1957 Swindon's first 'Inter-City' six-car set DMUs with buffets intended for the Glasgow-Edinburgh shuttle, temporarily worked from Snow Hill to Swansea. In March 1958 the service was taken over by Swindon 'Cross Country' units, though as each set had a buffet and a train consisted of two or three sets, it was impossible and uneconomic to man each. In 1962 'Western' class diesel hydraulics took over from 'Kings', while the following year these in turn were superseded by Brush Class 47 locomotives.

Wolverhampton

The site of Wolverhampton station caused a fierce controversy when the Shrewsbury & Birmingham and the Birmingham, Wolverhampton & Dudley Railways both wanted the same area of land for a station. A compromise was reached, the companies dividing it using the canal as a boundary. Construction of the BWDR began in 1851 between Snow Hill and Priestfield Junction where it joined the Oxford, Worcester & Wolverhampton Railway 1½ miles south of the town. The BWDR together with the half-mile length of GWR north of Wolverhampton Low Level station linking Cannock Road Junction with Stafford Road Junction was completed and ready for the Board of Trade inspection in August 1854, when just before the visit, a 63ft span wrought iron tubular bridge between Soho and Handsworth collapsed, repairs taking over two months. The line opened for passenger trains on 14 November 1854. Both were double mixed gauge lines, standard gauge trains from Shrewsbury and Chester working through Wolverhampton to Snow Hill, while local services to Birmingham were broad gauge. From 4 February 1854 until 13 November the same year, the SBR used Wolverhampton High Level station and Birmingham New Street, but from 14 November diverted its trains to Wolverhampton Low Level and Birmingham Snow Hill. Wolverhampton

station was renamed Wolverhampton Low Level in April 1856.

Wolverhampton Low Level was built to the one-sided plan like Reading, Taunton and Gloucester, the up and down platforms being sited on the west side in order to be on the town side of the line and thus avoid passengers having to cross tracks to reach the platform. Like Reading, a platform was provided both sides of the train. The footbridge giving access was open with trellis work sides. The up platform for local services was situated on the conventional side of the line. Unlike Reading and Taunton, one of the crossovers was situated at the mouth of the 377yd-long Wolverhampton Tunnel, such a highly dangerous situation being somewhat ameliorated by the introduction of a primitive block system.

The break of gauge prevented through traffic being worked from the North to London, so a transfer was arranged at the Victoria Basin depot of the SBR. Oxley Viaduct, just north of Wolverhampton was the most northerly point reached by the broad gauge. From 1 November 1868 all passenger trains from Low Level to Snow Hill were worked on the standard gauge.

In 1858 the Great Western sold to the LNWR for £80,000 its interest in the joint High Level station acquired through its purchase of the SBR

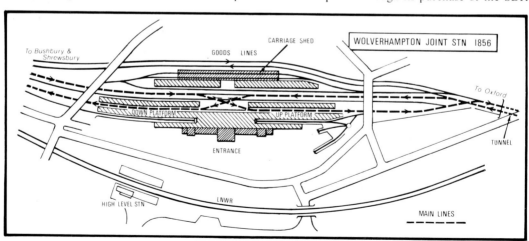

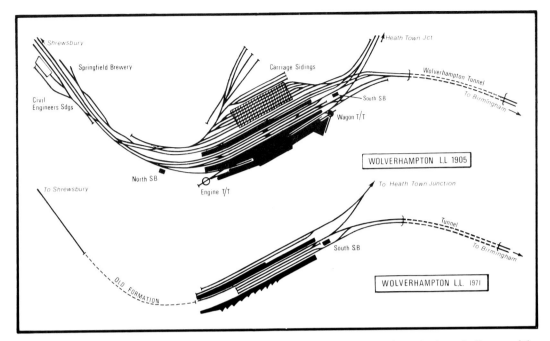

on 1 September 1854 and concentrated its traffic on Low Level jointly owned with the OWWR. From opening, both stations had been used by the GWR for down traffic, coaches from High Level being united with those from Low Level at Stafford Road Junction, No corresponding up service was run, all passengers from the North having to use the Low Level station.

The train shed roof with its timber gables was supported on brick walls and when the roof was removed and replaced by platform canopies, these walls remained. The offices were contained in a 'large town house' type of building of blue brick, with pediments above the windows as at Reading. A splendid feature was the lofty booking hall with two tiers of windows admitting light. An interesting feature found at Low Level and indeed at other early GWR stations, was the use of wagon turntables (which used less space than a set of points) giving access to short spurs at the southern end of the platform, while later in the 19th century, they were also provided at the other end.

Removal of broad gauge tracks in 1869 gave an opportunity for the station to be remodelled, with separate up and down platforms. For many years a dip in the centre of the platform gave access to a level crossing intended for luggage, but was also used by impatient passengers. The provision of a luggage lift allowed the crossing to be abolished. The 20th century saw the removal of the train shed and its replacement with platform canopies and umbrella roofing.

Track alterations through the years were remarkably few, the principal one being in April 1899 when a new carriage shed was built east of the station and the goods lines were diverted between it and the station. From 18 January 1970 the layout was greatly simplified when it became a terminal station, all passenger trains using the former down platform. On 6 April 1970 the up platform was converted to a parcels concentration depot at a cost of £30,000, its catchment and distribution area stretching to Walsall, Dudley and Kidderminster. The parcels service proved so successful that two sidings were laid on the formation of the former goods lines. A fleet of 50 delivery vans handled some 8,000 parcels daily. The main station door ceased to be used by passengers as DMUs only used the extreme southern end of the down platform, a blackboard announcing 'Passengers for Snow Hill to use entrance through Yard'. The station became a parcels depot only from 6 March 1972. The line through Stow Heath was taken out of use on 23 May 1973, the only approach then being from Heath Town Junction. The station closed as a parcels depot in 1981, the remaining tracks being taken out of use in October 1984 pending removal. At the time of writing the Borough Council has bought the site and is developing the station as the Wolverhampton Transport Heritage Centre, displaying examples of cycles, motor cycles, buses, trolley buses, lorries and vans made in Wolverhampton. It is hoped to obtain at least one steam locomotive which has been serviced or maintained at the former Stafford Road works. The building will be cleaned and restored, with Victorian-style gas lamps lighting the exterior and the stone block road outside.

Above left:
The approach to Wolverhampton from the north in mixed-gauge days pre-1869. Features of interest include the overall roof of the train shed, and that the common rail of the mixed-gauge track leading into the bay changes sides beyond Wednesfield Road bridge in order to bring standard gauge trains alongside the platform. From left to right the lines are: two goods lines; through; up; down; bay. *L&GRP (17793)*

Left:
This exterior view circa 1910 shows the very solid appearance of the station building. Note the GWR buses just visible in the background, far right.
Wolverhampton Public Libraries

Above:
Double-framed 'Barnum' class 2-4-0 No 3216 stands at the north end of the up platform next to the road bridge in 1925. *H. Robinson*

Above right:
No 3218, another 'Barnum' class 2-4-0, stands beneath the overall roof at Wolverhampton on 3 March 1929. When the roof was demolished, the supporting walls were left in place.
P. F. Winding collection

Right:
No 6003 *King George IV* receives attention after arriving at Wolverhampton with the down 'Inter-City' on 21 July 1954. *Brian Morrison*

Above:
Restored No 3440 *City of Truro* **heads a Stephenson Locomotive Society excursion to Swindon Works at Wolverhampton on 16 June 1957. The West Midland line train to Stourbridge Junction, Kidderminster and Worcester waits in the bay with '5101' class 2-6-2T No 5106. On the far right of the picture can be seen the carriage shed, situated to the east of the station, with the freight lines running between the two.** *G. F. Bannister*

Left:
The imposing interior of the booking hall, photographed in April 1956. *Ian Allan Library*

Top right:
BR Standard Class 4MT No 75003 in lined green livery passes through the station on 31 August 1961 with an up freight. *M. Pope*

Centre right:
'Castle' No 5070 *Sir Daniel Gooch* **draws out of the bay platform with the 2.10pm to Stourbridge Junction via Dudley on Whit Monday 11 June 1962. The locomotive had arrived at Wolverhampton on the up 'Cambrian Coast Express'.** *M. Mensing*

Right:
The up 'Cambrian Coast Express' pulls away from Wolverhampton behind No 6025 *King Henry III* **in the final summer of the 'King' operations.** *A. W. Smith*

Left:

On 27 August 1962, green-liveried 'Western' class diesel-hydraulic No D1005 *Western Venturer* waits in the up through road with four gleaming maroon Mk 1 coaches which it will add to the up 'Cambrian Coast Express' before taking the train forward from Wolverhampton. *M. Mensing*

Below left:

During the rundown of steam, grimy 'Castle' No 7001 *Sir James Milne* waits for departure with the 12.05pm from Wolverhampton, the southbound 'Pines Express' on 7 May 1963. *Ian Allan Library*

Below:

A fine cast iron lamp column is visible in this photograph of a porter loading a bulky consignment on the first stage of its journey to New Zealand in May 1963. *Ian Allan Library*

Top right:

A Gloucester RC&W single-car diesel unit arrives at Wolverhampton Low Level as the 17.48 from Snow Hill in June 1969. *N. D. Griffiths*

Right:

The 17.48 from Snow Hill once again after arrival at Wolverhampton on 11 May 1970. With the end of through services, much of the station had by now been given over to parcels traffic. The down platform line and the through roads have been lifted beyond the footbridge where they terminate in buffer stops. *G. F. Bannister*

Below right:

The north end of Wolverhampton Low Level on 11 May 1970 after conversion for use as a parcels depot. The remaining local passenger trains use only the cut-back remains of the down platform, whilst the up platform line is used solely for parcels traffic. *G. F. Bannister*

Engine Sheds and Locomotives

The OWWR built a standard gauge three-road shed south east of Low Level station in 1854, but this closed nine years later after amalgamation with the GWR. In November 1854 the GWR opened a broad gauge shed at Stafford Road about a mile north of Low Level station and adjacent to Dunstall Park station. A standard gauge shed was added in 1860. As the site was required for the expansion of the locomotive works, the shed was closed c1881 and three roundhouses built on the other side of the Stafford Road with parallel road sheds at the rear. This complex closed in September 1963. Oxley shed, built in brick and of the standard two-turntable unit type, was of similar construction to Old Oak Common, but because of site constrictions, the sheds were placed in tandem. Opened in July 1907 it accommodated freight locomotives, passenger types remaining at Stafford Road. It closed in March 1967.

The works at Wolverhampton were the Northern Division locomotive headquarters dealing with standard gauge locomotives and broad gauge engines working north of Oxford, and was allowed considerable autonomy. Locomotive building ceased in April 1908, the works thereafter simply being repair shops. With the rundown of steam, it closed in June 1964.

Following the GWR takeover, ex-OWWR 2-4-0s and 2-2-2s were joined at Wolverhampton by 'Sir Daniel' class 2-2-2s. It became the practice for locomotives working between London and Wolverhampton to make one journey via Worcester and the other via Banbury, this rostering continuing until World War 1. By the early 1880s the service was worked by larger 2-2-2s of the '157', '999' or 'Queen' class. Around the turn of the century, these in turn were replaced by the handsome Dean 'Achilles' class 4-2-2s. Gradually representatives of all the GWR standard classes appeared, but 'Kings' were not allowed to work north of the town until clearance tests in 1959. All London expresses changed engines at Low Level, at the same time up trains being strengthened and down trains shortened. 1962 saw the last of the 'Kings', and from then on 'Western' class diesel-hydraulics were responsible for expresses. Local services had been worked by DMUs since the summer of 1957.

Below:

A view inside Wolverhampton Works on 6 August 1932. A variety of locomotive types can be seen under repair, with double-frame 4-4-0s particularly in evidence in the foreground. *Great Western Railway*

Right:

Near the end of its working life, No 5015 *Kingswear Castle* stands on the turntable at Stafford Road (84A), its home shed, on 20 July 1954. *Brian Morrison*

Below right:

Stafford Road shed in the 1930s. Locomotives present include two ROD 2-8-0s, a Churchward Mogul, a 'Hall', a 'Star' and two 'Dukes'. *M. E. J. Deane*

Bibliography

Ahrons, E. L., *Locomotive & Train Working in the Latter Part of the Nineteenth Century*; Heffer, 1952.

Allen, C. J., *Titled Trains of the Western*; Ian Allan, 1974.

Allen, G. F., *The Western Since 1948*; Ian Allan, 1974.

Beck, K. M., *The West Midland Lines of the GWR*; Ian Allan, 1983.

Binney, M., Pierce, D., *et al, Railway Architecture*; Bloomsbury Books, 1985.

Body, G., *Railways of the Western Region*; Patrick Stephens, 1983.

Bradshaw's Railway Guides, (various dates).

Clark, R. H., *An Historical Survey of Selected Great Western Stations, Vols 2 & 3*; OPC, 1979/81.

Clinker, C. R., *Closed Stations & Goods Depots*; Avon-Anglia, 1978.

Clinker, C. R., *Paddington 1854-1979*; BR (WR) & Avon-Anglia, 1979.

Cooke, R. A., *Track Layout Diagrams of the GWR & BR WR*; author.

Harris, M, *et al, Brunel, the GWR & Bristol*; Ian Allan, 1985.

Harrison, D., *Salute to Snow Hill*; Barbryn Press, 1978.

Jackson, A., *London's Termini*; David & Charles, 1985.

Lyons, E., *An Historical Survey of Great Western Engine Sheds 1947*; OPC, 1972.

Lyons, E., Mountford, E., *An Historical Survey of Great Western Engine Sheds 1837-1947*; OPC, 1979.

Macdermot, E. T., Clinker, C. R., Nock, O. S., *History of the Great Western Railway*; Ian Allan, 1964-67.

Potts, C. R., *An Historical Survey of Selected Great Western Stations, Vol 4*; OPC, 1985.

RCTS, *Locomotives of the Great Western Railway*; RCTS, 1952-74.

Searle, M. V., *Down the Line to Bristol*; Baton Transport, 1986.

Thomas, D. St.J., *A Regional History of the Railways of Great Britain, Vol 1, The West Country*; David & Charles, 1981.

Vaughan, A., *A Pictorial Record of Great Western Architecture*; OPC, 1977.

Vaughan, J., *This is Paddington*; Ian Allan, 1982.

Journals: *Engineering, Great Western Railway Magazine, Modern Railways, Railway Magazine, Railway World* and *Trains Illustrated*.

Acknowledgements

Grateful acknowledgement for assistance is due to: G. F. Bannister, M. E. J. Deane, B. J. F. Gant, Goodlands Ltd, B. Mills, J. Robson, N. W. Slipp, D. R. Steggles, P. A. and S. H. Taylor; also to the staffs of the reference libraries at Bath, Birmingham, Newport, Plymouth, Reading, Taunton and Wolverhampton.

The Power Of Eliminating Negative Thinking

The Life-Changing Self Help Guide - How to Stop Overthinking, Remove any Negativity in Your Life and Finding Joy in Every Day

Bryan Patterson

ISBN – 9798524298454

Table of Contents

SCAN QR CODE AND GET AUDIO BOOK

FOR FREE!

To my dear readers,

We are thankful that you decided to buy this book. As special gift we can offer you the audio book for free. Just scan the QR code and download for free on Audible:

Please scan with your mobile phone:

*Just possible for new Audible customers.

Introduction

Negative thinking is extremely common and can affect most people at one time or another in their lives. There are many types and severities of negative thought patterns. They can range from an occasional fleeting negative thought to constant and intrusive thoughts that prevent you from optimising the quality of your life.

Some experts believe that negative thinking is an intrinsic part of human evolution that we initially adopted to keep us safe from harm in prehistoric times. For example, if you faced dangers in the prehistoric world, fear, anxiety, worry and other negative thoughts could trigger your flight or fight mechanism and help you to evade any imminent peril. However, in the modern world, negative thinking is much more harmful than helpful.

If you are being plagued by negative thinking, then it may be time to make a change to the way that you perceive the world. Negative thoughts often originate from our past experiences, traumas and perceptions of ourselves and others. They can start to form a pattern and spiral out of our control, affecting us in a variety of areas.

The great news is that negative thinking can be eliminated from your life and in this book, you will learn about how negative thinking can originate, how to get to the root of your negative thinking patterns, how to spot negative thoughts when they start to affect you and how to change your perceptions to eliminate them from your mind. This is intended to make you feel better and revolutionise your life entirely. You can adopt ways to prevent yourself from overthinking and overanalysing situations and find ways to rediscover the joy in the world.

Packed with simple explanations that can help you to understand your thought patterns and containing helpful and useful practical exercises, you will be able to use this book to change some of the fundamental aspects of your thoughts and emotions. No longer will you need to suffer in silence with negative and detrimental thinking patterns.

Most importantly, you could see significant improvements to all areas of your life, including your self-confidence, self-esteem and self-acceptance as well as improved relationships, friendships and career prospects. Crucially, you can be liberated from restrictive thinking cycles and find joy and happiness in your daily life, allowing you to prosper and flourish.

How Does Negative Thinking Originate?

There can be many origins of negative thinking. Origins can range from childhood experiences to recent traumas. In many cases, negative thoughts are established through a pattern of bad or unhappy experiences periodically throughout our lives, either generally or in a specific area. For example, if you have repeatedly experienced unsuccessful or unhappy relationships, you might likely feel a negative attitude toward relationships in general.

Childhood experiences are an extremely common way that negative thought patterns form. Our personality tends to be mostly formed before we turn five years old. Therefore, bad experiences at a very young age can impact detrimentally on our lives as adults. For example, the loss of a parent through death or divorce when young can programme your brain to fear abandonment and to assume that people will always leave you, no matter what.

Of course, trauma, stress or upset at any age can lead to negative thinking or a tendency to overanalyse situations. Significant life events can often lead to negative thoughts or overthinking a situation and prevent them from focusing on the positives that would allow them to find joy in their lives. Humans often find the bad things easier to believe than the good things. For some people, one negative comment can erase all the joy that was brought by 100 positive comments in an instant.

While chronic negative thinking may be caused by a specific significant event or set of events in the past or present, it is also possible to go through periods where your thoughts take a negative turn simply because you are not feeling your best. For example, sleep deprivation, malnutrition, general life stress and even the common cold can cause your thoughts to take a turn for the worst. Hormones may also have an impact on your emotions and thinking patterns too.

Consequently, it is possible to see that there can be a multitude of causes that lead to negativity in your life. Naturally, in this book, we will aim to eliminate that negativity and replace it with positivity and the capability to rediscover the joy in the world. It is not always possible to pinpoint the causes of a negative mindset, but the most important focus should always be on transforming your mindset to a more positive one.

How Negative and Positive Thinking Can Impact Quality of Life

Negative thinking can impact every single area of your life. It can be detrimental to your family life and relationship, to your friendships, to your career, to your hobbies and even to your sense of self. It can strip you of your confidence and self-esteem and make you feel worthless, excluded from society and completely helpless.

Conversely, when you reframe your thoughts and transform your mindset to a more positive one, you can see improvements in all areas of your life. You may find that your friendships significantly improve. You might also start to see a closer bond with your partner or spouse and rediscover the affection that brought you together in the first place. Positive mindsets can lead to you feeling more motivated in your work and hobbies. Most importantly, you can reclaim your self-confidence and remember that you are a wonderful person with a lot to offer in the world.

Positive Thinking Can Transform Every Area of Your Life.

Positive and negative are two polar opposites and when one exists it will naturally eradicate the other. If you think of negative thoughts like ice cubes and positive thoughts like sunlight, you can see that positivity can help to melt away a negative mindset. Essentially, changing your mindset by reframing your perspective and using specially designed techniques can help to replace negative thoughts with positive ones. This can replace your faulty thinking patterns and cognitive distortions with healthier ways of viewing your life and the world around you.

So, what can a positive mindset bring into your life? Well, you may see that your romantic relationship with your partner begins to improve. If you have noticed there have been strains or stresses within your marriage or relationship, there is a chance that your negative mindset may be contributing to this. People tend to be like sponges and when you put out negative energy, your partner may absorb this. If you are single, it is much easier to find a partner when you radiate positive energy because positive people are enjoyable to be around.

Your career can also enjoy success from a radical shift in your mindset. Your boss and co-workers are more likely to value someone who has a positive perspective on work and life because you are contributing something great to your team. Similarly, you may find renewed energy and confidence to pursue the hobbies and pastimes that you have enjoyed in the past. When your thoughts are on a negative downturn, you may feel fatigued and lacking in the motivation to engage in your favourite interests. On the other hand, an intrinsic sense of positivity can imbue you with the getup and go to participate in the things that you love doing.

Overall, your negative mindset has simply pushed the pause button on your journey to life successes. In this book, we will ensure that you can get back on track and give your life the kickstart toward positivity that you have been craving.

There is a direct correlation between a positive mindset and improved quality of life!

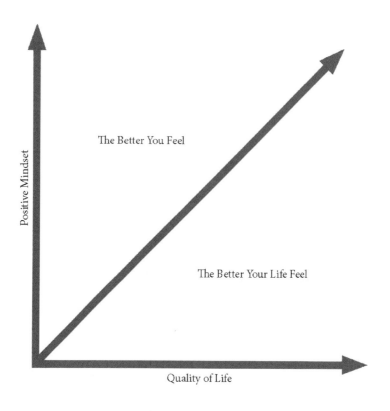

The Psychological and Physical Impacts of Overthinking

Mental health conditions and negative thought patterns are inextricably interlinked. Often, when people suffer from mental health problems, even mildly, this can cause them to have negative thoughts. Similarly, negative thoughts can lead to mental health conditions too, such as anxiety and depression as well as other mental health conditions like eating disorders and OCD. Often, negative thinking or overthinking can cause social isolation because you simply do not have the energy or drive to be around other people. This, in itself, can further exacerbate your negative thought cycles.

By eliminating negative thoughts from your life, you can significantly reduce the risks of suffering from conditions like anxiety and depression. You can also alleviate some of the symptoms of these mental health conditions if you already suffer from them by transforming your thought patterns from negative to positive.

While negative thinking can be disastrous for mental wellbeing, it can also have a catastrophic effect on your physical health too. When you fall into patterns of negative thoughts, this can raise your stress levels and trigger the release of excessive levels of hormones such as cortisol. At the same time, levels of endorphins and other "happy hormones" can become depleted. With the brain's hormone levels completely out of balance, you might notice that your stress becomes chronic.

Chronic stress is associated with a plethora of detrimental physical conditions, including raised risks of heart disease, obesity and a less resilient immune system. Simply put, your body has lowered defences against all kinds of diseases and is not as strong as it could be to fight them off.

By shifting your mindset from its current negative one to a happier and more positive outlook, you can rebalance your hormones, boost your immune system and give your body the best level of resilience against disease and illness. Your psychological and physical wellbeing could experience a substantial boost in health, allowing you to experience holistic improvements in all areas.

It's Okay Not to Be Okay

There is a common misconception in society that we must be strong and happy all the time. However, the climate has started to shift as celebrities and even Royals have openly talked about the mental health issues that they have faced in the past and present.

Remember: it's okay not to be okay!

The first step to recovering from any kind of mental health or wellbeing problem is to admit that you are suffering. Do not suffer in silence. Try and be open about it, even if you are only open to yourself. Once you have recognised that a problem exists, then that problem can be examined, explored, worked on and improved.

Remember: just because you are not okay today, it does not mean that you cannot be okay in the future.

In life, we have a limit as to how much we can take before we "burst." Psychologists sometimes refer to this as the **Stress Bucket.**

A stress bucket represents your mind and the "water" that goes into it represents the strains, stresses and worries that accumulate in your mind. Your daily stresses can build up and a single specific setback can cause your stress bucket to overflow. Remember that past or recent traumas can also reduce your resilience against stresses too and shrink your stress bucking giving you a lower tolerance against stress.

Essentially, if you have a lower tolerance against stress, this means that you are more vulnerable to your stress bucking filling up more quickly. When your stress bucket becomes full, it can overflow. This overflow is likely to manifest as stress, worries, anxiety, depression, overthinking, overanalysing and negative thinking.

While the periods that this lasts for are more likely to be short compared to chronic negative thought cycles, they can be extremely distressing when they occur and it is essential to use helpful techniques to alleviate this distress when it happens.

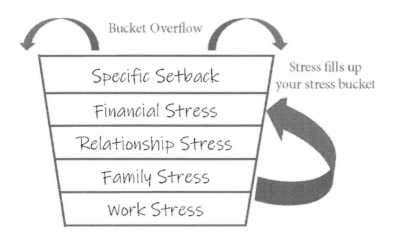

STRESS BUCKET

Bucket Overflow

Specific Setback

Stress fills up
your stress bucket

Financial Stress

Relationship Stress

Family Stress

Work Stress

Your stress bucket is filled with the various stresses in your life. When you subsequently face a specific setback, this can cause the bucket to overflow, leading to negative thoughts, anxiety and even depression.

By finding ways to poke holes in our stress bucket and prevent our stresses from building to unmanageable levels, negative thinking patterns can be broken. We will discuss stress management; problem-solving and worry management techniques later in the book to arm you with effective tools that can help you to "poke" holes in your stress bucket and relieve the various daily stresses that can build up and manifest as negative thinking patterns.

Remember that worrying can be transformed into problem-solving. Overthinking can be overcome. While you might feel at a low ebb right now, there is always a light at the end of the tunnel. Of course, that does not make it wrong to not feel okay right now. Your feelings are valid but it is also essential to remember that there is hope.

Many people go through hard times in their life and they overcome the obstacles in front of them to thrive and flourish in the future. You can draw your own stress bucket to see which areas of life are contributing to your worries.

Identifying Negative Thought Cycles

Negative thought patterns can come in a variety of guises. Often, they are hidden beneath the surface and you may not even be consciously aware of them. Consequently, this makes it difficult to break free of negative thought cycles. Therefore, when you notice a negative thought, making a written note of it allows you to track your thoughts more effectively.

Thought Diary

EXAMPLE OF A THOUGHT DIARY:	Negative thought(s)	The occurrence that caused the thought	Feelings and emotions	Behavioural reaction
Monday	I look really fat today.	I could not fit into an old outfit.	Sadness, disgust, self-hate, anger.	I skipped breakfast and lunch.

Tuesday	I'm useless at everything.	I made a mistake at work.	Annoyance, guilt, inferiority.	I didn't meet co-workers for drinks after work.
Wednesday	I'm a terrible parent.	I forgot to wash my child's gym kit for school.	Self-hate, guilt, upset.	I drank too much alcohol this evening.
Thursday	I never do anything right.	My spouse mentioned that I forgot to put the bins out for collection.	Annoyed, worthless, tired.	I purposely started a fight with my spouse to get back at them.
Friday	Nobody likes me.	My friend cancelled our lunch date.	Excluded, lonely, unlikeable.	I blocked my friend on social media.
Saturday	Everything goes wrong for me.	My car got scratched when I was parked at the shops.	Angry, irritated, annoyed, frustrated.	I drove home extremely fast and recklessly.
Sunday	Everyone else is happier than me.	I found out that my friend is getting married.	Jealous, upset, self-hating.	I yelled at my spouse.

Now that you have seen the example thought diary, here is one to fill in yourself. By keeping these regular records of your thoughts, feelings and resultant behaviours, you can start to understand what triggers negative thinking patterns to occur in your daily life.

	Negative thought(s)	The occurrence that caused the thought	Feelings and emotions	Behavioural reaction
Monday				
Tuesday				
Wednesday				
Thursday				
Friday				
Saturday				
Sunday				

As you can see from the example thought diary, negative thoughts and feelings lead to negative actions that can be extremely self-destructive and self-sabotaging. In these examples, the resultant behaviours do nothing to improve the situation and only lead to more negative thinking. Before you can transition from negative to positive thinking, it is important to identify the root of the negative thought patterns.

Now that we have an understanding of how negative thoughts can manifest, it is easier to see how negative feelings can lead to negative thoughts and then subsequently transform into unhealthy and counterproductive behaviours.

The Negative Thought Cycle

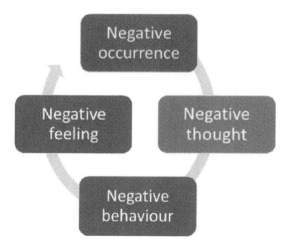

The fundamental problem with the negative thought cycle is that it constantly feeds back into itself. When something that you perceive as "bad" happens to you that leads to unhappy thoughts. These thoughts make you feel depressed or anxious or guilty. Consequently, that can cause you to behave in an unhealthy way. Your behaviours can then lead to more negative occurrences happening and the cycle continues.

To ensure that you can transform your life, you need to break the cycle. However, it is essential to remember that you cannot control everything. For example, if someone scratches your car when it is parked on the street, you have no control over that. It is impossible to prevent bad things from happening sometimes. Of course, you can minimise the risks of bad things occurring but they will still happen regardless.

Similarly, feelings are automatic and autonomous. It is very difficult to stop a feeling from flooding your brain and body in the aftermath of a negative event. Our feelings are a part of human nature and sometimes they are extremely difficult to control. However, where the change can be made is at the level of how we perceive the feelings.

For example, when you feel guilty because you forgot to pack an apple in your child's lunch, there are multiple ways that you can perceive this:

"I'm a terrible parent and I always do everything wrong. I hate myself!"

"I made a mistake but I intend to learn from it and use this as an opportunity to grow. Tomorrow I will make a to-do list so I do not forget again."

As you can see, with the first statement, your thought is likely to lead to self-punishment and potentially unhealthy behaviours that will not help you to improve as a person. On the other hand, the second example is much more positive. You are acknowledging that you made a mistake, but you are also learning from it and using it as a chance to improve yourself. Your manner of thinking directly impacts your behaviours.

If you were to allow yourself to think the first statement, the chances are that you would not make any changes and this can lead to another negative event. If you train your brain to think in the style of the second statement, that automatically encourages you to make the necessary changes to prevent the same kind of negative event from occurring in the future. You can use the techniques of **cognitive restructuring** that we will explore later in the book to help with changing your thought patterns.

One of the great things about changing the way you think is that this can also gradually positively impact those automatic feelings that have plagued you in the past when a negative event occurs. Once you have broken free of the negative thought cycle, your feelings might not be so negative following an unhappy event. The thought cycle can run both ways. Negative thoughts can also lead to negative feelings and vice versa. Liberating yourself from this cycle can allow you to interpret events differently in both the way you *think* and the way you *feel.*

As we have already discussed, negative thoughts can come from a variety of sources. They can be triggered by an external event or they can be an internal intrusive thought. They can also arise from your childhood or recent traumas that you have endured. Whatever the source of negative thinking, the effects that it has on you *right now* are the important points to note. Once you know what you are thinking, you can start to understand the patterns of your thinking and learn how to overcome unhealthy thought patterns as we will discuss in the next chapter.

What are Cognitive Distortions and How to Overcome Them?

Cognitive distortions are unhealthy and negative ways of thinking that often exacerbate a situation. There are several of these distortions that may be affecting you daily without you even realising that you are experiencing them.

Some examples of cognitive distortions are:

"My friend is late to meet me for lunch. They have probably had a terrible accident and they can't even call for help."

"I didn't get that job promotion. I'm terrible at my job and I should just quit now."

"I missed out on getting that last parking space. I never have any luck and my timing is always the worst."

These kinds of thinking patterns are causing you to view the world in a distorted way and they often occur when your interpretation of events is not accurate. They can cause you to feel terrible even when the truth is that your friend may be stuck in traffic or you didn't get the promotion simply because your boss doesn't feel that you're quite ready for it yet.

Researchers and scientists have often tried to identify where these distorted thinking patterns originate. Some experts believe that they evolved as a survival mechanism during prehistoric times. Back then, they helped people to evade the many dangers that they faced. However, in the modern age, these lines of thinking can be severely detrimental to our lives.

People tend to use them as a coping mechanism to deal with the daily stresses and strains of life. If they are allowed to continue unchecked, they can cause their own sets of problems.

Some of the most common cognitive distortions include:

- **ALL OR NOTHING THINKING:** Also known as polarisation or black and white thinking, this kind of cognitive distortion can prevent you from seeing the grey areas in life. It causes you to believe that things must be either one thing or another and they cannot be anything in between.

For example, you may believe that someone loves you or hates you but not that they simply like you. You might think that your life is destined for extreme success or abject failure but not that you can simply live an enjoyable and comfortable life as most people do. Similarly, when you meet new people, you may categorise them as angels or devils rather than accepting they can be a combination of good and bad. It is a distortion that focuses on the extremes which are not reflective of the reality of life.

- **CATASTROPHISING:** Generally, when people engage in catastrophising, they focus on the worst possible scenario that they can think of and it often spirals out of control.

For example, if your spouse is late to return home from work, you may start to believe that they have suffered a car accident and are lying in a ditch somewhere. This can then lead you to believe that you have lost the love of your life and not only that but that you will no longer be able to pay your mortgage because there will be no money coming into your household. Therefore, you will lose your home and become homeless.

While this is an extreme example, this type of catastrophising can afflict many people. It often develops in the wake of past negative experiences, such as childhood traumas.

- **PERSONALISATION:** This type of cognitive distortion involves taking things personally even when they are not your fault or aimed at you. Often, people take things personally when the situation is unconnected to them.

  For example, they may pass a colleague on the street and greet them with a wave. Their colleague doesn't smile or wave back at them. They will then assume that their colleague has intentionally ignored them and they must have done something wrong to warrant that response.

  In reality, their colleague may have not noticed them because they were lost in their thoughts or thinking about something that was going on in their own life. Often, when people suffer from anxiety or depression, this can be a common thought pattern.

- **OVERGENERALISATION:** This is the practice of taking your conclusions about a single event and then applying that conclusion to all events. For example, if you have one romantic relationship that goes wrong, in your mind you may believe that all your romantic relationships will go wrong and subsequently form a belief that romantic relationships are a waste of time and will never be successful. Many people who suffer from anxiety and various forms of PTSD are more susceptible to this cognitive distortion.

- **IGNORING THE POSITIVES:** Most people experience both positive and negative occurrences in their lives and this is natural. However, when you are stuck in negative thinking patterns, you may put more weight on the importance of negative events. If something good happens, you might explain it as a lucky coincidence that is unlikely to be repeated. For sufferers of this cognitive distortion, it can make them feel helpless, powerless and demotivated.

- **MIND READING:** Sometimes people can assume that they know what other people are thinking, without using any evidence to support their thoughts. It differs from empathy because it does not involve gaining an understanding of other people's thoughts. It is merely an assumption and usually a negative one.

For example, if you are out shopping and you see someone staring at you, your first thought could be to assume that they are looking at you because you are ugly and they are disgusted by your appearance. Logically, this is very unlikely. In reality, they may be looking at you because they think they recognise you from somewhere or simply because they like your clothes and wish they could find an outfit like that.

- **LABELLING:** When you label yourself, you restrict your entire being and sense of self to a single descriptor like "worthless", "fat" or "failure in life." This can trigger emotions of self-hatred and profound unhappiness. The Danish existentialist philosopher, Søren Kierkegaard once said: "Once you label me, you negate me." This is true for yourself too. When you label yourself, you are disregarding the complex elements that comprise your overall being. It is important to remember that you are more than any labels you assign to yourself.

- **EMOTIONAL REASONING:** If you believe that your emotions are always the same thing as the truth, then you may be experiencing emotional reasoning. For example, if you feel that someone does not like you, without any evidence to support that belief, this can be emotional reasoning.

  Of course, emotions are extremely important and your instincts can sometimes be correct. However, if you find that you have a repeated pattern of allowing your feelings to determine your thoughts without stopping to question the logic behind them, that can become problematic.

- **MENTAL FILTERING:** In some ways, this is similar to the cognitive distortion of *ignoring the positives* but it has fundamental differences. For people who use a negative mental filter through which they view their lives, the positives simply do not exist to them. Anything that happens that is good is instantly pushed aside and ignored and their minds are then refocused on the negative events. This can be one of the most extreme types of cognitive distortions and can lead to severe depressive disorders if it goes unchecked.

- **FALSE EXPECTATIONS:** Societal and cultural expectations are all around us and it is easy to fall into a thinking pattern that we "should" act in a certain way or "must" do specific things or "ought" to be a particular kind of person. By putting these kinds of restrictions on yourself and labelling yourself in a certain way, you can place an unrealistic burden on your shoulders.

  For example, "I should never make any mistakes at work" is a commonly held belief by many people. However, the truth is that you are human and humans are not perfect. With this line of thinking, one little error could shatter your self-belief. Ultimately, if you do not live up to your own standards, you may believe that you have "failed" and suffer a loss of confidence and self-esteem.

Transforming Your Thoughts

While these distortions can cause traumatic feelings and consequences to your mental and physical wellbeing, the great news is that you can change them. To achieve this, there are steps you can take and techniques that you can use to stop yourself from distorting a situation and helping yourself to alter your perceptions.

Identify the Distortion

When you notice that you are experiencing a cognitive distortion, it is important to actively recognise it. For example, if your old friend from school fails to send you a birthday card and your start to think: "they didn't send me a card because they hate me and they'll never speak to me again," actively recognise that this is an example of a cognitive distortion. You have no logical or concrete evidence for your thought.

Next, it is a good idea to identify the *type* of cognitive distortion that you are experiencing. In the example of your friend's failure to send you a birthday card, you may be using a combination of emotional reasoning, mind reading and catastrophising. You feel sad and ignored because your friend didn't send you a card and believe that the way you feel is the absolute truth. Additionally, you are assuming what your friend is thinking without really knowing. As you believe that the lack of a card means that your friend will never speak to you again and that they have ended the friendship, you are also catastrophising and predicting the worst possible outcome for the situation.

You are doing all of these things without any evidence to back up your thoughts and feelings!

Reframe Your Thinking

When you are caught up amid cognitive distortions, it can be understandably difficult to reframe your troublesome thoughts. However, with patience and practice, it is very possible to start to alter your perceptions.

In the example we have used concerning your friend and the birthday card, focus on some alternative explanations as to why you might not have received a card from your friend.

- They simply forgot because their own life is very busy.

- They are on holiday and were unable to send the card from their destination.

- They sent the card but it got lost in the mail.

When it comes to the catastrophising part of your thinking, you can even reframe these thoughts to alter the outcome of your thinking patterns.

- Even if my friend didn't send me a card because they are angry with me, that does not mean the friendship is over. Friends sometimes fight and they still makeup and continue their friendship.

- Even if the friendship does end, I have other friends and meaningful people in my life and the world does not end because a friendship is over.

Consider the Pros and Cons of Your Thought Patterns

As mentioned earlier, many people likely develop cognitive distortions as a way to cope with the trials and tribulations that life throws at them. In the heat of the moment, they might make you feel like you have a modicum of control in a powerless situation. They may also help you to feel like you are rationalising a situation. However, it can be necessary to focus on your thoughts and decide whether these are *healthy* coping mechanisms. Do these thoughts have a positive or negative outcome for your wellbeing?

Chances are, that you will notice that they are negatively impacting your feelings. When you have weighed up whether or not they are helping you, this can motivate you to change the way you think and realise that you can feel significantly better when your thoughts start to change.

Use this table to help you with cognitive distortions:

What was my thought?	What kind of cognitive distortion is it?	How did I feel?	How can I rationalise it?	What is my new thought?

Cognitive Restructuring

Cognitive restructuring involves identifying the maladaptive cognitive distortions that we talked about in the previous chapter. It can also be extremely useful for other negative thinking patterns as it allows you to take the time to find a more logical perspective for your thoughts and feelings. So, how can you restructure your thinking to ensure that it is more logical and does not cause you extreme anxiety or destructive behaviours?

Take a Breath

Take a moment to calm yourself. You can use some of the breathing techniques, such as square breathing, which you will learn about in more detail later in the book. You can breathe in and out while remaining focused on your breaths to allow yourself to take a step back from the situation.

When you experience a cognitive distortion or other forms of negative thoughts, it can be all too easy to get caught up in the moment and allow your thoughts and feelings to overwhelm you. By taking a moment to calm down, this can give you the time and space that you need to refocus and recentre yourself.

Identify Triggers

Identifying the triggers that caused you to think and feel the way you do can be extremely helpful. You can use the table from the previous chapter to write down what it was that has affected you. In some cases, there may be multiple triggers. By seeing it in writing, you can often gain a better understanding and start to rationalise the situation subconsciously.

Again, taking this step back and giving yourself the time to explore the events that have just happened in a little more detail can be extremely beneficial. It allows you to take a more objective viewpoint on it rather than getting caught up in a negative thought pattern.

You can ask yourself several questions to help to identify your triggers:

- What happened when I got upset? By recalling the situation, you may be able to identify the trigger more effectively.

- Where was I? Your surroundings at the time that you became upset and started to experience the negative thoughts and feelings can provide clues to your trigger. Sometimes a physical environment can cause an upset if it has negative associations for you.

- Who was with me or around me at the time? When you recall who was with you or around you, then you may be able to identify if anyone said or did anything that upset you. It may even be that you saw someone who reminded you of a different person who causes negative feelings for you.

- When did I start to notice the negative thoughts and feelings? Was it immediate, later that day, or sometime afterwards?

Be Self-Aware

Once you have identified the events that caused your thoughts and feelings, it is a good time to analyse the situation. A careful balance must be achieved here because you do not want to *overthink* the situation. Try and take an objective standpoint, as if you were listening to a friend's problems. Consider the feelings that were triggered by the situation itself and the resulting thoughts and feelings that arose from that situation. Write them down.

It is also important to notice any automatic or intrusive thoughts that you experience as a result of the situation. These are spontaneous thoughts that infiltrate your mind without you realising it. Being more self-aware and identifying these thoughts can help you to garner a better understanding of the way that you think. When you understand how you think, it is easier to change it.

Rate the Intensity of Your Feelings

On a scale of 1-10, with 1 being the lowest and 10 being the highest, note just how intense your feelings are as a cause of the situation or event that caused you to think negatively. It is also important to identify the type of feeling that you are experiencing. For example, are you experiencing worry, anxiety, anger, frustration, sadness or some other sort of feeling? You may be simultaneously experiencing multiple negative feelings.

When you know what you are feeling and you have rated the intensity of your feeling or feelings, it is possible to start to change the way that you think and generate different thought patterns. This can be the start of breaking those patterns of negative intrusive thoughts that are causing you to feel bad and experience distress.

Change Your Perspective

When you have gone through each of the previous stages of taking a few moments to step back from the situation and breathe and you have identified your triggers, thoughts and emotions, you can embark on reframing your perspective on the situation.

For example: if your friend is late to lunch, you might normally react by thinking: "I hate her, I cannot believe she's ditched me and didn't even bother to call." You might feel sad, angry, frustrated and let down. This could then prompt you to leave the restaurant immediately and block her on social media or ignore her calls later that night.

When you use cognitive restructuring techniques, you can revolutionise your thoughts, feelings and actions to achieve a healthier and more productive outcome.

What was your trigger? In this scenario, the trigger is fairly easy to identify at face value. But why did that trigger you so deeply? Is your friend often late and it annoys you? Have you been let down by other people before? Do you feel insecure about your friendships?

What were your automatic thoughts? You reacted by feeling hate and annoyance towards your friend.

How did you feel? You felt sad, angry, frustrated and let down. Essentially, you felt disrespected by your friend's lateness and lack of a phone call to notify you.

Your trigger, thoughts and feelings then led to negative actions. This kind of deep, visceral and negative reaction is an example of unhealthy thinking patterns.

Let's reframe the situation.

Yes, your friend did not show up to your arranged lunch date and did not call, but you can think differently about the situation. Maybe she was stuck in traffic and did not want to use her phone to call you while she was driving. Maybe something urgent came up and she was not able to call. Maybe that is just the type of person that she is. Remember, you cannot change other people's personalities. Some people are persistently late or flaky and they do not understand how their actions affect others.

In terms of your feelings, they will automatically change when you reframe your thoughts. You might even see a little humour in the situation if she is something who is always late as that is just her typical behaviour and you choose to be friends with her regardless of any foibles in her personality. You might feel calmer because you think that she is choosing to prioritise safety and not call you while she is behind the wheel. You may even feel compelled to call her and check that she is okay. Your behaviours may also change to more positive ones in light of your new way of thinking and feeling.

Re-Rate Your Emotions

Now that you are in a better place, mentally and emotionally, it is time to rate your emotions again. Before, they might have felt extremely intense. You might have been a 9 on the anger scale, an 8 on the sadness scale and even a 10 on the frustration scale. So, with this in mind, rate each emotion again.

In almost every case, your emotions will have lessened in intensity. While they might not be at 1 or even at 2 or 3, there is a very good chance that you will feel substantially calmer than before. At this point, it is essential to notice how much relief you feel from the reduction in the intensity of your emotions. Feeling calmer and less negative is a *great* thing. It is liberating. Make a mental note of this feeling because the relief that you are experiencing at this moment is the crux of the reinforcement. In other words, as this technique has helped you and make you feel good, your brain will urge you to use it the next time you're experiencing negative thoughts.

While you will not necessarily automatically adopt this method immediately, the more times that you consciously use it, the more you will train your brain to use it subconsciously. Eventually, your brain can be retrained to automatically use this method without you needing to work through the steps in this same structured manner. Of course, that takes a little effort and some practice. For some people, their brains can be retrained in a matter of weeks. For others, it can take months. Remember to keep trying as your brain needs the time and training to learn this new method of thinking. Your brain is like a muscle and the more you work on it, the more toned and honed it will become.

Overcoming Your Schemata

Schemata are patterns of thinking that our experiences condition us to hold. A schema is part of the mental structure of our mind. When you experience negative thinking, this may indicate that your schemata are maladaptive.

There are many types of maladaptive schemata:

Schema	Belief
Mistrust	Other people will intentionally hurt, betray, manipulate, lie or treat you terribly.
Emotional deprivation	Nobody can meet your emotional needs.
Social alienation	You are not a part of society or specific groups within society.
Abandonment	Other people will abandon you or leave you and those others are unreliable.
Defectiveness	You are worthless which can often manifest as feeling inferior or

	being hypersensitive to any negative external force
Failure	You are unable to succeed at anything and will always fail when you try.
Incompetence	You will never succeed alone and require other people's help.
Underdeveloped self/self-sacrifice	You must make others happy even if it causes harm or detriment to yourself. This is often known as "people-pleasing."
Pessimism	Overemphasising the negative aspects of your life and neglecting the positives.

Schemata tend to be thought patterns that form at an early age but the good news is that they can be overcome. While they are often an intrinsic part of a personality, they do not need to define us. When you have a better idea of the schema that is affecting you and influencing your thoughts and behaviours, it is easier to ensure that you take steps to overcome it. Maladaptive schemata often lead to extreme worrying or anxiety and in the next chapter, we will explore ways to break the worry cycle.

How to Break the Worry Cycle

Worrying, ruminating, overanalysing and overthinking are all intrinsic elements in a negative way of thinking. It is very easy to fall into a cycle of worrying and overthinking. You may know someone that is *always* worrying about something. It might be a worry about their health one day, their job the next, their kids the next and so on. You may be that person who is always worrying.

The problem with the worry cycle is that people will often avoid tackling the specific worry as avoidance can bring short-term relief. Avoidance can be tempting because it is an easy solution except that it is *not* a solution at all and can prevent the ultimate resolution of the problem. Avoidance is an unhealthy coping mechanism that many people fall into. Ignoring a problem does not make that problem disappear and will exacerbate your anxiety levels.

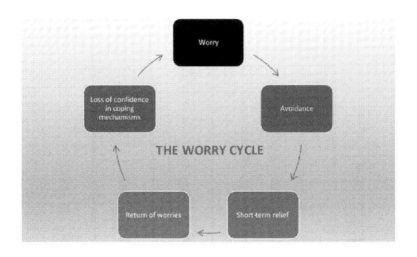

The longer the worry cycle continues, the worse it can feel. Therefore, it is necessary to try and step off the merry-go-round of overthinking your worries by addressing them at the very first stage. Essentially, *you should avoid avoidance*!

This method allows you to categorise your worry as being realistic or unrealistic. In other words, can you do anything to change what you are worrying about and if you can do something to change it, is it possible to do something about it *right now?*

A worry can be real and it is essential to validate that. Many people have worries and stresses in their life that are extremely potent and cause levels of anxiety. However, instead of avoiding the worries, tackling them can give long-term relief rather than the short-term relief you will experience from avoidance.

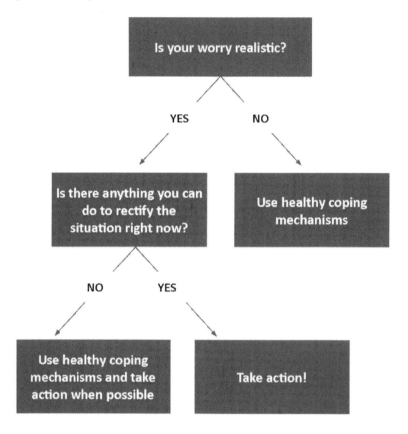

This flowchart demonstrates a healthy way of dealing with worries. The truth is that everyone has worries in their lives but when those worries become intrusive and stop you from happily living your life, then it can be the right time to do something about it.

For example, if you worry that the earth may be destroyed by a passing asteroid, it is unlikely to be a realistic worry. While this could potentially happen at some point in the future and there have certainly been many movies with this premise, it is not *realistic* right now. Therefore, you can start to use healthy coping mechanisms (which will be discussed later in the next chapter) to soothe yourself.

However, if a worry is genuine, then you may be able to address it, so it is necessary to ask yourself the question: "Can I do something about this worry *right now*?" For example, if you have just opened a letter from a debt collector telling you that they need you to call them but it is currently 10 pm, you cannot do something about it *right now* because their offices will be closed so you cannot call them.

While it is a realistic and valid worry, continuing to worry about it until you can do something about it will only increase your anxiety and cause you to overthink and overanalyse the situation. Therefore, it is wise and helpful to engage in some of the healthy coping mechanisms that we will discuss next. However, when you *can* do something about the situation, it is essential not to fall into avoidance patterns at that point.

On the other hand, if you open that same letter at 10 am and the debt collector's office is open, it is essential not to fall into avoidance patterns as that will only lead to more worry. This is when it takes some inner strength to address the situation.

When trying to find that inner strength to ensure that the situation is addressed immediately, you can ask yourself some questions:

- Will avoidance lessen my stress levels?

- Has avoiding upsetting situations in the past worked out well for me?

- Would I not rather rectify this situation so that I can be free of worries?

- Will I continue to overthink the situation if I do not take action now?

Taking immediate action breaks the worry cycle and allows you to lessen your anxiety. It will also remove the tendency to overthink because you will not have the time to start overanalysing the situation. By keeping the focus on solving the problem, you are lessening the need to overthink the situation which can actively prevent you from resorting to worrying or thinking negatively.

Healthy Coping Mechanisms

Learning to find healthy ways to cope with the stresses, worries and strains of life is an essential part of eliminating negative thinking from your life. The truth is that we all face obstacles and it is impossible to entirely prevent those obstacles from occurring. However, we can change the way we react and how we deal with them.

When you are under stress or you feel like you cannot cope, using healthy coping mechanisms is a way to prevent yourself from resorting to unhealthy or destructive behaviours.

Distraction Techniques

Utilising distraction techniques is an emotion-focused coping strategy and is excellent at helping people to focus their minds on something other than the negative thoughts, ruminations or worries that are causing them distress.

There is no doubt that it can be difficult to distract yourself in a *healthy* way when you are stressed, anxious or caught up in a negative thought cycle. Many people resort to unhealthy distractions such as drinking, drugs or gambling. However, those are not productive ways of distracting yourself and can lead to their own set of problems.

Instead, it can be necessary to focus your attention on doing something that you enjoy and takes your mind away from the worry at hand. For example, if you have a movie or a television show that you love, watch it. If you enjoy painting, take out your canvas and paints and start your masterpiece. Get out of the house and go for a walk. Arrange a meeting with friends. Even calling a family member can be a way to distract yourself from the negative thoughts or worries.

Self-Soothing

When you find that you experience intrusive negative thoughts, this can be the perfect opportunity to try and soothe yourself with some sensory experiences. Sensory experiences can often also be extremely comforting and allow you to practice mindfulness and being present in the moment rather than overthinking your situation.

Some examples of self-soothing can include taking a hot bubble bath or walking barefoot on the grass in your garden. They can also be experiences such as mindfully eating your favourite foods or drinks, listening to a song that uplifts you or spraying your favourite fragrance onto your skin.

Unfortunately, when you are in a state of high anxiety, it can be difficult to bring to mind exactly what kinds of things will make you feel better. Consequently, it is an excellent idea to put together a box of sensory self-soothing materials that you can turn to when you are not feeling at your best. Having this box preprepared means that you can easily open it and calm yourself instantly.

When preparing your self-soothing box, it is a good idea to choose objects that feel familiar and comforting to you and will not spark any further anguish. For example, if you had a beloved family pet who passed away, a photograph of your pet could generate memories of happier times. However, do not include a picture of your pet in the box if you feel that will lead to more negative thoughts.

Select items that satisfy all the senses, including sight, sound, taste, touch and smell. This gives you a complete sensory experience and is a fantastic way to boost your mood and distract you from worries, stresses and any tendencies to overthink a situation.

Sensory Self-soothing Box

Sense	Object
Sight	A picture of your loved ones.
Sound	A copy of your favourite CD.
Taste	A non-perishable item of your favourite food.
Touch	An item that feels nice in your hands or against your skin.
Smell	A bottle of your favourite scent or essential oil.

Managing the Problems

This is a type of adaptive behavioural coping strategy and focuses on solving the problems that are causing your distress. For example, if you are feeling down because of a fight with a friend, rather than ruminating on the situation alone in your home, call your friend and try to resolve the problem.

Another example of where this coping strategy could effectively be used is in the workplace. Many people deal with setbacks at work or with workplace bullying or harassment that puts them in a negative mindset. While it can be tempting to suffer in silence or to use other coping techniques such as distraction, these do not deal with the root of your problems. Using this specific coping strategy, you could address the colleague or colleagues that are causing you stress, talk to your boss or contact your HR department.

Essentially, this coping strategy allows you to take back the control in your life. It focuses on seeking information on how you can improve a situation and then evaluating the benefits and risks of acting on what you have learned.

Of course, you may not always be able to use this strategy as not all problems can be resolved by addressing them directly and not all problem-solving is within your control. In these cases, the other coping strategies that we have discussed may be better suited to your needs.

Seek Support

Communication is key when it comes to seeking support with intrusive negative thoughts, feelings and anxieties. . If you have a trusted partner, friend or relative, share your problems with them. The adage of a problem shared as a problem halved is especially true when it comes to overcoming negative thoughts and behaviours.

Initially, it can be difficult to open up to others about your problems. Some people believe there is a stigma surrounding mental health issues. However, suffering in silence will only exacerbate your problems. In some cases, it may be easier to communicate anonymously with a stranger. There are various telephone helplines and internet forums dedicated to supporting people who have anxieties, worries and mild to moderate symptoms of depression.

When you open up about your struggles, whether you talk to a friend, colleague or stranger, try and keep your explanation simple. It can be tempting to want to divulge every detail but in the initial stages, communicate your basic thoughts and feelings. You can expand or elaborate later but you need to remember that the other person needs to process what you're telling them. Overwhelming them with too much information does not give them the time to actively listen to what you're telling them. Staying brief also reduces the chance of becoming overwhelmed.

Stay calm when you talk to them too. While it is natural to become emotional when you express your problems, it can be extremely distressing to you if you allow your emotions to overwhelm you. At the same time, it is essential to be direct and honest so they can get a complete picture of what you're experiencing.

Tips for Talking

- Stay calm.
- Be brief.
- Be direct.
- Be honest.
- Be open.
- Listen to their responses.

Find the Humour in a Situation

It can be tough to find humour in a difficult situation, but laughter truly is one of the best possible medicines. Laughing can have a positive effect on your mental and emotional wellbeing and can also be conducive to better physical health. It can help to relax your muscles, increase the oxygen levels in your bloodstream and help to release endorphins which can make you feel better.

If you take life too seriously, it can impact the way that you feel in your mind and body. Sometimes, even if you are feeling down, watch a comedy show or put on a humorous movie. This can trigger your laughter response and ease the pain that you feel about the stresses in your life. Ultimately, it can lighten your load and allow you to find humour in places and situations where you would not have found it before.

Using Breathing Techniques to Combat Anxiety

Anxiety can occur in many situations, both positive and negative. However, it can be extremely difficult to focus on a task when you are overwhelmed by anxiety. When your anxiety builds up, it can overwhelm you, especially if you already have other stresses that are negatively impacting your life. If you cannot calm yourself at that moment, your stress can overflow, as in the example of the stress bucket that we discussed earlier in the book.

Remember, your body experiences the same physical sensations when you are excited as when you are anxious. It is your brain that interprets these sensations differently. Therefore, if you can refocus your attention, it is possible to retrain your brain not to interpret your anxiety as a negative emotion.

One excellent technique that can help to calm you and refocus your mind is **Square Breathing**. Square breathing works by rebalancing your and allowing you to find your centre. Firstly, breathe while counting to four (or less if you cannot manage to make it to four.) Next, hold your breath in for four beats. Exhale for four beats. Count to four before inhaling again. Focus on your breathing and counting as you inhale, hold, exhale and hold. Continue to repeat this until you feel calmer and your mind appears clearer.

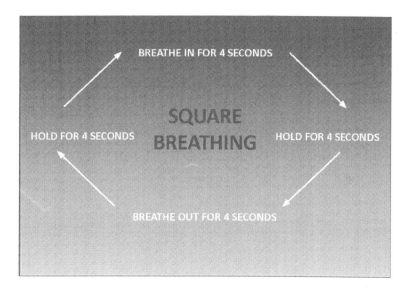

Breathing exercises, such as square breathing are excellent for incorporating into your daily routine. You can find time in the morning or evening to try it so that you can prepare yourself for your day or calm yourself at the end of a tough day. However, they can also be used in a moment of negativity, worry or stress. For example, you might remember that we explored the power of **cognitive restructuring** earlier in the book. When you experience an event that triggers negative thinking, you can use your square breathing techniques to remain calm and to help you take a step back from a stressful situation. Square breathing can defuse the triggers that lead to an overwhelming wave of negative thoughts and emotions.

Another exercise that you can also try is **mindful breathing**. In this technique, you focus on paying close attention to the pattern of your breath.

The Benefits of Self-Care

When you're feeling negative, it can be easy to neglect self-care. Self-care is different from basic hygiene rituals like brushing your teeth or washing your hair. Self-care focuses on caring for your *inner* self by using various activities to nourish and repair your soul.

Self-care works on the principle that when you do something you love, it can make you feel happy. Feeling happy makes you feel more motivated. When you feel motivated, you are more likely to spend time doing more of the things you love. You can create a positive cycle that will help to eliminate some of the more negative cycles that you may currently fall into.

There are many different ways to practise self-care such as:

- Take a hot bath or shower.

- Go for a walk or run outside.

- Eat a healthy diet to ensure that you are getting all the necessary nutrients to boost mental and physical health.

- Play sports.

- Get a massage.

- Visit a beauty or hair salon.

- Eat a healthy meal.

- Get some good quality sleep.

- Engage in some guided relaxation.

- Spend time in nature at a park or local woodland beauty spot.

- Cuddle up to your loved ones such as your spouse, children or pets.

- Listen to feel-good music.

- Watch one of your favourite movies at home or the cinema.

- Go to a café (either alone or with a friend.)

- Engage in a positive pastime that makes you feel happy.

At first, doing something purely for your enjoyment may feel unnatural because many people get used to doing things for others and putting themselves last. This can breed subconscious resentment that leads to a river of negativity bubbling just below the surface.

When you start to take care of your own needs, it allows you to find moments of joy in life's smaller things and rejuvenates you so that you have the energy and motivation to take care of others too.

Rediscover Your Joys in Life

One of the most detrimental consequences of negative thinking is that it can become all-encompassing and overwhelm every aspect of your life. This means that when you are caught in a negative pattern, the time you have to enjoy life decreases. In essence, your world shrinks and your brain has no time to process happy thoughts because it is constantly focusing on the unhappy ones.

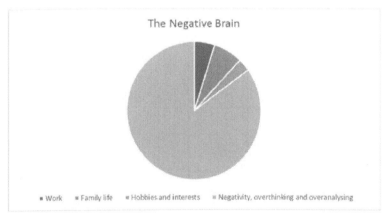

The Negative Brain

■ Work ■ Family life ■ Hobbies and interests ■ Negativity, overthinking and overanalysing

It may be necessary to retrain your brain, using some of the techniques that we have already discussed in this book as well as others that we will discuss later, to readjust the time that you spend concentrating on worries. This can allow you to have more time for joyful pursuits and happy thoughts.

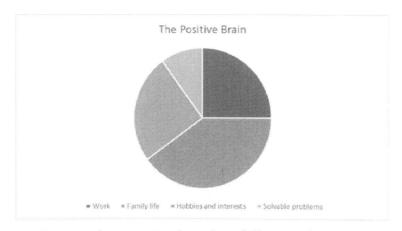

You may have noticed one key difference between the negative brain and the positive brain, aside from the percentages that comprise the content. While a negative mindset concentrates on negativity, overthinking and over-analysis, a positive mindset will encourage someone to solve any problems that arise. When you have a positive mindset, general life problems are not barriers that hold you back. Instead, they are obstacles that you can overcome.

Remember: thinking about problems and overthinking problematic situations are two different things. In the former scenario, you are looking for solutions. In the latter scenario, you are ruminating on the issues at hand without actually addressing them. To address your problems or worries, refer to the flowchart on managing worries that we explored earlier.

If you are currently in a state of anxiety or stress, you can also try techniques such as square breathing or mindfulness which can help to recentre your focus on the present moment and eradicate intrusive worries that may be affecting you and preventing you from relaxing. We will go into mindfulness in more detail later in the book.

Once you have managed to clear some of your worries and have achieved a more neutral mindset, it is the right time to find joy in your life again. Joy can be achieved in several ways and can transform into full-blown happiness or be a series of euphoric moments that boost your mood and wellbeing.

So, you may currently be asking the question:

"How do I rediscover the joys in my life?"

As we discussed in the last chapter, taking care of yourself and practising self-care can help you to find joy in the small things in life. However, it is important to employ a holistic approach to rediscovering the joy in your life. Getting your emotions back on track can require a structured approach, particularly if you have been mired in negative thinking patterns for a prolonged time.

Of course, it is very possible to restore your thinking to a more positive outlook and start to find the joys in your life once again. It can take some time and practice to become adept at it, so do not become disheartened or give up if you do not manage to achieve this immediately.

1. Become more connected with your inner self.

When you are disconnected from yourself, experiencing those euphoric moments of joy is almost impossible. Therefore, it is essential to try some techniques that can help you to know yourself again. One great way of reconnecting with yourself is to try meditation. There are many resources for guided meditation available for free online. When you meditate, ensure that you are in a calm and quiet environment and that you will not be interrupted.

2. Focus on your goals.

Achieving goals that you set yourself can bring you extreme moments of joy and allow you to gain some self-confidence too. When you set goals, make them SMART goals. They should be:

- Specific
- Measurable
- Achievable
- Relevant
- Time-Bound

In short, you should make sure that your goals are specific rather than vague. For example, "I would like to take a holiday is very vague." However, I would like to take a holiday in Paris is specific.

You should also be able to measure your progress in achieving this goal. If your goal is to take a trip to Paris, you can measure your progress by keeping track of how much money you have saved up or whether you have booked the hotel and travel to get there.

A goal should always be achievable. The goal to visit Paris is very achievable for most people. On the other hand, if your goal was to take a holiday on the moon, that is not achievable unless you are an astronaut for NASA and maybe not even then!

Your goal should always be relevant to your ultimate objective, which is to find joy in your life. Your Parisian holiday can help you to do that. Setting a goal that is negative or does not help you become more joyful is not relevant to your objectives.

Lastly, a goal should be time-bound. This means that you should set a specific deadline for its achievement. It can be a great objective to want to holiday in Paris, but if you do not set a deadline, you may not have made any progress towards achieving it in 20 years. Therefore, set a finite date for when you want to realise your goal.

You can even write out a "joy" list of all the things that you want to experience and work through it so that you can keep making goals and keeping bringing new joyful experiences into your life.

3. Dedicate time to your passions.

Everyone has at least one passion in their life. Whether yours is spending time with your family, playing or watching sports, taking long walks or simply slipping into a steaming-hot bubble bath, you can find joy in your life in this way.

The problem arises in this case because when you are feeling negative, it can be hard to motivate yourself to do something you enjoy. Therefore, it is essential that you have already worked through the techniques in this book to clear your mind and make a path for rediscovering your passions again.

4. Find positive people.

The positive energy that positive people radiate can be extremely energising and allow you to find joy in things that might otherwise pass you by. The joy that positive people have can rub off on you meaning that you could become more joyful, even when you are not around them.

Positive people are easy to identify when you know what you are looking for. Seek out the people who are always smiling, even in the face of adversity. Seek out the optimists who always enjoy a glass-half-full attitude in their lives no matter what.

Eliminating Toxic External Influences

While negativity can often come from within and from the way we think, there can also be external influences that bring negativity into our lives. Sadly, many people have a friend or a relative who is pessimistic or toxic. For example, you may know someone who is always trying to "bring you down" with comments or jibes, even when you are feeling relatively upbeat. *These types of people are toxic influences.*

There are many names to refer to toxic influences, such as emotional vampires or mentally draining acquaintances. Whichever term you prefer, it doesn't change the reality that they do not bring positivity and light into your life. If you feel that someone you know is like that, ask yourself whether they are improving your quality of life or being detrimental to your quality of life. If the answer is the latter, it could be the right time to cut ties.

Yes, of course, it is not simply that easy. The toxic influence or emotional vampire could be someone you simply cannot cut out of your life. It could be a parent or a parent-in-law. It could be your boss. It might even be an estranged spouse with whom you share children and therefore must maintain contact. Therefore, it may be necessary to find ways to manage your interactions with them so that they do not drain your positive energy or bring you down with their negative energy.

When you have a friend or relative who is bringing toxicity into your life and damaging your mental wellbeing, the best thing is to remove them from your life if that is possible. For example, if you have an old school friend on your social media who is constantly posting comments that make you upset or make you feel bad about yourself, it may be the right time to remove them as a friend.

On the other hand, you could have an ex-spouse who brings toxicity into your life. This could be because they are mean, sharp or cold in the way they act when they are around you or there could simply be some residual hostility left from the breakdown of your relationship. However, it might be necessary to see them or talk to them concerning your children. In this case, you can likely minimise the contact between the two of you, only seeing them or speaking to them concerning the kids. On the occasions that you do need to see them, you can use some of the coping strategies that we will discuss later in this chapter.

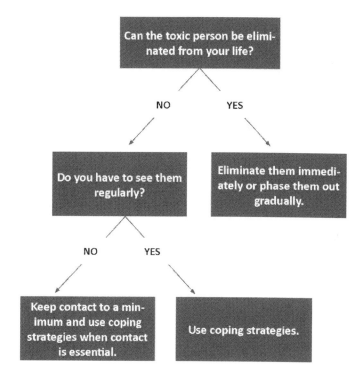

The hardest toxic influences to eliminate are the ones that you need to have contact with regularly or even daily. These could be people like your boss or toxic colleagues who unwittingly upset you or are intentionally nasty. When it comes to dealing with these people, it might not be possible to eliminate them from your life. However, you can eliminate the negativity that they bring into your life. This is possible by using the coping strategies that we will explore next.

In the case that you need to use coping strategies, these methods are intended to help you put up barriers to stop other people's negativity from affecting your mindset. It can sometimes take practice to fully achieve this.

- **Do not take their negativity personally**. Just because someone else is negative and acts or talks in a negative way does not mean that it is aimed at you. They may have their own problems in life. This can be difficult when it comes to dealing with an ex-partner because there may be some underlying bitterness on their part. However, remember that the problem is *theirs*, not yours.

- **Do not overreact**. It can be easy to feel triggered into an emotional reaction when someone is being negative around you. However, remember that you are strong and do not need to absorb their ways of thinking. Negative energy can be guarded against.

- **Put up barriers**. In some ways, it may be necessary to develop a type of mental shield, especially if you absorb other people's energy easily. You can do this by repeating a mantra to yourself such as: "it is their problem, not mine."

- **Spend time with more positive people**. If you have been in a situation where you have been around one or more negative people for a significant amount of time, you can offset this by spending time with positive people as soon as possible. This can prevent you from slipping into a negative cycle of thinking and refocus your mind on happier and less stressful thoughts.

Ultimately, negative influences are all around us, but all we can do is shield ourselves from them as much as possible. With time and practice, you will become extremely adept at ignoring the negative influences that you experience and focusing on the positive ones instead.

Start a Journey Towards Wellbeing

Connect with Your Loved Ones

Connecting with the people that you love has been proven to boost wellbeing, improve mood and raise general levels of happiness. You may want to connect with the people that you love by simply spending time with them or enjoying various activities with them like a walk in the park or a meal in a restaurant. You can also boost your mental wellbeing by being more physically affectionate such as through cuddling your children, hugging a friend or physical intimacy with a partner.

Additionally, connecting with other people, in general, is also extremely beneficial. A random chat with a passing stranger at a bus stop can inject a little joy into your life. Simply put, connecting with others helps to satisfy our belonging and love needs. As we will talk about later when we discuss Maslow's Hierarchy of

Needs, a sense of belonging within the structure of society is an essential requirement within human nature.

Learn New Skills

The power of learning is often underestimated in mental health but it has many intrinsic benefits. Firstly, learning a new skill can be beneficial in keeping your mind focused on a healthy and productive activity. In some ways, learning a new skill can act as a distraction technique. When your mind is processing this novel activity, it is not focusing on any negativity.

Learning a new skill can actively restore your self-confidence. When you embark on learning something new, it might be daunting at first, especially if your confidence levels are depleted. However, if you choose a programme with supportive staff, you may quickly discover that you are extremely good at whatever project you have embarked on. Consequently, this can translate into renewed self-belief and a realisation that there are many things you are extremely good at.

The new skill that you choose to learn will likely depend on your personal preferences. There are many different skills and it could be something as simple as learning to paint. You could take a music course, learn a new language or even choose to start a degree online. With a plethora of options, it is simple and straightforward to get started on learning a new skill.

Be Physically Active

The psychological benefits of exercise have been well-documented in multiple academic and scientific studies. When you exercise, your brain releases endorphins and other feel-good chemicals. This can give you an essential boost and provide you with the right amount of positivity that will start to shift your thinking from negative to positive.

Negative thinking ⟶ Positive thinking

Regular exercise

Another benefit of exercise when it comes to eliminating negative thinking can be that you actually look and feel better. If your negative thoughts are connected to your body image in any way, exercise can help to rectify the root cause of those issues.

Most importantly, being active encourages you to spend time outside and connect with nature. Nature is very calming and being outdoors rather than surrounded by the same four walls of your home or workplace is a liberating experience that can reset your thinking and push the pause button on intrusive negative thoughts.

Allow Yourself to Be Mindful

Mindfulness focuses on being present in the moment. When you are mindful, you are concentrating on the here-and-now rather than anything that has occurred in the past or may occur in the future. By focusing on the current moment, your brain cannot think about negative thoughts. You will not worry or ruminate.

Mindfulness can sometimes take practice before you become fully skilled at it. If you are used to being caught up in patterns of negative thoughts or overthinking, then your mind may initially wonder when you start to practice mindfulness techniques and this is normal and natural, so do not be put off if that happens.

As you become more skilled at mindfulness, it can start to be second nature to you. In the first instance, it is a good idea to start by practising mindful activities such as mindfully listening to a song, mindful eating or mindful walks in the woods. In the example below, you can try out mindful drinking. This example uses sparkling water as there are many sensations for all the senses but you can try it with your favourite drink if you prefer.

Mindful Drinking

- Take a glass out of your cupboard and notice how the glass feels cool and hard against your fingers.

- Lay it on the countertop in your kitchen and listen to the sound it makes as it touches down on the worktop.

- Open a bottle of sparkling water and hear the fizz and pop as you open the bottle cap.

- Pour the sparkling water into the glass, listening to the glug of the water as it hits the bottom of the glass and fills it up.

- Lift the glass and look at the bubbles slowly rising to the surface. Take note of the tiny splashes in the glass as the bubbles pop when they reach the top.

- Put the glass to your lips and be aware of how the rim of the cool glass feels against your skin. Take notice of any slight scent of the water.

- Take a sip of the sparkling water and hold it in your mouth for a moment. Pay close attention to the sensations that the fizzy water creates as it passes over your teeth, tongue and gums. Notice the taste and flavour of the water.

- Swallow the water and concentrate on the feeling as it slides down your throat.

Give Something Back

It is extremely easy to fixate on your problems and constantly think about the negative things in your life. However, sometimes you can break your cycles of overthinking by giving something back to others. Volunteering is an excellent way to give something back to your local community. Most areas have volunteer programmes where you can do anything from helping to grow local produce to rescuing mistreated animals. You can check out local opportunities online to see if there are any current openings in your area.

Helping others can be an inspiring and cathartic experience that may also put your problems in perspective. When you are alone with your issues, it can be all too simple to inflate them to a level where they are the worst thing in the world. However, when you spend time around people who have had even worse experiences, it can often make you realise that while your stresses and worries are valid, they are also not necessarily as bad as you might have believed.

Be Your Own Best Friend

Are you extremely critical of yourself? Do you often berate yourself for little mistakes that you would never dream of criticising other people for making? Do you set unreachable standards for your achievements and then fall into a cycle of guilt and self-hate when you fail to achieve the unachievable? *Would you stay friends with someone who talked to you the way you talk to yourself?*

If we don't love ourselves, how can we expect other people to love us? The reality is that there is nothing wrong with showing yourself a little compassion or care. There is also nothing wrong with loving yourself. Self-compassion is a very healthy mindset.

Doing something nice for yourself, in the same way that you might do something nice for your best friend, can allow you to value yourself proactively. It can also be a fantastic way to find some joy in your life. Why not treat yourself to a massage or buy a box of your favourite chocolates? When you realise that you *deserve* a treat, then you can start to befriend yourself again.

Sometimes, to ensure that we can truly love ourselves, we need to also ensure that our needs are fully satisfied. The American psychologist, Abraham Maslow devised a hierarchy of needs that need to be satisfied to ensure that we are fully fulfilled. When you are feeling negative, it can be easy to neglect getting these needs met. At the same time, if these needs remain unmet, it can throw us into negative patterns of thought.

Needs include:

- Physiological and biological needs (food/water/warmth/sleep).

- Safety needs (safety/security).

- Love and belonging needs (friendships/intimate relationships).

- Esteem needs (respect/status/self-esteem/accomplishments).

- Self-actualisation needs (achievement of full potential).

Maslow's Hierarchy of Needs

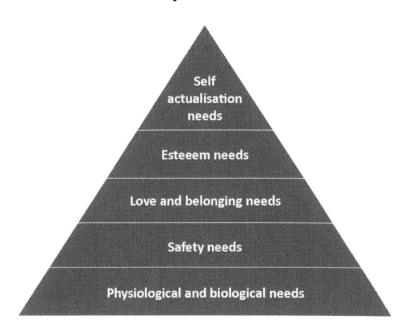

This hierarchy relies on each level being met before satisfaction of the next level can be achieved. So, for example, if you have your physiological and safety needs satisfied but you do not have a sense of belonging or love, it can be difficult to feel an adequate degree of self-esteem and accomplishment in life. This can lead to negative thinking patterns and it may be necessary to rectify the gaps in your needs where they are not being fulfilled.

Loving yourself means taking care of yourself. Taking care of yourself means ensuring that ALL your needs are fully met. When your needs are fully met, you can achieve a sense of self and relish in your achievements. Recognised achievements help transform a negative mindset into a positive mindset.

So, if you do feel some areas may be lacking when it comes to your needs, identify them and this is an excellent starting point to begin ensuring that they are completely met so you can achieve a sense of self-actualisation.

Identify Unmet Needs and How to Change This

Example:

	Which needs are not being met?	How can I change this?
Physiological	Not applicable	Not applicable
Safety	Not applicable	Not applicable
Love and belonging	Love – my partner does not show me any physical affection.	Talk to my partner and tell them how I'm feeling. Work out a plan to spend more

90

		intimate time together.
Esteem	Accomplishments – I do not feel like I'm progressing in my career.	Identify promotion opportunities and ask my boss or team leader for help with promotion applications.
Self-actualisation	Achievement of full potential.	Improve my love/belonging and esteem needs as self-actualisation can be realised once the other two are fulfilled.

Now, here is one for you to try:

	Which needs are not being met?	How can I change this?
Physiological		
Safety		
Love and belonging		
Esteem		
Self-actualisation		

The Power of Positive Affirmations

Positive affirmations are a way of complimenting yourself rather than berating yourself. If you have been stuck in a negative thought pattern for some time, there may be some types of thoughts that have become accustomed to. For example, you may often tell yourself that you're not good at something, not attractive enough, not smart enough or even worthless.

Stop Now!

You *are* **good at what you do. You** *are* **attractive enough. You** *are* **smart enough. You are** *worthy!*

The brain is essentially a giant biological computer. Our experiences are the coding that programmes our brains to function. Your past experiences and traumas have programmed your brain to function in a specific way and the output may currently be a negative one.

Positive affirmations are designed to retrain the brain and make new connections so that you think differently. Even if you do not initially believe the affirmations, the more you say them, the more your brain will start to process them as being the *truth.*

"I am smart and capable."

"I am worthy of love."

"I am good looking."

"I am good at my job."

"I am popular."

At this point, it is a good idea to return to the negative thought diary that you recorded earlier to recall some of the negative thinking that you have experienced. Take those negative thoughts and turn them around. For example, if you are recurrently telling yourself that you are a bad parent, switch it around and tell yourself that you are a good parent.

One of the primary things to remember about positive affirmations is that you must repeat them to yourself consistently and frequently. It is a good idea to set aside a time every morning or evening to stand in front of a mirror and say these affirmations to yourself. You can even write them on post-it notes and affix them to the wall so that you can see them and have easy access to them if you feel that negative thoughts are starting to intrude on your mind.

You can use the table below to make a list of your positive qualities (the first two examples are filled in for you). Sometimes, people struggle to think of positive qualities about themselves when they are stuck in a negative thought cycle, so it is a good idea to ask a friend or relative to help you. Ask them to tell you what they like about you and list some of your good qualities. This can also have the benefit of reinforcing that other people positively regard you and it can help to break through those negative and self-effacing thoughts.

Positive Quality	Affirmation
I'm good at running.	I'm an excellent runner and I can succeed at whatever I try to succeed at.
People enjoy the food I cook.	I'm a wonderful cook and people love eating my meals.

You can fill in the rest of the table with positive affirmations that are personal to you. Remember to repeat these affirmations **as often as possible.** They can be even more important if you experience a negative setback in your life.

For example, if you do not get the promotion you wanted, you still have many worthy skills to offer in your job and it is important to refocus on the positives rather than focus on a single negative. In this example, look at achievements that you have made in your career and remind yourself that you are **great** at what you do.

When is the Time to Seek Professional Help?

While self-help can be extremely useful and revolutionise your life, there may come a time when it is necessary to seek further help from a trained medical professional. Negative thinking or overthinking to an extreme degree can be a sign or symptom of a more serious mental health problem.

Sometimes, these types of issues require therapy with a psychologist or counsellor to resolve the causes that are at their root. Various types of psychological therapy solutions are available.

One of the most popular forms of therapy is **Cognitive Behavioural Therapy** (CBT.) This is a type of talking therapy that can change your thought patterns and behaviours. Generally, it is used for anyone suffering from symptoms of anxiety or depression. CBT can help to liberate you from the vicious interconnected cycle of negative thoughts, feelings and actions. A therapist can guide you through transforming this cycle into a more positive one.

Exposure therapy is used to help free people of anxieties surrounding specific fears or intimidating situations by exposing them to their fears in a safe and controlled way. If you have negative thoughts or fears about a certain situation or action, then this type of therapy could be helpful to you.

Another helpful form of therapy is **Acceptance and Commitment Therapy** which is a type of psychotherapy. It utilises strategies of mindfulness and acceptance to increase the flexibility of your thinking and ensure that you can communicate unpleasant thoughts and feelings more effectively. Essentially, it is aimed at gaining a more thorough understanding of your ultimate values and goals.

Dialectical Behavioural Therapy is a form of CBT that focuses on a range of specific skills. It concentrates on transforming negative thought patterns to achieve more positive behavioural changes. If you have noticed that your negative thinking leads to destructive or self-sabotaging behaviours and actions, this could benefit you.

A traditional and well-established type of therapy is **Psychoanalytic therapy.** Based on the model set out by Sigmund Freud, you work collaboratively with a therapist to explore some of your fears, thoughts and needs. It focuses on gaining a better understanding of your emotional problems that are at the root of your current thoughts, feelings and behaviours. It can be very effective at treating prolonged problems of negativity and overthinking.

Interpersonal therapy can also be a good option to help resolve some of the underlying issues that might be leading to negative thinking patterns. It can help to treat conditions such as depression.

A large majority of people will be able to resolve their negative thinking or stop themselves from overthinking simply by using the techniques that have been outlined in this book. However, if you feel that you have deeper issues that cannot be resolved alone, seeking help is a viable option that can allow you to enjoy a better quality of life.

Conclusion

Negative thinking is a cycle that can be broken with work, commitment and practice. It is not something that needs to last forever and patterns can be changed and reframed. In this book, you have learned to identify and understand your negative thinking patterns, how to transform them into more positive ways of thinking and some coping techniques that can help you to manage worries and anxieties that can result from your thoughts and feelings.

What's more, you have hopefully learned how to see the joy in your life once again and how to find the little things that make you happy. However, the work is not over. It is essential to keep going with these techniques as change takes time and does not happen overnight. Permanent changes require gradual and prolonged steps to ensure they are cemented in your new mindset. Do not be tempted to rush as you are only at the beginning of an extremely successful journey.

With time and patience, you can achieve all the goals that you set out to achieve and ensure that you reap the rewards of your hard work. As you continue along your path, you will notice that many significant areas of your life begin to improve.

You will likely notice that your romantic relationship becomes more closely bonded with your partner and that you can achieve higher levels of good quality communication and intimacy. Your friendships will strengthen as people enjoy being around you with your revised positive mindset. As your self-confidence and self-esteem improve, your career prospects may also follow suit. Positive thinking and stress reduction can even improve your life expectancy!

Ultimately, this book has provided you will all the tools you need to be more positive, stop detrimental patterns of overthinking and rediscover all the joys that the world has to offer. If you suffer setbacks on your journey, do not worry as that is natural. Lapses happen and the best thing to do is to get back on track as soon as you can. Use your new tools to help you and do not be disheartened.

You can do this!

SCAN QR CODE AND GET AUDIO BOOK

FOR FREE!

To my dear readers,

We are thankful that you decided to buy this book. As special gift we can offer you the audio book for free. Just scan the QR code and download for free on Audible:

Please scan with your mobile phone:

*Just possible for new Audible customers.

Disclaimer

This book contains opinions and ideas of the author and is meant to teach the reader informative and helpful knowledge while due care should be taken by the user in the application of the information provided. The instructions and strategies are possibly not right for every reader and there is no guarantee that they work for everyone. Using this book and implementing the information/recipes therein contained is explicitly your own responsibility and risk. This work with all its contents, does not guarantee correctness, completion, quality or correctness of the provided information. Misinformation or misprints cannot be completely eliminated.

Printed in Great Britain
by Amazon

Walter Morrison: A Millionaire at Malham Tarn

GORDALE SCAR: ONE OF SEVERAL LIMESTONE SPECTACLES OF THE MALHAM DISTRICT.

Walter Morrison:
A Millionaire at Malham Tarn

by W. R. Mitchell

Inheriting the Malham Tarn Estate when he "came of age", Mr Morrison found so much pleasure at Tarn House, his "mountain home", that for over 60 years he spent part of each year here. He gloried in the spectacular limestone scenery such as Gordale Scar (pictured left), or in the greystone beauty of Malham village (pictured below).

The map is set against photographs showing the road by the Tarn, ''Lister's Arms'' at Malham and the village as it was in Victorian days.

Contents

Illustrations:

Thanks are extended to the many people with Malhamdale associations who loaned photographs.

Front cover—Walter Morrison (about 1910). Billy Towler with a horse offered at a sale at High Trenhouse, and Malham Tarn, with the House seen among trees.

Back cover—A late Victorian print of an angling party on Malham Tarn. One of the Brayshaw brothers with a fine trout caught in the Tarn.

This page—A Victorian photograph of the old house now occupied by the Warden of the Field Centre.

Page 1—Two-horse carriage in the yard at Malham Tarn House. Holding the horses on this occasion is William Skirrow, the butler.

The photographs on page 15 appeared in the sale catalogue of 1927. *(See page 48 for the main details of this sale).* Picture of Malham (page 24) courtesy of Walter Scott.

Typeset and printed by J.W. Lambert & Sons, Station Road, Settle, North Yorkshire, BD24 9AA. Published by W.R. Mitchell, 18 Yealand Avenue, Giggleswick, Settle, North Yorkshire, BD24 0AY.
© W.R. Mitchell, 1990.
ISBN: 1 871064 09 0.

Foreword

by

Mary Reckitt

The Half Hunter gold pocket watch that belonged to Walter Morrison.

MY LATE HUSBAND, Paul Holmes, was the first warden of the Field Centre established at Malham Tarn when the house and some adjacent land were leased to the Field Studies Council by the National Trust. Tarn House and later Shepherd's Cottage were home to us for nearly 20 years.

I am therefore delighted to have been asked to write the Foreword to this memoir of Walter Morrison. Of course, I never knew him, but his influence could be felt in Tarn House and throughout the neighbourhood. Stories of his charitable actions and, indeed, of his eccentricities, abounded.

Over the years, thousands of students have passed through the Field Centre. They still do, coming from schools and universities or privately for the many diverse courses — everything from botany to archaeology, from art to biology.

The National Trust, who acquired the Estate in 1946, have extended its size in recent years. Their warden/naturalist lives on the Estate and works with the Trust's farm tenants to maintain the landscape and wildlife of the area.

I am sure that Walter Morrison would have been pleased if he could have known that the House and estate of which he was so proud, and which he loved, are so well used and cared for today. This limestone countryside is an inspiration to both young and old.

ACKNOWLEDGEMENTS: Thanks to Margaret Mary Alderson (whose father, William Taylor Chapman, was Mr Morrison's farm bailiff); Mrs Bronte Bedford-Payne; Mrs G.M. Chapman, Mrs Dorothy Clack; Alister Clunas (National Trust); Mrs Frank Coates (who with her husband once farmed Middle House); Mrs Edith Cowgill (a daughter of Mr W.W. Thornber, a corn merchant with many friends on Malham Moor); Jack Heald, Editor of "The Craven Herald"; T.H. Dugdale.

Mrs Enid Ellis; F.H. Ellis (garage proprietor at Settle who recalled Mr Morrison's early days as a car-owner); Miss Dorothy Fairburn (Managing Agent, Malham Tarn Estate); Peter Fox; Mrs Doris Hartley of Settle; Mrs Jane Hoyle (who walked three miles a day to and from Capon Hall to Malham Tarn School); Mr Kingsley Iball (Warden, Malham Tarn Field Centre); Mrs Ingham of Malham (whose mother was a maid at Tarn House); Mr and Mrs Frank Lowe (for memories of James Usher, gamekeeper at Malham Tarn); Jim Nelson; Mrs Bob Preston; Mrs F. Robson (who was brought up at Gordale Farm); Mrs V. Rowley (whose late husband, Dr Geoffrey Rowley, was a Notable Craven historian); Mrs Lettice Sharpe (one of the 12 children of Alfred Ward); Mrs Doris Thompson (who as Doris Carr was Headmistress of Malham Tarn School in the 1930s); Garry Thornton (who made available on loan Elinor Pike's memories, in manuscript, of Settle 1915-18), Miss Barbara Ward (whose childhood was happily spent at Malham Tarn), John Geldard read through the draft.

A LAMENT by J. Clayton,
a former Editor
of ''The Craven Herald'':

To my keen regret, Mr Morrison refused to be what he termed ''interviewed''. I had suggested that the recollections of his world-wide travels, his store of antiquarian and literary lore, his acquaintance with celebrated men, and particularly his knowledge of their peculiarities and characteristics, should be placed on record for the benefit of posterity...

The answer came back: ''I refuse. In the first place, I never kept a diary and I never kept a letter. In the second place, I hate snobbery; and to give publicity to one's scattered recollections is a form of snobbery that I abominate.''

Walter Morrison (right) with his Steward,
Mr Winskill, in a local hayfield.

The Road to Malham Tarn

WALTER MORRISON knew virtually every yard of the road from Bell Busk Railway Station to Tarn House, his ''mountain home'' in High Craven. As a millionaire, he had a coachman, horses and an assortment of vehicles at his disposal on his visits to his Yorkshire estate. He preferred to walk and he did so at a steady, mile-eating pace—through Airton, Kirkby Malham and Malham, then up the hill beside the Cove to Malham Moor.

Mr Morrison, pedestrian, is recalled as being ''a big man, baldish on top, with a bushy beard. He walked with his hands behind his back and his chest sticking out. He was indifferent to other people and seemed to be living in a world of his own.'' The wealthy man, who could have indulged any whim, favoured the simple life. He was known, when returning to Malham Tarn, to call at a shop in Settle to buy a leg of mutton, which he bore triumphantly home!

His return to Malhamdale was announced by a telegram received at Malham Post Office. The Misses Baines wended their weary, sometimes painful way to Malham Tarn House

7

to deliver the message. ''They had a little terrier and it seemed to enjoy the walk more than they did. It made for the Kennels at Malham Tarn and upset all our dogs,'' recalls one of the Ward family. ''The telegram was left at our house. Grannie used to make the Misses Baines a cup of tea. She'd tell them: 'One of t'kids 'll tak yon telegram up to t'hall.'

Walter Morrison, a wealthy bachelor, lived on a family fortune built up by activities as varied as Argentinian railways and the manufacture of black crepe, which the Victorians used extravagantly at funerals. Walter had a London house and another in Devonshire, but—fresh air fanatic that he was—he had a special regard for Malham Tarn House, ''my mountain home.''

On Malham Moor, at an elevation of about 1,200 feet, he could be himself. He had a large estate, an assured social position and a reputation of being generous to deserving causes. In truth, his needs were simple—for food, clothing, good footwear and a road enfolding between walls made, Pennine style, of unmortared stones.

He walked for hours in an area where the day was punctuated by the bleating of the horned sheep and by the calls of the upland waders, including the long-nebbed curlew, a bird with a bubbling call, and the lapwing that gave an exuberant shout before tumbling in the air, to recover its equilibrium when, it seemed, it would hit the ground.

Mr Morrison's estate in Yorkshire lay on a small part of the largest outcrop of limestone in Britain. He gloried in the cliffs, gorges and outcrops that brightened up the landscape, having been licked smooth by wind and rain. The south windows of his home framed Malham Tarn. He liked nothing better than to show off the expanse of water and the grey-green countryside to his guests.

Mr Morrison might disembark from a train at Bell Busk, at Hellifield or at Settle. He preferred to walk to Malham Tarn rather than travel in the estate horse and trap. He strode along a road system that was still largely water-bound, dusty in dry weather and puddly when wet.

This tall, stiffly-built man with the bent head and the grey beard sweeping his chest was recognisable at a range of half a mile. He tended to wear formal clothes, with a square-shaped grey flat hat. From Settle, he would take either the footpath way to the top of

Right—Old Malham, from a postcard sent by Mr Coates of Rainscar to Mr Chester of Low Trenhouse. The card was No.1 of a local series that proved very popular with visitors.

Left—Janie and Annie Banks, of Capon Hall, going down Lings. The unmetalled state of the roads enabled horses to ''keep their feet'' on gradients. Walter Morrison preferred to walk!

Capon Hall — known locally as Capna — was not part of Malham Tarn Estate, though Walter Morrison passed it whenever he walked to and from Settle.

Langcliffe Brow or go by horse and trap.

He did not care much for the people of Langcliffe. When he had competed as a candidate in a local Parliamentary election, and changed his political allegiance from the Liberal cause beloved by most voters at Langcliffe, he was stung by the shouts of villagers: "Old Turncoat!" Feelings ran so high, it was even rumoured that he had intended to provide Langcliffe with almshouses and decided, instead, to build a domed school chapel at Giggleswick.

The road between Settle and Malham Tarn meandered across the high ground, offering spectacular views of Ribblesdale and Penyghent, before descending at Cowside, from which there was a steady pull up Henside (locally known as "Hensit") Lane, crossing the watershed and passing "Capna" (Capon Hall).

So to Malham Moor, which William Bray, an 18th century traveller, had approached from Kilnsey, along Mastiles Lane. Mr Morrison had a copy of Bray's *A Tour into Derbyshire and Yorkshire,* which was published in 1783. Curiously, Bray did not mention the limestone. "This ride is truly wild and romantic; nature here sits in solitary grandeur on the hills, which are lofty, green to the top, and rise in irregular heaps on all sides, in their primeval state of pasture, without the least appearance of a plough, or habitation, for many miles."

Walter Morrison was not averse to riding when the spirit moved him. He would instruct his coachman, Robert Battersby, to prepare the horse and landau and off they would go. In the early days, when Mr Morrison was known to stay at Malham Tarn for Christmas, he was being taken for a horse-and-carriage ride, with Battersby and Skirrow, his butler, on the box, when they noticed an inebriated postman lying beside the road. The postman had received his dinner and an excessive amount of drink while visiting Malham Tarn House!

At Mr Morrison's insistence, the carriage was stopped and Mr Skirrow disembarked to attend to the recumbent man. He was told to say as little as possible or he would incriminate himself. Mr Morrison was told that the postman had been taken ill. Clearly, said Mr Morrison, he had a most exacting postal round. The landowner promptly wrote to the General Post Office suggesting that they shorten it.

The approach to Gordale Scar, near Malham. Today, a durable footpath discourages walking at random.

A Most Secluded Dale

A VICTORIAN visitor to Malhamdale was advised against a direct approach from Settle. The author of *A Practical Guide Book to Malham and its Surrounding Scenery,* published in Blackburn, 1886, noted:

It is a toilsome walk over the hills from Settle, and difficult to find. But a conveyance may be taken from Settle by Hellifield. Malham is reached within 13 miles.

This 12-page guide, one of the earliest of its kind, mentioned Malham's remoteness from railway stations—five miles from Bell Busk, seven from Hellifield and six from Settle. Those with means might order a conveyance from the *Buck Hotel* or the *Lister's Arms* at Malham and the *Victoria Hotel* at Kirkby Malham.

In 1903, McFarlane's Illustrated *Guide to Malham,* published at Skipton, mentioned as "the usual road" that which goes from Gargrave, through Eshton, Airton and Kirkby Malham adding: "The old village of Malham has long been accustomed to the visits of strangers; the hosts [of the local inns] are never deaf to the sound of carriage wheels nor inattentive to the wants of their customers."

The writer of each guide could scarcely contain his eagerness to lead the newly-arrived visitors on to the natural wonders around the head of Malhamdale. I refer to Malham Cove, Janet's Foss, Gordale Scar and Malham Tarn.

To William Bray, in 1783, the Tarn "has nothing beautiful in its shape or borders, being bare of trees and everything else to ornament it, except two or three small houses at the further extremity, but there is a very peculiar circumstance attending it; at one corner it runs out in a small stream, the only outlet from it, which in a short space rushes in full current into a leap of loose stones, and is there lost.''

A century later, when the tourist age was well under way, and descriptions had a romantic aspect, Malham Tarn was being described as occupying ''a most picturesque situation among the trees'' and Walter Morrison was mentioned as ''one of the best of landlords''. He was also a big-spender. At Tarn House, in 1903, ''nothing is wanting that taste could suggest or art could effect to render this an agreeable abode.''

Listers and Morrisons

BEYOND the curving cliff of Malham Cove stands the expanse of Malham Moor, part of a limestone plateau from which rise the mountains of High Craven. Malham Tarn is the central feature of a township of rather more than 11,000 acres; the highest point of the Moor is Fountains Fell, at 2,191 feet.

Early peoples were living in this limestone countryside when elsewhere the terrain was marshy and densely wooded. Norse folk kept sheep on the moor and, in the 12th century, their distinctive pastoral way of life was incorporated in that of the vast monastic estate of Fountains Abbey. Malwaterhouse, on the north-west side of Malham Tarn, would be one of the monastic lodges.

By the early part of the 14th century, Fountains was noted for such non-religious activity as wool-production, using vast summer grazings on Malham Moor and elsewhere in highland Craven. The settlement near the Tarn was first mentioned in the Memorandum Book of Fountains Abbey in 1454, wherein it is stated that a pig had been sold to William Tollar ''de Malwaterhous''.

On the Dissolution of Fountains Abbey, Malham Moor and a good deal of Malham were purchased by Lambert of Calton, and in due course—through inheritance or purchase—came into the possession of Lister of Gisburn. The Listers developed a large sporting estate. Their grand shooting ''box'' was built on a site prepared by excavating a hillside and spreading the spoil to create a tract of flat ground.

Thomas Lister (1752-1826) was created baron in 1797 in recognition of his services in raising three troops of yeomanry. He took the title Baron Ribblesdale of Gisburn Park but was more widely known as Lord Ribblesdale. He spent much of each summer at Malham Tarn. This ambitious man had the notion of so extending his estates he might ride from Gisburn Park to the Tarn without leaving his own land. The distance, as the crow flies, is some 12 miles. He did not achieve this ambition but his love of his property led him to plant a large

A mounted shepherd near the outflow of Malham Tarn. It is believed that he was Abraham Banks.

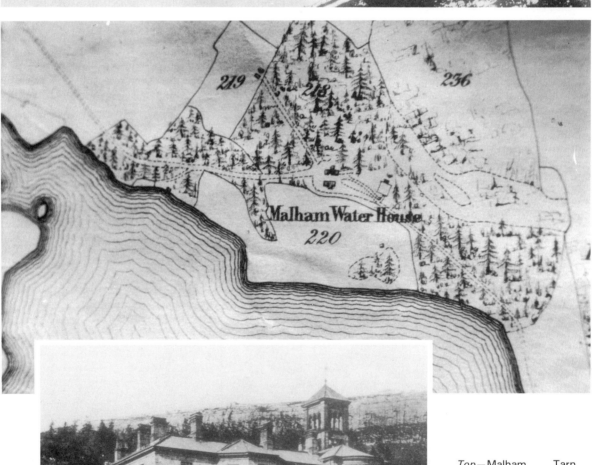

Top—Malham Tarn. *Centre*—An old estate map of the eastern shore of the Tarn as it was in the days of the Listers. *Bottom*—Tarn House, as it was in the days of Walter Morrison.

number of trees—oak trees at Gisburn, with spruce and larch by the north shore of Malham Tarn.

About 1802, Lord Ribblesdale appointed the Rev Thomas Collins, who had been a friend during undergraduate days at Oxford, as his agent at Malham Tarn. Collins moved from Gisburn Park, where he had assisted on the estate, and soon the old house had been transformed into a fine sandstone building with bow windows and a lake view.

A large stable block was built some way up the hill from the house and became known as the High Stables. Collins was kept busy. Unaided, he attended to the affairs of the estate, including the mines; he became a JP in 1802 and entertained visiting fellow magistrates, among them Yorke of Halton Place and Wilson of Eshton Hall.

In 1852, the Malham Tarn Estate was purchased from the Listers by James Morrison, of Basildon Park, Berkshire. The Morrisons were shrewd businessmen. James Morrison (1790-1857), a native of Hampshire, had a Scottish ancestry. He amassed a fortune as a draper and on his death he was a millionaire four times over. (His eldest son, Charles, inherited half his father's fortune and lived to quintuple it, dying in 1909 at the age of 92 years).

Walter Morrison was the fifth of seven sons; he was born in London on May 21, 1836 and inherited the Malham Tarn Estate from his father on his 21st birthday. Walter's appeal to the folk of the district rested partly in his status as a millionaire, and partly because he not only made "brass". He hung on to it!

The ornate tower which Walter Morrison added to Tarn House

A "Mountain Home"

WALTER MORRISON had a privileged upbringing. He was one of three brothers at Eton and Balliol. He went down from Oxford in 1858 and promptly undertook the Grand Tour, which he extended to take in Egypt, Syria and the United States.

At the age of 25, he won the first of several Parliamentary victories. He was to represent the far-flung Skipton Division for many years, though his political career was not helped by his public speaking. Geoffrey Dawson, a neighbouring landowner, who was also a distinguished Editor of *The Times,* respected Morrison as a man and philanthropist but wrote of him as being "a rare and rather tedious speaker."

Young Mr Morrison took over a tract of outstanding limestone country, the focal point of which was the Tarn. The House stood on its man-made ledge above a Tarn that had its level raised four feet when the Listers dammed the outflow in 1791. During Mr Morrison's lifetime, a scheme was put forward, but not accepted, for installing a ram to pump water from the Tarn to a dam on the scars, from which the water would flow back into the Tarn by way of a turbine, which would provide electricity for the House and outbuildings.

Judged by modern standards, Malham Tarn House was bare and comfortless. "Walter Morrison never seemed to notice or care for comforts," wrote Geoffrey Dawson. "Yet, like Morrison himself, it was solid and substantial . . . with big rooms, big windows and a big outlook."

His house was badly damaged by fire in April, 1873. No time was lost in re-building. Readers of *The Pioneer* were informed on July 26, 1873, that "the country seat of W. Morrison, Esq., M.P., situated on the shores of the lake at Malham, [a seat] which a short time ago had a narrow escape of being destroyed by fire, is now undergoing thorough renovation and repairs. The portion damaged by the fire is being rebuilt and the work has been carried on with alacrity."

Mr Morrison contributed the eastern side of the House—with Entrance Front and an Italianate bell-tower [the latter dismantled about 1963]. The construction work was carried out with fine sandstone ashlar. To the south front was added a verandah, with cast iron columns springing from stone pedestals to support a glazed canopy.

This photograph of Walter Morrison is seen by visitors to the Library at Malham Tarn House, which is now a field centre.

A major part of the "big outlook" mentioned by Geoffrey Dawson when describing the House was the Tarn that lapped on a bed of impervious Silurian rock. The Tarn is quick to freeze over in a cold snap. In 1860, not long after Mr Morrison claimed his Yorkshire inheritance, a Grassington carrier unwittingly took a short cut across the lake with his horse and cart. When, in 1881, a foot of ice covered the water, one of Morrison's men rode across it on a horse and woodmen transported timber across the icy surface by sledge.

Malham Tarn House was the big man's "mountain home". He rejoiced in the freshness of the air. As a young man with consumption, he had been sent by the doctors to Pau, "a very malarious district under the Pyrenees." He insisted on going up to the snow line, despite the doctor's comment that if he did, he would be dead in 48 hours. Not only did he remain alive, he "discovered that fresh pure air is good for consumption before any doctor found it out."

Walter Morrision became a fresh-air fanatic. He had a good many illnesses in following years but never went to doctors to cure them. "I do not take medicine," he said. His love of pure air led him to consider the "ozone" treatment of wounds and the discarding of bandages.

Solitude never worried him. He spent many a solitary evening at Tarn House with his books and his pipes, "which were very nearly as numerous as his books." This is not to say that he disliked human company. "At the same time he was the most gregarious and talkative of men. His hospitality was boundless . . .," noted Geoffrey Dawson.

A Slaidburn man who accompanied his employer to Malham Tarn at grouse-shooting time recalled that Walter Morrison greeted his guests at the front of the hall. "As a typical country squire of the period, no one could have filled the bill better than Mr Morrison. About 5ft 6 inches tall and well-built, he wore a frock coat which came to below his knees, and a round hat which was of the same material and colour as his suit. He had a round, jovial face with brindled whiskers . . ."

Right—From the catalogue of the sale of Malham Tarn Estate in 1927.

THE HOME OR WATER HOUSES FARM (Lot 2).

THE SHEPHERD'S
COTTAGE & BOTHY
(Part of Lot 2).

THE GARDENER'S
COTTAGE
(Lot 2a).

THE CHAUFFEUR'S
COTTAGE
(Part of Lot 1).

COTTAGES AT MALHAM TARN.

THE BUCK HOTEL
(Lot 15).

THE LISTER ARMS
(Lot 20).

IN MALHAM VILLAGE.

Victorian Visitors

Malham Tarn,

~~Bell Busk,~~

Settle ~~Leeds.~~

Oct 27th

1897

Yours truly

G. Morrison

Above—Charles Kingsley, a visitor to Malham Tarn House. *Right*—Address and signature from a letter written by Walter Morrison.

A LIST of eminent Victorians who visited Malham Tarn House includes Judge Hughes, author of *Tom Brown's Schooldays.* Hughes arrived with his son-in-law and daughter, Mr and Mrs Coates, who were to be passengers on the ill fated *Titanic.* Charles Kingsley was so entranced by the local landscape, by the clarity of the streams and by the excellent trout fishing in the Tarn he included some delightful word pictures of the area in his best-selling children's book, *The Water-Babies.*

Kingsley was no stranger to Yorkshire; in 1845 he accepted from the father of an old college friend an honorary canonry of the collegiate church of Middleham. Visiting Wensleydale, he sent his wife some rare flowers he had picked. Thirteen years later,

he was at Burley-in-Wharfedale, Bolton Abbey, the Strid and Malham Tarn House. He described the scenery at Malham as "a constant joy" and the trout fishing as "the best in the whole earth."

With regard to *The Water-Babies,* his tale of Tom, the Chimney Sweep who, escaping from a hard master, entered the underwater world, Walter Morrison used to tell visitors: "The mansion down one of whose flues little Tom came into little Ellie's room, was doubtless Ovington House. Thence Kingsley came on hither, found that we used the Itchen flies, but much larger and went on writing *The Water-Babies.* 'Vendale' is Littondale, with bits of the Yoredale rocks, etc., from Ingleborough thrown in; while 'Lowthwaite Crag' is Malham Cove, whereon you can see the black mark made by little Tom as he slipped down it in a state of profuse perspiration."

John Ruskin stayed at the *Buck Inn* in Malham; he painted a water colour of Middle House Farm and wrote of "the quiet hills of Malhamdale". Ruskin's *Parable of Jotham* contained his impressions of Malham Cove, where

. . . the stones of the brook were softer with moss than any silken pillow; the crowded oxalis leaves yielded to the pressure of the hand and were not felt; the cloven leaves of the herb-robert and robed clusters of its companion overflowed every rent in the rude crags with living balm . . .

A Busy Estate

WALTER MORRISON was content to leave the running of the Estate to his agent, John Whittingale Winskill, who like Collins, the agent of the Listers, appears to have achieved a great deal with virtually no back-up in the shape of an assistant or clerk. Mr Winskill mirrored his employer in his Englishness and had administrative ability. His range of interests extended from tree planting to establishing a trout hatchery for the replenishment of the fish stock in the Tarn.

The policy of tree-planting begun by the Listers was continued. About 10 per cent of the trees survived. Harry Speight discovered that since Mr Morrison had acquired the estate, at least 500,000 trees, ''in perhaps fifty kinds'', had been planted under various conditions and by various methods. Yet out of these ''probably not more than 50,000 are alive.''

Mr Frank Hodkin, the mason, plumber and handyman of later times, was a Sheffield man who lived with his family in accommodation adjacent to the School. He had a motor-bike with a twin-Jap engine in a Sunbeam frame but his handiness with estate matters did not extend to dealing with the machine. ''He got it a bit hot one day, when he was checking it. He threw a bucket of water at it. Cast iron will not stand cooling off quickly—and he cracked the cylinder barrels!''

Labour was brought in from Malham, Settle and Arncliffe. Both the joiner and handyman came from Settle, having accommodation in ''the lodgings'' from Monday until Saturday. ''They brought their own jock [food] and cooked for themselves during the week.''

The most exceptional service was given by Mr John Greenwood, of Malham, who was gardener at Malham Tarn House for 57 of his 78 years. He walked to and from work daily, averaging 40 miles a week. George Petyt, a gardener in later times, walked from Arncliffe. He was assisted by Dickie Bates and Ted Banks, who lived in Malham and walked to the Tarn daily. When Mr Morrison decided to drive a new road through rock to replace the traditional approach along the north-western shore

John Whittingale Winskill.

of the lake, there was an accident and Ted Banks lost an eye.

Richardson, the carter, went to Settle every day with a two-wheeled cart and one, sometimes two horses. A second horse was needed to ''trace'' up Langcliffe Brow if there was a big load. Any of the Malham-Tarners who wanted to go to market travelled in the cart!

The front lawn of the House was mown by a machine drawn by a pony called Happy Jack. Small leather shoes were placed over the iron shoes so that they would not mark the lawn.

Left—John Winskill and his wife.
Above—Four Little Maids from Tarn House.
Below—Alfred Ward, gamekeeper, with his wife and family, photographed during the 1914-18 war shortly before his eldest son returned to the Army after leave.

At the Big House

WILLIAM SKIRROW, the butler, presided over the house in Cromwell Road, London. He travelled to Malham Tarn House when needed. In moments of relaxation, Mr Skirrow enjoyed smoking a pipe. Mrs Skirrow, housekeeper in London, was the former Martha Duxbury, of Settle. Her brother had a confectionery business in Cheapside. She was house-proud. Under Martha's supervision, spring-cleaning was almost a daily occurrence.

The position of housekeeper at Tarn House was occupied by the equally conscientious Miss Lodge. It was said that before the Derby Brights coal was put in the scuttle in Mr Morrison's drawing room, each piece was washed and polished. Miss Lodge ruled her little staff with firmness. "She was very much the lady when Walter Morrison was not there, when she would invite local children to the House," I heard from a former resident at Low Trenhouse. "My mother was among them. When she was about to be married, Miss Lodge presented her with some teaspoons."

William Skirrow, who off-duty was a keen pipe-smoker.

Miss Lodge, housekeeper, maintained a firm hold on domestic matters.

Helen Ward, one of the gamekeeper's children, used to take milk up to the house, where she was welcomed by Miss Lodge. Helen discovered that the housekeeper had a kind heart. "Always she would give Helen a cup of milk. She seemed to grow strong and fit because she had this milk in Miss Lodge's kitchen every day of her life."

Helen's father, Alfred Ward, who was the gamekeeper, had courted Ellen (Ellie) Earnshaw, a native of Calton who became the cook at Tarn House. Alfred proposed marriage to her and then informed Walter Morrison that he would have to leave his employ for he would require a better cottage than he had. When Morrison discovered that the gamekeeper was going to marry his cook, he was quick to provide the desired accommodation—the cottage called Sandhills which is now "Hilary's Cottage". After marriage, Ellen helped out at the house during busy periods, such as when a shooting party arrived.

Annice Holmes (nee Sidwell), whose family had a confectionery shop in Settle, recalls visits to the shop by Walter Morrison. He would disembark from his horse-drawn trap and, wearing formal clothes, with top hat and elastic-sided boots, enter the shop for a chat and some purchases. "He was a gentleman— and we treated him as such," says Annice.

The Duxburys and their successors, the Sidwells, catered for the shooting parties at Malham Tarn, supplying such tasty items as oyster patties and lobster patties. The food was transported from Settle to Tarn House by horse and trap. When the work was done, Mr Battersby sometimes took the girls to the boathouse and rowed them on the Tarn for an hour or so. Mr Morrison invited Annice and her sister Rosa to stay at his London home, No. 77 Cromwell Road, so that they might attend an exhibition of French cookery and learn more about Choux pastry. The girls were welcomed to London by the Skirrows and given a memorable stay in the Capital.

Robert Battersby, as coachman, met visitors to Malham Tarn House at Settle railway station. Mr Battersby, "a little old man who had a big white beard," was greatly respected. He had a superficial resemblance to Walter Morrison and he liked people to think he was the owner of the Estate. Indeed, both Mr Battersby and Mr Winskill were sometimes mistaken for "the idle rich". They dressed up like gentlemen. Mr Morrison employed three grooms, one of whom was Harry Gill.

The carriage used by Robert Battersby when collecting visitors at the station was "one where you sat two at the front and two at the back; it was drawn by one horse, a hackney." One summer, Mr and Mrs Skirrow had brought some London maids up to Yorkshire for the summer. The girls had been promised that, on arrival at Settle, they would be taken out to a cafe for afternoon tea.

The train arrived at 3pm. Mr Battersby was in the station yard with the horse and landau. When told that the girls were to be taken out for tea, he demurred at the delay and said that he had lots to do on his return to Malham Tarn.

Mr Skirrow said: "You go home, then, Robert."

A somewhat corpulent, elderly Walter Morrison riding in his special low-slung carriage. The horse is being held by the faithful Mr Battersby.

Above—The new farmhouse at Low Trenhouse, provided by Walter Morrison, seemed very cold and draughty by comparison with the old.

Left—High Trenhouse, a typical Pennine longhouse.

"And how will you get home?"

"Oh, we'll hire a conveyance."

"And who will pay for it?"

"Mr Morrison, of course."

The coachman waited. He and everyone else knew that Morrison might be a millionaire but he didn't like throwing his brass about!

Mr Battersby was a much-loved personality but on one occasion he said to Alf Ward's sons: "If you lads'll watter me horses, you can go up in t'loft and get yourselves an apple apiece." The lads had to pump all the water. They then found that the apples were old and wizened, having been bought specially for the horses.

"One of the lads said to his brothers: 'I'll cure 'im. So he went up into t'loft and got his apple and put it in t'end of t'pump. He was pretending to be pumping away. Mr Battersby came and said: 'Nay, lads, get on wi' it; you haven't got any watter in there.' So the Ward lad gave the pump an extra jerk—and out shot the apple, followed by gallons of water, which soaked Battersby. He had to go indoors to change his clothes."

In later years, the corpulent Walter Morrison found it difficult to clamber into the standard horse-drawn vehicles and so he was taken for a ride on the Estate by Robert Battersby using a small, four-wheeled carriage which one of the Ward lads called a "chariot". Drawn by a single horse, it enabled Mr Morrison to tour without having the reek of a car's exhaust in his nostrils. By this time, Mr Battersby's beard was long and white. "Our Jimmy thought it was froth from separated milk."

Just before the 1914-18 war, Walter Morrison bowed to the inevitable. He bought a car.

A Motor Cab in which a Malham Moor bride was taken to Church for her wedding.

Infernal Combustion Engines

ROBERT BATTERSBY had a rapid transformation from coachman to chauffeur when his master, who for long had denounced motor cars as nothing but "toys of the idle rich" — decided to become mechanised." He seemed to have had a sneaking admiration for the car. "If anyone who had such a vehicle came to Malham Tarn for the shooting, he'd always beg a lift home."

Once he accepted the principle of using a car, he did not rush into car ownership. "First of all, Walter Morrison hired a Wolesley car from the *Golden Lion*," said Fred Ellis, a pioneer garage proprietor at Settle. "He would have it for a week or so at a time, and go off to the Lake District. All he did was go up and come back in it; that car was doing nothing during the day."

Then he got a Fiat. It was supplied by a Settle mechanical genius and eccentric known as Billy Slinger. "Walter Morrison was a big chap, so it was a great big car. Walter didn't intend to drive the car himself, and so he sent his coachman, then aged 75, to Billy Slinger to have driving lessons. Billy soon lost his patience, and if he was not driving well, he would rebuke Battersby by kicking his foot off the clutch."

After two or three circuits of the town, Mr Battersby was judged proficient at driving a car. The man who had brought a horse and carriage down to Settle now returned at the wheel of a Fiat. It is said that when he arrived almost at the place where the horses turned to go into the yard, he shouted: "Whooa, lass! Whooa!" The car did not stop — it travelled straight ahead, crashing into a gatepost and smashing one of the lamps. "I don't remember it, but I've heard them talk about it . . ."

The Fiat was succeeded by a Lexington, from America. By now, the 1914-18 war was in progress. When a spare part was needed for the Lexington, Mr Morrison was helped by Geoffrey Dawson, who had inherited the

Langcliffe estate and, as related, was also Editor of *The Times*.

Some gearing was at fault, and the Ellis family, who had the West Yorkshire Garage at Settle, had difficulty in locating a spare. Geoffrey Dawson contacted the London agents of the car firm, only to be told that the latest consignment of spares lay under water in London Docks. The ship had been sunk by enemy action.

When the identity of the inquirer was known, the part was promptly taken from a new car in the agent's showroom. Meanwhile, the garage had a new gear made by an engineering firm in Leeds. The car was tested on the steep road to Malham Tarn, and as it descended the hill a frightful sound—like a siren—was heard from the back axle where the gearing had been fitted. One of the teeth was slightly out of line. Happily, the new part soon reached Settle from London.

Fred Ellis told me that Walter Morrison was never garrulous. ''When his car was driven to the garage for petrol, the staff would see Walter almost filling the back seat, his head buried in a newspaper. He wouldn't know if he'd stopped or not.''

Raising dust on the water-bound roads of Malham Moor, in the pioneering days of motor transport, was the Sentinel Steam Wagon hauling a cart with coal up to Malham Tarn. ''It took two tons at a time; a horse and cart could manage only half a ton.''

Top—The first motor car to be seen at Settle stops outside the Naked Man Hotel. *Middle*—Mrs Miller, the Halton Gill schoolmistress, with a car she called Auzzie. *Bottom*—Morning's rabbit catch at Capon Hall. *Left*—Mr Cox, the dealer from Burnley. *Right*—the farmer, William Blades.

Scenes from an Old-Time Summer at Malham

On this page, we see Malham as it was in ''Morrison time''; Abraham Banks, one of the patriarchs of Malham Moor, who lived at Capon Hall; young stock at Middle House when it was farmed by the Coates family; and Mr Frank Coates on a single-horse mowing machine.

"Drinkings" at High Trenhouse; the Banks family of Low Trenhouse haytiming with sled; a champion tup and *(bottom right)* three veterans, Abraham Banks, Mrs Chester of Low Trenhouse and Tom Cowgill of Malham (photographed in 1925).

"MALHAM TARN NIGGER MINSTRELS"

A Country Life

MR MORRISON was shown all the estate and household accounts, not because he distrusted his staff but simply because he loved figures; he was curious about all that was done in his name. It is said that when a sheep died he insisted that his accounts must be debited with a sheep and credited with the fleece of the dead sheep.

His delight was to go out and about, preferably on foot: across the Moor or down to Settle (where his association with Martins Bank, as a director, was strong enough for his photograph to be hung on a wall) and on to Giggleswick School for a governors' meeting. He was not educated at Giggleswick but found such pleasure in his association that he donated a School Chapel. In return, the School hung his portrait in the hall of Big School.

As a Member of Parliament, he was frequently asked to use his vote and influence to support various causes, such as Mr Stevenson's Total Sunday Closing Bill of 1887. One who petitioned his support received a letter as follows:

I have advocated Sunday Closing for many a year. Perhaps I am a bit selfish in this respect. The Sunday drinking at Malham is a great nuisance here, though the great majority of trippers are decent sober people.

I have always maintained that you must open places for dinner and tea, say for an hour for each meal, to enable the very large numbers of persons (in towns particularly) who have but one room to live in, and who cannot cook in it, to procure those meals. House-owners take meals on Sundays, and lodgers must have the same privilege too.

It is the long hours which cause drunkenness on the idle day; men do not get drunk in an hour.

The Grand Old Man of Craven welcomed organised parties and had a special ten-minute talk about Malham Tarn. At other times he kept himself pretty much to himself. He always had a brief word for any child he passed and was amused when he heard about one of the Ward children who, while carrying out the daily inspection of traps set for rabbits, was approached by a titled lady who wished to walk through the Estate. The boy told her it was private. She must not go beyond the gate.

She said: "Do you know who I am?" The lad replied: "No—but if you were t'Prince o'Wales I wouldn't let you through. It's private property." He stood at the gate, preventing the lady and her posh companions from going further. "Old Walter did nowt but laugh over that!"

He enjoyed the company of Alfred Ward, who now presided over a family of 12 children. For the record, as they say, these children were Helen, Gladys, Mary, Beatrice, Lettice, Barbara, Dorothy, Alfred, Harold, James, Geoffrey and Jack. The gamekeeper was paid only a modest wage but had a free house, free coal and a kitchen garden.

Mr Morrison found special pleasure in repeating any Yorkshirisms that took his fancy. If an angler, talking poshly, used the word "water", Morrison would say: "Don't call it water; it's watter! Ask Alf, if you don't believe me." He once said to his gamekeeper that he was lucky to have a family, adding: "You'll have somebody to leave your money too." And Alf Ward promptly replied: "You can always leave your brass to me!"

Jim Ward recalls the meals of country fare— of woodcock, snipe, grouse, trout: all sorts of delicacies that were beyond reach of townsfolk. "In those days, long before

Walter Morrison, as he was in 1909. Mr Morrison enjoyed the company of the Dalesfolk, and especially that of his gamekeeper, Alfred Ward, knowing that the latter's speech would contain many of the old dialect words and expressions.

myxomatosis came along, rabbits were a good feed."

On at least one occasion, Walter Morrison went caving. Living in classic limestone country, he was familiar with the subterranean drainage and the presence of caves and potholes. He was fascinated when it was reported to him in 1867 that a cave had been found beneath the farmstead of Darnbrook and, with his head gardener, Thomas Coulthard, he went underground. By the light of a lamp, they scratched their names and the date on a wall of rock.

Swans on Malham Tarn.

Towards the end of his long life, Walter Morrison visited Tarn House from August until early December. His nieces, Misses Effie and Eva Freshfield, had been here, with their own staff, since the beginning of May, and they usually left in September. The nieces had a governess, which greatly benefited the head gamekeeper's children, some of whom were taught by the governess. ''They got a better education than if they had been to school.''

It seems that Mr Morrison had been ''best man'' at the Freshfields' wedding, and they were thus welcome visitors to Malham Tarn House. It also followed, he being a clergyman, that a service was held in the House on Sunday, the usual venue being the billiards room, with the Freshfield girls, who were talented musicians, providing the accompaniment for the hymn-singing.

''Anyone could go to the service,'' recalled a woman brought up on one of the Estate farms. ''When I was a child, I went. I daren't move a muscle. My mother had an umbrella and if you moved a muscle in Church, she'd prod you with it . . . There was a big three-seater couch against the wall and a lion-rug on the floor. Mr Morrison used to sprawl on the couch. Many a time, in his later days, he was asleep for half the service.''

The Freshfield ladies enjoyed helping in the hayfield. ''They did their best. They usually held their rakes all wrong. Dad, who wasn't a picker of words, would say to 'em: 'You're going ass-first.' '' (One of the Freshfield ''girls'' owned a cottage and barn adjacent to Prior Hall at Malham. In the house lived Ben Kearby, a workman from the Tarn Estate. The barn was used as a joiner's shop for the Estate. Ben, who

Left—Malham Tarn House and the Boathouse.
Below—The Staff at Malham Tarn House. The three men were (from left to right) Mr Lupton, chauffeur, Mr Battersby, former coachman, and Mr Skirrow, butler. Of the women, Mrs Skirrow is first left and Miss Lodge, housekeeper, is the prominent figure in the foreground.

was no longer lish [nimble] was driven to Tarn House on Monday morning in the trap belonging to T.H. Geldard, who also brought him back home on Friday afternoon. Mr Geldard was indeed a good neighbour).

Helen Ward had letters written by some of the wealthy ladies who visited Walter Morrison's "mountain home" in summer. One letter accompanied a parcel of clothes sent to the gamekeeper's children. The writer hoped that "little legs will be kept warm by thick woollen stockings."

Christmas had a special flavour at Malham Tarn, where at 1,200 ft the snow lay deep and crisp and even, changing the familiar contours of the landscape and reflecting back the yellow light from stable lamps as groups went carolling. With Walter Morrison away from Malham at this time, the estate folk could truly relax. A choir was formed by members of the well-known families—the Wards, the Chapmans, the Hodkins, Mr Percy from Giggleswick and Edgar Brown, the joiner, who had a particularly fine voice.

For the children, the most popular winter sport was sledging. "We sledged down one steep hillside, across the old Roman road and up the other side. We hadn't a proper sledge; we used a piece of zinc sheeting."

School by the Tarn

MALHAM TARN Subscription School, established in 1872, had a committee of seven who were elected annually in Easter Week. Needless to say, Walter Morrison was the chairman; a copy of the rules and regulations shows pencilled amendments to the list of committee members but the name of Walter Morrison is unbesmirched.

Between 1896 and 1917, the teachers were, successively, Mrs Barker, Miss Offer, Miss Isabel Jackson, Miss Yeoman, Mrs Michael, Miss Hollywood, Miss Hargreaves, Miss Duckworth and Miss Jackson. The number of children on the register ranged from 18 (in 1896) to 13 (in 1906). There followed Miss Phyllis Thornber, Mr Bilton and, from 1932 to 1941, Miss Doris Carr.

Miss Yeoman, who lived at Langcliffe and was to be recalled as "a kindly woman", taught at Malham Moor School at the turn of the century. John Hilton, who had a motor bike and sidecar, transported her in that sidecar on a Monday morning; she stayed at school, occupying some upper rooms, until Friday afternoon, when she returned to Langcliffe.

In the summer of 1900, Her Majesty's Inspector reported most favourably on the School. "Improvement has been effected in all

The oldest known photograph of Malham Tarn School was taken with the forms set out in the school grounds to catch every scrap of light. Third from the right on the front row is Jane Hoyle, who walked from Capon Hall. *Below*—Children having a nature study class on the shores of Malham Tarn.

Above—Malham Tarn School in 1927. From left to right: Frankie Chapman (who was to be killed by lightning), Cecil Banks, Ethel Taylor, Barbara Ward. At rear, Mary Hoyle, Hugh Nowell, Harry Taylor.

Adventure by the sea. A school trip to Morecambe, c1928.

subjects and in recognition thereof the highest principal grant is recommended.'' Miss Yeoman was at Malham Tarn House in December of that year supervising a performance by her scholars, part of a Christmas entertainment. They presented action songs, drill, recitations and tableaux. The *Craven Herald* reported:

The idea of a concert in this scattered hamlet on the Moors originated with Miss Yeoman and Miss Winskill. Mr Morrison, ever ready to help forward anything for the benefit of his neighbours, kindly allowed a large room at the Hall to be used for the purpose . . . The proceeds of nearly £4 were to go for prizes and a Christmas tree for the children.

The teacher's accommodation upstairs was spare. ''There was one of those little desks, a table and some chairs, an oil stove and, in a little bedroom, just a bed, a wardrobe and dressing table.''

The school consisted of a single room, with a table and some desks; the heating was by coal fire, not a stove. Jane, one of the Coates family of ''Capna'' (Capon Hall), began school in 1900 and was here until she was 14. At the age of six, she began to walk the one and a-half miles to school with a similar distance to walk

Above — Miss Doris Carr, on ponyback, waves to the children of Malham Tarn School before returning home to Lee Gate, in the mid 1930s.
Below — An outdoor lesson.

when lessons were over. She was taught the Three R's — Reading, 'Riting and 'Rithmetic. At midday, teacher boiled a kettle to make tea. ''After we had our dinner, which was mainly sandwiches, we went down to the beck to wash our hands. I can remember rubbing them with sand.''

Nature walks along the edge of the Tarn introduced the children to birds and flowers. ''We once found a pheasant's nest in a tree.'' Farm children took time off in haytime; they

included Nowells and Banks from Capon Hall, Chapmans from Tennant Gill and Coates's from Darnbrook.

Miss Duckworth came from Colne, and talked "reight Lancashire''. The daughter of a farmer's wife who did "bits o'washing'' told me: "Miss Duckworth would come to our house to pay for it and our lads 'ud be there. When she spoke, they sometimes laughed. She was so broad it sounded like swearing. Mother told them off about it.'' Miss Dorothy Jackson was "very nice—she let me make model aeroplanes out of cardboard on Friday afternoons,'' one of the scholars was to recall. Miss

Two more studies of Malham Tarn School as it was between the wars. *Above*—A genial horse. *Below*—Members of the Popay family with (right) Phyllis Thornber, schoolteacher.

Phyllis Thornber was yet another of the indomitable women who served at this remote school.

Mrs Coates, of High Trenhouse, taught at Malham Tarn now and again. "She'd been a teacher afore she was married. She used to get concerts up. I remember one concert because I had a right bad heel. I couldn't get a shoe on and I went in my slippers. Another time, we

gave a special performance at Capon Hall, where t'farmer had fallen off his horse and broken his leg. He had to stay in bed. We thought brekking a leg was an awful thing. Nowadays, they don't think much about it.''

Sometimes, Walter Morrison visited the school and asked to read out the names on the register. The children had to reply as the names were called. "We used to call Mr Morrison 'Grandad'—though not to his face! He was a nice old man; he loved children and if he saw you playing, as he walked near the house, he'd come and talk to you.''

If something was required for use at school, the teacher usually approached Mr Skirrow at the House; he then approached Mr Morrison. Just after the 1914-18 war, there was a desire to take children for an outing. Someone mentioned it to Mr Skirrow, who said to his master: "I think it would be a nice thing to take all the children to Morecambe; would you pay for the trip?'' And, of course, he did. The children were conveyed to Giggleswick railway station in the Fiat car and others were transported in horse-drawn traps.

Mr Winskill, the agent, had a large walking stick "and when Christmas parties were held, he used to get us all standing round him. Then he'd say: 'I'm going to set my rocket off to the moon.' He pretended to light it and then threw his stick in the air. Somebody would get clattered with it as it came back to earth.''

The Malham Moor school outlived Walter Morrison by many years. In the 1930s, when Miss Doris Carr, of Lee Gate, was the teacher, and there were eight scholars, she preferred to go home each evening rather than occupy the teachers' accommodation at Malham Tarn. For some time she walked, almost six miles a day, and then, at the insistence of her father, she began to use one of the ponies.

She taught at the school near the Tarn for 12 years and ''enjoyed them all.'' There was but one room, with a coal fire. The children's outer clothes were hung to dry on a rack above the fireplace. The furnishings were half a dozen twin-desks, a stock cupboard in one corner and another cupboard by the fireplace. ''I had a tall desk—just four legs and a top.'' The age range was from five to 14. While Kathleen, Dorothy and Doris

A ''cricket team'' on the lawn at Malham Tarn House. Mr Winskill is fourth from the left on the back row and Taylor Chapman stands on the extreme right.

were being taught arithmetic, Jean, Gordon and Laidler, studied history, and the two infants, Doreen and Nellie, would be having a good time with the plasticine. The playground was a grass field with some rock outcrops to attract the more adventurous.

Events of the Farming Year

WALTER MORRISON'S long residence on Malham Moor and his retentive memory gave him an extraordinary detailed knowledge of local life and traditions. He was always relaxed in the company of the farmfolk who sustained a farming way of life that was little changed for 1,000 years—a life concerned with sheep and a few cattle.

Mr Morrison, a ''model landlord'', took pity on his tenants at a time of industrial depression and reduced the rents by up to 50 per cent. Those tenants had mixed feelings about the new farmhouses he was building early this century. He employed a London architect, who used an alien style, with deeply pitched roof of Welsh slates. At Low Trenhouse, Mr Banks and his family exchanged their cosy little Dales farmhouse for a new building that was so cold and bleak ''false teeth froze in the glass in the bedroom in winter.''

Walter Morrison sometimes walked through the farmyard at Low Trenhouse and had a chat at the doorway of the house with Betty Banks, who was a great reader, with a fondness for books written by Victorian novelists. They discussed literary topics for hours.

The Banks of Low Trenhouse had a mare which was due to give birth to a foal. It was considered unlucky to watch the birth of a foal so the family stayed in the farmhouse and left the mare in the High Close. With a horse, the birth process is exceptionally short; if not, there is some complication. In this case, both the mare and foal died. Walter Morrison promptly replaced the mare.

It was this grey mare that the daughter of the family, Margaret, used when she wished to visit Malham. She rode to the Post Office one day in 1918 to be greeted by an excited Postmistress, Mrs Wiseman. ''So pleased to see you, Maggie,'' she said. ''There's a telegram for you. We know what's in it, but we can't tell anyone else till you've seen it, because it's yours.'' The telegram was the first intimation Malhamdale had that the war was over. Margaret jumped on her horse and went round all the farms on Malham Moor with the gladsome news.

The farmers on Malham Moor kept to an old routine. In November, a special salve was applied to the skins of the sheep ''to keep them warm''; then there was tupping, leading to lambing in the laggard Pennine spring. It was customary to wash sheep about a fortnight before clipping. ''We washed in Jennet's [Janet's Foss]. We picked a time when t'dub were full. In those days, Jennet's sank a bit and in a dry season water would be going out faster than it went in. I remember going to the top of the waterfall in dry weather. We put sods across and got 51 trout out of the pool. All Malhamdale got trout that summer!''

When the sheep had been clipped, they were spained [lambs separated from the ewes] and the surplus stock sold. Hoggs that were to be retained were driven to the coastal marshes for their first winter.

''Dad cut across country wi' t'sheep; he'd go by Sannet Hall and down the old green lane to Helwith Bridge and on to Austwick. He stayed overnight at Whoop Hall [near Kirkby Lonsdale] and go on to Morecambe Bay next day. In

Top—Calves at High Trenhouse. *Middle*— Laidler and Jean Coates at Middle House. *Bottom*—The Chesters moved from Malham to Drebley, where this picture was taken in the 1930s.

Spring, he'd set off again to collect them. We used to go and meet dad when we thought he'd be nearly at Cowside. If my young brother said to Dad, 'That sheep had two lambs last year', or something like that, Dad was suited no end because he kenned [knew] his sheep.''

Then it was tupping time again on Malham Moor; new life was implanted in the ewes as the year died grandly with flurries of snow to chase the crisp autumn leaves.

A woman who, aged five, clearly remembered ''flitting'' from Malham to a farmhouse on Malham Tarn Estate, told me: ''In the wagon were two boys; our Len was only a baby. Me and our Kate sat back to back with mother and dad; we were tied in for safety. We landed to High Trenhouse. Mr Coates was a big pal of my dad. He said: 'We haven't sin t'furniture go by yet. Come and have a cup o'tea. So they loose t'horse out and we went in for a drink. Mrs Coates said: 'Leave two girls here while you get a bit straight.' Mother said: 'I haven't brought their night clothes.' Mr Coates, who was always saying silly things, said: 'Well, they can have my shirts.' I wasn't having that. But our Kate stopped.''

Mr Morrison, being mainly a summer visitor, was familiar with haytime—with the mowing of the meadow grass, its drying by wind and sunshine and the storage of hay in the many barns. He doubtless watched cows being milked by hand, and milk being churned prior to being made into butter and cheese.

He was fond of visiting his tenants at their farmhouses and of sitting in the kitchen, listening to the homely wash of dialect while holding one of the children on his knee. Thomas and Betsy Newhouse, of Gordale Farm, saw him on days when he had visitors who were keen to see Gordale Scar. He brought them to the farm, pointed out the footpath way to the Scar and then entered the farmhouse for a cup of tea.

It was a typical Dales farmhouse, with two kitchens, one containing a set-boiler and the ''backstone'' on which oatcake was made by Betsy. She would spend a whole day at it and fill a drying rack in the living room with the oval pieces. Her niece remarks: ''Oatcake was eaten for supper, with loads of butter.''

This niece recalls sitting on Mr Morrison's knee. ''In the autumn, a gentleman from

Darnbrook Farm, in the remotest part of the Moor.

Mr Winskill and Mr Chapman at Darnbrook, following a big flood.

The dogs owned by Major Morrison being walked from Tarn House to Middle House.

Garstang arrived to buy the draft ewes; he gave me a shilling. Mr Morrison called the next day and he gave me sixpence. I can remember telling him: 'Mr Sanderson gave me a shilling.' It didn't make any difference; he didn't reach into his pocket again!''

Thomas Newhouse did not usually drink, but who could resist the odd drink when it was free of charge, as at the *Lister's Arms* in Malham on Rent Day? ''It was the only time I knew grandma to be cross with grandpa. He came back a bit merry.'' Less merry were those who walked to and from Malham daily to work for the Estate. Among them were Mr Wiseman, Mr Baines and Mr Brown. Each was paid £1 in wages per week.

That was before the 1914-18 war shattered the old social order. It was a time when a visitor to Malham Cove or Gordale saw goats kept by the farmers. The kids were born early in the year, which meant that the nanny goats had a good flow of milk available if a farmer had an orphan or weakly lamb. ''The farmers brought down the goats in spring. Woe betide you if they drove them through the farmyard and there were some billy goats. You could smell them long enough after!''

A Sporting Estate

MALHAM TARN was highly regarded as a fishery by Fountains Abbey. Some of the trout were transported by moorland ways to the great Abbey by the Skell, near Ripon. The Listers improved the fishery. When Walter Morrison owned the estate, sporting visitors were glad to have the help and advice of the Wards, father and son, who had records of fish caught in the Tarn since 1864.

The Tarn's delights were appreciated by Charles Kingsley, who on July 5, 1858, wrote: ''My largest fish to-day [a cold North Wester] was 1½ lb., but with a real day I could kill 50 lb. Unfortunately it wants all my big lake flies, which I, never expecting such a treat, left at home.'' In a succeeding letter—that in which he described the fishing as ''the best in the whole earth''—the author of *The Water-Babies* was now researching a book on ''The Pilgrimage of Grace'' [a book that was never completed]. Kingsley included a note that ''wonderful Malham Tarn will come into the book and all around it.''

Tradition endowed the resident fish with extraordinary dimensions and characteristics. Mr Morrison was never known to turn down an application to fish but he insisted that all trout caught under a pound in weight should be returned to the water. On the one and only occasion he fished the tarn himself, he managed to bag a small, quarter-pound trout—and, ignoring his own regulation, he took it back to the House.

Anglers who took out the boat at Malham Tarn in the 1850s and 1860s returned to the shore with double figure catches. Then, as more and more permits were granted, the numbers fell away. An angler had to be

Malham Tarn, showing one of the robust boats. In Mr Morrison's time,
the craft were made in the Lake District.
Right—Mr Winskill, who was so keen on maintaining a good stock of
trout in Malham Tarn he opened a hatchery at Tennant Gill.

satisfied with a brace of takeable fish.

By 1872, this decline in the number of fish was being reflected in the impressive sizes of some that were being caught, the average weight being 1½ lb, with 2 lb fish being caught occasionally. In the 1880s and onwards, many fish that made the scales dip at over 2 lb were being recorded. The record fish, one of 6lb 8 oz., was landed in 1924, being taken on a nightline that had been set for perch.

T.K. Wilson, who knew the Ward family well, and was able to consult their records, asked Alfred Ward about his best catch, to be told that it was taken early one morning when he was fishing from the shore almost in front of the House. He hooked and landed, in quick succession, seven trout, their total weight being 21 lb.

A good many Malham Tarn trout had a deficiency in the operculum, or gill cover. Mr Morrison encouraged the belief that these fish were a distinct breed. Then it was whispered that when Thomas Lister, the first Lord Ribblesdale, had Malham Tarn (from 1790 to 1852) he had introduced Loch Leven trout. They became afflicted with a similar malformation. No one who has fished the Tarn has left a record of a blind trout; it was once claimed that many older trout went blind because a yellow film covered their eyes.

With regard to perch, Tim Wilson was told by Alfred Ward that the largest catch in a day, at 886, was recorded in 1861. Mr Ward could not remember the circumstances of that, but he remembered the next best, of 857, in 1911. Ten men from Long Preston fished from four boats; throughout the time they were afloat, the fish never went off the feed.

The Malham Tarn boats, which were robustly made for Mr Morrison in the Lake District, were much in demand. Alfred Ward, when taking out young people, sometimes amused himself by rocking the boat to scare them.

Mr Ward bought in pheasant eggs and hatched them out under broody hens for subsequent release into the woods. He was also in charge of the famous local grouse moors.

Walter Morrison was fond of recalling the days before grouse were driven. Shooters walked the moors and shot any birds that were flushed by the dogs. Later, grouse-driving became popular. Malham Tarn Estate included three big moors—Penyghent, Rainscar and Darnbrook. Walter Morrison kept three gamekeepers and each autumn was enacted the ritual of grouse-driving. Walter Morrison dutifully joined his shooting guests in the butts but shot without any great enthusiasm. "He did shoot, but didn't crack on it so much. It was more a case of something for his friends."

Walter insisted that if anyone joined the grouse-shooting party, they were expected to shoot. He had the billiards balls locked up when, it seemed, some of the guests might prefer the dry comfort of the house to a wet day on the Moor!

A Slaidburn man recalled: "A day's shooting with Mr Morrison was always on a grand scale. We would leave our horse at Rough Close Farm and then make our way on to the fell by way of Tennant Gill. Here Mr Mark Frankland was brought up. I remember he used to join the beaters on the fell of whom, including gamekeepers, there would be about 20 in all. I, too, was numbered amongst them, but usually I was allotted to the lower ground where the going was easier.

"It would usually be September before Mr Morrison's invitation arrived. By then his friends from London would have joined him. They were supplemented by local gentry such as Mr Proctor, Mr Atkinson and others from Settle, Langcliffe and Stainforth. Lunch was brought from the hall and partaken at the shooting boxes up on the fell, with the coachman and butler in attendance. Altogether, the warm September days went by very pleasantly . . ."

On shooting days, when the visitors went on to the moor, Mrs Holmes, who was then the cook—she was a maiden lady but had the

Walter Morrison was proud of the Malham Tarn fishery and supported the idea that the trout were distinctive, having a deficiency in the gill cover. He went to great pains to ensure there was good sport on the grouse moors, but he himself was not especially keen on shooting.

courtesy title of 'Mrs'—prepared food to be taken out to the shooting hut. One who helped to prepare that food said: "I used to fair hate mekkin' meat or cheese sandwiches for all that lot. I used to bake for 'em an' all. They loved my currant loaf; it was not like teacake. I cut that currant loaf into slices. They all had a little pastry as well."

A few days before the Glorious Twelfth [the start of the grouse-shooting season], Mr Winskill would call at the Craven Bank in Skipton to ask for the names of the staff. Several days after shooting had begun, each person received a brace of grouse.

A note issued by the Craven Bank. It features an engraving of the celebrated Craven Heifer.

Head of the Bank

WALTER MORRISON became Chairman of The Craven Bank in 1905. His association was to be recalled by W.B. Carson, who entered the Bank's service at Head Office in Skipton in 1898. The Bank had eight Directors. They met periodically in a room above the banking office, with a break for lunch, served in an adjoining room by the wife of the caretaker.

Mr Morrison disliked licking envelopes, possibly because his correspondence was heavy. Mr Carson remembered when, on a visit to the Bank, he would ask for a glue pot and spread envelopes, flaps open, on his [Mr Carson's] desk. He then proceeded to brush and daub the envelope flaps thoroughly, "making my desk a sticky mess."

He never took advantage of his directorship. Now and again he would telegraph from his London home a request to overdraw £5,000, adding "REPLY STATE YOUR TERMS". In

April, 1906, when The Craven Bank had been amalgamated with the Bank of Liverpool, he—as Chairman—could be sincere in his declaration at a shareholders' meeting that it was in their best interests.

"Memory conjures up a picture of his huge frame beside mine on the railway station platform where I hurried to deliver his pass book to him. He chatted as the train approached and I am sure his kindly attention would not have been more gracious had he known that the junior clerk at his side would one day become a chief general manager."

Mr Morrison was the most important client of Messrs Charlesworth, solicitors, Settle. Elinor Pike, who worked in the office in the 1914-18 war, remembered him as "rather a remote figure". Many stories, some true, were told of him. "The one and only time I saw this great man was in the office. On arrival, I saw a tall, shabbily dressed and stooping figure who was ushered at speed into the private office of Mr Charlesworth. Hearing who he was,

I tried to keep out of sight—thinking he might disapprove of females. I busied myself in untying knots in some of the red tape. Later, still with my head down, I saw feet coming towards me.

"Seeing what I was doing, the great man patted me on the arm and said: 'Well done, young lady! I always undo knots in string, never cut them; keep it up!' His words must have made an impression upon me as even now, in old age, I scarcely ever cut string, but I have never become a millionaire! Ah, well . . .''

Speaking in Public

MR MORRISON was a tireless traveller and speaker at election time. The local newspaper reported his every word with appropriate responses from the audience—such as (hear, hear) or (applause). In the pre-television age, people were prepared to listen intently to long political speeches which, today, would be considered dreary.

Walter Morrison was not one of the best speakers, but wherever he was billed to appear as a candidate in an election, it was certain that the hall would be packed. Now and again a few hecklers might be heard. The speaker impressed by his great stature and, of course, the possession of money impressed those who had little of it.

In the elections of 1886 and 1892, the main topic was Home Rule, In 1900, standing before a packed audience in the Town Hall at Skipton, he "expounded his views on the paramount question of the day, viz., the South African crisis." Helen Ward recalled that when he changed his political allegiance from Liberal (yellow) to Conservative (blue) he also changed the colour of the crockery at the House. The yellow crocks were buried near Sandhills (besides the dead horses!)

In 1900, when he had been at Malham Tarn for some 40 years, he had a memorable year, cutting the first sod of the Yorkshire Dales Railway, between Skipton and Grassington, and on another day rising at the Craven Show

Mr. WALTER MORRISON

RESPECTFULLY SOLICITS

THE FAVOUR OF YOUR

VOTE AND INTEREST.

luncheon at Skipton to propose the toast of the organising Society and its Officers.

He went on at length about—butter. He complimented the many farmhouse producers of butter but believed the time had come when it would be sensible for them to "imitate their neighbours across the Irish Channel" and establish creameries in every district where a considerable quantity of milk was available.

He also had a suggestion to make about prize-giving. Having been at the North Ribblesdale Show at Settle, he saw the Shorthorn judges spend two hours discussing which of two cows should receive the first prize. Eventually, they had to call in one of the other judges to help. "Why should they not in such an instance bracket the first and second prizes and let half go to each animal," said Mr Morrison.

No "hear, hears" and no "applause" greeted this suggestion. Taking a long time over a decision is all part of the judging game!

Outdoor Occasions

MUCH could be written about his political life and his great love of military matters, especially his involvement with the Yeomanry. But my brief is the Walter Morrison of Malham Tarn—a mainly rural topic. In 1898 he was appointed president of the Yorkshire Geological Association and took part in the survey of Malham's underground waters.

He welcomed parties of geologists, journalists and naturalists to his Estate, as in the 1890's, when his guests for the day were members of the National Union of Journalists. Two motor omnibuses, supplied by the enterprising firm of Chapman, Ltd., of Grassington, and two private cars, awaited the journalists at Skipton Railway Station. Both the Malham hotels—the *Lister's Arms* and *The Buck*—had been requisitioned for lunch. There followed a three-hour walk to Malham Tarn, with stops to listen to a commentary by Mr Jonas Bradley, of Stanbury. Then, of course, followed a meeting with Mr Morrison and his celebrated ten-minute talk about the area.

The Yorkshire Geological and Polytechnic Society held a Spring excursion at Malham, with Mr Morrison as guide. "Mr Morrison is a resident in the locality and when not required in the perturbed atmosphere of the House of Commons he retires to his pretty mansion amongst the hills overlooking Malham Tarn. Every foot of the rugged moorlands that lie for miles around the wooded oasis in which his residence is sheltered from the biting winds is known to him . . ."

After a visit to Kirkby Malham Church and a morning ramble, luncheon was served at Malham Tarn House and the geologists then visited Malham Cove and Gordale Scar. Next day, Mr Morrison was with them as they visited the fine series of scars which mark the lines of the Craven Faults between Malham and Settle. On they went to Victoria Cave, thence to Giggleswick School to see the museum that held items taken from the famous "bone cave".

Mr Morrison took a particular interest in the investigation of underground waters at Malham and Clapham. In 1899, Mr G. Bray of Leeds and John Winskill, Mr Morrison's agent at Malham, put into a spring a dye that went green. They were hopeful of tracing the flow of water by marking the point of egress. "The results were disappointing to the observers generally, but they show that the problem is not nearly so simple as was previously supposed . . ."

In 1910, the Yorkshire Naturalists' Union held its Meet at Malham. "Mr Walter Morrison, on whose estate some of the most charming scenery of the district lies, took a keen interest in the gathering. He entertained several of the members at his home for the week-end, and shared some of the walks, beside throwing open to the investigators his wide domain, and lending his boats for a thorough searching of the Tarn . . . Afterwards, the party walked across the moor and descended by Malham Cove, finding the Alpine Bartsia on the heights and Jacob's Ladder in its ancient haunt at the Cove—the very spot on which Ray and Martin Lister found it as long ago as the 17th century."

One of the last photographs to be taken of Walter Morrison, as he welcomed a party of visitors to his Estate.

Mr Morrison's Benefactions

WALTER MORRISON drew the most astonishing reverence from the Malham folk. He had been so long at Malham Tarn he was "one of us". He had a Victorian piety and attended Church regularly. It is recalled that on Sunday mornings he went to Kirkby Malham Church. "If guests were staying with him, he would walk and the guests would ride. The servants came by dog-cart."

His benevolence towards the Church was legendary and included meeting most of the cost of the restoration in 1879-81, a restoration which pleased everyone at the time but has its critics among those who do not care for Victorian "improvements".

Walter Morrison was a Trustee of the Organ Trust Fund, which paid £16 per annum to the organist and £1.10s to the organ blower, and of the Church Hall Fund, under which the major expense was £9.15s.2d for "coal and lamp oil". Walter presided over the Kirkby Malham Reading Room, was a manager of Kirkby Malham School, of Kirkby Malhamdale United Schools and, of course, the Malham Moor School.

Indeed, it was at his initiative and expense, in 1872, that a site was bought to accommodate a new Dale school and headmaster's house. The land cost £50 and he expended £2,874 on the building work. Two existing schools, those at Kirkby Malham and Malham, were now accommodated under one capacious roof. French and Latin were taught and Walter Morrison was fond of hearing the senior pupils speak in French—doubly elated when the scholars did well for a guest at Tarn House, who was a Frenchman.

The Rev. D.R. Hall, reporting on Church affairs in 1909-10, noted that Mr Morrison had given a subscription of £10 towards Church expenses.

"Our esteemed friend and neighbour, Mr Morrison, passed through another serious illness last winter. But thanks to a good constitution and regular habits he has been able again, notwithstanding the stress of a busy life, to stand the strain of a very trying illness".

Reporting to his parishioners a year later, Mr Hall mentioned the death of Thomas Coulthard, of Malham Tarn, "for 50 years the faithful, conscientious and true servant of his master here [Morrison] as he was of his Master in Heaven.''

In the chapel that Mr Morrison provided for Giggleswick School the donor appears in stained glass, with a model of the chapel under his arm. ''It was,'' as Geoffrey Dawson was to write, ''his first and last piece of self-advertisement.'' His subscription portrait painted by Sir Hubert von Kerkromer, and now hanging in Big School at Giggleswick, ''well suggests''—as one writer had it—''the kindliness, humour and generosity that are the distinguishing features of Mr Morrison's character.''

His last great act of benevolence was the production of a book *Craven's Part in the Great War;* he worked closely with Mr J. Clayton, Editor of ''The Craven Herald'' and he defrayed the cost of production. The book featured all those who had served, and a copy was given to every returning soldier and also the relatives of those who had been killed.

Interior of the Church, the restoration of which was paid for by Mr Morrison.

The Last Years

THE CRISP AIR and attractive walks in High Craven contributed to Mr Morrison's long life, though he and death were close together one day when he was on his way through Settle to catch a train. He dashed into a tobacconist's shop, removed from the shelf what he thought was a jar of tobacco, asked someone waiting in the shop to tell the owner that he had taken some of his favourite brand from its usual place, and resumed his hurried journey to the station.

When the tobacconist discovered that Morrison had taken in error the drug latakia, used in minute portions for blending, the railway company were contacted and told to contact him. On no account must he smoke the substance. They did. He didn't. And all was well.

Walter Morrison, as a feeble old man, attended a meeting at which money was being raised for the peace rejoicings after the 1914-18 war. ''One day, when I wouldn't be four years old, I was taken to a meeting by granny, recalls one who was taken there. ''Granny daren't leave me at home, of course.''

Walter Morrison was there. He was asked for a donation. ''I can see him now, fumbling in his pocket, slowly pulling out sovereigns and looking closely at them, one by one. At the finish, he gave 10 sovereigns. They represented a lot of money in those days. It had all to be written down in the accounts: Walter Morrison, donation £10.''

The 1914-18 war brought out his fighting spirit, though he was unable to fight. He served on the Settle War Relief Committee. It was ''Morrison money'' that defrayed much of the expense of providing a special ''welcome home'' to the Servicemen in August, 1919. He himself was too ill to take part, though it was recalled that 60 years before, in that month, he had inaugurated the Settle Voluneers. ''It would have been very fitting indeed if on the anniversary of such an event he could have

Mr George Jenkinson
Black Horse Inn
Giggleswick
Settle

But you do not stand alone, most families at home have paid their toll of blood to the same grand cause.

Believe me

Yours faithfully

W. Morrison

Mr George Jenkinson

A page from a letter of condolence written by Walter Morrison.

extended the hand of welcome home to the volunteers who have so worthily taken a part in the Great War,'' the *Craven Herald* observed.

Writing from ''Malham Tarn, Langcliffe, Settle'' on October 26, 1915, the Grand Old Man brought some words of comfort to Mr George Jenkinson, of the *Black Horse* at Giggleswick, who had lost his son on active service. ''You must feel that he could not have given his life for a nobler cause.''

In 1920, after some years of indifferent health, and being unable to stand the rigours of a Pennine winter, he bought a house in Sidmouth. He died here in the following year. Mr Morrison had last been seen in Malham less than two months before his death and his last public appearance, in the previous autumn, had been when he attended a distribution of the war memorial volumes, *Craven's Part in the Great War*.

When his death was announced, tributes were paid to him as a businessman. He was a director of the Carlton Iron Company, of the Improved Industrial Dwellings Company and of the Yorkshire Dales Railway Company. His long political career was recalled. There had been two political terms—12 years as a Radical and social idealist and 14 years as a Liberal Unionist of Conservative leanings; the two having been separated by a space of a dozen years, when he immersed himself in business.

He was buried in the yard at Kirkby Malham Church. His workmen had already collected a large flat stone from Penyghent. It was now inscribed by Jim Hodkin, the estate mason. The stone was moved by horse and cart to Kirkby Malham.

On funeral day, ''our Ellie [Ward]—then aged 15—stopped behind and looked after all the kids on the Moor. We kids didn't know there was a funeral. All we knew was that for some reason Our Ellie had to take care of us. She said: 'Come here, I'll show you something.' We went on to the front of the house and looked across Malham Tarn. You could just see a little bit of road—and the hearse on its way to the Church.''

The man who had lived simply was buried without great ceremonial. His oaken coffin was plain and unpolished, with heavy brass fittings. It was lowered into a plain earth grave. A correspondent of the *Pioneer* wrote:

The day was bleak and dour, as though nature herself joined in the expressions of sympathy for the death of one who loved her second to none.

Among those attending the funeral were Abraham Banks, of Capon Hall, his oldest neighbour and William Skirrow, who had been Mr Morrison's valet for over 30 years. Robert Battersby the coachman, had to remain at home, having broken a leg shortly before. The "funeral tea" was held at the Lister's Arms at Malham.

Wrote the Editor of "The Craven Herald":

The passing of Mr Walter Morrison, full of years and honour, is a wrench that the people of Craven feel with painful acuteness. There was nothing meretricious about him. He was genuine; a fine type of Nature's gentleman. . . His patriotism was a burning passion. . . Straight in all his dealings, he had no place for the man who did not "play the game". . . Believing in the cause, he supported it with a magnanimity that sometimes staggered his friends. Of his private benefactions, no one will ever know their usefulness or extent. . Craven mourns its "Grand Old Man", one whose like we shall ne'er see again.

Walter Morrison's last journey. The cortage leaves Kirkby Malham Church for the grave.

Detail from the cocked hat Walter wore when he visited the palace.
Right—Four generations: John Winskill, Annie Coates (daughter), John Coates (grandson), Enid (great granddaughter).

After Walter Morrison

HE DIED plain Mr Morrison. He did not like a big fuss, though when he was presented at Court he had felt disposed to order a special black velvet suit with silvery buttons. He strode to the Palace with a "cocked hat" and silver buckles on his gleaming shoes.

Mr Morrison, who never married, left a gross estate to the value of £2m. Apart from the large bequests to his relatives, he left £1,000 to John Winskill, £1,000 to Robert Battersby, £3,000 to William Skirrow; £3,000 to Martha Skirrow and £1,000 to George Petty, gardener at Malham Tarn. Other servants, who had been in his employ for two years or more, shared in a fund of £5,000.

Walter Morrison left his personal belongings to the ever-faithful Skirrow. He and Madge

retired to West View, Settle, where—60 years ago—visitors to the house could see many objects that once had adorned Malham Tarn House. Among them were two French sandalwood chairs, one of which became riddled with woodworm.

He devised the estate to his nephew, Major James Archibald Morrison, DSO. For a little while longer, the sporting aspect was maintained according to tradition by James William Usher, a Northumbrian, who was appointed head gamekeeper. One of his assistants, William Lund, was known locally as Mowdy Bill through his prowess as a mole-catcher. When John Winskill retired, Mr Usher took over his work as agent as well as his own tasks as gamekeeper.

Major Morrison soon disposed of the southern portion and in 1927 sold the remainder in lots to various purchasers. Mr E.W. Fisher, of Oakfield Lodge, Huddersfield, paid

£28,000 for:

MALHAM TARN (the mansion and the lake) extending to about 448a.1r.24p Included were old-world gardens (planned with sloping lawns leading to the Tarn itself); kitchen gardens; the lake, covering 152 acres and two boat-houses; High Folds Scar Wood; keeper's cottage; chauffeur's cottage and the school and schoolhouse, together with the sporting rights over almost the whole estate. Also: The Home or Waterhouses Farm, area 1001.2r.28p, situated north-east of Malham Tarn, together with shepherd's cottage fronting the road leading to Malham Tarn; the tenancy in hand; and Cottage, at present occupied temporarily by the estate gardener, offered with vacant possession.

The sale of the contents of Malham Tarn House—nearly 300 lots—took place in the large hall. Among the chief purchasers was Mr F. Laycock, of Skipton, who bought for 55 guineas a Jacobean oak Court Cupboard with canopy. A set of eight Queen Anne walnut dining chairs with cabriole club legs realised 220 guineas. A local woman who went to the sale of furniture and fittings bought the red satin curtains. ''I got a pile of curtains for £1. There was satin on the inside, a winceyette lining and more satin on the outside. I took the lining out, washed it and made my grandma three nighties out of it.''

Mr Fisher is recalled as ''a nice man''. I was told: ''He took over on our Beatie's wedding day. When he heard that the bride and her guests would not be permitted to go through Malham Tarn Estate, and would have to go the long way round by road on their way to Church, he ordered Hodkin to open the gate and let them through, saying: 'If they want to go down there on their way to Kirkby Malham Church, they will go. . .'.''

It was in 1924, during Mr Fisher's ownership of the Estate, that electric lighting was installed in the House. ''He was such a nice man, was Mr Fisher. They found him dead in bed about six months after he had arrived''.

The new owners of the Estate were the Hutton-Crofts, she being a niece of Walter Morrison. The family had extensive property in Hampshire and East Yorkshire. Malham was used only during the shooting season. The Hodkin family had been installed as caretaker/housekeeper, and James Usher continued with his various duties.

Daily, in fair weather or foul, Usher tramped with his dogs over the fells. A Lancashireman, Frank Lowe, often accompanied him. ''Walk on the grass,'' he was told by the gamekeeper, who added, ''it saves your shoes.'' It was on Fountains Fell one day that Frank mentioned the prevalence of black rabbits thereabouts and learned that these animals had been introduced to make it more difficult for poachers to dispose of any they had acquired.

Mrs Hutton-Croft left the Malham Tarn Estate to the National Trust in 1946. Shortly afterwards, the House was leased to the Field Studies Council.

The grave of Walter Morrison.

47

By Direction of Major J. A. MORRISON, D.S.O.

WEST RIDING OF YORKSHIRE

6 miles from Settle; 12 miles from Hellifield.

Illustrated Particulars with Plan and Conditions of Sale

OF THE

HISTORICAL, RESIDENTIAL, SPORTING, AGRICULTURAL & MANORIAL ESTATE

OF

MALHAM TARN

situate in the parishes of Malham, Malham Moor, Langcliffe, Halton Gill,
Litton and Arncliffe, including

THE COMFORTABLE MANSION

delightfully placed on the edge of THE MALHAM TARN LAKE,

**Simple and Inexpensive Old World Gardens,   Stabling and Garages,
STAFF COTTAGES,   TWELVE EXCELLENT SHEEP FARMS,
TWO FULLY LICENSED HOTELS,**
"The Buck Hotel" and "The Lister Arms" and

**THE MANORS or REPUTED MANORS of MALHAM, DARNBROOKE and
FOREST OF KNOUPE.**

Mineral Rights,

The whole extending to about

12,716 acres,

With Manorial Rights over a further area of about 2,100 acres.

FIRST-RATE GROUSE SHOOTING over the Estate,

AND

EXCEPTIONAL TROUT FISHING in the Lake and Streams

To be offered for Sale by Auction, as a whole or in Lots, by Messrs.

KNIGHT, FRANK & RUTLEY

(Sir Howard Frank, Bart., G.B.E., K.C.B.; Alfred J. Burrows, F.S.I., F.A.I.;
Arthur H. Knight, F.A.I.; Charles Phillips, F.A.I.)

At The DEVONSHIRE HOTEL, SKIPTON,

On Thursday the 11th day of August, 1927,

at 2 o'clock precisely

(unless previously sold by private treaty)

A Child's Prayers Matter to God

A Child's Prayers Matter to God

What Every Child should know about Prayers

Funke Ogunoiki

For my husband, Dr Adebola, and children;

Modupé Anna and Tobi Matthew

Acknowledgements

I would like to thank the Holy Spirit for instructing me to write this book. I have enjoyed pouring my heart and the wisdom of God into this book.

Throughout the writing of this book, I received a great deal of support and assistance from my husband (Dr Adebola Ogunoiki). Thank you for editing and formatting this book. Thank you for looking after the children while the book was being written.

I would like to thank my children for being patient with me throughout the time of writing this book. My children's morning and night time routine triggered the writing of this book.

I would like to thank my parents for introducing me to Jesus Christ from a very young age.

Finally, I would like to thank the children's teachers at the Redeemed Christian Church of God, Bethel Model Parish, Olomore, Abeokuta, Ogun State, Nigeria; they played an important role in my faith in Jesus as a child.

Contents

Preface

What could be more important than giving our children the tools to connect them to Jesus? Sometimes, as adults, we are often short of words when praying to God and we sometimes require help in talking to God more confidently. Have you ever thought about your children's feelings when they are talking to God? Have you thought about helping your children to increase their daily conversations with God?

This prayer book provides a guide for children when they are talking to God. The prayers within this book are applicable to all aspects of children's lives.

Introduction

Hello God's child,

Do you know that you are very special to God? In the bible, Jesus said: "***Let the little children come to Me, and do not forbid them; for of such is the kingdom of heaven.***" (Matthew 19:14). Jesus also said that nobody must stop you from talking to Him (Mark 10:14).

God also said that you can call upon Him and He will show you great and mighty things that you do not know (Jeremiah 33:3). God is always available for you and He is never too busy.

Do you know that God cares about your prayers? He would like to talk to you every day and He would like you to talk to Him as well.

Sometimes, you may be short of words while you are praying to God; this is why I have written this book to help you with your daily conversations with God. This book will help you speak out your prayers to God more confidently. It will also help you learn how to talk to God and it includes some of the things that you could say to Him.

This book has one big message: God cares about you and He would like to listen to your voice every day.

A Guide for Parents

Teaching children to pray is an important part of introducing them to Jesus and building their direct relationship with Jesus.

Introducing prayers to children from a young age helps them to make praying to God a part of their daily routine and it will also teach them that praying to God should be a part of their daily lives.

You could start teaching children how to pray even before they can speak coherently by praying with them as part of their daily routine (morning and night routines).

Encourage your children to use the prayers within this book to pray. However, remind them that they are free to talk to God about anything; absolutely anything. The same way your children have daily conversations with you, is the same way that they can talk to God about anything.

Let your children know that God is interested in all aspects of their lives, such as:

❖ Who they are

❖ Their family members

- ❖ Their friends

- ❖ Their Pets

- ❖ Their teachers

- ❖ Their house

- ❖ The news that they listen to

- ❖ Their siblings

- ❖ The weather

- ❖ Their school work

- ❖ Their meals

For Your Preschoolers (3 - 4 years old)

Encourage your preschoolers to get used to saying the following phrases to God:

- ❖ Thank you God for my food and drink

- ❖ Thank you God for my mummy and daddy

- ❖ Thank you God for my eyes, hair, hands and legs

- ❖ Thank you Jesus

- ❖ I love you Jesus

- ❖ I am sorry Lord

- ❖ Thank you Jesus for my grandparents

- ❖ Lord, bless me

- ❖ Lord, bless mummy and daddy

- ❖ Lord, bless (insert their siblings names)

- ❖ Praise God

A Guide for Children

Are you wondering what Praying to God is all about?

❖ It's about you talking to God about anything

❖ It's about you having a conversation with God

❖ It's about you having a chat with God

Do you know why you need to pray to God?

❖ Praying to God will help you to appreciate Him for all the wonderful things that He had done and is still doing for you

❖ Praying to God is a way for you to build your relationship with God, and for you to get to know Him more

❖ Praying to God is a way for God to know more about you

How can you pray to God as a child?

There are different ways in which you could talk to God as a child. This includes:

❖ Praying before going out and after you have returned home

❖ Praying on your meals

- ❖ When you wake up in the morning, you could lead your own prayer or you could ask your mummy and daddy to pray with you. Also, you could use this prayer book as a guide

- ❖ You could pray with your eyes closed or open; whichever you choose, ensure that you are focusing on God and not distracted

- ❖ You could pray to God anywhere, as God is everywhere. He is omnipresent, which means He is present everywhere and He would hear you from anywhere

Let me share some examples of people in the bible who prayed at different places:

- ❖ Daniel prayed in the lion's den (Daniel 6:10-28)

- ❖ Peter prayed on the water and under the water (Matthew 14:28-30)

- ❖ From inside the fish, Jonah prayed to God (Jonah 2:1)

- ❖ Jesus Christ prayed on the mountain (Mark 6:46, Luke 6:12 and John 6:15)

You can pray to God at any time and in any position. You can pray to God on your bed, in the bathroom, at school, in the car, whilst sitting down, whilst walking, whilst playing, etc.

Creating a Prayer Routine

Do you know that there are different ways of praying to God? This could be through singing, playing an instrument, talking to God, writing a poem or a letter to God, drawing pictures, and many more.

Here is an acronym (**T.H.C.A.T**) that you could use when praying to God as part of your daily routine.

The use of **T.H.C.A.T** will be very useful when you are praying to God.

T stands for **Thank God** (Mention the things you are grateful to God for like; Thank you God for sleeping and waking up, Thank you God for being with me, Thank you God for my family).

H stands for **Honour God** (Say something beautiful to God).

C stands for **Confession unto God** (Say that you are sorry to God for any wrong doing).

A stands for **Ask God** for anything.

T stands for **Thank God** (Thank God for listening to your prayers).

Biblical Affirmations

Here are some biblical affirmations about your identity in Christ Jesus.

1. I can do all things through Christ who gives me strength.

2. I am more than a conqueror through Christ who loved me.

3. Greater is He that is in me than he that is in the world.

4. Nothing shall be able to separate me from the love of God.

5. I am the light of the world

   I will not be hidden

   I will be a leader through the help of God.

6. I am wonderful

   My health is wonderful.

7. I am awesomely and wonderfully made because Christ made me.

8. I am precious to God

   I am important to God.

9. I am amazing

   I am special to God

   I am loved by God.

10. I am the righteousness of God in Christ Jesus

    Sin has no power over me.

11. The wicked flee when no one is pursuing them

    But the righteous are bold as a lion

    I will be as bold as a lion.

12. As I obey all of God's word

    I am the head and not the tail

    I am the light of the world

    I will follow the light of God

    I will never walk in darkness.

13. The Lord is my shepherd
    I will always have everything that I need.

14. The Lord is my shepherd
    He gives me everything that I need.

15. The Lord is my light
    I will not be afraid, as God watches over me at all times.

16. As I put my faith in the Lord
    The Lord will renew my strength
    I will soar on wings like eagles
    I will not grow weary
    I will walk and not faint
    I will live by faith and not by what I see.

17. My God shall supply all my needs
    According to His riches in glory by Christ Jesus.

18. My body is a temple of the Lord
    I will not let sin reign in my body.

19. I have been born of God

Therefore, I have overcome the world.

20. I am the light of the world.

It's Time to Pray

Prayers of Adoration

1.   Holy, Holy, Holy, Lord God Almighty

Early in the morning

Our songs shall rise to thee.

2.   O Lord,

I lift Your name on High

I Praise Your Holy name.

3.   Blessed be the name of the Lord

Who lives forevermore

Who reigns forevermore.

4. O Lord,

   Your works are wonderful and beautiful

   You are a wonderful God

   You are a Great God.

5. Who is this King of glory?

   The Lord strong and mighty

   The Lord mighty in battle.

Good Morning Prayers

6. Good morning Father

Good morning Jesus

Good morning Holy Spirit.

7. O Lord, come into my heart today

Come into my heart to stay

Come into my heart Lord

In Jesus' name

Amen.

8. Thank You God for sleeping and waking up

Thank You God for watching over me and my family

Thank You God for sound sleep

Thank You God for protecting my family and I

In Jesus' name

Amen.

9. Dear God,

   Thank You for a good night rest

   Thank You for rest and shelter of the night.

10. Dear Lord,

   As I start today, please help me

   Guide and lead me

   In Jesus' name

   Amen.

11. Good morning Jesus

   Good morning Lord

   I know You come from heaven and above

   Your Holy Spirit is in me

   Good morning Jesus

   Good morning Lord.

Good Night Prayers

12. Dear Lord,

The night has come

It is time to sleep

Please watch over me

Keep me safe

In Jesus' name

Amen.

13. Dear Lord,

Thank You for all that happened today

Thank You for keeping me and my family safe

Thank You for all that I have learned today

Please grant me sound sleep

Please watch over me as I sleep

In Jesus' name

Amen.

Grace (Prayers before You Eat)

14. O Lord,

I present You my food

Bless my food

Come and dine with me.

15. O Lord,

Bless this food

O Lord for Christ sake

In Jesus' name

Amen.

16. Thank You God for my food and drink

Thank You God for blessing me with food and drink

Let this food nourish my body

In Jesus' name

Amen.

17. Dear God,

I thank You for my daily food

Thank You for farmers; for producing our food

Thank You for shopkeepers; for selling our food

In Jesus' name

Amen.

Prayers of Thanksgiving

18. Thank You God for creating me

Thank You God for creating my family

Thank You God for knowing all about me.

19. Thank You God for my home

Thank You God for water

Thank You God for electricity

Thank You God for gas

In Jesus' name

Amen.

20. Thank You for my home

Thank You Lord that I can keep warm or cool inside.

21. Thank You God for the rain

Thank You God for the wind

Thank You God for the sun

Thank You God for summer

Thank You God for winter

Thank You God for autumn

Thank You God for spring.

22. Thank You God for all that You are doing for me

Thank You God that I can smile

Thank You God that I can sleep, jump, play and eat

Thank You God that I can empty my bowel.

23. Thank You God for the Holy Spirit that is inside me

Thank You God for helping me to be kind

Thank You for helping me to be calm

Thank You for the spirit of gentleness that is inside me.

24. Dear Jesus,

Thank You for your death on the cross of Calvary for me

Thank You for the freedom that I have in Christ

Thank You for loving me.

25. Dear Lord,

Thank You for my neighbours and all those that live around me

Thank You for watching over us

Thank You for protecting everyone in my neighbourhood.

26. Thank You God for your good plans for my life

Plans to prosper me

Plans to give me a hope and a future

In Jesus' name

Amen.

27. O Lord,

Thank You for always providing for me

In Jesus' name

Amen.

28. Thank You Jesus for creating animals

Help us to look after them

Help us to care for them

Please, watch over all the animals in the world

In Jesus' name

Amen.

29. Thank You God for my school

Thank You for all the teachers

Thank You for the school cleaners

Thank You for the kitchen staff

Thank You for everyone at my school.

30. Dear God,

Thank You for being my Jehovah Shammah

Thank You for always being there for me.

31. Dear Lord,

Thank You for my church

Thank You for every Christian in the world.

Prayers for God's Protection

32. Dear God,

I commit today into Your hands

Lord, guide me

Help me in all that I do

In Jesus' name

Amen.

33. O Lord,

Protect all the children that do not have any parents

Provide for them

Watch over them

Guide them

Be with them

In Jesus' name

Amen.

34. O Lord,

Will You watch over my sister?

Please keep her safe

In Jesus' name

Amen.

35. Christ be in my thoughts

Christ be with my going out

Christ be in my speaking

Christ be with me always

In Jesus' name

Amen.

36. Christ be with my Mum and Dad

Christ be with me at school

Christ be with my going out and coming in

Christ be with my friends.

37. Christ be with my cousins

Christ be with my uncles and aunties

Christ be with my grandparents.

38. Dear Lord,

Keep me from all evil

Keep my life in Your hands

In Jesus' name

Amen.

39. O Lord,

Please look after everyone in my family

Watch over my Mum, Dad and my brother

Protect us from danger

Keep us safe

In Jesus' name

Amen.

☑ **EXCELLENT**

☐ **GOOD**

☐ **AVERAGE**

Prayers for Excellence

40. O Lord, make me wiser than my years

In Jesus' name

Amen.

41. Dear Lord,

Help me to be excellent in all my school work

Let the excellent spirit that was upon Daniel be on me

In Jesus' name

Amen.

42. Dear Lord,

Help me to be excellent in my character

Let my character be pleasing unto You

In Jesus' name

Amen.

Prayers on Your Birthday

43. Dear Lord,

Today is my birthday.

Thank You for keeping me to see another year

Help me to be who You want me to be

In Jesus' name

Amen.

44. Dear Lord,

Thank You for the fun that I had today

Thank You for providing for my Mum and Dad

Thank You for other children in the world who were born today

I give You praise and adoration

In Jesus' name

Amen.

45. Dear Lord,

Today, I am (*insert your age*)

Thank You Lord for keeping me to see another year

Thank You for watching over me.

End of School Term Prayers

46. Dear Lord,

Thank You for helping me through this term

I appreciate your help.

47. Dear Lord,

Holiday is coming

It's time to rest and refresh

Thank You for keeping me to see another holiday season

Please watch over me during the holiday season

Please watch over my family and friends

In Jesus' name

Amen.

Prayers for Help

48. Dear God,

Help me to be great in life

In Jesus' name

Amen.

49. Dear Lord,

Do something new in my life

Something wonderful in my life

Something glorious in my life, today

In Jesus' name

Amen.

50. Dear Lord,

Help me to continue to believe in You

In Jesus' name

Amen.

51. Dear Lord,

Help me to grow in the fruit of the Spirit

In Love, Joy, Peace

Patience, Kindness, Goodness

Faithfulness, Gentleness and Self-Control

O Lord, fill me with your love

Teach me to love like You

In Jesus' name

Amen.

52. Dear God,

Breathe Your Spirit on me

Let me be who You want me to be.

53. Dear God,

To those that are sick, heal them

As You are the Jehovah Rapha (The Lord that heals).

54. Dear Lord,

Please, keep sicknesses and diseases away from me

Let me have good health

In Jesus' name

Amen.

55. Dear Lord,

When trouble comes, I will be strong and courageous

In Jesus' name

Amen.

56. O Lord,

Let Your peace reign in the world

Let Your love reign in the world

In Jesus' name

Amen.

57. Dear Lord,

Help me to seek after You at all times

In Jesus' name

Amen.

58. Dear God,

Help me to feel Your presence at all times

In Jesus' name

Amen.

59. Dear Lord,

Help me to make good choices at school

I will not make wrong choices

In Jesus' name

Amen.

60. Dear Lord,

Lord, help me to receive uncommon favour from all my teachers

In Jesus' name

Amen.

61. Dear Lord,

Let your wisdom rest upon me

In Jesus' name

Amen.

62. Dear God,

Teach me how to manage my emotions

Let me be who You want me to be

In Jesus' name

Amen.

63. Dear Lord,

Please, help me to tell my friends about You

Let me only speak to them when You want me to speak

Teach me what to share about You with my friends.

64. Dear God,

Help me to be at the right place at the right time

Order my steps every day

Keep me safe

In Jesus' name

Amen.

65. Dear God,

Let Your mercy speak for me

In Jesus' name

Amen.

66. Dear Lord,

Help me to always remember that you love me and care about me.

67. Dear God,

I know that when I am scared or worried about anything

I can talk to You and I know that You will hear me

And You will take away my worries and fears.

68. Dear God,

Let the blood of Jesus speak for me

Let the blood of Jesus be upon me.

69. Father God,

Please write my name in the Book of Life

In Jesus' name

Amen.

70. Dear God,

Jesus was an obedient child

Help me to be an obedient child to You and to my parents

In Jesus' name

Amen.

Prayer Journal

Do you know that with God, you can be creative? God loves creativity. I would like to introduce you to this interactive journal which you could use to write down things that will help you to talk to God more.

1) What are you thankful to God for?

2) Psalm 23

1 The Lord is my shepherd;
I shall not want.

2 He makes me to lie down in green pastures;
He leads me beside the still waters.

3 He restores my soul;
He leads me in the paths of righteousness
For His name's sake.

4 Yea, though I walk through the valley of the shadow of death,
I will fear no evil;
For You are with me;
Your rod and Your staff, they comfort me.

5 You prepare a table before me in the presence of my enemies;
You anoint my head with oil;
My cup runs over.

6 Surely goodness and mercy shall follow me
All the days of my life;
And I will dwell in the house of the Lord forever.

What is your favourite verse in Psalm 23 and why?

3) Write a poem to God about anything that you like (It could be about your family, your school, your love for God; anything of your choice).

Recite the poem to God.

4) Who is God to you?

5) Find out and write down 5 names of God and their meaning.

6) Write the nine fruit of the Spirit around the fruit tree. The fruit of the Spirit can be found in the book of Galatians 5:22-23. (It would be lovely for you to memorise the fruit of the Spirit).

7) Write down who you are to God, using 'I am'

I am ....

I am ....

I am ....

I am ....

I am ....

I am ....

I am ....

I am ....

I am ....

8) Do you listen to Christian songs? Write down the title of 5 Christian songs that you listen to. With the help of an adult, find out and write down bible verses that can be linked to your favourite Christian songs.

9) What is on your heart today? (Tell God about it by writing it down. You can even draw a picture)

Date: ....

....

....

....

....

....

....

Draw your picture here

10) Write down anything interesting you have found out from reading the bible.

11) Has God answered any of your prayers? Write down what the Lord has done for you.

Printed in Great Britain
by Amazon

61984696R00036